INNOCENCE AND FIRE

"Don't talk, Amelia," he said. "Don't talk. Just feel." With that he caressed her gently.

Enjoying his touch, she closed her eyes and sighed softly. When she opened them again ⸱e was smiling at her.

Unable to help herself. ⸱ ⸱is face in her hands and pulled him⸱

Daniel moane⸱ ⸱s in a kiss that fueled t⸱ ⸱eat spiraled through her ⸱ ⸱on overwhelmed her, lifting he⸱

"Yes, Ameli⸱ ⸱ed. "I knew you would be like this. You're ⸱ ⸱ and sweetness. I love touching you."

She ached for something she couldn't name. The sensations pouring through her were so sweet, yet so wild, that she felt as though she were coming undone . . .

Books by Candace McCarthy

WHITE BEAR'S WOMAN
IRISH LINEN
HEAVEN'S FIRE
SEA MISTRESS
RAPTURE'S BETRAYAL
WARRIOR'S CARESS
SMUGGLER'S WOMAN

Published by Zebra Books

SWEET POSSESSION

Candace McCarthy

Zebra Books
Kensington Publishing Corp.
http://www.zebrabooks.com

For Kevin and Keith—once again and for always
. . . and for Nana.

ZEBRA BOOKS are published by

Kensington Publishing Corp.
850 Third Avenue
New York, NY 10022

Zebra and the Z logo Reg. U.S. Pat. & TM Off.

First Printing: February, 1999
10 9 8 7 6 5 4 3 2 1

Printed in the United States of America

Prologue

The Northwest Territory
1832

The quiet afternoon shattered as a woman's shrill screams mingled with the wild shrieks of an Indian war party. A half mile away, Daniel Trahern heard the noise, dropped the dead rabbit he'd shot for dinner, and started to run toward the sound. The scent of smoke hung heavy in the afternoon air, making his blood chill, as he hurried home to a log cabin beyond the woods.

Jane! Susie! His mind spun with the frightening mental images of a woman and child being tortured. The smoky smell grew stronger as the man crashed through brush and bramble, shoving bushes and branches out of his way in his haste to get to the scene.

Gasping, he broke from the forest into a clearing and saw the burning barn. Orange flames shot up through the wooden roof, crackling and popping and sending sparks high into the damp air. Dark smoke billowed out of the loft door and windows.

The screaming had stopped. There was no sign of the attackers or his family. Daniel started toward the fiery structure until he caught sight of the log cabin's splintered door.

"Jane!" he cried. "Susie!" A renewed leap of alarm propelled him toward the house. His heart thundered within his chest as he burst into the cabin. "Jane, where are you! Susie? Answer me!"

The house was in a shambles. The intruders had destroyed two of his hand-carved chairs; the matching pair lay on the farside of the room several feet from the table. The midday meal had been swept from the table onto the floor. Broken dishes and food lay in a heaped mess where already flies had found the spilled porridge. The buzz of the insects broke the silence as eerily as a vulture's cry interrupting the still quiet of an afternoon.

"Jane?" he whispered, his throat tight with pain and guilt. "Susie?" He shouldn't have left them alone. *"Where are you?"*

His heart jerked beneath his breast. There was no sign of mother or child.

It was raining as he exited the cabin. The storm had come quickly, out of nowhere. The clouds opened up, soaking Daniel as he hurried toward the burning barn. The fire hissed and choked and began to die beneath the driving rain shower. Daniel searched but found no sign of life. No sign that two females had been murdered and left to burn.

His insides frozen with horror, he checked the rest of the yard. Rain plastered his blond hair to his scalp, and his clothes were drenched within seconds, but he didn't care. He was oblivious to the storm, to the discomfort. Although he feared what he would find, Daniel continued to search for Jane and Susie, behind the cabin and in the fields, beyond the fields to the surrounding woods.

It was dark when Daniel headed toward the house. The charred remains of the barn looked ghostly in the moonlight as he passed the building. The smell of smoke lingered heavily in the damp night air.

His chest hurt, and his eyes stung with emotion. Balling his hands into fists, Daniel fought the rage that built within him, a hatred toward the savages who were responsible. As he viewed the destruction, he vowed to find out who had done this and why.

His stomach churning, Daniel entered the cabin. There was enough moonlight filtering in through the window for him to light a candle, which he held aloft after it was lit. He saw the pile of blankets that had been torn from Jane's bed, and felt the instant pinprick of tears. He gasped when he turned to inspect the room. Someone had slashed the mattress on Susie's bed. The child's doll lay on the floor, its cloth head torn from its little fabric body.

Who would do this? he wondered. Whoever did this were monsters. A shiny object on the dirt floor caught his glance. He bent and picked up a broken arrow. He recognized the marks on the piece of shaft. *Sioux.* He experienced a chill. When Daniel was a boy, his father had worked closely with the Ojibwa Indians. During his childhood, Daniel had witnessed the horror left after a Sioux raid that had wounded and killed many of his Ojibwa friends. This attack on his family was one more reason for him to fear and loathe the Sioux.

Frowning, he looked from the arrowhead to the toy on Susie's bed and became choked up by the image of a terrified little girl. *Susie. Jane.* He should have been here to protect them from the Sioux.

"Lord, have mercy on them!" he breathed. He was not a religious man, but Daniel closed his eyes and began to pray.

A sudden sound caught his attention. He thought he'd heard a whimper, then he imagined a rustling sound.

Glancing toward the larger bed, he listened for the noise. The second time he heard it was when he saw a shift in the pile of bedcovers. Daniel tensed, and his hand went to the knife tucked in his legging strap. He slowly approached the bed with the blade raised to strike.

The night was still. Nothing moved in the muted light. Daniel's heart pumped hard as he stared at the blankets and wondered if he'd only imagined movement. He waited for a few moments. Then, he inched closer, with blade poised to defend. He bent silently and suddenly jerked away the blankets, exposing the underside of the bed . . . and found himself gazing into the blue eyes of a sleepy little girl.

"Susie!" Joy made Daniel dizzy.

The child spied the knife, and her gaze widened with fear. Daniel cursed softly beneath his breath as he hurried to put away the weapon.

"Susie—" Daniel reached for the little girl. Susie shrank back under the bed in terror. He dropped his hands and stepped back. "It's okay, honey. They're gone," he soothed. "The bad men are gone."

Susie blinked as if focusing her gaze as she looked up at him. Daniel offered her his hand. "Come out, sweeting," he urged softly. "I'll take care of you. No one is going to hurt my Susie."

The child stared at Daniel's hand a long moment, then placed her small fingers within his grasp.

Murmuring soft words, Daniel tugged the child from under the bed and scooped her into his arms to cradle her closely. "It's all right, sweeting."

Susie's cheeks were smudged with dirt and tears shed earlier. Her blond hair was baby-fine and felt silky against his rough skin. She was a tiny thing, barely any weight at all.

The little girl burrowed her head trustingly into his broad shoulder. Daniel murmured to her soothingly while she shuddered and shook and relived her fears. Suddenly, Susie lifted her arms and hugged his neck. "Bad men," she sobbed.

"I know, sweeting, but they're gone now."

She rose back and gazed at him with tear-filled beautiful blue eyes. "Momma," she whimpered.

"I know," Daniel whispered, his throat aching.

Susie leaned into him and began to cry in earnest.

While he stroked the little girl's hair and tried to comfort her fears, Daniel lost the battle and wept his own silent tears.

One

August, 1836
The Wisconsin Territory

The clink of iron against metal disturbed the stillness of the morning near Trahern's Blacksmithy. Daniel Trahern heated the iron rod in the fire, then set it on the anvil to hammer it into shape. His blond hair was cut short and glistened golden beneath the glow from the forge fire. He had rolled up the sleeves of his blue linen shirt, revealing muscled forearms that flexed as he worked, transferring iron from fire to anvil, where he manipulated the hot softened metal with his tools. A leather work apron about his waist protected his dark breeches from fire and metal. His expression was intense; he took his work seriously, striving for perfection with each job.

Within a few yards from where the man worked were two men. Rebb Colfax stood idly, watching his friend work, occasionally making a teasing comment to the blacksmith and the third man that frequented the shop. Jack Keller owned the trading post across the road. When business was slow or whenever the mood suited him, he visited the blacksmithy to socialize and lend Daniel a hand. Today, he pumped the bellows whenever the forge fire needed to be stoked. Standing together, the three men were a contrast in age and color, from Daniel's fairness to Jack's dark hair with Rebb's wiry gray beard and locks in between. Jack and Daniel were close in age, while Rebb was older by more than fifteen years.

"Would ya look at that?" Rebb said. He had moved to the open entrance of the blacksmithy. A vehicle had just pulled up to park before Jack's trading post across the road. "We've got visitors. City folk by the look of 'em."

"Visitors?" Jack asked casually. He didn't appear in a hurry to leave.

Rebb looked back at his friend. "There's a female."

"A female!" Intrigued now, Jack left the forge area to join Rebb at the door. He caught sight of the woman and whistled. "Daniel," he called, "come and get a look at the lady."

Daniel Trahern warmed the iron rod in the fire, then set it on the anvil and continued to work it. He glanced at his friends, then went back to the task at hand.

"Daniel, come 'ere," Rebb insisted.

"I don't have time to be idle, Colfax," Daniel replied. "Can't you see I'm busy? Besides, they're likely here to see Jack."

Jack turned from the door to address his friend. "Not this time." He sounded disappointed. "This business is yours, Daniel," he said. " 'ppears these good folks are in need of a blacksmith."

"Then why did they pull up over there?" Daniel asked.

"I don't know." Jack's gaze returned to the man and woman. "Looks like something's broke on their wagon. Maybe they're afraid to move it."

"Wagon rolled in easily enough," Rebb commented.

Jack shrugged. "As I said, they're city folk."

Rebb nodded, as if the explanation was a good one. Everyone knew that city folk didn't have a lick of sense.

Ignoring the exchange between the two men, Daniel took over Jack's job, using the bellows to heat up the fire, then he returned the partially formed metal into the fire. The misshapen piece turned red then white in the flame, and he quickly transferred it to the anvil for hammering. The *clink-clank* of the four-pound cross peen hitting iron filled the blacksmithy as Daniel continued to work at his craft. His friends still hadn't left the doorway. He glanced at them—one gray-haired bearded rascal and one younger more attractive fellow with an eye for the ladies and a dimpled smile. The two men's fascination—especially Jack's—with the newcomers annoyed him.

"Jack, you going to give a hand with this fire or not?"

Jack glanced back. "I'll be there in a minute."

"Forget it," Daniel growled.

"Ah, come on, Dan," his friend replied. "I said I'd help. Come over here and look at this first, will ya?"

With a grunt of frustration, Daniel set down the black metal and his tools to approach his friends. "What?" he asked sharply. "What's so interesting that you've pulled me away from my work? You know I'm busy." He had a lot to do, and he hoped to get the majority of it done before sunset.

Rebb gestured toward the wagon. Daniel saw the vehicle, before his glance fell on the newcomers—a man in a dark suit and a woman wearing a fancy gown. The man was helping the woman out of the wagon. The blacksmith narrowed his gaze on the woman, then looked away.

"So?" He denied any interest; and with a bored look on his face, he went back to work. "Just a couple of missionaries," he said with disgust. "Maybe if we ignore them, they'll leave."

He cared little for the missionaries and less for new recruits with their enthusiastic fervor for "taming those wild savages." Those wild savages were his friends, the Ojibwa, and Daniel took exception to the way the whites were forever trying to change the Indians' way of life.

The furrow across his forehead deepened. Why couldn't the Indians be left alone to live in peace? He'd known the Ojibwa for a long time. He'd opened his blacksmithy before the treaty signed in March by the Indians and US government officials. The agreement guaranteed two new blacksmith shops in the region as well as improvements to the established, but run-down blacksmith shop at Michilimackinac. Those promises and a bunch of others had seemed like a good idea to the Ojibwa at the time, but Daniel knew better.

Daniel's father had been a blacksmith, and Daniel had served as an apprentice to his father at Michilimackinac after the Treaty of 1826, ten years earlier, when the Indians had given up the mineral rights to their land. As missionaries and more settlers moved into the area, he began to realize that the Indians were being manipulated into giving up more of their rights and their land. These good missionary people had come to "improve" the Indians. Their work as well as news of the government's future intent made Daniel angry for his friends. He understood the Ojibwa, and now that he understood what the government planned to do, he'd lost all respect for the missionaries and the US government officials. First the white men ensured that the Indians had become dependent on them for goods, supplies, and blacksmith services, then they used that dependency as a bargaining tool to change the People and take their land.

"They're coming this way," Rebb announced as he left the door to approach the forge area of Daniel's shop.

Jack Keller followed him. He returned to the bellows and pumped up the fire until it burned red-hot. Daniel systematically moved the iron from the anvil to the fire and back again, hammering the metal into shape, using different hammers and specially crafted tools of his own design. The mood of Daniel's friends was expectant. Daniel felt irritable.

The doorway darkened as someone entered the shop, blocking out the bright afternoon sunlight. Daniel didn't glance up as Jack greeted the person. There was a low murmur of conversation between Jack and the stranger. Then, Daniel heard his name.

"Mr. Trahern?" The stranger had approached the forge area, but kept well out of Daniel's way.

Daniel slowly lifted his gaze. The stranger stood within a few yards, an older, thin gentleman with salt-and-pepper hair. The blacksmith noted the man's white shirt, dark tie, and dark waistcoat. *City folk from back East,* he thought.

"You're the blacksmith, Daniel Trahern?" the man asked as he stepped closer. He looked tired.

Daniel narrowed his gaze for a moment. "No, I'm an Ojibwa war chief. This here hammer is my war club," he said sarcastically. The stranger's expression made him instantly contrite. "Bad joke," he grumbled. He glanced away. There was an awkward silence. "I'm Trahern, the blacksmith," he finally admitted. He switched tools as he went back to work.

"I've got trouble with my wagon," the man said, loud enough to be heard over the clink of metal. "Can you fix it?"

Daniel paused with raised hammer. "I can fix anything that needs fixing."

"Will it take very long?" a young feminine voice asked. A woman stepped into Daniel's line of vision. She must have followed the man inside.

Daniel stared at her, startled that he hadn't immediately

become aware of her presence. In a blue gown that was totally inappropriate for wear in this rugged wilderness, she looked like a misplaced debutante.

"Depends on what needs doing," Daniel drawled, "and if I got the metal." He noted the woman's shiny brown hair, which was drawn back severely and pinned in a bun at her nape. He saw glistening brown eyes and pink lips before he glanced away. *Easterners,* he thought with disgust. She wouldn't last more than a fortnight before she'd be clamoring to go home.

"And if the iron is available, Mr. Trahern?" she asked impatiently.

Daniel pointedly ignored her to address the man. "I'll have a look at her in a minute and let you know if I can fix it today or not." He sensed the woman's anger.

"Is there an inn?"

Daniel raised his eyebrows. "This isn't a town, Mr.—"

"Dempsey."

He nodded. "As I was saying. This isn't a town; it's a trading post. We don't get many folks looking to spend the night." He ran an assessing gaze over the man, then the woman, who bristled under his regard. "Where're you headed?"

"The mission run by Allen Whitely," the woman said tightly.

Jack and Rebb exchanged glances before looking to check Daniel's reaction. A muscle ticked along Daniel's jaw, but otherwise there was no indication of his thoughts. "Missionaries are you?" Jack asked.

The man smiled. "Actually I'm a physician. My name's John Dempsey," he said, offering Jack his hand as he introduced himself. "And this is my daughter, Amelia. We were told the mission needed a doctor to treat injuries and illness among the Indians and the settlers."

Daniel studied the man more closely. "Doctor? What made a doctor like you decide to take up residence in the wilderness?" The man might be a doctor, but he'd lay odds that his daughter had other intentions. She was clearly someone who considered herself superior to the Indians and to workingmen like himself. A missionary. "What about you?" he asked her.

The woman straightened her spine. "I'm here to help my father—not that it's any of your business."

With casual slowness, Daniel continued to work on the iron tool, firing it and hammering it, and shaping it with other specially handcrafted tools. He neither made a move to look at the wagon nor did he answer the man's question about a hotel.

He could feel Amelia's hostile stare as he addressed her father. "Can she make it across the road?" he asked, referring to the wagon.

The man understood. "I suppose so. I'll get her." He made a move to leave.

Daniel set down the unfinished tool along with his own. "I'll move her." He was the best judge of what was wrong.

"It's a *thing*, Mr. Trahern, not a *her*," Amelia said through tight lips.

He flashed her a mocking glance before he left, aware of her angry gaze, as he crossed the street and examined the wagon.

The repair would be minor, Daniel deduced. He climbed into the wagon and moved it into the open area of his shop which was used for carriage and wagon repairs. There he unhitched the horses and led them into the stable out back before returning to inspect the wagon further. Satisfied that he had the metal he needed for the job, Daniel reentered the shop through the side door. The

Dempseys were by the main door by the forge, waiting for his return, but he didn't approach them. He went back to work as if he hadn't left it.

"Well?" Amelia asked. She had turned and spied him by the forge. Daniel looked up and saw her standing with her arms folded across her chest, scowling at him. Her brown eyes glistened with fire.

He stared at her hard and saw a prim and proper, well-dressed woman. She wasn't exactly a beauty, but there was something compelling about her features . . . about the confined brown hair and snapping brown eyes. There was a spark of something in her expression that made him wonder about her.

If she didn't spend so much time frowning, Daniel thought, she'd be almost pretty. He had to stifle the urge to grin. Wouldn't she be furious if she could read his thoughts?

John Dempsey joined his daughter by the forge. "You didn't answer my question . . . about an inn?"

Daniel was only too happy to focus on the father, for his preoccupation with the daughter disturbed him. "Jack here," he said while gesturing toward his friend, "may have a room for the night."

Jack looked surprised, but recovered himself quickly and nodded. "I've got a spare room above my trading post," he said. "You're welcome to stay there."

John and his daughter exchanged glances. Amelia spoke first. "How long will this repair take?"

Daniel shrugged. "Got to finish this here tool before I can get to your wagon. Hour, maybe two, maybe six."

"Six!" Amelia gasped. "Six hours?"

Jack and Rebb started to grin. "Daniel Trahern never took six hours to do anything," Rebb said.

The woman scowled.

"How far is it to the mission?" John Dempsey asked.

"Half hour—hour at worst if the weather's bad," Jack said.

"We'll wait for the repair, then go on to the mission," John said.

Daniel nodded. "Suit yourself." He eyed the woman with narrowed eyes. "Move back from the fire. Don't want to see that fancy gown of yours catch fire."

Amelia glared at him, but stepped back.

"You be needing any supplies before you head out?" Jack asked. The father nodded. "Come over to my post, and see if you can find what you need."

Amelia looked only too happy to leave the forge. The Dempseys and Jack left, leaving Rebb and Daniel alone.

"I've not known you to be rude to a lady," Rebb commented.

Daniel scowled. "We don't need her kind around here. Some straight-laced female determined to influence the savages."

Rebb scratched the crown of his head where his dark hair had gotten thin. "Father's a doctor. What makes you think the lady's out to change the Ojibwa?"

The blacksmith raised his eyebrows as he met his friend's gaze. "Why else would a woman come to Indian territory? Doctor or no, the Dempseys are here to work at the mission. In my way of thinking, that makes them missionaries. Probably think they can save the devil's children by ministering to them." He paused to wipe his forehead with the back of his hand. "Trouble, if you ask me. Those two are going to be trouble."

Rebb looked surprised. "Why?"

"The woman," Daniel stated. "What woman in her right mind would willingly come to live in this godforsaken territory?" When his friend shrugged as if he didn't have a reply, Daniel smiled grimly. "None, at all. That's why this woman's gonna be trouble."

"Is Mr. Trahern always so rude?" Amelia asked Jack Keller as she and her father walked with him toward the trading post across the street. She had a mental vision of the blacksmith—blond hair that glistened in the firelight, symmetrical features that caught and held one's attention: a straight nose, eyes as blue as the clear azure sky, and a mouth that was perfectly formed. *And his arms.* She blinked. She couldn't forget how they moved as he worked. *Strength and purpose,* she thought, stunned by her thoughts and the odd little tingling she felt along her spine. She tensed.

"Daniel?" Jack echoed with an odd expression. "He's not normally rude." He looked at her and grinned. "Must be the weather."

His tone and the look on his face made Amelia relax with a chuckle. "You're teasing me," she said.

He nodded, and his teeth flashed as he widened his grin. "Part of my charm, I'm afraid."

"Charm apparently lacking in your friend, the blacksmith," she replied dryly. Jack didn't deny it, so Amelia figured it must be true. "He doesn't like women much, does he?" She frowned. "Or is it just me he doesn't like?"

"You?" Jack shook his head. "Surely not. Daniel's just in a surly mood."

"Does he have a mood often?"

"Only when he sees someone new at the mission," the man told her.

"Why?"

"Because he doesn't agree with their work."

"Why?"

Jack opened the door, and Amelia entered the man's building and looked around. Her father followed right behind her. "It's a long story," Jack answered.

Amelia fought against satisfying her curiosity about Daniel Trahern and studied her surroundings instead. The room housed a collection of furs and tools and trinkets. There were dishes and bowls, fabric and food items, all placed in some haphazard order. Squash, herbs, and other dried vegetables hung from the rafters above. Hats hung on wall pegs, and Amelia spied a pair of moccasins on the floor next to an old pair of leather boots. She wrinkled her nose as she checked along the back wall. The air inside the building was musty but not wholly unpleasant, because of the fragrant herbs. She noted all this and more; yet, still, in the forefront of her mind lingered thoughts of Daniel Trahern.

"What bothers Mr. Trahern about the missionaries' work?" her father asked, much to Amelia's relief.

"He doesn't like the way the whites are trying to change the Ojibwa. The missionaries as well as the government want to civilize the savages, only Daniel thinks their idea of civilizing means taking away the Indians' freedom and their land."

"And is he right? Is the government trying to take their land?"

Jack shrugged. "Could be. Each month more settlers come from back East. The settlers don't want to share the land nor do they want to acknowledge the Indians' way of life or their right to live here."

"And I remind him of the injustice to these Indians?" Amelia asked. She frowned. She found the man's logic incredible.

"You remind him of that and other things," Jack said.

He quickly changed the subject by showing the Dempseys several items he had for sale.

While Jack Keller and her father worked out a deal for the supplies, Amelia walked about the trading post, inspecting items for trade and sale, and fighting thoughts of the blacksmith. She couldn't put him out of her mind. His image returned again and again to annoy her.

"He took one look at me and decided I'm the enemy," she murmured beneath her breath. And she got madder by the minute. He didn't know her or her father; yet, he'd been quick to judge them after one brief meeting.

Amelia scowled. How dare Daniel Trahern sit in judgment of her. She had come to assist her father, a doctor with only the best intentions . . . despite what the blacksmith believed.

Two

The mission had been built on a river and within distance of the rugged shoreline of a beautiful huge lake. There were five residences, a church, the infirmary, and a gathering hall, made from sandstone and set in a forest clearing.

As her father steered their wagon toward the largest structure, Amelia took stock of her surroundings. They had come all the way from Baltimore, through harsh weather and good, by water, rail, and land . . . over rugged country, flatland, and hills. Finally, they had reached their destination.

John Dempsey had wanted this change in his life. Amelia had come along to look after her father. They'd left family in Maryland—Amelia's sister Rachel and Amelia's aunt, Bess, John's sister. Amelia's mother had died when her girls were young. The two little girls had been raised by their father and Aunt Bess.

When John had made his decision to leave Baltimore, Amelia had chosen to go, while her sister had elected to stay behind with Aunt Bess. Rachel was younger, more beautiful, and of marriageable age. When Amelia left, Rachel had been enjoying herself in Baltimore with a series of eager-to-please beaux. Amelia was plain compared to Rachel. She had lost more than one beau to her younger, more beautiful sister. Amelia had nothing to keep her in Baltimore: no beaux, no husband, no work. When her father had announced he was heading west, Amelia couldn't find any reason why she should stay.

As her father assisted her from the wagon, Amelia wondered how Rachel was doing. Had she found a husband yet? Or a steady beau? It hadn't seemed that Rachel would ever be satisfied with only one young man. Had she finally found the right one?

Amelia studied her surroundings as she waited while her father checked the supplies in the back of the wagon. A young man came out to greet them as her father straightened and returned to her side.

"John Dempsey?" The man smiled at them both and offered a hand to her father. After shaking John's hand, he turned to his daughter. "Miss Dempsey, it's a pleasure to have you here. My name is Allen Whitely. I'm the minister in charge. I can't tell you how grateful we are that you decided to come to our mission."

Amelia studied the young man with surprise. He was the minister?

"It's our pleasure to be here," her father said. "I was pleased to hear from your brother, my good friend James Whitely. He said you needed a doctor, but he wasn't ready to leave the city yet. He knew I needed a change, so he asked me."

Allen smiled. "How is James?"

"Well, but busy. He's taking over the care of my patients in Baltimore."

"You must be hungry and tired after your journey," Allen said. "Come and I'll show you the infirmary and your living quarters."

The Reverend Whitely led the way across the yard to a smaller building with an extended roof over the entrance. John Dempsey looked at it approvingly. Amelia was reserving judgment until after she'd seen the inside.

The interior was dark after entering from outside. As Amelia's eyes slowly adjusted to the dim light, Allen Whitely proceeded to explain what each room was as they walked through it.

"This front area is the infirmary. As you can see, there is a small alcove right inside the entrance for waiting patients. This back area," he said, gesturing as he spoke, "has a cabinet for supplies and two beds for the very ill."

Amelia, better able to see, noted the work area and started to envision where she would put her father's instruments and supplies.

"Beyond this room, through that door," Allen said, "is your living area. There are two bedrooms, a small parlor area, and a kitchen/dining area in the very back." He looked apologetic as he spoke. "It's not spacious, I'm afraid."

"It will do nicely," Amelia said with a smile. "Thank you." The young man grinned, relieved.

"Miriam Lathom, one of our missionaries, can help you when needed. Miriam has some knowledge of the area's herbs and plant life. If you need a particular ingredient for your medicine, Miriam can find it for you. Also, she understands some of the Chippewa language, and may be able to help you with your Indian patients.

"To tell you the truth," he continued, "the Chippewa have a great knowledge and skill of healing, so you may not have many Indian patients. Those who come will do so simply because they are too far from their home for treatment. There is an army fort about a day and a half's ride from here. It's likely you will have some patients from there . . . then, of course, there are those of us who live here at the mission. You are our only source of medical help. You may get problems from everything from something simple like a splinter or insect bite to a more severe injury like a severed arm."

John Dempsey nodded and asked a few questions; Amelia barely heard the two men's conversation as she wandered about the living quarters, envisioning ways to make the starkness of the place more livable.

"If you need any tools," the good reverend said, "there is a blacksmith shop about a half hour's ride from here. Daniel Trahern can make anything you want; he is a skilled craftsman. This mission is filled with hinges, tools, and other articles he made. If you decide you need something made or repaired, let me know, and I'll send one of my men to take you. There's a trading post there as well."

Amelia's attention had caught as soon as she'd heard the word *blacksmith*.

"Actually, we just came from there," her father was saying. "We had a problem with our wagon. Mr. Trahern was gracious enough to fix it for us."

"Gracious, my foot," Amelia muttered beneath her breath.

"Excuse me?" Allen asked.

Amelia forced a smile. "Nothing really. I'm sure we won't need a thing."

The young man nodded. "Well, after you get settled, you might think differently. I just wanted you to know that we're not totally isolated out here. We can get supplies and we have the services of a blacksmith."

"Thank you," Amelia said. "I'm sure we'll be happy here." *Over my dead body will I go to that iron-hearted Trahern man for help!*

It was evening, and Daniel was done at the forge for the day. He had cooked supper and cleaned up the dishes.

This next hour would be his favorite time with Susie before he tucked her in bed for the night. It was their special time together, when Susie would sit on his lap and he would tell her stories. In the summer, they'd sit outside under a starry sky, and in the winter, before the fireplace in the main room of the cabin.

"Pa?" a soft voice called.

Daniel glanced toward a bedroom doorway and saw seven-year-old Susie. He smiled. "All ready for a story?" She beamed as she nodded. "Which one shall it be?"

"Tell me about Black Hawk's great bear hunt."

"Shall we sit outside or in?"

"Inside," she said.

He pulled a chair out from under the dining table. Once seated, Daniel patted his lap, and Susie climbed up and made herself comfortable within his arms.

"As you probably remembered, Black Hawk was just a boy when he went on his first hunt . . ." In a deep voice, Daniel told the tale of how his Ojibwa friend had killed his first bear, a great beast that stood up on its hind legs and roared when Black Hawk shot an arrow into the animal's hindquarter.

"And there began the chase. Black Hawk had gotten separated from the rest of his hunting party . . ." Daniel went on to describe how the angry bear had chased the young brave, until Black Hawk had found a hiding place where he could prepare his bow and arrow for his next shot. "Then, he left his hiding place to face the bear. While the bear roared at him, Black Hawk shot another arrow. This time he hit the bear's neck." Daniel saw Susie's rapt expression and smiled. "You like hearing about Black Hawk, don't you?"

She nodded. "I like Black Hawk. He's always nice to me."

Daniel smiled. "Because he's your friend."

"Tell me what happens next," Susie urged.

Daniel went on to finish the story, which ended in Black Hawk's great victory over the bear. He explained how the people of Black Hawk's village had called the brave a true warrior. "Because of his bravery, Black Hawk was deemed a man, and everyone within the village came to respect him."

As he described the celebration in the Ojibwa village, he saw Susie's head nod. He continued the telling in soft tones. When he saw that she was sleeping, he ended the tale and stood with the little girl in his arms.

He put her to bed in the back bedroom, covering her with a blanket which he tucked tightly around her. Then he studied her with a tender smile for several minutes before leaving. She was seven, four years older than she'd been when Jane was kidnapped. He was pleased to note that Susie was finally past having nightmares. She had become more open and loving as the horror of what she'd seen on that terrible day faded with the passing of time.

As he stared down at Susie, he saw how much she resembled her mother. She had Jane's blond hair and fair skin. She had Jane's blue eyes and her smile.

Susie was Daniel's niece, not his daughter, but he had no objection to the child calling him "Pa." He was more like a father than her own had ever been. Susie's father hadn't been present at, or even nearby, his daughter's birth. In fact, the man had come home only twice during the first three years of Susie's life. An officer in the US Army, Daniel's brother-in-law had given little thought to his wife and child. It had been Daniel who had been Jane's rock when she needed one, staying near all through Jane's delivery of Susie.

After the death of his wife, Pamela, Daniel had given

up his home and gone to live with his pregnant sister, where he'd remained until the day the Indians had attacked. Finding Susie alive beneath Jane's bed had been a godsend, but Daniel still hadn't given up the hope that someday he would find his sister and reunite Jane with her child. Since Richard, Jane's husband, hadn't come home for a long time before the attack, Daniel had no choice but to assume that the man had died, killed in the line of duty.

Daniel had taken Susie to the settlement at Michilimackinac in the Michigan Territory, where the first blacksmith shop had been available to the Indians. He'd worked with two other men, making weapons, household items, and other metal objects wanted by both the Indians and the whites. When word reached the settlement that the US government had promised to open and maintain two more shops, Daniel had left to set up a new shop in the northern part of the Wisconsin Territory. He and Susie settled near Jack Keller's trading post, which had been there for less than a year. Jack had been glad to welcome the blacksmith and the little girl. He was grateful for the company and enchanted by Daniel's niece. The men became quick friends, then later, they regarded each other as family. When Rebb Colfax showed up at the blacksmithy one day, sent by the government with a load of firewood for Daniel's forge, he was invited into the Keller and Trahern's family circle.

There was a good relationship between the three men and the little girl. When the missionaries came with business for all three men, they were welcomed and assisted as they adjusted to this rugged life. But as time passed and more settlers moved into the area, most of them within a day's ride from the trading post, Daniel realized what the government was trying to do with the help of the settlers and the missionaries. Daniel's opinion of all of them fell, and he became a champion for the Indians who had become his friends.

As he left Susie's room and headed to his own, Daniel thought of John and Amelia Dempsey and what their arrival would mean to the Indians, especially his friend, Black Hawk, an Ojibwa war chief.

John Dempsey had claimed to be a physician. A discussion with Jack after the pair left confirmed that the man had purchased supplies that only a doctor might need. And he had a medical bag, which Jack saw when he'd helped load their wagon with supplies.

Daniel believed John Dempsey was who he said he was, but the daughter Amelia . . . He had a mental image of sable brown hair tucked back in a knot at her nape . . . brown eyes in an unforgiving face, and pink lips that looked too full and too sweet to belong to a pious woman.

Amelia Dempsey had told Jack she thought he was rude. Had he been rude? Daniel wondered. No, he hadn't been rude, he decided. Just cautious and a mite unfriendly, because he didn't want to encourage them to stay.

The doctor's daughter reminded him too much of his late wife Pamela. Not in looks, for Pamela's coloring had been much darker than Amelia's. The similarity came in their behavior. Amelia was a woman who considered men like himself inferior. She was a woman like Pamela who teased a man and played with his affections until he was hooked and well on his way to hell. He'd managed to put Pamela from his mind; he would do the same with Amelia Dempsey.

"Go home, Miss Amelia," Daniel murmured as he stripped off his shirt, then tugged off his breeches. "Go home where you belong and leave us and the Indians to live in peace."

* * *

Miriam Lathom was a dark-haired young woman with kind eyes. When she arrived at their door the morning after their arrival, John and Amelia took to her immediately. She had a soft voice and a graceful way of moving. Her face could have belonged to an angel; it had a glow that seemed to come from the inside. While her features radiated warmth, her manner would calm even the most disturbed soul, Amelia thought.

There was much that needed to be done to make the infirmary and the back rooms more livable and patient-ready for Dr. Dempsey's work. Miriam came each day to help as Amelia unpacked and arranged her father's instruments and tools, and attempted to make the barren back rooms into a home.

As the Reverend Whitely had said, Miriam knew all the places to find herbs and other medicinal plants that grew wild in and around the mission. The two women spent an entire afternoon roaming through the forest, identifying and gathering medicinal plants.

Three days after their arrival, Amelia saw her father's first patient at the infirmary. It was a young woman, a missionary wife. She had burned herself while cooking when the grease from a cook fire had popped and splattered across her hand. It wasn't a serious burn as far as burns go, but Dr. Dempsey treated it carefully, because even the most simplest injury could fester if not tended properly. The woman was pregnant, which meant careful monitoring of the wound, as John Dempsey wanted no injury to the mother to endanger either woman or child.

Amelia saw her father's face as he ministered to Mary Black's hand, and recognized a happiness in his expression that she'd not seen in a long time. Later, when she mentioned it to him, he'd looked at her and admitted that he felt he could do more good in this remote area than he ever could in a city the size of Baltimore, Maryland, where people rarely appreciated the assistance he gave them, while others treated him as their personal physician, becoming angry when he wasn't immediately available for their sole use.

"As if I was a possession instead of a human being," her father said.

Amelia placed her hand on her father's shoulder. "I never realized they treated you that way."

There was new spring to John Dempsey's step, a new interest in life. Amelia thought that it was worth giving up their comfortable lifestyle in Baltimore to see the utter contentment on her father's face.

If it was rough on Amelia to make the adjustment to a life that was much different than the one she'd left behind, she didn't mind it at all. She missed her sister and wondered how she was doing. She missed Aunt Bess and the gruff woman's warm, generous affection. But she was here with her father, and her love for him and her enjoyment of working beside him overshadowed the sadness of leaving her old life behind.

"Amelia," her father called from the front room, "do we have any camphor? I can't find it."

She entered the infirmary and went right to the appropriate shelf in the cabinet. If it were any closer to her father, it would have jumped up and bitten him.

"Right there, was it?" John said with a smile. He patted his daughter's arm awkwardly. "What would I do without you, daughter?"

Amelia grinned. "I don't know, Father, but I suspect you'd manage to get along just fine . . . just as you'd done before you married Mother."

A look of sadness entered John's deep brown eyes. "Wonderful woman, your mother. I miss her."

"She looked like Rachel does now, didn't she, Father?" Which meant she was not only a kindhearted woman, but a beautiful one as well.

John nodded. "But you've got her heart, girl." He smiled as he reminisced. "Such a kind and giving heart it is, too."

Yet I haven't found a man more interested in a kind heart than a pretty face, Amelia thought.

"It looks like we need a few supplies, Father. I'll take Miriam with me to Keller's Outpost." She glanced around the otherwise tidy room and was satisfied that everything was as it should be. "Will you be needing me this morning or shall I go ahead and leave with Miriam?"

"Go, daughter. I'll be fine here alone." His gaze held genuine affection. "See if Jack has any of that maple syrup he let us taste the last time we were in."

Amelia nodded. "Anything else?"

"I could use another one of these," he said as he held a pair of forceps. "Find out from Daniel Trahern how much it'll cost for him to make one of these for me."

Amelia stiffened. "He's probably extremely busy," she hedged. She didn't want to talk to Daniel Trahern; she didn't even want to see him. Her father was making it difficult for her to escape both things.

"Just get a price then, girl. I don't need it tomorrow."

There was nothing she could do but agree to visit the blacksmith. Unless she could ask Miriam to run the errand while she herself ordered supplies from Jack.

Amelia's spirits brightened. Miriam wouldn't mind taking care of that unpleasant matter for her.

But, later, as she spoke with Miriam, it seemed that the young woman was too busy to accompany Amelia to the post. The journey to the post wasn't a particularly long one. Amelia could certainly make it alone.

She scowled. Now the task of conferring with Daniel Trahern lay firmly within Amelia's hands.

Three

It was a beautiful, warm day without a cloud in the sky. With a young missionary's help, Amelia readied the wagon for the journey to the trading post. Besides their own supplies, there were a few items Amelia needed to purchase for some of the missionaries, including Will Thornton, the young man who helped her hitch the horse to the wagon—a smaller conveyance than the one she and her father had brought to the mission.

Amelia knew she'd have no trouble with the vehicle; she had driven the larger one on their way there. As for the journey to the post, there was a direct road from Keller's to the mission. It was a short simple trip, during which Amelia knew she wouldn't get lost.

With a wave at Will, Amelia left the mission, taking the dirt road that meandered through the forest toward the trading post and Trahern's Blacksmithy. She enjoyed the scenery as she drove. It was such a lovely time of year—not too hot, not cold. The trees were a lush shade of green. The sky was so blue and the sun so bright they nearly hurt her eyes. Amelia gave no thought to any dangers along the way. She didn't worry about encountering Indians, soldiers, or worse. The day was too bright and cheerful; such dark thoughts were dismissed as soon as they occurred to her.

When she pulled the wagon before the trading-post

building and climbed down from the seat, she noticed that someone had tied a couple of horses to the rail of the trading post's front porch. Amelia secured her own horse, then entered the log structure.

Once her eyes had adjusted to the dark, she saw Jack Keller, who waved to her as she came in. Smiling in return, she left Jack to finish with his customer while she wandered about the post. She picked out the items her father wanted, then chose the things that Miriam, Will, and the other missionaries requested. She smiled at Jack as she approached several times and placed the selected items on the counter. She felt a prickling along her spine, knew she was being watched, but refused to meet the other customer's gaze.

After a time, the stranger's obvious stare made her angry, and she glanced his way. She controlled a grimace as she took note of his appearance then quickly averted her gaze. He was a dirty, grubby fellow with unkempt hair, a scruffy beard, a large nose, and small eyes. She experienced a shiver of revulsion as he shifted closer and she caught a whiff of some horrible smell.

"Jack," the man said, "ain't you gonna introduce us?"

Amelia shot Jack a wary look. Jack, catching it, understood immediately. "Not in your life, Kertell. This here is a lady, too good for the likes of you."

Amelia didn't hear the man's reply as she moved to put distance between the malodorous man and herself. Finally, she heard Jack bidding the man farewell, and she was able to approach the counter.

"Thanks," she said.

Jack smiled. "My pleasure. Kertell did not seem like someone you wanted to know."

"You thought correctly." She pretended to shudder. "Who is he?"

"Name's Thomas Kertell. He's a fur trapper. Comes to the post regularly, about every three to four weeks."

"Are there others like him? People who come here to trade once a month or so?" she asked.

Jack shrugged his shoulders. "Few trappers, some Indians, and a couple of soldiers."

Amelia saw a gleam in his eyes. "You're teasing me."

"Just a little."

"A lot," she insisted.

He grinned. "All right. A lot." He pushed her gathered items in a pile on one side of the counter. "What else do you need?"

She gave Jack her list, and he helped her select all the necessary items. After she settled up, he assisted her in carrying the goods out to the wagon.

"Thank you, Mr. Keller," she said.

He smiled. "You are very welcome, Miss Dempsey."

Amelia became aware of Daniel Trahern watching from the open door to his shop across the road. Her heart beat a rapid tattoo as she looked at him, then glanced quickly away. She sensed his continued stare as Jack helped her climb up onto the wagon seat and as she drove the vehicle away.

She glanced back once, saw that he was still watching her, and felt a warm fluttering in the pit of her stomach.

What was it about the man that made her feel as awkward as a young girl?

She scowled. It was a certainty that she and Daniel would cross paths again. There would be other encounters. How could there not be when the comforts of life depended on the tools and other metal objects of necessity that he alone in this wilderness created?

She drove the vehicle into the forest and tried to appreciate the beauty of her surroundings, but her mind kept returning to Daniel Trahern and how uncomfortable he'd made her feel. There was one item on her list she hadn't gotten. A small medical instrument for her father, one that only a blacksmith could make.

What excuse could she give her father if she returned to the mission without at least having ordered one made? That Daniel Trahern made her so nervous that she avoided him like the plague?

Amelia pulled on the reins to stop the horse. Then she steered the wagon back to Trahern's Blacksmithy. She wasn't going to let the man intimidate her! He was only a man after all.

A disturbing man, she thought. *An attractive man.*

Thomas Kertell came out from behind a copse of trees and cut off the wagon, making Amelia draw back on the reins to stop it. His abrupt appearance frightened her horse, and it took a few minutes for Amelia to calm the animal.

The filthy man was grinning at her when she'd finally gotten the horse under control.

Amelia eyed Kertell warily. "You could have caused an injury! What do you want, Mr. Kertell?"

The fur trapper beamed at her. "You know who I am. You must've been askin' 'bout me."

She shook her head. "I didn't ask. Jack Keller told me."

The man's tiny eyes narrowed. "What'd he have to say?"

"Just that you're a fur trapper."

He nodded. "A damn good one, too."

"That's nice," she said. "Now if you'll move your horse, so I can get through, I'd appreciate it."

Kertell's smile revealed missing and black teeth. "How much?"

"Excuse me?"

"I want to know how you're gonna show your appreciation if I let you through?"

She scowled at him. "Let us not play games. Please move, so I can continue."

His grin faltered. "In a bit. I thought maybe you and me can get better acquainted."

"I'm sorry," she said. "I don't have time. There are people waiting for me at the mission."

He refused to move. "Why you heading back to the post then? Forget something at Jack's?"

"At Daniel Trahern's," she answered calmly, although her heart had picked up its pace and her stomach was beginning to burn with apprehension. "Let me pass, Kertell."

He shook his head as he nudged his mount closer to the wagon.

"If you don't move, I'll have to run you down." Her hands shook on the reins, but Amelia knew she would do it if she had to. It was a matter of survival—hers.

The fur trapper blinked with surprise, then his lips curved into a slow smile of delight. "So ya wanna be difficult, eh?" He chuckled. "Go ahead and run me over. See if you can."

Amelia stiffened for a brief moment. "Hiyah!" she shouted and slapped the leather reins against the hindquarters of the horse. The animal danced, then finally started to move. She knew the man could easily catch up with her, but she spurred the horse on, hoping to get back to the trading post where there was help.

She got about fifty yards, before Kertell was beside her. He hopped onto the wagon and jerked the reins from her hands. Amelia screamed and fought to shove him from the seat. Kertell cuffed her across the head with his fist. Her head spun, and Amelia saw stars. She nearly fell off the wagon as she clutched her head and blinked to clear her vision. Kertell grabbed her and shoved her onto the wagon seat.

Amelia thought she heard Kertell trying to calm her horse, which was skittish. She got up and tried to push the man off the wagon. With a growl, he hit her again. She gasped as tears filled her eyes, and she blinked to clear them.

A gunshot ran out in the stillness of the forest. "Leave her alone and get off the wagon, Kertell!" a deep male voice commanded.

The fur trapper froze. "This ain't your business, Trahern."

Through a painful haze, Amelia saw the blacksmith.

"I've made it my business. She's coming to see me," Daniel said.

The stench of Kertell was awful. To Amelia, the man smelled of combined body odor, filth, and rancid animal fat.

Amelia's head cleared, but continued to throb painfully. She saw Daniel Trahern about ten feet from the wagon. He had the barrel of a rifle aimed at Kertell's head. His hard blue gaze never left the fur trapper for a second. Amelia wondered if the blacksmith was a good shot or if she should somehow get out of the way of the gun. She wasn't afraid; somehow the appearance of Daniel Trahern had instilled a new calm. She had no doubt he would win this fight against the fur trapper. She knew instantly that Thomas Kertell would be no match for the blacksmith's intelligence and wiry strength.

She sensed movement by the man beside her as Kertell's hand inched slowly toward his waistband.

"Daniel! He's got a weapon," she cried, and threw herself off the wagon to put herself out of Kertell's range.

Daniel tensed. Quick as a flash, Kertell had drawn his knife, but to his relief, Amelia was out of reach before the man could use it against her to gain his freedom.

With Amelia out of the way of harm, Daniel raised the gun barrel and clicked back on the trigger. "Drop the knife, Tom," he said softly. "And don't try to use it."

At the outer margin of his vision, he saw Amelia struggle to get up from the ground. He didn't go to her, as he wanted. He kept his gaze and his gun on Kertell.

Anger filled Daniel, making him want to teach the fur trapper a lesson he wouldn't soon forget. He held his temper because Amelia was present.

"Get on your horse and ride out of here," he told the fur trapper. "I'll give you thirty seconds to move. If you're not on your horse by then, I'll blast a hole the size of a goose egg right through that soft head of yours."

Amelia heard the deadly menace in Daniel's voice and shivered. This was not a man one wanted as an enemy. Still, she moved away from the wagon toward him. She stayed out of the range of his rifle and well away from the invisible line between the two men. She should have felt threatened by Daniel's anger, but she didn't. She felt safe instead.

Thomas Kertell apparently understood the reality of Daniel's threat. With frequent glances toward Daniel's gun, he dropped his knife, slowly climbed off the wagon, and got on his horse.

With his gun still trained on the fur trapper, Daniel moved closer to the man's horse. "Don't come back, Kertell. Ever. Your presence and your business are no longer wanted here."

"What?" The man looked furious. "Because of her? A female?"

Daniel's eyes narrowed. "A lady, Kertell. The woman's

a lady . . . not that you've ever come in contact with one before. You don't mess with a lady, Tom." He lifted his gun higher and sighted down the barrel with one eye. "I don't see you moving, and your thirty seconds are up."

"I'm going!" the trapper cried, suddenly nervous.

As Kertell turned the horse, Amelia saw the man's hand move to his side. "Daniel, he's got a gun!"

Kertell immediately released the weapon and raised his hands above his head in plain view. "Don't take my gun, Daniel. You've already got my knife." He shot Amelia a nasty look that made her feel chilled.

"Get a move on. If you're gone before I count to three, I'll think about letting you keep that gun and your life."

"Can I have my knife?" Kertell knew when he'd been given a chance.

"One . . . two . . ."

The trapper kicked his mount and fled without his knife but with his rifle.

Amelia watched Kertell ride away, then closed her eyes and breathed a sigh of relief that he was gone. With a smile on her face, she turned to thank Daniel Trahern.

"Are you all right?" he asked gruffly as he approached her. His gaze seemed to catalog every inch of her from her hair, which was a mess, to her dirty face and hands, down to her shoes. Anger lit up Daniel's eyes as he looked at her face, and she realized she must be bruised where Kertell had hit her.

"I'm fine—"

"You're not fine, woman!" he burst out with fury in his voice. "Look at yourself. You've been hit and thrown about, and you're saying you're fine!"

His outburst startled her until she realized that his anger was rooted in his concern for her. She stepped closer. "I am fine," she said softly. "Yes, I've been hurt, but I'm alive, and I'm not seriously injured." She reached out to touch his arm but he jerked out of her reach.

"Daniel," she said, hiding her hurt, "thank you for coming to my rescue."

"I shouldn't have had to rescue you," he said.

Amelia smiled. "Yes, I know, but—"

"Why were you coming back, Amelia?" He scowled. "Better yet, why did you come here alone? Didn't you realize that this country isn't safe for a woman traveling alone?"

She blinked. "It's a straight road and only a short distance."

"A distance long enough to be trouble to anyone, Miss Dempsey."

She liked it better when he'd called her Amelia. It'd been the first time she'd heard her name on his lips, and she found she liked hearing him say it. Hearing it did strange things to her insides. "I didn't give it much thought," she admitted.

"Obviously."

She frowned at his scathing tone. "Daniel—Mr. Trahern," she amended quickly when she saw him frown. "I want to thank you for coming to my rescue."

"You shouldn't have needed a rescuer."

She still didn't like his tone. "I know. You said that—"

"What in the devil were you thinking of in traveling to the post all alone?"

"We needed supplies—"

"Are you a fool?" His blue eyes flashed with angry fire.

Amelia felt as if she were the guilty one, the one under attack. "I—"

"Even a child would have sense enough to realize the danger of these woods."

"We needed supplies!" she shouted before he could interrupt her again. "Miriam couldn't come. The rest were all busy."

Daniel's eyes narrowed. "Of course they were."

Amelia's back went up. "I'm trying to thank you for coming to my aid, but you're making it damn difficult!" She spun away and marched toward the wagon. Amazingly, through all the commotion, her horse hadn't run away. While the humans were arguing, the animal chomped grass.

She had not gone very far when she felt someone grab her shoulder from behind. She shrieked, and Daniel instantly released her. She spun to face him.

"I'm not done talking with you."

"I'm the victim here," she cried. "Why do I feel as if I'm the criminal being punished?" His nearness generated a heat inside her. She felt wounded and vulnerable, and she didn't need him yelling at her.

"Have you thought about what would have happened if I hadn't followed you?"

She saw red. "You followed me?" He nodded. "Why?"

"I'd seen Kertell, and I'd seen you. I knew it was only a matter of time before the man made a pest of himself to you."

"Pest?" She was outraged that he thought of her confrontation with the fur trapper so lightly. "The man is more than a pest, Daniel Trahern. He's a menace to society."

A half smile formed on Daniel's lips. His gaze was mocking. "You may have had some *society* in the city of Baltimore," he said, giving away the fact that he knew and remembered from where she'd come. "Here in Wisconsin, there aren't any society folks. It's just us poor working folks whose only desire is to survive in this rugged land."

"I didn't mean—"

He interrupted her again. "Once you've done all your trading or buying or whatever it is that needs doing at Jack's, then you'd best hurry home. Ask Jack to escort you back."

She glared at him. "I was coming to see you." She went to the wagon and reached under the seat. She pulled out a small metal instrument and extended it toward the blacksmith. "Father needs you to make one of these for him."

Daniel held her gaze for a long moment before he transferred his attention to the object in her hand. She held it out farther, and he took it. He didn't study it; he just looked at her. "You should not have come here alone."

"Can you make one of those or not?" she asked, fuming inwardly, but unwilling to show it.

"I can make it." Once again, his blue eyes captured her attention. Heat rushed through her veins as she steadily held his gaze.

"Good," she said. "Now if you'll excuse me, I'll be on my way." She was mad, but didn't show it as she climbed up onto the wagon as if she hadn't a care in the world. She was conscious of how disheveled she looked and of the pain in her head and at the site of her other injuries. "When will it be ready?"

The man shrugged as he approached the wagon. "Tomorrow—late. Have your father pick it up the day after."

"My father's extremely busy—what are you doing?" she exclaimed as Daniel climbed onto the seat beside her and grabbed the reins from her hands.

"I'm taking you home."

"No, you're not."

He glared at her. "You believe Kertell went away quietly. He didn't. He's out there right now, waiting to see if you're alone as you head back."

Amelia couldn't suppress a shiver. "You think he's waiting for me?"

Daniel nodded. He studied her face and his expression softened. He touched her forehead where Kertell had left a bruise. "Does it hurt much?"

It was almost as if he really cared. Mesmerized by his tender expression, she could only shake her head.

"Don't come back here alone, Amelia," he said quietly and with authority. "I may not be around the next time you get yourself into trouble."

Her jaw snapped. "I didn't invite the fur trapper's attentions!"

He inspected her from head to toe. "Just your being here is enough temptation for any man."

Amelia laughed harshly. "Hardly that, Mr. Trahern." She didn't think he would be so cruel.

"Daniel," he said stiffly, then he appeared to be annoyed at himself. "There aren't many women out here in this territory. A few at the mission, but none others like you. Your presence here alone is an invitation to a man."

Incensed, she lifted her chin. "That's not true, and you know it. For some reason, you've chosen to dislike me on sight. You know nothing about me or my father; yet, you'd made up your mind as soon as you met us." She was disconcerted by his continued study of her.

"You're a beautiful woman, Amelia. Surely, you must know that."

Beautiful? she thought. She wasn't the beautiful sister; Rachel was. What would he say after meeting her? "I'm neither beautiful nor stupid, Mr. Trahern, and I don't appreciate the cruel jokes at my expense." She tried to grab the reins from his hand, but he held them out of reach.

Daniel gazed at her, intrigued. Was it possible that she actually didn't recognize her own attraction? Then, he remembered he'd been blinded to it at first. Studying Amelia now, he wondered how he hadn't seen her true beauty immediately.

When she reached for the reins again, he allowed her to take them. He didn't make any attempt to climb down from the wagon. After a long, hard look, Amelia clicked her tongue to spur the horse on. She headed the vehicle toward a clearing where she could turn it around to head back to the mission.

"You're going the wrong way," he drawled with a smile of amusement.

"I'm turning the vehicle around, Mr. Trahern," she said haughtily.

He could feel her anger; it reached out to him in taut waves, but it was something else about her that affected him greatly. Sitting next to her made him very much aware of her femininity. His skin tingled, and he was conscious of her every movement . . . the sharp little intake of breath she made when he shifted closer and his knee touched hers . . . the angry sound she uttered when despite her pointed suggestions he refused to leave her to travel back alone.

She was tense, and he could feel it. She was angry, and he responded with amusement and respect.

Amelia pulled into the clearing and felt satisfied when she managed to turn the wagon around. They traveled for a time in silence. She had to admit to herself that she was glad that Daniel was with her. She had been nervous that she might encounter Kertell again. Daniel's presence made her feel safe and protected. If he had been nicer about things, she wouldn't feel the need to strike back at him.

She glanced his way. "Thank you again for the rescue, Daniel," she said sweetly—too sweetly. The fact that he'd scolded her still stung.

She was satisfied to see his gaze narrow. "Don't return alone, Miss Dempsey," he said, acknowledging the barb with one of his own. "I don't want to have to kill a man because you were too foolish to listen to good reason."

That was the last of their conversation until they reached the mission. Daniel helped her carry the items she'd bought into the infirmary. "I'll be on my way now."

"How will you get back?" Amelia asked.

"I'm going to walk, Miss Dempsey."

"But that'll take you hours."

"An hour actually. Not so very far at all."

John Dempsey overheard their conversation as he exited the building. "Thank you, Mr. Trahern, for escorting Amelia home. I appreciate it."

Daniel acknowledged the man's thanks with a nod. "Your daughter had a bit of trouble near the post today. I suggested to her that in the future she not travel anywhere alone. It's dangerous out there, more so for a lone woman."

John Dempsey gazed at his daughter. "I thought Miriam was going with you."

Amelia blushed. "She couldn't make it."

"So you decided to go alone?"

She nodded.

"That wasn't a smart thing to do," her father said.

Anger made her eyes sparkle and her fists clench. "I'm not a child, Father! I realize now that I shouldn't have gone alone. You and Mr. Trahern don't have to keep at me about it!"

With that, she went off in a huff to get away from both men.

"She's got a temper, I'm afraid," John Dempsey apologized.

"Nothing wrong with a little temper," Daniel said politely. "I've got a bit of one myself."

John Dempsey followed Daniel outside and to the wagon. "I'll have your tool ready the day after tomorrow," Daniel said as he brushed off his hands.

John nodded. "Thanks. I appreciate it."

"Your daughter—she's not all that helpless," Daniel said. "Today I think she realized that she has a lot to learn about the dangers of living in this area."

"She's always been a headstrong young woman," the doctor admitted with a sigh.

"Nothing wrong with being headstrong," Daniel said, "as long as one doesn't allow one's bad sense to outweigh the good."

Four

It was the first time that Amelia had ever seen an Indian, and she was shocked by the sight. She didn't know exactly what'd she expected, but it wasn't a near-naked man.

She'd been helping her father in the infirmary when the brave had come in with an injured hand. Amelia tried not to stare at him as she handed her father the things he needed. But she couldn't help looking at the warrior. She'd never seen a man in a loincloth. He was bare-chested and muscled. His dark hair fell past his shoulders. He had dark eyes that regarded her with curiosity whenever she happened to look his way. He made her uncomfortable. In her brief glances his way, she'd noted tattoos across his chest and shoulder and tiny metal rings through the lobe of each ear. He looked primitive and dangerous. She was both frightened and fascinated. She knew it wasn't polite to stare and worried about what was proper, but she looked anyway.

The Indian didn't flinch while the doctor worked on his hand, although the wound and her father's ministrations must be causing him pain.

"Amelia, hand me another strip of cloth," her father said.

She immediately gave him the bandage strip.

"Keep the wound clean," John Dempsey told his patient. "I've cleaned and stitched it. Come back in a few days, and I'll check it for you. If you can't return, have someone take out these stitches."

The brave nodded and mumbled a few words. The Indian obviously knew English. He handed something to John Dempsey, then with one last look in Amelia's direction, the Indian left. Amelia relaxed only after the man left the building. She peered outside and watched him join up with a band of six Indians.

"Amelia," her father said, drawing her attention, "come away from that window. It's not polite to stare."

She blushed. "I wasn't staring. I was just looking." She shuddered as she glanced outside again at the fierce-looking group of men. "I think I know why some people call the Indians savages."

John Dempsey smiled. "Did he make you nervous?"

She nodded. "I don't know what I'd expected, but it wasn't someone like him." She moved away from the window to clean and straighten her father's work area. "Apparently, he understands English." Her father nodded. "Who is he?"

"His name is Rain-from-Sky. He is brother to the Ojibwa war chief, Black Hawk."

Amelia felt a chill. "War chief?"

John inclined his head. "His brother is. When there's trouble between Indian tribes, Black Hawk leads the Ojibwa against their enemy. Rain-from-Sky is a great warrior, but he is not a chief."

"How do you know all of this?"

"From Reverend Whitely. Some of the Ojibwa are frequent visitors to the mission. He also said that Daniel Trahern and Black Hawk are friends."

Her heart skipped a beat at the mention of the blacksmith. She could easily picture Daniel with an Indian. Daniel was fair while the Ojibwa was dark, but there was something about Daniel that seemed as wild and untamed as his Indian friends. "With Daniel's influence, I'm surprised that the Ojibwa come to the mission at all."

"They don't come to be taught the word of God, although the missionaries have apparently tried to convert them. They come to trade with the people here."

"I would have thought they'd do their trading at Jack Keller's place," Amelia said.

"Oh, they do that, too."

"I don't understand—"

"Some of the Indian women like the crosses the missionaries wear about their necks. They bring furs and other items to trade for the necklaces the missionaries make for them."

Amelia cleaned off her father's worktable. "I see."

The doctor smiled at his daughter as he studied the object in his hand.

"What's that?" Amelia asked.

Her father held up a beaded pouch on a string long enough to be worn over the shoulder or around the neck. "Payment for services rendered."

The colorful beadwork was beautiful. Amelia was fascinated and approached for a closer look. "It's lovely!"

He handed it to her. "You take it. You can use it to carry whatever it is you ladies like to carry."

The beads felt warm beneath her fingers. "Thank you. I've never seen anything like it."

"They do beautiful work, don't they?"

Amelia agreed. "They do. It's hard—" She bit her lip. She'd been going to say that it was hard to believe a savage could make something so beautiful, but the unfairness of the statement got to her before she'd been foolish enough to utter it.

"The blacksmith said my forceps would be ready today."

"Yesterday actually."

"I could certainly use them," he said. "Do you know if anyone is heading that way?"

She didn't know, but told him she would ask around. She went in the back rooms to prepare her and her father's lunch. She heard the doctor talking to someone in the front room. A new patient must have entered the infirmary. She left the kitchen to check if her father needed help. She saw a young man—a soldier. He sat on the examining table while her father looked at his arm.

"How did you do this?" the doctor asked.

"Nicked it on a briar bush."

"It's festered."

The young soldier nodded. "It didn't seem too bad at first, but once I noticed the red swelling, I figured I'd better get it looked at." He noticed Amelia, who had quietly come up behind her father.

"And not a moment too soon," John said. "I'm sorry—it's going to hurt while I clean it, but it can't be avoided."

The young man nodded. "Hello," he said to Amelia with a smile.

"Ah, Amelia, good you're here," her father said without glancing back. Then, he told her what he needed, and she assisted him quietly, efficiently, feeling sympathy when the soldier winced with pain.

"Is he always this brutal?" the pale young man asked her after her father finished cleaning the wound and spread a salve on it to battle infection.

"Always," Amelia said with a teasing smile. "Sometimes he's even worse."

The soldier shuddered and closed his eyes. "Then I pray I never get shot."

"Bandage the wound for me, will you, Amelia?" her father said. "I have something to do in the back."

"Certainly, Father." She collected the supplies, then smiled at the patient as she bandaged his arm.

"Keep the wound clean, and put this on it to fight infection." The doctor handed the man a jar of cream.

"Thanks, Doc."

Her father nodded and left.

"Is your fort nearby?" Amelia asked.

The soldier shook his head. "No, it's two days' journey from here. We're camped nearby about a mile away." He watched her wind the strip of fabric carefully about his arm. "Amelia."

She looked at him. He wore the navy military jacket and pale blue pants that were the uniform of a US soldier. His dark brown hair had been cropped short, but he had long sideburns and no beard. His eyes were gray, fringed by thick dark lashes. His mouth looked too soft, his face boyish. He couldn't have been much more than eighteen.

"Pretty name," he said.

"Thank you. It was my grandmother's name."

"I'm Cameron Walters."

"Hello, Mr. Walters," she said. "It's a pleasure to meet you." And it was, Amelia decided. The young man was pleasant, respectful, and quite good-looking although he was young.

"Cameron, please."

"All right, Cameron." She picked up a second fabric strip and began to wind it over the first. "And you may call me Miss Dempsey," she said. Her eyes twinkled as she met his gaze.

He grinned, but took her at her word. "Miss Dempsey, you're new here. When did you and the doctor arrive?"

"Oh, you've been here before?"

He nodded. "A couple of times, but I would have remembered seeing someone as lovely as you."

Amelia met his gaze with raised eyebrows at his lavish compliment, believing it to be false. The soldier blushed and looked away, while mumbling an apology. His horrified look earned her sympathy.

"Tell me, Cameron, are you or any of your friends—I assume you're with your troop and haven't come here alone." The man nodded. "Are any of you planning a trip to the trading post?"

His expression perked up as he studied her. "Why, are you in need of some special item?"

"Actually, my father is, but not from Keller's—from the blacksmith there, Daniel Trahern."

"I could go there if you'd like."

"That's extremely nice of you."

"If you will be so kind as to accompany me there."

"What about your superiors? Don't you have to report back?"

He shrugged. "I don't see why, since I've been given the rest of the day free."

Amelia didn't know if she wanted to see Daniel again so soon, although she'd regretted their last exchange. The blacksmith had saved her and escorted her back to the mission. He had scolded her, but it had been for her own good; yet, she had repaid his kindness with anger. She knew she should apologize to him. She just didn't know if she felt ready enough to do that.

If you don't go and get it over with, you'll never rest, she thought. "All right, I'll go with you," Amelia said, and she hoped she wouldn't be sorry she'd agreed to go.

It was a pleasant afternoon for the ride to the trading post. Cameron was good company, and Amelia was glad for the escort. The memory of her encounter with Thomas

Kertell chilled her. She couldn't help wondering what would have happened if Daniel hadn't come to save her.

She stole a glance at the young soldier beside her. If Kertell stopped her again, would Cameron be able to protect her? Cameron was a boy compared to Daniel. She hoped he was a good shot. He was a soldier; he should be. His confident manner made her question her fears.

The journey to the post took little time. Amelia was glad when they made it safely with no sign of Kertell or any Indians. Her first encounter this morning with an Indian had been enlightening. She didn't think she wanted to meet one when she was alone.

"Would you like me to come inside?" Cameron said as he pulled the wagon in front of the blacksmithy.

She shook her head. She wanted to apologize to Daniel Trahern without an audience. "I'll be fine. Go on to Keller's. Didn't you mention that you needed a few things?"

The young man admitted that he did. "Shall I wait here for you when I'm done?"

"That'll be fine, thank you."

Amelia stared at the blacksmithy a moment before venturing inside. She entered the building and immediately spied Daniel by the forge fire. She studied him a moment, found enjoyment in watching him work, then approached.

Daniel felt a tingling at his nape that alerted him that he was being watched. He glanced up, saw it was Amelia Dempsey, and quickly looked down again.

"Mr. Trahern?"

He straightened, set down his work, and faced her. "Miss Dempsey," he said. "Come for your father's forceps?"

She nodded. "And to apologize."

Daniel concealed his surprise. "For what?"

"You rescued me three days ago, and I was rude." She

gave him a tentative smile. "I'm sorry. I'm grateful you came by when you did. I'm not sure I would have escaped that horrible man if you hadn't. Thank you."

"An apology and a thank-you?" he said with a teasing twinkle. "I'm honored."

The effect of his smile on her was devastating. His blond hair was ruffled and appealing. His blue eyes glowed, and there were tiny crinkle lines at each outer corner. Her blood warmed. He really was an extremely attractive man.

"Have you settled in at the mission?" Daniel asked.

"Yes, we have, thank you. The people there seem friendly enough."

Noting something odd in her tone, Daniel looked at her. "You're surprised that they're friendly."

Amelia blushed. "I guess it's because of something Jack told me when we first came."

Jack? Daniel frowned. *Not Mr. Keller but Jack.* He felt a niggling of anger. "What was that?"

"He said that you disliked the missionaries, that you didn't agree with their efforts to improve the Indians' way of life. I met an Indian this morning, and I would think the missionaries could help them."

A muscle ticked along Daniel's jaw. "You think that, do you?"

She nodded. "Why they barely wore a stitch of clothing!"

"So the white lady was offended," he said mockingly.

"No, not offended exactly."

"Miss Dempsey, you know nothing about the Ojibwa people, least of all what's best for them." His voice was hard, angry.

She appeared flustered. "I'm sorry. I guess I shouldn't have spoken up. I was just making an observation. You are right; I don't know the Indians, so how can I judge what's best for them?"

She had surprised him once again with her answer. "Since you are here," he said, thinking it best to change the subject, "I assume someone accompanied you."

She nodded. "Cameron Walters, a soldier in the US Army. He sought medical help for an injured arm and was gracious enough to offer himself as escort."

He felt a flicker of some strange emotion. "I would think you would have preferred to come with your father," he commented.

She shrugged, bringing his attention to the curve of her neck. "Father was too busy to come."

"And so this soldier volunteered to escort you," he said, perhaps a little too sharply. He didn't want to put a name to whatever it was he was feeling.

She nodded, but looked confused by his tone.

He forced a smile. "Is there anything else your father needed?" He moved to a worktable and picked up the forceps he'd made for John Dempsey.

"Not that I'm aware of." She didn't move, but waited for him to return.

He went to her and gave her the medical instrument. As he handed it to her, his gaze fell on the beaded pouch. "Where did you get your bag?" he asked, intrigued.

"The Ojibwa brave gave it to my father as payment for tending his injured hand."

Daniel raised an eyebrow. "An Ojibwa went to your father as a patient?"

"Yes, why do you sound surprised?" Amelia frowned. "Tell me—are the Ojibwa and the Chippewa one and the same people?"

"They are actually. Many people around here prefer *Chippewa* over *Ojibwa*." He rubbed his right wrist with his other hand, as if the wrist pained him. "Have you noticed how much alike the two words sound? *Ah-jib-ah-wa. Chip-ah-wa.*" He reached out to touch the strung beads. "As for your first question, I'm surprised because the Ojibwa people are skilled in the medicinal arts. I'd trust my life to an Ojibwa shaman before I'd go to an American doctor. I've seen them heal patients. Their skills are amazing. They know more about healing with plants and herbs than any white man I've known."

Amelia raised her chin. "My father is not just any white man," she said, sounding put out.

Daniel was amused. "No offense to your father. I'm just telling you how it usually is."

She relaxed and gave him a slight smile. To his satisfaction, she seemed in no hurry to leave. "What are you working on?" she asked, glancing toward the fire.

She'd amazed him once again. "You really want to know?" he asked. She nodded. "Come closer to the forge area, and I'll show you."

She started to approach when she heard a wild shriek from outside. "What is that?" Before Daniel could answer, she was out the side door, peering out into the yard behind the roofed, but open area Daniel used to fix wagons. The sound came again, and Daniel saw Amelia take several steps toward the noise. He followed with a smile on his lips. The sound was familiar to him. It was Susie playing.

A small figure ran back and forth in the yard on the side of the building. Amelia got a quick mental picture of dark hair, dirty face, and dirty clothes. She hurried forward as the figure disappeared. In a moment, the figure ran past again. Amelia realized, from the size, that it was a child.

She went out to the edge of the building and saw the child, singing and playing and howling shrilly, apparently engaged in some kind of game. It was a young girl, she realized. Amelia watched her a few minutes, wondering where the little girl came from.

She sensed Daniel's presence behind her. Amelia was appalled at the child's condition. She looked a mess.

"Who is she?" Amelia asked without turning. "A better question is why she's here. Surely, this is no place for a child. Where are her parents? And look at her, I'll bet she hasn't had a bath in well over a month."

She felt Daniel tense as he moved to her side. After a brief glance in his direction, she was surprised by the anger in Daniel's expression. "I'm sorry. I guess I shouldn't have said anything, but it bothers me to see a child that way."

"What way?" he asked tightly. "Happy?"

She gazed at him in astonishment. "You think it's appropriate for a little girl to be covered with mud and screaming like a wild Indian?"

"What I think is that you're too quick to judge. You're in unfamiliar territory. You understand little about our life here. We find our happiness in simple things. Susie is having a wonderful time at play. What's wrong with that?"

"Who is she?" Amelia asked a second time. She got her answer when the little girl suddenly turned and spied the adults.

"Pa!" she cried. She ran and launched herself into the man's arms.

Amelia froze in surprise. *Pa?* The child was Daniel's daughter? She closed her eyes as she realized that she'd offended Daniel once again. When she opened them again, it was to see Daniel slowly, carefully lowering the little girl to the ground. Amelia bit her lip as she watched father and daughter. On close inspection, she could see the resemblance between the two as Daniel smiled and ruffled the child's hair.

"Been playing in the dirt again, Susie?"

She nodded briskly. "I was playing warrior, Pa. Practicing for when I visit Conner. Last time Conner's grandma made us finger cakes, and we got to eat them outside."

Daniel winced. "I hope that your hands were cleaner when you ate than they are now."

Susie smiled up at her father and nodded. As if she had just suddenly become aware of Amelia's presence, the little girl turned and locked gazes with her. Amelia found herself staring into eyes so like Daniel's that it took her breath away.

Five

"Hello," the child said.

"Hello," Amelia replied. *Daniel is married with a child,* she thought. It was a sobering revelation. She hated the disappointment she felt.

"Amelia, this is Susie," Daniel said, watching her intently. He had his arm about the little girl. "Susie, this is Miss Dempsey."

"But, Pa, didn't you just call her Amelia?"

To Amelia's amazement, Daniel's cheeks reddened. "I'm an adult. Adults sometimes call each other by their first names. You're a child. Children should call adults by their proper name, using Miss or Mister."

"I call Jack *Jack* and Rebb *Rebb,*" Susie pointed out.

"That's because Jack and Rebb gave you permission," Daniel said. "Miss Dempsey hasn't given you leave to do so."

Amelia smiled as Susie stared at her as if considering. "You may call me Miss Amelia, if you'd like," she said.

Susie grinned at her, then turned a gaze full of satisfaction toward Daniel. "She has given me leave, Pa."

Daniel nodded. "Then it's all right then."

"Where did she come from?" Susie asked her father.

Amelia saw an odd look cross Daniel's expression. "It's all right, Mr. Trahern."

"She called you Mister, Pa. Why—when you called her Amelia?"

"I was just teasing your pa," Amelia explained, noting with amusement the change of expression that crossed Daniel's face. She grinned at the child. "I'm from Baltimore, which is a long, long way from here. My father and I live at the mission now."

The light in the child's blue gaze dimmed. "You live at the mission?"

Frowning, Amelia nodded. "Yes, that's right."

"Oh." There was a new wariness in Susie's expression.

"I'm not a missionary," Amelia said. "My father is a doctor."

Susie's brow cleared, but a hint of the wariness remained in her eyes. "Why did you come? Are you his helper?"

"Yes, I am." Amelia lowered her voice conspiratorially. "Actually, my father needs looking after."

Susie shot Daniel a brief glance. "Daughters should look after their pas," she said.

The two females grinned at one another.

Daniel wasn't happy with Amelia. The woman could feel the tension between them, but she doubted Susie did.

"Run inside and get washed," Daniel said to the little girl.

"Aw, Pa—"

"Now, Susie."

"All right." Susie hung her head as she went past Amelia and Daniel to get inside.

The tension reached unbearable limits as the little girl left Amelia and Daniel.

"Daniel—"

"No, don't say it," he replied coldly. "You've already expressed your opinion."

"It wasn't my intention to offend anyone."

"Again, you're too quick to judge."

Amelia flushed and felt severely reprimanded. She didn't know what else to say that wouldn't anger the man further. "I guess I'd better be going."

He didn't encourage her to stay. She felt sad that their newly made truce had already ended. She was drawn to Daniel. She didn't know why when they'd barely been able to speak kindly to each other. Each one had insulted the other from the first moment of their meeting. For a little while, she'd hoped that if not friends, she and Daniel would have, at least, been able to obtain a certain level of peace between them.

There was still the matter of payment for her father's instrument. She felt her cheeks warm as she realized that there would be no gracious way to leave.

Amelia picked up the beaded pouch and extracted a silver coin. She extended the coin toward Daniel. "Thank you for filling my father's order."

His features were hard as he took the coin. She flinched and turned away. "Good afternoon, sir," she said.

Although the wagon was across the street, Amelia chose to leave from the yard and walk around the building.

She'd gone several feet when she felt the strongest urge to glance back, but she didn't. She could feel the animosity of his stare and knew she wouldn't like his expression.

Daniel has a wife, she thought. Why hadn't that fact ever occurred to her? The existence of his daughter had startled her, but it was the new knowledge of his wife that distressed her the most.

I have to learn to think before opening my mouth, she thought. She had gotten into trouble for her frankness before; she should have learned her lesson a long time ago.

The appearance of the little girl had stunned her. She

might not have been as surprised if the child had been a boy. But a girl? She'd never before seen a little girl so filthy and disheveled. She was astonished that Susie's father seemed unconcerned with the child's appearance. What about Susie's mother? Did she feel the same way? Didn't she mind that Susie ran around looking like a grubby little boy?

Cameron Walters was waiting for her in the wagon when she came around the outside of the blacksmithy. "I almost went inside to fetch you," the young man said. "Did you get what you needed?"

Amelia nodded. Cameron jumped down from the wagon to help her climb up and get comfortable on the seat. A brief glance in the back had shown her that Cameron had bought or traded for what he'd needed. "I see you bought a few extra things," she said.

"I did." Cameron smiled. "Anyplace else you'd like to go?" he asked.

"Just back to the mission, please." She could sense someone's hard stare as Cameron turned the wagon around to head back to the mission. Amelia glanced toward the blacksmithy to meet Daniel's angry gaze. She turned quickly away, shaken.

She shouldn't have come. She hadn't made things any better between her and Daniel Trahern.

Why should I care? He's married with a child.

But deep in Amelia's heart was the realization that she wanted his respect if she couldn't have anything else.

Daniel saw red as he watched Amelia and the soldier drive away. The woman was outrageous! Too quick to judge, too haughty and confident for her own good. How dare she insult his upbringing of Susie! Susie was a happy child, despite the terrible horror she'd endured the day of her mother's kidnapping. He didn't think he'd done such a bad job raising her.

He returned to the forge, then decided to quit for the day. He put everything in its proper place and went inside to Susie. He found the little girl kneeling on a chair, bent over a basin on the table. She apparently had just finished washing up, but had only succeeded in streaking the dirt on her face, hands, and arms. Susie dried her dirty hands on a towel. He took one long look at the child, then at the soiled towel, and felt a niggling of uneasiness. Susie was filthy and wore the worst garments. Amelia's comments about this being no place for a child hurt him; but as he studied Susie through Amelia's eyes, he began to wonder if the woman was right.

"Susie," he said, "you're going to need a bath, sweeting." With a smile, he went to a cabinet and pulled out a small looking glass. He brought it to the little girl. "Take a look."

Susie peered at her reflection and started to laugh.

Her amusement was contagious, and Daniel started to chuckle. "Do you like playing in the dirt?" he asked.

She nodded. "When Conner and me are playing warriors."

Is Amelia right? he wondered again. Susie was a little girl, who had no feminine influence to teach her what it is to be a female. As he warmed water on the iron stove, then went to pull out the hip tub, he began to worry that he'd not done right by Susie.

She was seven years old. She needed a woman to help her bathe, a woman to teach her how to fix her hair, someone to see that she had clothing besides the buckskin tunic and leggings she enjoyed wearing. Without a woman's influence, how was Susie to grow up to be the kind of a woman who would find a man to love and care for her, to have a family with?

When the water was hot, Daniel poured it into the tub, then added cold water. He gave Susie a bar of soap, some clean towels, and told her he'd wait outside while she washed. He'd bathed her when she was a baby. Now that she was older, he didn't think it was appropriate.

His house was next to the forge, and he sat on the front porch while he waited for Susie to tell him she had bathed and dressed again.

She was a little girl now, but what was to happen when she was a young woman? "Jane, I wish you were here for Susie," he whispered. "I know nothing about womanly things. I'm trying my best, but what if my best isn't good enough?"

He could hear Susie in the great room, singing and splashing, enjoying herself once she'd climbed into the bath. She sounded happy. Surely, that counted for something? Surely, he'd done something right?

Still, he couldn't forget the look on Amelia's face when she'd gazed at his little Susie. Amelia had managed to smile past her shock and dismay, but he knew she'd been appalled.

He'd had more than one anxious moment during which he'd worried about the child's welfare. Amelia's comments brought his doubts back, his concern for a little girl growing up among a small settlement of mostly men. He allowed Susie to visit the Ojibwa village occasionally to play with the children there and learn things from the Indian women. He trusted Black Hawk and his people. The women were generous to Susie, treating her as one of their own. *But Susie isn't learning what it is to be an American woman,* he thought with concern.

"I'll wager, Amelia, you'd be horrified to learn that

Susie spends time with Indians!" he muttered beneath his breath.

Susie came to the door. "Pa, I'm finished."

Daniel turned around and froze. She had put on her soiled clothes after taking a bath. She looked clean about the face, neck, and arms. He looked down. Even her feet were clean, he noticed. But she hadn't washed her hair, which was so coated with dirt and dried mud, that her blond hair was brown.

"Ah, sweeting, you forgot to wash your hair."

She shook her head. "I can't see when I wash my hair, and I don't like it 'cause I get soap in my eyes."

"It needs to be done, Susie. Change into some clean clothes, then I'll wash your hair for you, so you won't get soap in your eyes."

She made only a token protest and sat in a chair while she waited for Daniel to empty, then refill the washbasin. After he'd rinsed her hair, Daniel fixed supper. After they had eaten, he told Susie another story.

When it was bedtime, he tucked her in and kissed her good night. He gazed at the sleepy little girl with affection. "Susie, you're happy here, aren't you?"

She reached out a hand and touched his cheek. "I'm happy, Pa." Her eyes fluttered closed. Unable to stay awake, she drifted off to sleep.

Daniel left the room, thoughtful. Somewhat encouraged by a little girl's love, he sat in his favorite chair and wondered about her future.

Cameron Walters chatted nonstop during the journey back to the mission. Amelia, disturbed by her confrontation with Daniel, said little or nothing as the soldier talked about his time in service, about his childhood in Pennsylvania, and about his life in the wilderness.

The young man didn't seem to notice Amelia's lack of response, for which she was grateful. She felt terrible. She had offended Daniel with her observations about his little girl. The knowledge that Daniel was married with a child was upsetting to her.

"Then the captain," Cameron was saying, "he orders the man shot." The young man's horror finally pierced Amelia's conscience where nothing else could. "The bloke was only seventeen."

Amelia blinked. "Your commander shot one of his own men?"

Cameron nodded. "He'd run away, he had, and he'd taken all of our rations, too. Captain Milton, he was furious. He wouldn't rest until he'd found Peter Upton. He kept us moving for twenty-four hours straight. I, for one, was exhausted. By the time we'd found Peter, I had murder on my mind. Only it was too late, 'cause Peter had already drowned in the river."

Amelia frowned. "I thought you said the captain shot the young man."

Cameron nodded. "He did right enough, only Peter was already dead. Captain knew it, too, only he was enraged and needed to release his feelings." The young soldier looked at her with a residual of his own shock and fear. "He turned Pete's body over—he'd been lying facedown on the riverbank, you see. Well, he turned Pete over, then raised his gun and shot Pete between the eyes, not once but three times. The captain looked as if he'd been taken by the devil. He scared me, scared all of us. After that, none of the men would dare to desert."

Amelia shuddered. "Your captain sounds like a horrid man."

Cameron shook his head. "No, that's the thing of it. The captain's good to us. We'd not seen anything like that before Pete, and we haven't seen anything like it since."

Still, Amelia didn't think she wanted to make the man's acquaintance.

She was glad when they reached the mission. Thoughts of what Cameron had just told her lingered in her mind. The mental images that Cameron left with her were disturbing, and after thanking Cameron for his escort, she went to her bedchamber to be alone. Once in her room, she was bombarded with unsettling thoughts. Cameron's story had bothered her, but it was her embarrassment with Daniel and her distress over her attraction to a married man that she struggled to come to terms with.

She sat on her bed and had visions of a dead man with three bullet holes in his head intermingled with images of Daniel's expression after she'd been foolish enough to insult him.

She had gone to the blacksmithy to make peace with Daniel Trahern, but the only thing she'd accomplished was to alienate him further.

Six

"Amelia!" The harsh whisper accompanied by a gentle shake of her shoulder jolted Amelia awake in the middle of the night.

She blinked in the darkness and saw her father silhouetted against the soft light filtering in from the next room. "Father, what's wrong?"

"Patient," he said, and turned away.

Without another word, Amelia sprang from her bed and pulled a dressing gown over her nightwear. She was familiar with such a summons; she'd helped her father often enough with his medical practice back in Baltimore. Her heart gave a lurch as she hurried to the front room. She had immediate thoughts of Daniel Trahern. Was he sick or injured? It had been over a week since she'd seen him, and although he was married, she couldn't seem to get him out of her mind.

At the door to the infirmary, she was pulled up short at the sight of her father's patient. It was an Indian brave, looking so much different than the other Indians she'd met. *A different tribe,* she guessed. She became aware there were others in the room. She checked her surroundings and was taken aback by the number of Indians who had come with the patient. She did a quick mental count. There were eight of them, all watching her father from various positions about the room.

She drew a sharp breath and entered the infirmary. Several pairs of dark eyes pinned her as she reached her father's side. Her gaze fell on the patient, and she had to conceal her reaction of surprise. The brave, merely a boy, had suffered a gunshot wound. The young Indian held himself erect, trying hard not to flinch or make a sound, as John Dempsey examined and probed the wound with his fingers. She felt instant sympathy for him.

Without a word from her father, Amelia left his side to gather the supplies and instruments he would need to remove the bullet and properly tend the wound. First order of business was to clean the injury and the surrounding area. She handed her father a cloth and the solution he'd need. He accepted the items with a nod of thanks, and with a frown of concentration on his face, got to the task at hand.

While her father was thus engaged, Amelia set up his instruments—a lancet, a probe, and the new pair of forceps—where John Dempsey could reach them. As she worked, she was aware that the Indians watched her. Tense, she refused to meet any of their gazes. She kept her eyes on her work, her father, and their young patient.

Her father caught and held her glance. Amelia nodded at the silent message and went to prepare a dose of laudanum for the boy's pain. She poured the proper amount into a glass tumbler and brought it to the patient to drink. As she extended the glass toward the boy, a hand shot out to clamp about her wrist.

Amelia gasped and almost dropped the glass. Her gaze shot to the Indian who'd grabbed her, an older warrior with red-and-black stripes painted across his chest and forehead, and tattoos circling his wrists and upper arms.

The angry brave muttered something in his own lan-

guage. Petrified, Amelia looked at him, then at her father.
"Father—"

"It's all right," he said in English, as if it would do
any good when the Indian didn't understand. "Taking out
the bullet is going to hurt. We just want to ease the boy's
pain."

A second Indian murmured something to the one who
held Amelia's arm. The brave released Amelia, and it was
all Amelia could do not to drop the glass. He stared at
Amelia hard as he moved back against the wall to the
position he'd been in before he'd rushed forward.

"He did not mean to frighten you, doctor's daughter,"
the second Indian said, causing Amelia to start. "Runs-
with-the-Wind feared what was in the cup. I explained to
him that it was something to make Little Cloud feel less
pain."

"You speak English," she said.

He nodded. "So, too, do Morning Eagle and Walks-
with-Big-Stick." He gestured toward two of his friends,
both behind her.

She nodded. "Thank you."

The Indian smiled. "Little Cloud is Runs-with-the-
Wind's son. He is concerned for him."

Amelia murmured that she understood. While curiosity
prompted her to ask more questions, she kept silent instead, feeling that it would be somewhat inappropriate to
pry into the Indians' affairs.

She waited until her father was done deciding the best
way to extract the bullet, then she again extended the glass
toward Little Cloud. He reached for it with his one free
hand, raised it to his lips, and made a face as he swallowed it. He handed the glass back to her. She looked,
and there was a little bit of the contents left in the glass.

"Drink all of it," she said. Her gaze went to the Indian

who spoke English. "Make him understand that if he doesn't drink enough of it, it will not help him with the pain."

The older Indian spoke rapidly to the boy. The boy answered, and the man answered. The boy hesitated, but then he drank the remainder. He gasped when he was done, and his eyes watered.

Amelia smiled as she took back the glass.

"More, Amelia," her father said.

She froze. "But, Father, he's just a child."

John Dempsey seemed to consider that. "All right. We'll wait a few minutes to see how the medicine affects him."

Amelia nodded, relieved.

When the boy closed his eyes and started to doze despite the pain he must have been feeling in his shoulder, the doctor proclaimed the patient ready for the operation.

It had always bothered Amelia seeing people suffer, but she'd been able to do her job, because she knew they were trying to help them to heal. But on this occasion Amelia had to admit that she'd never felt a patient's pain as much as she did with this young Indian. He didn't cry out or whimper. Rather it was his courage and attempt to hide the pain he felt that garnered her sympathy and respect.

All the while her father was digging into the child's shoulder for the bullet, Amelia was conscious of the other Indians in the room, especially the boy's father, Runs-with-the-Wind. She tried not to think what the Indians might do to them if the boy became ill or died under her father's care. She offered up several silent prayers asking for Little Cloud's quick recovery.

Once while the doctor poured whiskey into the wound in an attempt to clean it, she'd met Run-with-the-Wind's gaze and felt a chill shiver along her spine as he stared back at her without emotion. When she transferred her gaze to the Indian who helped her earlier, she found the same stoic expression unbroken by a smile.

Amelia felt a pooling of relief when John Dempsey finally lifted the bullet with his forceps. He examined the bullet, then set it in a glass dish. After her father had stitched the boy's wound closed, Amelia was able to relax, as she felt some of the tension leave the room.

With a silent nod, the doctor instructed his daughter to put a plaster on the boy's shoulder. Then he addressed one of the English-speaking braves. "The boy needs to sleep," he said. "He shouldn't be moved."

"We cannot stay," the man replied. "We must move him."

John nodded, as if he understood. "Then you must move him carefully and find a safe place for him to recover. He is young and should mend well, as long as he doesn't take infection."

The Indian translated, and the father answered.

"We will find a safe place for him to heal," the man said.

"Good," the doctor responded. He gazed down at the bullet on the stand next to the examining table. "How did it happen?" He raised his gaze to the friend.

"While he slept, the boy was shot by a white soldier."

Amelia gasped, having overheard. Her gaze was full of warmth and sympathy as she studied Little Cloud.

The friend, noting Amelia's reaction, smiled at her. "You think this wrong. Perhaps only a savage would shoot a child while he was sleeping."

"Only an evil man would hurt an innocent child," she responded softly, drawing a respectful nod from the Indian.

The Indians left shortly afterward, their needs making

it imperative they leave before dawn. John and Amelia Dempsey looked at each other. They should have been exhausted, but neither one felt tired. With a soft smile, Amelia embraced her father, then started to clean the surgery. With a thoughtful expression on his face, her father quietly began to help.

"Father, who are they?" she asked, remembering her first impression that these Indians were not Ojibwa. "Why wouldn't they stay?"

John Dempsey paused in the act of putting away the unused bandages. "Sioux," he said.

Amelia frowned. "Sioux? Aren't they—"

"Yes," her father said, interrupting her. "The enemy of the Ojibwa, and they have ventured into Ojibwa territory."

Suddenly, Amelia understood why the Indians had departed quickly and why, while at the infirmary, they'd been totally on their guard.

He couldn't stop thinking about Amelia . . . how she looked, what she'd said about Susie, how much he'd missed sparring with her. As one week then two passed since he'd last seen her at the post, Daniel wondered if something was wrong. He'd been upset at their last meeting, but from his brief experience with her, he'd learned that it wasn't like her to avoid a challenge.

He'd given a lot of thought to her words about Susie and had come to the conclusion that Amelia was right. This was no place for a little girl. But he wasn't about to send Susie away, and it wasn't the wildness of this place that was bad for Susie. It was the lack of a woman's influence in her life. Susie needed someone to teach her proper manners; although he tried his best, he didn't know all a lady needed to know. He'd never imagined such a thing could be important out here in this vast wilderness of the great lake. He hadn't thought ahead to Susie's future, where her life might take her, how ill prepared she'd be for a more civilized place should fate lead her there.

As he viewed his beloved little girl through Amelia's eyes, Daniel had to admit that he'd failed in doing all that he should have for Susie. He planned to rectify the matter, and he hoped Amelia would help him. He was going to ask Amelia to educate Susie in the ways of being a little lady.

With Susie safely with Jack for the morning, Daniel headed toward the mission to speak with Amelia. Would she help him or be angry that he'd dared to come?

He didn't know how she'd react, but there was only one way to find out—and that was to ask her.

He arrived at the infirmary, expecting to find her inside, but spied her coming out of the building across the yard, accompanied by a young man. Daniel's narrowed gaze failed to recognize her caller. He searched his memory but couldn't recall a name.

Was that why she'd stayed close to the mission? To spend time with this young man?

Daniel felt a burning in his gut. Surely, he couldn't be jealous. It didn't make sense, but he could find no other name for this feeling.

He heard her laugh at something the man said, felt the burning intensify, and Daniel turned away, unable to watch, afraid of what he might do or say if he confronted her.

His intentions forgotten, Daniel left the mission before Amelia could see him. His feelings troubled him, and he needed time to think about them.

He didn't get too far from the mission when he heard a horrific scream. Heart racing, fear clutching his breast, Daniel ran back.

Seven

As he broke, running, from the woods, Daniel saw that the mission was being attacked. *Sioux!* he thought. He jerked a knife free from the sheath tucked into his legging string. The scene was terrifying. Men, women, and children ran screaming from their assailants. He watched with horror as a brave chased down a sobbing woman and sank a tomahawk into her back. He heard her death shriek as she fell dying in the middle of the yard.

A child's ear-piercing cry of terror captured his attention. He turned and spied a little boy as he was being swept away by a Sioux warrior. Daniel rushed forward to help the child, but it was too late. The warrior and his captive had disappeared from sight.

His blood humming with fear, Daniel searched for Amelia, but couldn't find her about the yard. He saw a brave struggling to retain his grip on a young man. Daniel hurried to help the missionary. Approaching the Sioux warrior from behind, he plunged his knife into the Indian's side. The warrior cried out and released his captive to clutch the area of his injury. The young white man flashed Daniel a look of gratitude before he escaped into the church.

Daniel continued to search for Amelia, his heart thundering in his chest, his body tense when he couldn't find her. The victims' cries for help from all directions within

the settlement made it difficult to decide whom to help
next.

And then he saw her at the door to the infirmary building, fighting off a Sioux brave as he dragged her from
the building. Amelia kicked out at the man with her foot,
then cried out as the Indian retaliated with a heavy-handed
cuff across her face. She stumbled, looking dazed, but then
her vision cleared as the warrior grabbed her. She kicked
and swung her arms in a valiant attempt at escape.

Daniel bellowed with outrage and raced toward the
struggling pair, his knife raised for attack. "Amelia!"

She saw him. "Daniel! Help me!" Her gaze was wild
with fear. The Indian whooped triumphantly as he caught
hold of both of Amelia's arms. The savage twisted them
behind her back, making her cry out with pain.

Daniel slipped his knife into its sheath, and, with a wild
shriek of his own, went after the Sioux warrior. He
grabbed the savage with one arm, locking him in a choke
hold. The brave released Amelia to pry away Daniel's arm.
The two men struggled. The Indian broke free. Daniel
withdrew his knife. He and the warrior crouched defen-
sively and began to circle each other with their weapons
raised to defend.

With her heart in her throat, Amelia studied the com-
batants, saw the way their knives glinted in the sunlight.
She feared for Daniel's safety; the Indian wore the look
of someone with the intent to kill.

Then, she caught sight of Daniel's savage expression,
realized that the brave had met his match. Daniel was not
just any unskilled white man.

She watched the two men with mounting horror as
knife blades arched in the air and slashed, often missing
their target, but a few times nicking flesh and skin. All

about them came the bloodcurdling cries of the Indians and the terrified shrieks of their helpless victims.

The warrior bent low and thrust his knife toward Daniel's stomach. In a sudden defensive move, Daniel spun, then returned to deflect the attack with a direct hit to the warrior's arm. The Indian lunged a second time, causing Daniel to trip. Amelia held her breath as Daniel quickly rolled backward and sprang to his feet again, with knife ready to defend.

Amelia's gaze went beyond the two men toward the churchyard as she searched frantically for a glimpse of her missing father.

"Go back inside, lock the door," Daniel ordered, as he and the Indian continued to dance about each other.

"No, I won't leave you!" she cried.

"Now!" he growled as the Indian's knife grazed his arm.

Amelia hurried inside the infirmary, locked the door, and rushed back to her father's room to look for his flint-lock pistol. She found it in his bed stand, grabbed it from the drawer, and spent precious seconds trying to load it. When she had loaded both barrels, she ran back to the door, unlocked it, and slipped back outside again. The first Indian had fallen, but Daniel was fighting another. Holding the long-barreled gun awkwardly, she found the trigger, then aimed toward the sky, off toward one side, and discharged a shot. The loud crack made by the gun startled both men, who drew instantly apart.

Amelia aimed the barrel at the Indian. "Let him go or I'll shoot!"

"He doesn't understand English," Daniel said.

"That's why I fired a shot."

The Indian narrowed his gaze, looked at Daniel and the smoking gun in Amelia's hands, then fled.

After he'd gone, Amelia lowered the gun with shaking hands. Daniel came to her quickly and eased the weapon out of her grip. "You did fine, Amelia," he said softly. "But what would you have done if he hadn't run when you've already discharged your shot."

"The gun fires two shots. I had one left to blast him with," she said.

Reaction set in, and she began to shake. She looked stunned. Concerned, he slipped his arm around her and pulled her to his side.

"Come on," he urged gently. "We've got to get out of here."

Amelia shook her head. "My father—"

"He wasn't inside?"

"No," she replied. "I don't know where he is!"

"Amelia," he said, "we'll find your father, but right now we have to get out of here. If we're killed or captured, we won't be able to help him."

She blinked up at him with trusting eyes. "The missionaries," she whispered with a dawning look of horror. Her attention caught by a fallen, dead woman several yards away, she shuddered.

"There is nothing we can do for her or any of them now," he said. "Come. Later, I'll see that they receive a decent burial."

With a quick check of their surroundings, Daniel hurried Amelia away from the mission and the carnage.

Amelia didn't say a word, but every so often Daniel heard a soft sob or a whimper.

She halted suddenly. "Miriam!" she burst out.

Daniel frowned. "When was the last time you saw her?"

Tears filled Amelia's eyes. "In the yard," she whispered. "She was running from a savage."

He felt a sharp pain in the pit of his stomach. "We have to believe that they didn't hurt her, that she's alive and a captive." He didn't want to tell her what the Sioux might do to one of their prisoners. He didn't really know, but could imagine.

"Oh, God," she breathed with closed eyes. "May the Lord have mercy on them both."

He took her away from the scene, to his house near the forge. She didn't say much during the journey. Daniel understood that she was shocked by what had occurred and deeply worried about her father and her friend.

It was as they reached the trading post that she seemed to come alive, asking questions, worried about the safety of a place so near to the attacked mission.

"Will they come here next?" she asked, her voice trembling.

"Anything is possible, but I think it's highly unlikely." He stopped at Keller's to warn Jack and get Susie. He told Jack what was happening at the mission, and Jack pulled out some guns from his stock and handed Daniel and Amelia a supply of ammunition.

"Pa!" Susie greeted him with a hug and a smile.

"Hello, sweeting," he said. "Miss me?"

She nodded. "Uncle Jack said I helped him good."

Daniel's gaze went to his friend. "He did, did he?"

"I did." Jack smiled at the little girl. "Susie girl was helping me straighten out this front room." His glance flickered to Amelia, noted with a frown her bruised face. "Hello, Miss Dempsey."

"It's good to see you, Mr. Keller."

"If not under the best of circumstances," Jack replied quietly.

Amelia nodded, then followed Daniel as he took her to his home. Her whole being cried out to find her father, but she needed to talk with Daniel about it. She'd have little chance against the Indians should she return to the mission and find them still there.

The horror clung to her, imprinting images in her mind, leaving the memory of screams that continued to ring in her ears long after she'd reached the silence. Tears filled her eyes as Daniel opened the door for her and gestured for her to enter his home.

If she hadn't been so upset, she would have appreciated the house as a home. Then, suddenly, Amelia tensed as she recalled Daniel's wife. Would she object to her presence? Amelia wondered. Her gaze sharpened as she studied her surroundings. She thought about the woman who had made Daniel a home, gave him a daughter.

She looked at Daniel, who had stooped to Susie's level and talked with her quietly in words Amelia couldn't hear. The little girl nodded while her gaze focused on Amelia with an intensity that was surprising for a child.

"You need something for your cheek," he said, then left the main room.

Susie approached her. She stared at her. "You've hurt your face." She reached up to tentatively touch Amelia's bruised cheek.

Before the child had a chance for questions, Daniel reappeared with a wet linen towel. He pulled out a chair and gestured for Amelia to sit down. When she'd complied, he gently placed the cool, wet towel over her injured cheek. The towel felt good against her skin. She wondered if her face would swell, but realized that she didn't care if it did.

Susie moved to stand on the opposite side of the table. "Miss Amelia," she said in a mature-sounding voice, "Pa said you'll be staying with us a while."

Amelia's gaze flew to Daniel before returning to the child. "Yes, I guess I will be."

"You don't have to be scared here," the little girl said. "Pa will protect you. You won't have to worry about bad men as long as you're with Pa."

"Thank you, Susie. I'll try not to worry anymore." She managed a slight smile. "I appreciate you sharing your home with me."

Susie nodded, then headed to one of the back rooms.

"I can't stay here," Amelia told Daniel. "It's surely an imposition." She glanced toward the back of the house, searching. "Besides, what will your wife say?"

Daniel looked stunned. "I have no wife," he said. A muscle twitched along his jawline. "She died years ago."

Amelia caught herself staring. "I'm sorry. I didn't know." The realization that she was staying in the house of an unmarried man came to her like she'd been kicked in the stomach. Her mind raced with confusion.

Daniel has no wife, she thought, startled by the sudden burst of gladness she felt. She frowned. Sharing his house wasn't a wise thing given that she was attracted to the man. She couldn't stay with him. It couldn't possibly be proper for her to remain.

He was looking at her oddly, speculatively. She held his gaze for a moment, wondering if he could read her thoughts. As a glimmer entered his blue eyes, she blushed and looked away.

She studied the room with more interest, then saw what she hadn't seen at first glance. There was nothing about the room that displayed a woman's touch, nothing except a small vase of wildflowers, picked no doubt by a little girl.

"I should go back to the mission," she murmured, knowing that it would be too dangerous for her heart if she stayed.

"You can't go back," he said. "It's not safe."

"But my father!" she argued. "And what about Miriam? And all of the others. What if there is someone hurt but alive, who might die if they don't receive medical attention?"

"Amelia," he said patiently as if speaking to a child, "the only thing you'll do by going back to the mission now is to put yourself in danger. Do you want to end up kidnapped or dead?"

"No, of course not."

He touched her cheek, clearly startling her with his caress although he noted that she didn't pull away. "I promise I'll go back tonight as soon as it gets dark." He'd realized something disturbing about the attack, something he had to think about further.

"You will?" She had a childlike look of trust in her beautiful brown eyes.

He nodded. "Will you trust me?"

Her eyes filled with tears as she inclined her head. "Yes," she whispered.

With a soft groan, he pulled Amelia into his arms, held her tightly while she wept quietly. He understood her pain; he remembered his own that wouldn't go away. He recalled the smell and sight of blood . . . envisioned savages as they attacked their innocent victims.

He held her to comfort, and found comfort of his own. He enjoyed the feel of her warm softness against his muscled hardness, the silkiness of her hair against his chin.

They stood together until silence reigned in the house and a little girl came from the back room to touch Amelia's arm.

Amelia raised her head from Daniel's chest, realized where she was, and blushed as she pulled away. She met Susie's gaze with a sad smile.

"It will be all right," the child said. "Pa will take care of you."

The woman had to blink back new tears. Susie looked up at her with empathy in her pretty blue eyes. As she gazed at the little girl, Amelia realized what she hadn't noticed before, that the child was clean, that her hair was blond not brown, and that she had the most beautiful blue eyes fringed with thick lashes.

Amelia touched Susie's shoulder. "Thank you, Susie."

She nodded, then faced Daniel. "Pa, I fixed up Miss Amelia's room."

"Thank you, Susie," he responded with a gentle smile. "You're an angel." Susie beamed. He addressed Amelia. "Susie will show you to your room."

She didn't feel right about staying there. "Daniel, I'm sorry for this inconvenience."

He gave her a halfhearted grin. "Who said you're an inconvenience? I've got a problem, and you may be the solution. But we'll talk about that later."

Amelia tilted her head, intrigued.

"Go along with Susie now," he urged.

The woman smiled at the child and followed her toward the back of the house.

The room that would be Amelia's was cozy and had a four-poster bed large enough for two that was covered with a beautifully handcrafted patchwork quilt. A window on the farside of the room allowed the muted afternoon light to filter in past chintz curtains in soft shades of rose, pink, and green. A washstand stood in a corner holding a white-and-blue porcelain pitcher and basin. A clean linen towel had been placed over the wooden rack that was part of the stand. A bar of lye soap sat next to the basin within easy reach of the bather. Not far from the washstand, a looking glass hung over a beautifully made dresser.

Amelia stared in shock at the lovely room. She wouldn't have been surprised to see such a bedchamber in Baltimore, but such comfort out here in this wilderness home was totally unexpected to her.

Had this room been Daniel's wife's? Had he left her things here as a memorial?

With a vague sense of uneasiness, Amelia went to the dresser, opened a few drawers, and felt relieved when she found nothing in them.

She realized that Susie was watching, wondered if the little girl thought her strange for opening and closing dresser drawers. She smiled at Susie and told her the truth—what a wonderful room it was.

"It's beautiful," she said with a smile of pleasure. "Where do you sleep?"

Susie pointed toward the left wall. "In there. Would you like to see it?"

Amelia nodded and followed Susie to her room, then praised her on how neat she'd kept it. It didn't look like a young girl's room, but it was obviously a child's room, with a child's treasures on the dresser and washstand: a smooth stone, a pretty bird feather, a pair of beautifully handcrafted, beaded and quill-adorned moccasins.

"It's a wonderful room," she said sincerely. Amelia felt tiny butterflies in her stomach. "Where does your pa sleep?"

Susie gestured toward the right wall. "Pa sleeps in the room on the other side of yours," she said. "Would you like to see it?"

"No," Amelia said quickly, "it's not necessary. I'm glad I'm not driving someone from their room."

"You aren't," Susie assured her. "Are you hungry?" she asked as they returned to the great room.

Amelia wasn't, but she didn't say so. "Would you like me to fix you something to eat?"

The child shook her head. "Pa's making stew."

There was a small kitchen beyond the great room. Susie and Amelia found Daniel there, preparing a meal. Amelia watched him as he chopped meat and vegetables, then put them into a large iron pot. He had started a fire in the cookstove. He continued to add ingredients as the contents of the pot simmered.

He glanced at them as they entered the room. His gaze sharpened as he studied Amelia, then Susie, before he turned his attention back to his guest. "Is your room all right?" he asked casually, but Amelia heard the underlying concern.

"It's wonderful. I'm sure I'll be very comfortable there, but, Daniel, I really shouldn't stay."

His expression dimmed. "I thought we discussed this, and you agreed that it wasn't safe for you to go back yet." He paused to toss in some wild rice. "I told you I'd check back there tonight." *Not that I'll find anyone alive,* Daniel thought. There was little hope that anyone had been left behind alive.

"I want to go with you," Amelia said.

Daniel scowled. "No. Absolutely not. It's not safe. I want to slip into the mission and get out again as quickly as possible. Let me handle this. You'll only slow me down. I promise—I'll check everywhere." He softened his expression and his voice. "Trust me."

"I do."

He was satisfied with her answer. "Are you hungry?" he asked.

Amelia sniffed appreciatively. "It smells wonderful."

"It's not roast turkey, but it will satisfy a man—or woman's—hunger."

"Can I help?"

He shook his head. "I'm nearly done. You just relax. You've had a trying day."

She glanced down at herself and grimaced. "I'm afraid I don't have a change of clothes."

Daniel couldn't help himself; he took his fill of her, studying her from her head to her shoes and back again. For a long moment, he stared at her mouth, saw it quiver, and met her glistening gaze. He was startled by what he saw in her expression, felt his own instant response to her desire.

"I'm sure I can find something for you to wear," he said huskily. He would rather see her without a stitch of clothing. Her shocked little gasp told him she had read his expression or his mind.

"I'd like a drink of water," she said in a raspy voice.

"Whatever you desire," he said with a gleam in his blue eyes. He filled a glass for her, and noted the way she trembled as she accepted his offering.

"Thank you," she murmured without meeting his gaze.

"The pleasure is mine," he replied. And it was. He hadn't counted on this strong physical attraction between them.

It would be a test of his strength to keep his hands off her.

Eight

The stew was delicious, and Amelia found that she was hungry once she started to eat. After she finished, she felt terribly guilty for enjoying her meal, as the events of the afternoon came back to disturb her.

Tears filled her eyes as she worried about her father and Miriam. As she helped Daniel wash, dry, and put the dishes away, she asked him about the Indians who'd attacked.

"Sioux," he said. He got a look on his face that told her he was troubled.

"What's wrong?"

He shook his head, as if debating with himself over an issue that had bothered him only one other time. "I don't understand why they attacked during daylight. It's not like them to do so. The Indians are usually careful to wait until night and strike under the cover of darkness."

Amelia thought about it and saw what he meant. "They weren't afraid of resistance," she said.

He looked at her, surprised yet pleased with her understanding. "Yes. It is not like the Sioux to venture this far. The Ojibwa and the Sioux have been enemies for some time."

"Why?"

"Hunting rights. Land. As the US government acquires more of the Indians' lands, the Indians are pushed west-

ward. Ojibwa find themselves in Sioux territory. The
Ojibwa have been trading with the American Fur Company for years. Beaver pelts are considered the most valu-
able of the furs, and were at one time plentiful in this
region. But as the beaver were killed for trade, they started
to become scarce, so the Ojibwa went to other places for
the beaver. The Sioux felt they were infringing on their
land." He smiled at her as he took a dried dish from her
hand and set it in a cabinet in the kitchen area. "It's ironic
in a way, as the Indians actually believe that no one owns
the land. It is a gift from the Great Spirit that they may
use while they are here. But I suppose it's not actually
the land itself that came between them but their right to
the gifts granted to them by the land spirits."

Amelia looked interested. "Spirits of the land?"

Daniel nodded. "To the Indians, everything has a spirit.
The deer they kill and eat has a spirit. The trees and sky
and the grass that grows beneath their feet. When an
Ojibwa hunter kills a deer, he burns an offering of tobacco
in thanks to the spirit of the deer. He thanks the deer for
giving up his life so that his family may eat and be
clothed and have all the wonderful things they use made
from the deer's bones and hooves and body."

"They don't kill needlessly."

Daniel smiled. "They treat all creatures with respect.
As barbaric as some of their practices may seem, they
actually have a code of honor and respect."

"You like them," she said.

"I like and respect them. I'd trust Black Hawk with my
life."

"Black Hawk?" The name sounded familiar to her. She
remembered why. "Does he have a brother named Rain-
from-Sky?" He nodded. "He's the one who gave Father
this—" She reached for the small beaded pouch that she

wore about her neck. "It's gone! My beautiful bag is gone!" Tears filled her eyes as the events of the day returned to hurt her. "My father and my friend are missing, and I'm crying over a lost pouch." She sniffed and wiped her eyes.

Daniel's face softened. "You're crying because of everything that's happened, not over a lost bag," he said gently.

She nodded. The tenderness in his expression nearly undid her. "I'm sorry."

He looked surprised. "For what?"

"You didn't need me to invade your home."

"I invited you into my home," he pointed out.

"You did?"

He inclined his head. "Besides, I need you here. I have a proposition for you that I hope you'll consider."

She stiffened her back and flushed a bright red.

His lips twitched with amusement. "It concerns Susie."

"Susie," she echoed, while trying to assimilate what he'd meant.

He got a look on his face that told her he was concerned. "I promise I'll search for your father—and I'll find him, too. While you're here, I'd hoped you'd teach Susie what it is to be a little lady."

"Excuse me?" Amelia wasn't sure she'd heard him correctly.

It was his turn to blush. "A lady. I want you to teach her manners and all the things a little girl needs to learn to make her way in society."

Amelia controlled the urge to gaze at her surroundings. "You want her to act like a lady." She paused. "You want her to wear dresses?"

Daniel gave it some thought. "Does she have to wear

them all the time?" He sounded uncertain, and Amelia loved him for it.

"No, of course not," she said. "It wouldn't be practical for a young girl to always wear gowns out here in the wilderness." She recalled the Indians' practice of going with very few clothes. "As long as she is dressed, her tunic and trousers will be fine."

He looked relieved, and she had amazed herself by being sincere. There had been a time once when she would never have condoned ladies or little girls wearing breeches or trousers. Now she wished she had a pair of her own.

"Then you'll help me—us?"

She nodded. "I can't promise that Susie will take kindly to what I have to say, but I will certainly do my best to teach her proper deportment." She smiled gently when he looked confused. "Proper behavior for a young lady," she explained.

He seemed satisfied. "Thank you."

"You're welcome." Something occurred to her which gave her pause. "Daniel, is this because of what I said— the other day about this being no place for a little girl?"

"Let's just say that your comment got me thinking."

She felt contrite. She hadn't meant to offend or worry him. "I'm sorry. I see how much you love Susie." She held his gaze. "She's a lucky little girl."

A spark flared in his blue eyes. "Amelia—"

"I speak too quickly and often regret what I say," she said, interrupting him. "I just want you to know that about me . . . in case, you decide that I'm not the best one to be teaching Susie anything."

"I think she'll learn a lot from you," he said with eyes that glowed. "I have no problem with someone who speaks her mind."

"Most men find it quite tiresome after a while," she replied.

"I'm not most men."

A look passed between them that made Amelia's toes curl. Daniel Trahern was far too attractive for her peace of mind. *And you're staying in his house . . . in the room next to his.* It was a good thing that Susie was there as a buffer between them. Nothing could possibly happen; surely, they'd remember their place as long as they remembered Susie.

She saw it in his eyes—this physical awareness between them. Her skin tingled, and her face warmed. They were alone; Susie had gone to her room to play. Amelia closed her eyes, knowing she was in trouble. The knowledge of the child only a few yards away did little to deter the stark feeling of desire for the child's father.

She got up from the table. "I think I'd like to wash if I may," she said, sounding flustered.

Daniel rose to his feet as she stood. "Of course. Would you like me to heat up some bathwater?"

They stared at each other as his words registered, bringing with them mental images of water and a tub and naked bodies. Amelia swallowed against a suddenly dry throat. "No, that's all right. Perhaps another day. I'll just wash with the water as it is." She turned to leave.

Daniel stopped her with a hand on her arm. "Amelia," he said, his voice low and husky and intent, "if it's in my power, I'll find your father and your friend Miriam." He paused but looked as if he wanted to say more. "I'm glad you're here, although I'm not happy with the circumstances."

She managed a smile. "Thank you for saving my life, Daniel Trahern." She reached up and touched his cheek. "My life for yours," she said softly.

He raised an eyebrow.

"You saved my life, and so I will help what is yours." He still looked confused. "Susie," she said.

He grinned. "Will you join me for a while?"

Amelia shook her head. "No, I think I'll go to bed if you don't mind." She bit her lip. "I have nothing to wear but the garments I have on."

"I have a few things you can wear until I can retrieve some of your own clothes." He left the room and was back within seconds. He handed her a white shirt. "It's mine, but should serve nicely for sleeping."

She could feel herself blush as she took the garment. "Thank you." The thought of Daniel's shirt next to her bare skin made her stomach flutter.

She bit her lip. "You said you were going to return to the mission. Will it be dangerous?"

"Probably." He lifted a lock of her unbound hair, inspected it as it slipped from his fingers to fall past her shoulders. "But I'll be careful," he said. His gaze met hers. It had been just a few hours. Would there be anyone there who needed help? "I'll do what I can to help the survivors."

"The Indians wouldn't stay there?" she asked with concern.

"No. I'm sure they're gone by now." He held her gaze steadily. "But I'll not take chances."

"Be sure that you don't," she said in the softest voice.

It was late and dark when Daniel headed toward the mission with Jack Keller. They walked, they wanted no sound to announce their arrival. They couldn't be sure that the Indians had left. They crept through wearing moccasins taken in trade from the Ojibwa. The moon was a

crescent sliver in the night sky. The forest was alive with
the sound of summer insects. An owl hooted in the distance. An animal scurried through the underbrush, rustling
grass and leaves.

Hearing a strange sound, Daniel paused once to listen,
and Jack immediately froze behind him, his senses alert.
When there was no other noise, Daniel and Jack looked
at each other, nodded, and continued on.

It was dark at the mission settlement. At first glance,
it seemed that the place was deserted, until Daniel saw a
tiny light coming from a window in one of the buildings.
He and Jack crept into the settlement, looking for bodies,
and did not find anyone in the yard. Someone had taken
the dead, whether to bury them or not, Daniel had no
idea.

There was a strange combination of odors in the air.
The lingering smell of blood and death mingled with
smoke, the forest, and other outdoor scents. Daniel waved
Jack into the settlement. Then with his friend by his side,
Daniel moved to the lone building with the tiny light.

The building was made of sandstone, like the other
structures at the mission. Daniel went to a window and
carefully peered in. He saw a wounded white man lying
on a bed. Another white man sat in a chair next to the
bed, holding a cup while the injured man drank.

Daniel gestured to his friend to take a look. He moved,
and Jack took his place, studying the scene inside the
room.

"Think it's safe to go in?" Daniel asked. He hadn't
seen anyone who posed a threat, but he wanted his friend's
opinion.

Jack nodded. "No sign of Sioux. Looks safe enough to
me."

Daniel went first, skirting the building toward the main

door. He waited for Jack to appear, before knocking. "Stay out of sight," he said.

Jack agreed and moved to one side with his gun raised and his finger on the trigger.

When no one came to the door, Daniel knocked a second time. This time he heard a shuffling noise inside. He pounded on the door a third time and announced his presence.

"Reverend Whitely?"

The door swung open, and the minister blinked several times as he gazed up at him. He was cut across the lip where someone must have hit him. His eyes were red-rimmed as if he hadn't slept or he'd been crying. His expression was wary as he peered out into the night. "Daniel Trahern, is that you?"

"It's me, Reverend—and Jack Keller, too."

A sigh of relief escaped the man's throat as he moved aside to allow them entry. "Come in, please."

Daniel entered, and Jack came out of the shadows to follow him inside. "Are you all right?" Jack asked.

The minister nodded, but there were tears in his eyes. "Only two of us left. The Indians either killed or kidnapped the others." His green eyes were glazed as if he were reliving the nightmare of the attack.

"The dead," Daniel said.

"We collected the bodies and buried them in the churchyard. There were three. Anne Rose, Pete Holmes, and Arthur Grutchly—all good people who'd done nothing wrong." Allen Whitely's face crumbled. "I don't understand this! We didn't do anything to warrant the attack."

"The Indians were Sioux," Jack said.

The missionary looked to Daniel for confirmation.

Daniel nodded. "Saw them for myself. They weren't Chippewa."

Despite the fact that Daniel didn't like what the missionaries were doing, he thought highly of the reverend, for his intentions were better than most.

"I still don't see why the Sioux would attack us."

"Did they take anything?" Jack asked.

"Only our women and children—and some of our men," the man replied, sounding upset.

"There was a woman in the yard—" Daniel began.

"Anne Rose. I took care of her first. She was a wonderful, caring individual whom we'll all miss terribly."

"I'm sorry," Daniel said, meaning it.

The Reverend Whitely acknowledged Daniel's sympathy with a nod of thanks.

"Are there others who need burying?" Jack asked.

"Not here at the mission." The young minister looked pale. "There may be some in the forest."

Those who had tried to escape, Daniel thought. "We'll scout out that area in the morning." He didn't have to say that there was no need to look now, for they all knew that any attempt to escape would have meant instant death to the ones who'd tried.

Daniel glanced past the minister toward the figure on the bed. It was the young man who had sought shelter in the church after Daniel had stabbed his assailant. "Is he all right?" he said, gesturing toward the young man, who lay with his eyes closed.

"He has a shoulder wound. He got it when an Indian sneaked into the church and attacked him. The good Lord must have been with him, because the boy managed to get free and lock himself in the back storage area—a room with no windows. The brave didn't try to break in, nor did he wait until William left. Apparently, he had other victims to apprehend. Will stayed in that storage room until I found him later." Allen moved toward the bed to study the young man. "He was in that room for over two hours. Given the seriousness of his wound, it was amazing that he didn't expire."

"Can I take a look?" Daniel asked. Having saved him once, he felt a certain responsibility for young Will.

The cut was deep, but it was straight and it looked clean. Still, it looked like it needed stitching. "Reverend, that shoulder needs a couple of stitches."

The minister nodded. "Can you do it? I'm squeamish, I'm afraid." He shook his head, looking dazed. "If only the doctor was here—"

"Where is the good doctor?" Daniel asked.

"Missing," said Allen Whitely. "Indians must have taken him."

"And Miriam Lathom, too?"

Whitely nodded. "And poor Amelia Dempsey."

"Amelia Dempsey is safe with Susie."

The minister looked relieved. "Thank God." His glance fell on Will Thornton. "Perhaps Amelia can stitch up Will's shoulder."

"I'll stitch it," Daniel said. "I think it's best to keep Amelia away from here for a time. The Sioux could still be in the area. No sense risking her life."

Daniel began to ask for the items he'd need to tend Will. With Jack's help, Allen found what Daniel needed, then watched, white-faced, as Daniel, assisted by Jack, closed the young man's wound with neat, even stitches.

Nine

It was late when Daniel got back to the house. As he entered the cabin, he saw that Amelia was up. She was seated in the dark, at the table where they'd dined only hours before. A faint touch of moonlight filtered inside the room, making it possible to see her. She didn't appear to see or hear him when he came in.

Daniel frowned as he approached her. "Amelia?"

She didn't say anything. Concerned, he went to the stove and lit a candle in the embers of an earlier fire. He headed back to Amelia with the burning candle.

"Amelia?" he whispered. He didn't want to frighten her. The look in her expression worried him. She had her eyes open, but it appeared that she stared without seeing. There was horror in her brown gaze. He caught his breath as he saw tears trailing down her cheeks.

He set the candle down, then pulled out a chair and sat next to her. Her hands rested on the tabletop, tight white-knuckled fists. He felt an odd little pain in his midsection. The day had taken its toll on her. He wanted to help her, but wasn't sure how.

"Amelia." He reached out to cover her clenched hands with his own. She wore his shirt, which was several sizes too large for her, but it served her well as a nightdress. He raised his voice. "Amelia!"

She blinked, then gasped, scared until she recognized him. "Daniel!"

"I thought you went to sleep," he said gently.

She shook her head. "I tried, but I couldn't sleep. The mission. My father. Kidnapped. Dead." Her words were disjointed as she turned inward to her thoughts again.

He touched her shoulder, then rubbed her back. Her expression chilled him. He needed her to look at him, talk with him. He had to know if she was all right.

He released her back to take hold of her chin and turned her toward him. Facing her, he looked into her eyes.

"Amelia, I just came from the mission."

She jerked and met his gaze. "Did you find—" She paused to swallow hard. "—anyone?"

"Your father?" he said softly. He studied her with regret. "No." He touched her face, stroked her cheek. "The minister was there, and young Will Thornton."

Fresh tears filled her eyes. "That's all?"

He nodded and slid his fingers along her jaw to her ear, combed her hair back, then cupped the back of her neck. She blinked at him, her brown eyes overflowing with her tears.

Daniel felt a wrenching in his gut. He wanted to make her pain go away, to see her smile, even get angry. "Amelia," he said huskily.

She sniffed and closed her eyes. A tear pooled at the base of her lashes, then slowly trickled down her cheek. Daniel groaned and bent to kiss it away. "Amelia," he whispered, then his mouth found her lips in a tender kiss meant to comfort.

He ended the kiss and studied her. She sat with closed eyes, a vulnerable young woman overwhelmed by the day's events. Her lashes fluttered open and she looked at him. She appeared dazed, then startled, then embarrassed.

He reached for her, pulled her into his arms. She didn't resist. He slipped his arms about her waist and lifted her onto his lap. He heard her soft sob as she melted against him.

"We'll find him," he vowed with an intensity he'd never before felt. He'd lost Jane; he would find Amelia's father and her friend.

She cried quietly for a time as he held her. She felt good in his arms. The sweet scent of her enveloped him. She clung to him as if she would absorb his warmth and strength, which he was more than happy to give her. Her hair felt soft against his neck and chin. He held her as he would a child, but his feelings were anything but fatherly. There was little fabric between them. He stroked her hair, enjoying its silky texture against his rough hands. He rubbed her back as she turned her head and lay against him, her face buried in the curve of his jaw and shoulder. He became conscious of the warmth and softness of her body.

"You're not alone, Amelia," he told her gently. "I'm here, and I'll do everything I can to see that you and your father are reunited."

She raised her head and gazed at him with red-rimmed, tear-filled eyes. "But what if he's dead? What if the Indians—"

"Sh-sh," he soothed. He pulled her back against him, cradled her head with his hand while he caressed her shoulder and arm with the other. "Don't even think it. Believe that your father is safe. The fact that he is missing is a good sign."

"I must go to him." She lifted her head, started to get up, but Daniel held her firm. "My father is out there, and he needs me." A strangled sob burst from her throat. "He needs me!"

Daniel cradled her face with his hands, forced her to meet his gaze. "You're not going anywhere. Think! Do you honestly believe your father would want you traipsing off into the night to confront his captors?"

"You don't understand!" she cried. She struggled against his hold. He released her. "My father needs me!"

"I understand!" he exclaimed in a sudden burst of emotion that immediately caught her attention. "It's happened to me!" He shuddered as the memory, the horror, came back. His voice lowered to a hoarse whisper. "It's happened to me."

Stunned, Amelia stared at him with glistening brown eyes. "Daniel," she began, then halted at his pain-filled expression. He was a champion for the Indians, wasn't he? He believed in their rights and their freedom to live as they'd lived for centuries. Yet, here he was telling her that he understood what she was feeling, that the Indians had done the same thing to him. His anguish reached out to her, making her shudder and hug herself. She wanted to comfort him, but her own pain was too raw. And he clearly didn't want to talk about it.

Daniel closed his eyes to regain control. The events of the day had brought everything back to him, but he had managed to keep his emotions in line, to think, to reason, to plan. He didn't want her to see him this way. It would only add to her fears. He just wanted her to know that he wouldn't fail her as he'd failed Jane.

"Please," he said without opening his eyes. "No questions. Not tonight."

To his wonder, he felt her arms slip about his waist, heard her sigh, and felt her lean into him, her soft curves against his hard torso. Her hands fluttered at his back, then she was offering him comfort with the soft, light stroke of her hands on his shoulder and neck. One hand reached to touch his cheek. He shuddered and relaxed beneath her hands. She held him, and he laid his head in the curve of her neck, breathing in her fragrance, feeling his tension dissipate, his pain ease and slip away.

They held each other, drawing strength and comfort from their closeness. After a time, they pulled back simultaneously, looked into each other's eyes, then flowed together again in a kiss that began as the sweetest, most tender contact and quickly became a hot, searing fusion of mouths and breaths.

When they broke away, both were gasping; stunned by the force of their feelings, by the onslaught of desire that erupted between them; yet neither felt shame or regret. They were too caught up in an emotional whirlwind, which must have started when they'd met and spiraled after their horrific day.

Daniel didn't want to release her. His heart pounding in his chest, he gazed into her eyes, stared at her mouth, and wanted to kiss her all over again.

Amelia gazed back at him with the same longing in her eyes.

"It's late," Daniel said in the softest whisper.

She nodded and started to rise.

He caught her arm, battled the urge to kiss her, then gave in and drew her down for one more gentle kiss. When he released her, she straightened with eyes glowing and cheeks flushed. He felt like a brute for having taken advantage of her at a time when she was weak . . . until he realized that he was as vulnerable as she at that moment.

He smiled and touched her cheek. "Good night."

"Good night," she murmured. She seemed reluctant to go.

He stood, and she stepped back. "You'll be able to sleep?" he asked.

She nodded, but both knew that it was a lie, for he was sure neither of them would sleep well that night.

Daniel reached for the candle, snuffed out the flame with his fingers. The room plunged into darkness, but still Amelia made no move to leave.

He could hear her breathing, feel her presence in the tingling along every inch of his skin. He waited with bated breath for her to move.

"Daniel," she began, then stopped.

"Yes?"

"I—ah—thank you."

He suffered extreme disappointment. What had he expected her to say? That she wanted him to kiss her again? To make love? He knew then that the day had taken its toll on him to inspire such outrageous thoughts.

"Sleep late in the morning, Amelia."

"If I can."

He smiled in the darkness. His eyes had adjusted to the light, and he could just make out her outline, but he didn't need to see her to envision her in his mind. "I'll try to keep Susie from bothering you."

The mention of Susie seemed to have an effect on her. He felt her withdrawing from him emotionally as well as physically. The loss hurt him, bothered him in a way he'd never known.

"Good night, Amelia."

"Good night, Daniel," she returned in a shy little voice.

"Can you see?" he asked.

"Yes."

He could see enough to watch her enter her room and

close the door. A few minutes later, he left the lonely stillness of the room to seek his own bed—and the sleep that he was sure would elude him that night. He thought of her as he undressed and slipped into bed . . . then he dreamed of her as exhaustion took hold and he fell into a deep, fitful sleep.

Amelia woke to the delicious smells of breakfast. She stretched with closed eyes and wondered what Aunt Bess was cooking this morning. She caught the sound of a squeaking door, but kept her eyes shut, sure that it was Rachel anxious to tell her sister about an evening spent with her latest beau. She heard the door shut with a click and smiled. There would be time for her and Rachel later. She wanted these last few lazy moments in bed.

Amelia opened her eyes and saw the strange room. She heard a man's voice and a little girl's answer, and everything came back to her in startling, terrifying clarity.

The mission had been attacked. Her father was missing, and so was Miriam. Only two of the missionaries, and she, had survived.

Tears filled her eyes as she rose from her bed. She stared at the wall and cried for a time, until she had spent her tears and regained control of her emotions. She became aware of her apparel. She glanced down, saw that she wore Daniel's shirt, and the memory of last night came back to her in a rush. She could feel her cheeks warm as she blushed. Then, she recalled the comfort of his embrace . . . the warmth and tenderness of his kiss . . . the hot curl of desire as they'd clung together, their mouths seeking, their bodies straining toward each other as if they couldn't get enough.

She raised her hands to her cheeks, closing her eyes as

she wondered what had come over her, wondered what Daniel must think of her.

A niggling from the back of her mind gave Amelia pause. She recalled Daniel's promise to help her, his pain when he'd told her that he, too, knew what it was like to know fear and suffering like hers.

Something inside her responded to the memory. He'd been so kind, so gentle with her last night. Unable to sleep, she'd sat in the dark, reliving the attack, fearful that she'd never see her father again. Daniel had pulled her into his arms, comforting her with his strength, his presence, his soft voice. He had vowed to find her father, and she believed he meant what he said. His words had given her a small measure of comfort, but she was still worried. If her father was still alive, he might be suffering terrible tortures at the Indians' hands.

Anger replaced the self-pity. What had instigated the raid? Her father had shown only kindness to his patients. If Daniel was right, then the attackers were the same Indians as the young boy her father had tended, Little Cloud, the child with the bullet wound in his shoulder. As she got out of bed, Amelia thought of the men who'd stood like angry sentinels around the room as she and her father had worked. Had she done something wrong that night, something that incensed the Sioux?

Her hands hesitated on the buttons of Daniel's shirt. She wanted to do something, anything that would bring her father back to her, but Daniel had said he would handle it. Still, it was hard to sit still when everything in her being was telling her to get moving.

Amelia raised the hem of her makeshift nightdress. The morning air felt cool against her bare skin as she reached for the chemise and gown she'd worn yesterday, her only articles of clothing, except for the corset that she refused to put back on. She recalled how she could barely move when the Indian came after her, promised herself that she'd never again wear a garment that would restrict her movements—at least, not in this untamed land.

A soft knock on the bedchamber had her opening the door, clad in her gown but without having completed her toilet.

Susie stood outside her door, her blue eyes inquisitive, curiosity in her expression as she noted Amelia's unbound hair. "Pa has breakfast fixed," the child said.

"Thank you, Susie," Amelia replied. "I'll be out directly after I do something with my hair."

"You can use my brush if you'd like," Susie offered.

Recalling the filthy condition of Susie's hair the other day, Amelia thanked the child for the offer and told her that she'd manage without the hairbrush.

Susie stepped into the room, went to the dresser, and opened one small drawer that Amelia hadn't checked. She reached inside and pulled out an elaborate brush and comb set. "You can use my momma's," she offered as she held out the set.

Amelia felt a burning in her stomach. The brush set had belonged to Susie's mother, Daniel's wife. Just as she'd feared, she was using the woman's room, and if she accepted Susie's offer, she'd be using the woman's hairbrush.

"Please, she wouldn't mind. Neither would Pa."

Amelia eyed the silver set doubtfully. She met Susie's gaze and realized that the little girl didn't mind her refusing her own hairbrush but Susie would be offended if Amelia didn't use her mother's hair set. With eyes locked on the child's face, Amelia took the brush and comb. "Thank you," she said softly.

Susie nodded and looked pleased. "I'll tell Pa you'll be in to eat in a few minutes."

Amelia gave an affirmative jerk of her head and watched Susie leave. Her thoughts were in turmoil. She had taken the woman's room, kissed her husband in the dead of night; now she was using the woman's personal things. Her situation seemed unreal, but when she looked into the hand mirror and saw that she looked a mess, she started to comb then brush her hair until its silky smoothness crackled and sprang to life.

She looked into the looking glass one last time before leaving the room. She didn't recognize herself as the dewy-eyed waif with hair past her shoulders. She debated whether or not to pin back her hair and decided against it. She didn't have the energy to struggle with it this morning. After what happened yesterday afternoon, a pristine appearance no longer seemed important.

When she felt herself ready to leave the room, she set down the hairbrush, readjusted the skirts of her cotton gown, then inhaled sharply in an attempt to calm the wildly beating tattoo of her heart.

She opened the bedroom door, lingered at the threshold as she searched for Daniel and saw him immediately at the stove. He worked to finish breakfast, unaware that she was watching. She used the time to study him in a new light, as memories of the day before raged a silent battle in her mind.

Shocked that she could recall the kiss between them more clearly than the attack the previous afternoon, Amelia straightened her spine and left the bedchamber to approach where Daniel stood.

"Miss Amelia!" Susie exclaimed upon seeing the woman. "Come sit here. Pa's about to serve up our meal."

Susie's voice had made Daniel glance back. Amelia felt

his blue gaze assessing her with concern. She promptly looked away. She could feel herself blush as she joined Susie at the table. She didn't have to study him to be aware of Daniel's continued regard. She sensed that he still hadn't turned back to the stove.

"I hope you like eggs," Susie said with a gamine grin. "Pa fixes great eggs."

Unable to avoid it, Amelia looked toward Daniel with a raised eyebrow. He smiled at her, and she glanced away, startled by the quick rush of desire she felt as their gazes caught and held.

"Eggs?" she asked. "Where on earth did you get eggs?" She hadn't had them since she'd left Baltimore.

"Pa traded some beans from our garden to Rebb Colfax for some of his chicken eggs," Susie explained.

"I didn't know anyone kept chickens out here," Amelia commented with a smile in the child's direction.

"Just Rebb," Daniel interjected with a grin. He had dished out two platefuls, and he set one each before Amelia and Susie.

Susie began to eat as fast as she could swallow a forkful.

Amelia observed the girl with mixed feelings as she realized that she could teach something to Daniel's child.

She and Daniel exchanged glances. She nodded in silent assurance that she'd start working with Susie that day.

Daniel's eyes flashed with emotion in response.

Shaken by his look of desire, Amelia turned her attention to his child, but it was hard to pretend that she wasn't more interested in him.

Ten

"Army fort! I'm not going to any fort!" Amelia exclaimed. She was furious. Daniel wanted to take her to the nearest military fort; he wanted her to be locked up inside some stockade fence and watched over by a bunch of crude soldiers.

"Amelia, it's not safe here," Daniel reasoned. "You'll be protected at Fort Brady."

She glared at the man who had rescued her and now wished to send her away. "I'm not going. What about Susie's lessons?"

A dangerous look entered Daniel's eyes. "Susie's lessons can wait," he said.

"Because I'm a burden, is that it?"

"No!" he exploded. "You're not a burden. You've been a big help. It's not that at all." He lowered his voice. "I just want you to be safe."

Amelia suddenly spied Susie near the door to her room. The little girl stood, watching them with a frown. "Daniel, Susie—"

But he'd already seen Susie's interest. Despite the fact that they'd begun their discussion of the issue quietly, they'd quickly raised their voices in defense of their own viewpoints.

Daniel smiled at Susie and raised his arm. The little girl scurried from the doorway of her room to be hugged by Daniel. "Would you do me a favor, sweeting?" he asked. She nodded. "Run over to Jack's and see if he has any cornmeal."

"Are you and Miss Amelia fighting?" she asked with the candor of a child.

The adults looked at each other. Amelia answered. "No, we're not fighting, sweetheart. We're merely having an important discussion."

Susie looked to her father for confirmation. Daniel nodded, and the child looked relieved.

"See if Jack has any maple syrup," Amelia said to the little girl. "Okay?"

"Okay." But still Susie hesitated, reluctant to leave.

"Go on, Susie," her father urged.

With a concerned glance in Amelia's direction, Susie hurried off to the trading post.

Once the little girl had left, Daniel focused his beautiful blue eyes on the woman before him. She heard him sigh. "Amelia—"

"No, Daniel," she said stubbornly, folding her arms. "It's not fair of you to ask me to go. If it's too much trouble having me here, then I'll leave." She thought a moment. "I'll go back to the mission."

"No!" he burst out. "Don't you see? This is what I'm trying to avoid. I don't want you to return to the mission until I know it's safe."

"My father is missing," she said.

"Yes," he replied, "he is, but you won't find him at the mission or anywhere else within miles of here."

She paled. "How can you be so sure?"

His expression softened. "I can't. That's why I'm going to speak with Black Hawk. Once he and his men scout out the area, we'll know for certain."

"Daniel, please let me stay." To her dismay, her eyes filled with tears. "I promise I won't leave this area."

He regarded her through narrowed eyes. "I wish I could believe that." He continued to stare at her. "You'll remain right here until the Ojibwa say it's safe to leave?"

She nodded. She didn't want to go, and it wasn't just the fact of her missing father that kept her here. She didn't want to leave Daniel. He made her feel special and safe . . . and more of a woman than she'd ever felt before.

"I don't want you to go," he admitted.

Her heart thumped with gladness. "You don't?"

He shook his head as he stepped closer to her. He reached out and touched her cheek with his hand. She closed her eyes in enjoyment of his caress. "Amelia—"

There was a longing in his tone. She opened her eyes and saw sorrow in his expression, a pleading for understanding. She recalled his vehemence about finding her father, remembered how she'd realized that Daniel must have lost someone in a similar Indian attack.

"Susie's mother?" she guessed in a soft voice.

He didn't ask her to explain. He nodded and dropped his hand. Amelia longed for his touch. "Four years ago," he said. "There was a raid on our cabin. I wasn't home; I'd gone hunting—"

Amelia saw that Daniel was still beating himself up about it. She moved closer and slipped her arms about his waist, wanting only to comfort him. She gave him a hug, then moved back to look into his eyes.

"I heard them—the Indians—before I got there." His voice had become a monotone, without life. "When I arrived, the barn was on fire . . . and our cabin was in shambles. Jane was gone, and there was no sign of Susie." He paused to take a breath. "I checked outside, everywhere, and couldn't find either one. After a time, I gave up and went back to the house. I remember feeling empty inside, except for the pain." He shuddered. "I could barely breathe for the pain." He stared at her with glazed eyes. "Then, I heard a noise—from under the bed. I couldn't be sure it wasn't an animal, or an Indian for that matter. I got out my knife, ready to defend myself, and pulled away the blanket."

His expression brightened, and Amelia felt a lightening in her heart. "It was Susie, frightened, but alive and unhurt. She wanted her momma. Dear God, it hurt me to hear her cry out for Jane. I couldn't help her. I couldn't find her momma." He released a shaky breath and was able to smile. "But I'd found her, and I was so glad."

Amelia smiled even while she battled tears. She leaned into him, pressed her face against his breast, enjoying the closeness. Closing her eyes, she could see the scene as it must have happened, feel the pain of a man who'd lost his wife and child only to learn that he'd regained his daughter.

And Jane? she wondered.

"I was never able to find Jane. There was no sign of her—nothing. Her body was nowhere to be found."

Jane's body was never found.

Amelia's chest tightened. She released him and stepped back. *Could the woman be alive?* The realization that she could upset her. Not that she wanted the woman killed, but the existence of Daniel's wife complicated things for her . . . for their relationship. She cared for Daniel, more than she probably should. The idea hadn't seemed so terrible—her and Daniel together, but if he still had a living wife . . .

She shuddered and closed her eyes. She hadn't thought she'd feel more pain than she suffered when she realized she had a missing father. She saw things differently now,

understood more about the man before her. Her father had
been missing for only two days. What must Daniel be
feeling with his Jane gone for over four years?

"It's all right," he said with a smile. "I'm fine really."

Amelia gazed at him with a longing she tried desperately to hide. "I'm sorry you had to go through that."

He shrugged. "Do you understand why I don't want to
go through it again? That's why I wanted you at the fort.
Not because I wanted to send you away, but because I
wanted you to stay healthy and alive . . . where I knew
I could find you later . . . after it's all done."

Heat shot throughout Amelia's body. She didn't understand, but she thought he was telling her his concern was
rooted in something deeper than simple friendship. She
remembered their heated kiss that first night. She blushed.
That certainly wouldn't happen between friends. There was
more to their feelings, yet it was more than physical attraction. They sensed it every time they exchanged looks,
brushed hands, or shared the same room. They felt it when
they were apart and missing each other.

But what about Jane? Amelia knew that Daniel wanted
her now, but what was to happen if his missing wife made
her reappearance?

"Daniel—" She wanted to ask him, but was afraid.

His eyes glowed as he looked at her. Her body responded on instinct, without thought, because it felt so
right. She stilled, unwilling to make the first move, needing to be reassured that he did, in fact, desire her.

She didn't stop him as he pulled her into his arms. She
didn't stop him as he bent his head and kissed her—a
wild, sweet mating of mouths that stole Amelia's breath
and make her flesh tingle and come alive.

It was a brief kiss, too brief as far as Amelia was concerned, but it was probably just as well, because Susie

entered the cabin then. There was nothing about the two adults that revealed to the little girl their tumultuous thoughts or raging desire for each other.

"Jack had some cornmeal, but no maple syrup. He said to tell you that he expects some syrup later in the week after Rain-from-Sky comes to trade."

Daniel smiled at his daughter. "Thanks, sweeting. You've done well."

The child's teeth flashed, and she included Amelia in that good-natured grin.

Suddenly, Susie's expression became serious. "Is Miss Amelia going away?"

"No, I'm afraid not. It appears you're stuck with me."

Daniel nodded when Susie looked to him for an answer. "She's staying. I hope you like her company, because she's going to be around for a while." He looked at Amelia. "And she's going to teach you a few things."

"Teach me?" Susie asked.

Amelia nodded. "That's right," she said. "Your pa has asked me to show you some things that a woman—a lady—needs to know."

Susie appeared curious. "Like what?"

"She'll tell you all about it tomorrow," Daniel said. "Right now we've supper to think about. Any idea what you'd like to eat."

"Possum!" Susie squealed.

Amelia paled. "Possum?"

Daniel's lips twitched. "Never ate possum before?" he drawled with a thick, self-imposed accent, the likes of which Amelia had never heard.

"No, I can't say I have."

"Wait until you taste Pa's possum pie." The little girl seemed to take delight in seeing Amelia's face turn a sickly shade of green. "Jack and Rebb say it's the best thing they ever ate on this side of the Wisconsin Territory."

"Ah, well, if Jack and Rebb like it," Amelia said, sounding doubtful, "then I imagine I'll like it, too."

She glared at Daniel, who sniggered as he turned away.

"Please sit straight, Susie." Amelia paused in the act of brushing the little girl's hair. "You mustn't slouch. It's bad for your posture."

"What's posture?"

Amelia smiled. "It's how you hold yourself. You wouldn't want curved shoulders or a crooked back, would you?"

Susie seemed to give the matter some thought. She touched her shoulder. "I'm already curved."

Amelia chuckled. "I don't mean over your shoulder like this." She placed her hand on the child to demonstrate. She slid her fingers over shoulder to upper arm, then she released her and moved in front of the girl. "When I talk about curved shoulders, I mean this—" In an exaggerated display, Amelia hunched her shoulders and made a face.

The child stared at her with a frown. "Maybe I want curved shoulders," she said obstinately. "And maybe I like my hair messy and my feet dirty. Maybe I don't wanna be a lady."

"Susie—" Amelia had recognized early on that Susie was not going to be an eager pupil. And could she blame her? *No, I can't.* She herself had begun to have grave doubts about trying to change the little girl. She was a happy child when she was allowed to play outside and be herself. What right did she have to mold and shape Susie into something she was not?

Amelia decided she would have to rethink this arrangement. It was a certainty that Susie could benefit from a few lessons on manners and hygiene, although Amelia had been quite surprised with what Susie already knew.

Susie did not own a single dress. Amelia felt strongly that the child should have one, at least. A garment that she could wear for special occasions. Susie would not always be sheltered from society. She would most likely leave the area one day with a husband of her own. It wouldn't hurt to make sure that Susie was well prepared for that day.

Susie now sat with her arms folded across her chest, her chin thrust high into the air. Studying her, Amelia felt the urge to smile, for she recognized that look. On occasion, she'd worn a similar expression of her own.

"All right, Susie, I think you've probably had enough for one day." She smiled. "Would you like to make cookies?"

Susie lowered her arms, and her face brightened. "Is that what the maple sugar's for?"

Amelia nodded. It would be the cookies she'd enjoyed as a child. It would be their own special recipe, concocted from the ingredients that were available.

"Can I make the batter?" Susie asked.

"Are your hands clean?"

The child held out her hands, turning them for Amelia's inspection. "I can wash them again if you want."

There was not a spot of dirt on the dainty hands. Amelia smiled, pleased. Despite her reluctance to cooperate, Susie had apparently taken the lesson on hand-washing to heart.

"They look fine to me," Amelia replied. "Now let's go into the kitchen."

Suddenly, Susie looked suspicious. "This ain't another lady lesson, is it?"

"No. But you know it doesn't hurt for a lady to know how to bake."

"As long as I don't have to wear one of them aprons."

Susie had remembered the one Amelia had worn only last night when she'd offered to make supper. "An apron is used to protect a lady's gown."

Satisfied with Amelia's explanation, Susie nodded. "Then it's a good thing I got my buckskins on."

They went to the kitchen and pulled out the ingredients they'd need to bake. As she and Susie measured out the flour, sugar, and cinnamon, Amelia thought of her childhood, which called up images of her father. Tears filled her eyes.

"Is this good?" Susie asked. She tipped the bowl for Amelia to see.

"Yes, very good," Amelia answered huskily.

The little girl looked at her and saw her tears. "What's wrong?"

In an effort to control her emotions, Amelia turned away. "I'm fine."

"No, you're not," a deep voice drawled. Daniel had come into the room silently and had been watching the two for some time.

Amelia gasped and spun around, surprised by his appearance.

"She's crying, Pa," Susie exclaimed, sounding upset.

"I know she is, sweeting," Daniel said. He studied her thoughtfully. "Susie, you can finish up the batter, can't you?"

Susie nodded, looking proud. "Sure, I can, Pa—"

"Then finish up, and let me take Amelia into the next room."

"That's really not necessary," the woman protested.

Daniel captured her arm and gently pulled her toward the main room. "Be careful near the oven, Susie."

The child assured him she would, and Daniel tugged Amelia into the other room, where he gently pushed her into a chair. Then he took the seat next to her.

"This is ridiculous," she said.

He didn't say anything. He preferred to study her; the sight of her always brought him pleasure. And he found that pleasure increasing with each new day.

"Tell me what caused you to cry."

She shook her head, sending her brown hair flying. She had worn it down this day, and Daniel admired the silky locks, the rich warm sable color. Her eyes were red-rimmed, the lids puffy; yet, he'd never seen a woman more beautiful or appealing. "Amelia—"

"It's silly. I don't know why it came over me like that. It's not like I've learned anything new . . . anything to upset me."

"Your father," Daniel guessed.

She inclined her head. "Susie and I were making cookies when suddenly I remembered how it was when I was a little girl. My mother died when I was young, but we had Aunt Bess. She's my father's sister. Aunt Bess loved to bake, and Rachel and I would help her." Amelia's lips curved slightly up. "Father would put up such a fuss after he'd tasted one of our cookies. You'd have thought we'd fixed him a seven-course meal."

Daniel watched her without speaking, wanting to hear more. He enjoyed the vision of her as a little girl. She was probably a skinny little child with brown eyes as big as saucers in a face that would light up the world when she smiled.

He wanted to take away her pain, but he knew that he couldn't—not until he found her father. Still, he had to try. It hurt him to see her tears. "We'll find him, Amelia—and soon."

She started and stared at him as if he knew something that she didn't.

He recognized his mistake. "No, there is no word yet. I went back to the mission. There's been no sign of anyone who's been missing."

Her face fell, and he felt like a heel. He stood and drew her up next to him. Next, he pulled her into his arms. "You know I'm going to do everything in my power to bring your father back, to make you happy again."

She gazed up at him, her brown eyes swimming, her expression one of trust and admiration. He caught his breath. "No," he said, "don't make the mistake of thinking me more than a man. I don't have any special powers. I can't snap my fingers and make your father appear, but I can search for him. I can ask my friends to help." He brushed her cheek with his knuckle, wiping the tear that dripped from her left eye.

"It's going to take time," he warned. "Oh, I could easily ride out now and search, but I could just as easily get myself captured by the Sioux—or worse."

"No," Amelia breathed, "you mustn't." *I couldn't bear it if you were.*

"Then have faith," he whispered.

She nodded as she stared into his eyes. His tender look made her feel warm inside.

"Pa? Miss Amelia?" Susie appeared at the door, her face, hands, and clothes covered with flour and batter. "Can we bake the cookies now?"

"We'll be right in, sweeting." Daniel held Amelia's gaze for a minute longer. "Shall we?" he then said to Amelia when he'd sensed Susie gone.

She nodded. Amelia wiped the remainder of her tears and went back to the kitchen with Daniel following closely behind.

Eleven

After asking Jack to keep an eye on Amelia and Susie, Daniel slipped away early one morning to find Black Hawk. He found the Ojibwa village easily enough, but when he arrived, he learned that Black Hawk and a small band of his men were away from the encampment. The group wasn't expected back for a few days. Daniel spoke with Rain-from-Sky, asking that he send word upon Black Hawk's return. Then, he went home to Amelia and Susie, knowing that Amelia would be disappointed that he hadn't learned anything. He arrived at the cabin shortly after noon. Amelia and Susie were inside, preparing their midday meal.

"Pa!" Susie spied him first, running to jump into his arms. "Did you see Black Hawk? What about Conner?"

Daniel flashed Amelia a glance before he responded. "Conner was running about with Brown Bird."

Susie nodded. "Pa? When can we go back for a visit?"

The man shrugged. "As soon as we know it's safe enough to travel."

Amelia approached with a question in her brown eyes. "Daniel?"

He shook his head. "I'm sorry, Amelia, but Black Hawk wasn't there. His brother will send word as soon as he returns." He felt a sudden ache as her face fell.

"Susie?" Amelia said. "Would you please set the table?"

The girl looked reluctant to leave.

"Go ahead, sweeting," Daniel said. "I'll not be going anywhere for a while now."

The child dashed toward the cabinet where the dishes, eating utensils, and glasses were kept. Amelia waited for her to be gone from the kitchen, before she said what was on her mind.

"Has something happened to your friend?" she asked anxiously.

Daniel looked surprised by her question. "No," he said with a certainty that relieved Amelia's fears. "He's on a mission for his People. His brother Rain-from-Sky said that Black Hawk will be back in a few days." He touched her face and smiled. "I explained to Rain-from-Sky about the Sioux attack on the mission. He understands the gravity of the situation. We'll hear from the Ojibwa in a day or so."

Amelia felt the knot that had caught in her stomach ease away. She nodded. "Are you hungry?"

He grinned, but looked surprised that she'd cook for them. "Starved. What's for dinner?"

She blushed. "I'm afraid I'm not the greatest cook."

He fingered her jaw, then released it. "I'm sure the meal will be just fine. The cookies that you and Susie made were delicious."

"Baking is one thing," she said. "Cooking a meal is something else."

"Did Susie help?" he asked.

"Yes, of course," Amelia said.

"Then I imagine you've made flapjacks with maple syrup and Indian pudding."

She felt a flicker of surprise. "How did you know?"

Susie had shown her how to make the pudding. Amelia had seen her Aunt Bess make flapjacks back in Baltimore.

"They're Susie's favorites. She'll eat both every day if you let her."

Amelia made a face. "She may change her mind after she tastes the way I cooked them."

Daniel chuckled and hugged her to his side. "Let's go take a look and see if you're such a terrible cook."

Amelia was surprised how well the meal turned out. The flapjacks were light and airy, much like the ones she'd had as a child in Baltimore. The maple syrup sweetened them just enough to make the dish more of a treat. The pudding, made from cornmeal and other ingredients, was just as delicious. When the Traherns announced both tasty, Amelia beamed.

She felt Daniel's amused regard as she accepted a second helping. Susie chatted to her father about her morning, while Amelia remained silent, contributing to the conversation only when Susie or Daniel addressed her directly. She watched Daniel with Susie and felt a tug on her heart. Daniel was patient and loving toward the child. As she studied him, she felt herself responding to his gentleness, his capacity for loving his little girl. When Susie, at one point, left her chair to climb onto Daniel's lap, Amelia became caught in a memory . . . of herself and her father . . . of Rachel and her father when she and her sister were small. Fear for her father hit her hard as she could no longer put aside her concern or forget that her father could be in grave danger or dead. She blinked back tears. She didn't want to spoil the Traherns' afternoon. When she could no longer stifle her tears, she rose and left the room with the excuse of clearing the table.

Daniel followed her into the kitchen seconds later. She could feel his gaze on her as he set down some dirty dishes near the washbasin. "Thank you," she said without meeting his gaze.

She felt him hesitate. "Amelia—"

Amelia met his gaze. "I'm all right, Daniel."

He stared at her, and she felt herself respond to the warmth and sympathy in his beautiful blue eyes.

"I need to speak with Reverend Whitely and Will. I need to know if they saw anything—"

"Two days," Daniel said. "I'll take you there myself if only you'll wait two days."

"But what if they know something? What if two days is too late?"

He touched her arm. "I don't want you returning to the mission. Not until I've spoken with Black Hawk."

"But that's not fair! He's my father. I think Reverend Whitely was the last one to see him!" She felt an overwhelming panic. "Please, Daniel," she whispered.

Daniel frowned. "I'll see what I can do to bring him here."

She felt a rise in her spirits. "Thank you," she murmured. In a moment of gratitude, she gave him a hug.

"I can't promise they'll come, but I'll ask them. If they choose to stay at the mission, then you will wait until it's safe to return."

She nodded, pleased by this man who had initially stirred within her feelings of anger and dislike.

"I'll go back there tomorrow morning."

"Fine—"

"Amelia, tell me you won't leave this area. I need to know that you and Susie are safe."

Susie, she thought. "I'll watch over your daughter for you."

A strange look entered Daniel's expression and was gone.

"You two seem to be getting along," he commented after a silent moment.

"She's a wonderful little girl. She doesn't particularly like her lessons in becoming a lady. She refused to wear a dress, and she'll not wash her hair until I make her."

Daniel smiled. "It's the soap. She's afraid of getting it in her eyes."

"Oh, I didn't realize." There was much more that Susie objected to. She didn't want to play with dolls—a curious thing, Amelia thought. When she asked Susie why she didn't own any dolls, Susie's expression closed up and she wouldn't answer. Perhaps Daniel would know why Susie had no dolls.

". . . And the princess had hair of gold and eyes that were so blue they matched the clear summer sky."

Amelia stood for a moment at the doorway of Susie's room, watching as Daniel told his little girl a story. Moved by the scene and understanding that it was a special, private moment between father and daughter, she stayed only a minute before she turned away to wait for Daniel in the great room.

The sight of Daniel seated on the edge of Susie's bed, his blond head tilted to one side as he told Susie the story would forever be etched in Amelia's memory. She thought of her impression of Daniel when she'd first laid eyes on him, how she'd thought him an impossible, unfeeling man, and realized that she'd never been so wrong about anyone.

Susie was lucky to have Daniel. Amelia wondered about Jane, Susie's mother, Daniel's wife. Was she sweet and docile or spirited like her daughter?

Amelia recalled earlier that day when she'd attempted to show Susie the proper way to partake of an afternoon tea. Susie had been restless, not at all interested in dress-ing up or drinking tea, her mind wandering to outside, where the child preferred to be playing.

When she'd tried to instill in Susie the importance of learning how to conduct herself in polite society, the child had given her a look designed to kill, then she'd shoved back her chair and run outside, ignoring Amelia's request to rejoin her.

Susie had been sulky at dinner, but her sour mood had quickly passed afterward when Daniel had promised an extra story that night. The three of them had gone outside to sit on the front porch of the house, studying the moon and stars, while Daniel told a tale of a ship captain's ad-ventures on Lake Superior one stormy night two years ago.

It had been a pleasant time, with Amelia and Daniel seated side by side on a bench swing, Susie on Daniel's lap and snuggled within his arms. Amelia had listened to the deep melodic tone of Daniel's storytelling voice and had felt some of the strain of the last day ease. It could have been another time or place. Her father's kidnapping might never have occurred.

When the story was over and it was time for Susie to go to bed, Daniel carried Susie inside, and Amelia had remained on the porch swing, studying the night sky. When she finally roused herself to go inside, she had heard the low sound of Daniel in the other room and had gone to look in on the two briefly.

Now, as she waited for Daniel to rejoin her, Amelia was conscious of the quiet intimacy of the night, the fact that soon she would be seated with a man she was greatly attracted to . . . a man she desired. The thought made her heart trip and a warmth burn in her stomach. She recalled the previous night's kiss . . . and longed for another taste, a taste that could prove dangerous to her peace of mind.

She sat on the sofa before the fireplace. There was no fire, as the night was warm, but she could imagine the orange flames licking about the wood. She could feel the heat as if the fire were alive—and it wasn't her physical attraction to Daniel that made her feel warm and tingly all over.

Being separated from her father, not knowing what was happening to him at this very moment, was difficult for her, but she knew it would be impossible if it weren't for Daniel and his kindness and understanding.

She felt the sting of tears and fought hard against them, determined not to give in to sadness again. If anyone could help her, it was Daniel, and she would take comfort in the fact that he had promised to help her and that he had friends who could help her as well.

Amelia studied the room—the large beams across the ceiling, the stone fireplace . . . the smooth wooden floor. On the mantel, there was a vase of cut flowers. On the wall above the vase was Indian artwork, no doubt given to Daniel by his Ojibwa friends.

After the attack on the mission, it was hard for her to be open-minded about the Indians. She knew that there were different tribes, that one couldn't be blamed for the actions of another, but she wasn't sure how she'd feel if any Indian—Chippewa or Sioux, friendly or not—came through that front door.

She wondered if Susie was being difficult tonight. It was taking Daniel what seemed to be an inordinately long time with her. Perhaps Susie was complaining about Amelia and her lessons.

Feeling a bit sleepy herself, Amelia closed her eyes, sure that she would hear Daniel's return.

She must have dozed, because suddenly she jerked awake. Daniel sat beside her, his eyes shut, his face boyish in repose. He must have returned a while ago. She shifted uncomfortably, wondering if he had watched her while she slept. Then she realized that she really didn't care, for he felt comfortable enough to relax, to sleep, in her company.

She studied him—the bright blond wave that fell across his forehead, the lighter streaks of gold brought by the touch of the sun. He had changed his clothes, shedding his buckskins for a white linen shirt and brown breeches. His feet were bare, the tops with a smattering of golden hair, his toes nicely shaped and even.

Once again, she was struck by the power in his male form, in his arms and legs, in his upper and lower torso. Her eyes fell on a small scar on his right wrist. She wondered how he had gotten it, if he had others, and how he'd gotten them, too. Staring at him, she wondered what he had been like as a little boy, and was shocked by her musings, for no other man had ever inspired such questioning thoughts.

Her gaze wandered down to his waistband, and she felt herself blush as she wondered what he'd look like without clothes. She decided that he would be pleasing to her eye no matter what, because of the strength of her feelings for him.

Her attention returned to his face, and she found, much to her embarrassment, that he had awakened and was watching her through heavy-lidded eyes. She gasped, then managed to control her emotions enough to smile. He didn't smile, but just looked at her. Mortified, she rose to escape, but he reached out and pulled her back down, right onto his lap.

Her gaze flew to his face, and she saw that a grin had come to his lips and a mischievous twinkle lit up his eyes.

"Thought you'd get away from me, didn't you?" he said in a deep husky voice.

"Daniel—"

"No, Amelia," he said. The look in his eyes had changed. Desire flamed within the blue orbs. His expression held her captive; she couldn't look away.

She felt herself respond to his look, his hold on her. She shifted a little and heard him groan. The sound made her freeze until she realized that she hadn't hurt him. It had been a soft exclamation of pleasure.

He cupped her shoulder, then ran his hand down her arm. She trembled beneath his touch and briefly closed her eyes.

"Susie sleeping?" she asked, aware of how shaky her voice sounded.

Daniel nodded, his attention intent on his hands, one of which held her wrist, the other that hovered near the top button of her gown.

His eyes captured hers. She stared at him, her thoughts in turmoil, her body aching, but the doubts playing on the surface confused her. His wife was missing, but he still seemed attached to the woman.

She was here, but was it her that Daniel wanted—or was he pretending she was his Jane?

"I'm not your wife," she said, aware of how lame that sounded.

He jerked with surprise, then scowled. "I know you're not. Don't you think I know the difference? The last thing I think about when I'm with you is my wife."

There was an underlying harshness in his tone that surprised her. "Daniel—"

"Don't talk, Amelia," he said. "Don't talk. Just feel." With that he caressed the underside of her chin and jawline, ran a finger about her left ear, trailed a path around to the back of her neck.

Enjoying his touch, she closed her eyes and sighed softly. When she opened them again, he was smiling at her. His good humor reached his blue eyes, making them appear brighter, more blue.

Unable to help herself, Amelia lifted a hand to the side of his face. She rubbed his cheek, enjoying the rasp of light whisker growth. She touched where his collar dipped in the front in a V, wound her fingers lightly in the soft growth of exposed chest hair, then, aching, she cupped his face and drew him toward her lips.

Daniel moaned as his mouth captured hers in a kiss that fueled the spark of desire between them. Their lips touched and opened, their tongues dueled and dipped low to taste the sweetness of each other's mouths. Heat spiraled in the tips of Amelia's breasts, threading out to bring fire to her lower abdomen. She clung to Daniel and gasped as the sweet heat of desire overwhelmed her, lifting her higher and higher.

He raised his head, but then he touched her where no man had touched before. Cupping her fabric-clad breast, he caressed her, rubbed her nipple. Amelia's eyes widened briefly with surprise, before she closed her eyes and moaned softly with delight.

"Yes, Amelia," Daniel rasped. "I knew you would be like this. You're all fire and sweetness. I love touching you."

She arched into his hand. The sensations pouring through her were so sweet, yet so wild, that she felt as though she were coming undone.

She didn't protest when she felt his fingers again on her bodice buttons. She felt the air as he undid each button. She felt the backs of his knuckles against her heated skin.

Amelia ached to touch Daniel. She wanted to feel his heat, the warmth of his skin next to hers. While he worked to undo the last of her buttons, she struggled to get to him, tugging the hem of his shirt from his breeches, slipping her hands beneath fabric to feel the taut, sleek muscles of his stomach and higher.

His stomach contracted beneath her touch. He had started to open her gown bodice, but he froze as her fingertips reached his nipples. She was surprised to feel them harden into small buds, like her own.

"Let me touch you," she whispered.

He looked at her with a burning gaze. When he didn't move, she took it as his consent, and she tugged up his shirt. He released her in order to raise his arms, so she could rid him of the garment.

The heat of him enveloped her, even before she touched him. She caressed him and gave a soft exclamation of delight at the freedom to fondle and stroke his bare skin.

"Amelia—"

She met his gaze. "Don't you like it when I touch you?"

There was a flash in his blue eyes. "You know I do."

She smiled. "Good," she said, "because I like touching you."

"That's fine," he said softly, "but be prepared, for I'll not sit here inactive while you touch. I want to touch you as well—badly." He paused to dip his head, pressing his lips within the folds of the open bodice, above the lace edging of her chemise. Her breasts pebbled against the thin fabric of her undergarment. She gasped and grabbed his head, weaving her fingers within his blond hair.

When his mouth caught the area of fabric that covered

her nipple, Amelia cried out with shocked delight. She tried to pulled back his head, but as sensation exploded within her, she held on, pressing him closer, whimpering at the pleasure he was giving her.

He lowered her chemise to expose her breasts. He kissed her right nipple, then laved it with his tongue. Amelia moaned as he continued to taste and touch her.

Suddenly, she felt his hand on her leg, felt the fabric of her skirt rise and the puff of air against her exposed calf. She didn't try to stop him as he continued to raise the hem of her gown. She put her arms about his neck, tightened her fingers in the hair at his nape. She moved to help him raise her skirts.

Their breaths were labored. She could feel her heart beating wildly. She felt his pulse that echoed the thundering within his chest.

"No, Momma, no!" The cry of a little girl had them crashing back to earth again. "No! No! No!"

Daniel and Amelia sprang apart at the sound of Susie's cry, and Amelia stumbled to her feet, suddenly aware of where they were, what they were doing . . . and all the doubts and complications which would have prevented their actions if they'd only taken the time to think ahead.

"Nightmare," Daniel murmured as he dressed.

Sobered by the interruption, Amelia struggled to redo her bodice. She was afraid to meet Daniel's gaze, unsure of what she'd see. His silence told her that he, too, was uncomfortable about what had occurred between them.

"Momma!" Susie's high-pitched scream had Daniel rushing to her side.

Amelia wanted to follow, to see for herself that Susie was all right, but she was too shaken, her legs too trembly to take a step in the right direction. Instead, she sat on the sofa, leaned forward to cup her head in her hands, and struggled to overcome her embarrassment—and shame.

Twelve

When she'd regained her composure, Amelia put her embarrassment aside and went to Susie's room. She found Susie asleep, cradled within Daniel's arms. Traces of tears were still visible on the child's cheeks.

Sensing her at the door, Daniel looked up.

"Is she all right?" she mouthed silently.

He nodded. He shifted, setting Susie to lie down. He reassured her with a few soft words when she stirred in her sleep. He covered her up, tucked her in, then rose carefully from the bed. He brushed back Susie's hair from her forehead and left her side.

Amelia moved out of Daniel's way. "I heard her call for her mother."

Daniel nodded. "She had a nightmare." He looked concerned. "She hasn't had one for a lone time. I thought she was over them."

"Any idea what caused it?"

"I wish I knew." He frowned. "She dreams of the Sioux attack—the one Jane was taken in."

"Poor thing." Amelia felt sympathy for the child. Her own father was gone, and she, an adult, was upset. She could imagine how devastating it must be for a small child to lose a parent.

"It's late," he said.

Suddenly the shift in mood had come full circle. "Yes,

yes, it is." The intimacy was back. She could feel her heart beating wildly in her chest, as she waited for his lead.

He rubbed his nape as he looked away. "I've got a lot to do tomorrow. I guess I'll retire for the night."

It was the wisest choice for both of them to leave each other's company for the solitary sanctuary of their individual rooms. Still, Amelia felt a knot of disappointment.

"Well, good night then," she said softly.

"Good night." He didn't look at her, and it hurt.

She escaped the awkwardness of the moment by heading toward her room.

"Amelia?"

Pulse racing, she turned to meet his gaze. "Yes?"

"I'll be leaving for the mission before light. If you need anything or have any trouble, see Jack."

She nodded, then she continued toward the door of her bedchamber.

"Amelia, I'm sorry about what just happened," Daniel said, stopping her again.

She faced him with a steady gaze. "I'm not," she said. She disappeared into her room, closing the door quietly behind her.

Daniel stared at the door to her room, his thoughts racing, his body aching. *She isn't sorry.*

"A dangerous bit of knowledge, Daniel," he muttered. He wanted her; it was plain and simple. But a relationship between them would be foolish, a complication they didn't need.

There had been fire between them, and the passionate conflagration had burned hotter, brighter than he'd ever felt before.

Dear God, she didn't regret it! Daniel fought the urge to go to her, take her in his arms, and . . .

No, he mustn't allow desire to rule his head. He had to remember Pamela, his wife . . . his lovely, treacherous wife. She had lured him in with her charms, with her body, then in the end she'd betrayed him with another man.

As he entered his room, Daniel recalled with startling clarity when he'd first met Pamela. Pamela and her sister Janet had come to stay with her father, an officer at the fort at Prairie du Chien. Daniel's blacksmithy was a few miles from the fort, situated within a reasonable distance from the trading-post settlement.

He'd been captivated by both of General Randolph's daughters. Janet, the elder, was an attractive young woman with a ready smile and a look of caring in her hazel eyes. Pamela had been the younger sister. With dark hair that fell in waves down her back, she had green eyes, a coquettish grin, and a complexion of smooth white cream. Of the two sisters, Pamela had seemed the most interested in him, and Daniel was immensely flattered and pleased. They married within a month of their meeting, and Pamela moved out of the fort into Daniel's home.

Daniel had realized shortly after their marriage that Pamela had pursued him only because her sister Janet had shown an interest in him. It wasn't long after that Daniel sensed his wife's discontent. He hadn't realized it at the time, but Pamela had been a spoiled young woman who had played with his affections in order to win him from her sister. He hadn't guessed during their brief whirlwind courtship the calculation, the deceit, she'd used to convince him she was in love with him. He'd been enthralled with her beauty, with her attention. After their marriage, the harsh reality of their relationship had been sobering to him.

Things had looked up for the young couple for a time

when Pamela became pregnant. She seemed happy. She smiled more, as if she basked in the glow of impending motherhood. Daniel had been delighted with the change in his wife and the coming of his first child. Pamela's pregnancy seemed to transform her, making her the woman he'd thought he'd wed.

His world came crashing down on him one day when he returned home from a delivery to the army fort to find Pamela gone. She had left a note on their dining table, informing him that she'd gone away with her lover—the real father of her unborn child . . . his best friend, James Beck. Daniel was devastated by both his wife's and his friend's betrayal. He'd been cuckolded then abandoned, and worse yet, Pamela had lied about her child. Neither she nor James had possessed the courage to face him with the truth. Pamela had left him a note instead.

Daniel, I've left you. Gone to be with my lover—the father of my baby.

Something within Daniel had died that day. He'd hardened himself against the pain, but he'd become bitter, eyeing the world with a new icy disdain. When news reached him that Pamela had been killed in a carriage accident along with the driver of the vehicle, James Beck, Daniel's closest friend and Pamela's lover, Daniel had experienced sharp betrayal regarding his friend . . . then nothing. He'd been unable to care enough to mourn either one of them.

When his sister Jane had sent word that she was pregnant and afraid to be alone with her military husband, who was absent more often than not, Daniel decided to go to his sister in her hour of need. They'd always been close. In fact, she and her husband Richard had for a time lived nearby.

When his niece Susie was born and he held her in his

arms, Daniel had felt his heart begin to thaw, and he allowed himself to feel again.

His life with Jane had been a pleasant existence. He loved his sister and adored her child. Then came that terrible day, that afternoon that their cabin was attacked, Jane kidnapped, and Daniel had found his three-year-old niece hiding under the bed.

His search for Jane had been futile. Daniel and Susie managed to build a new life in a different place, far from the scene of Susie's terror. In the months and then years that followed, Susie had brought Daniel more happiness than he'd felt in a long, long while. It still upset him that after three years he'd been unable to find Jane.

The recent attack on the mission brought the memories, the pain of losing his sister, back to him. Had it stirred up bad memories for Susie? She hadn't been at the mission, but she'd learned about the attack.

His feelings for Amelia complicated things. Daniel hadn't expected to feel desire for a woman again, to respect her and value her friendship. The more he learned about her, the more he was convinced that Amelia Dempsey was unlike any other woman he'd ever known . . . intelligent, attractive, and caring . . . and a dangerous risk to his aching heart.

Daniel left the cabin when the day was but a hint of light in the distant sky. He started toward Jack's to tell him of his trip but then he saw Rebb Colfax's cart exiting the woods and heading his way. Spying him, the older man waved in silent greeting. Daniel changed direction to approach Rebb.

"Hey, Rebb, what are you doing out and about so early?" he asked.

Rebb gestured toward the back of his cart. "Need a few things. Maude wants me hanging around today, so I thought I'd rouse Jack and get my trading done early." The old man looked at Daniel thoughtfully. "Going someplace?"

"To the mission." He explained about the Indian raid and the destruction left behind. Rebb was shocked to hear about the kidnappings and the loss of life. Daniel told him about the two survivors at the mission and the woman who was staying at his house.

"Amelia's father is missing," Daniel said. "She wants to talk with Allen Whitely, won't rest until she does. I don't want her returning to the mission. It's not safe, and I won't feel better about it until after Black Hawk scouts the area and pronounces it safe."

"What did that black devil have to say anyway?"

Daniel frowned. "Why do you insist on calling him that black devil?"

Rebb spit a wad of chewing tobacco on the ground. " 'Cause that Indian is a black devil. He's got something inside him waiting to bust out. He's like a powder keg just itching to be lit."

"Does he frighten you?"

"Heck, yeah," Rebb said. "They all frighten me, but Black Hawk most of all."

"But you've broken bread with him."

The older man brushed the notion aside with a wave of his arm. "Course I have. I've no intention of making an enemy of him."

"You don't know the Ojibwa like I do," Daniel said.

"Well, I reckon I don't. And I suppose as far as Injuns go, the Ojibwa aren't a bad lot. That brave—Rain-from-Sky—he seems friendly enough. Once helped me get my wagon unstuck from the mud. I thought I'd just die when he first showed up, but then as silent as the night, the Injun and his friends pushed my cart free." Rebb shook his head, the memory a continued source of amazement to him. "I suppose for that reason I'll give the Ojibwa the benefit of the doubt. Rather encounter an Ojibwa than a Sioux any day. Haven't had much experience with the Ottawa and or any of the others."

Daniel, noticing the increasing daylight, realized that he had to get moving. He stifled his impatience as Rebb continued to talk. "I've got to go," he said. "How soon does Maude expect you back?" Maude was Rebb's wife. His friends rarely thought of her, as she never came to the post. Sometimes, Daniel and Jack wondered if she was a real person or a figment of their old friend's imagination.

Rebb shrugged. "Not for a couple of hours. Woman probably doesn't know I'm gone. I left before she woke up."

"Can you keep an eye on my house and the girls?"

"Sure can. Since I ain't in no hurry to get home, how about I sit on that front porch swing of yours and wait until Jack wakes up on his own?"

Daniel smiled. "Thanks, Colfax."

The man grinned. "Just remember my good deed when the time comes for me to need a new shovel made."

"I'll remember."

Daniel left, after returning to the smithy for Jack's horse, an animal that Jack allowed Daniel the use of. He rode to the mission, for he didn't want to be gone long. He felt no evil presence, nor did he feel any sense of doom as he broke from the forest into the mission clearing. As he headed toward the building where he'd last seen the Reverend Whitely and the young man, Daniel wondered how they were faring . . . and if they'd found any more of their missing friends.

* * *

When she got up and found Daniel gone, Amelia wasn't surprised, because Daniel had warned her that he'd be leaving early. She peeked into Susie's room and saw the child sleeping, then left for the kitchen to find something to eat.

As she checked the cabinets and pantry, she didn't reflect too deeply on the previous evening, for every time she started to remember, she suffered a sensation between embarrassment and excitement. Her feelings for Daniel confused and dismayed her; she couldn't afford to think of him right now. Her first and main concern at the moment was finding her father . . . and Miriam. She didn't know the young woman too well, but she had been helpful and caring, and she'd helped Amelia adjust to a life much different than the one she'd led previously.

She made herself a pot of tea, brewed from local plants and herbs, something Miriam had taught her. Grabbing a piece of bread and a handful of berries picked only yesterday, Amelia headed toward the door and the porch swing outside.

She opened the door and gasped, then shrieked, as she came face-to-face with an Indian. She held up her teacup as if it were a weapon. "Who are you? What do you want?" She started to tremble and was in great danger of spilling her tea and dropping her breakfast.

The brave didn't move, didn't speak. He stared at her with dark glistening eyes, and she felt a chill. She thought of Susie in bed behind her, and debated whether or not she could shut the man out and lock the door. The Indian wore little in the way of apparel, just a vest and a loincloth of dark leather with leggings to just above the knees, and moccasins with a puckered front seam. His jet-black hair hung past his shoulders; a small braid hung on each side of his face. He had riveting features. His high cheekbones were unpainted; she noted the lack of face paint and felt better, but only a little, for she didn't know much about the Indians. Amelia had encountered them only three times—and the third time had been the worst experience of her life as a band attacked, kidnapped, and killed people she knew.

The Indian still didn't stir, and Amelia found herself wondering what to do. Terror was clawing its way from her throat to her stomach, and she couldn't breathe. Then she heard movement behind her, knew she'd have to do something fast or Susie would be at risk.

"What do you want?" she demanded in a stronger voice.

The corner of his mouth curved slightly. Was she wrong or did she see a twinkle of amusement in his obsidian eyes?

She turned quickly to see Susie emerge from her bedchamber. "Susie, go back into your room!"

Susie, blinking sleepily, frowned. "What—" she began, then she spied the Indian. "Black Hawk!" she cried. To Amelia's shock, the little girl rushed forward. The woman watched as the Indian's expression softened as he held out his arms.

"Sus-sie," he said. "It has been too long since I've seen my little flower."

The child grinned and, to Amelia's surprise, said something foreign.

The brave's gaze returned to Amelia. "Little Flower says that this man wouldn't be a stranger to her if only he would come to his friend's lodge more often."

"Oh, I—"

"I'm Black-Hawk-Who-Hunts-at-Dawn" the brave said, "warrior of the *Anishinaabe,* friend to Daniel Trahern."

Amelia relaxed and let out a breath of relief. "Black Hawk," she said. "Yes, Daniel had told me about you. In fact, we have been waiting for your return."

He nodded. "As you can see, this man has returned." He glanced about, as if searching for his friend. "Where is my friend, Dan-yel?"

"He's gone to the mission," Amelia said. She explained about the attack, her missing father, and Daniel's part in rescuing her. "He said it was the Sioux."

Black Hawk's face darkened. A hard glint had entered his dark eyes. Suddenly, Amelia could see that he would make a formidable enemy. She was chilled, but not overly scared by the change in him.

"I must go to my village," he said. "Tell Dan-yel that he can find me there."

Amelia nodded.

The brave's expression softened as he returned his attention to Daniel's child. "You must come for a visit. *Enyan'?*"

Beaming, Susie nodded. *"Enyan',"* she said.

The warrior smiled. *"Mino,* Little Flower."

Then the Ojibwa met Amelia's gaze. "Until I see you again, Woman-with-Eyes-of-Deer."

Amelia started, then felt inordinately pleased by the Indian's name for her. He left her thinking, reevaluating her feelings once again about the red people the white men called savages.

Thirteen

Daniel paused on the threshold before entering the cabin. He had come back without the two men from the mission. Allen Whitely didn't want to leave Will Thornton, and Will wasn't fit enough to travel even a small distance yet. Amelia was going to be disappointed, he thought. He had questioned both men so he would, at least, be able to bring news if there was any, but he knew she wouldn't be satisfied. The attack had been so quick, so unexpected, that neither the minister nor his young friend remembered seeing what happened to John Dempsey, Miriam Lathom, or any of the other missing people.

He didn't see Susan or Amelia as he entered the cabin and quietly closed the door. Either they were in their bedchambers or in the kitchen work area in the back. He headed toward the kitchen first and was rewarded by the sound of their voices.

"It's important to wash your hands before eating, Susie," he heard Amelia say. He didn't hear Susie's answer.

"You don't want to become ill, do you?"

"I won't get sick just because my hands are dirty," Susie replied. Daniel frowned as he heard the obstinacy in the child's tone. "Everyone knows that a person gets ill when he washes too much."

"That's not exactly true," Daniel said as he entered the

room. He saw Amelia's look of gladness and gratitude. "You know that the Indians bathe daily, and none of them, Conner included, suffers any ill effects."

Susie turned to him with a closed look. "That's not the same thing."

Daniel arched an eyebrow, and his niece blushed. "What's the matter, sweeting? Why are you giving Amelia a hard time?"

Her mouth firmed. "I don't need to learn all these things."

"All what things?"

"How to dress 'like a lady.' " She scowled. "I'm already a girl. Why do I need lessons to be what I already am?"

"We know you're a girl, Susie," Amelia said softly. "I just thought you might like to know what to do if you're ever forced into polite society."

Susie, ignoring Amelia, asked Daniel, "What's polite society?"

Daniel had to stifle a smile. "There are people in the world who have certain expectations. They wear the right clothes, and they act the way others of their class expect them to."

"What's a class?"

Amelia thought about it and realized that she didn't know how to explain without making "polite society" sound like a terrible thing. She and Daniel exchanged glances. She looked at him, her expression relaying the silent message that the telling would be up to him.

"Pa?" The child looked from one adult to the other.

"Susie," he began with patience, "I asked Amelia to teach you a few things about what it is to be a woman, things your momma would be teaching you if she were here."

Susie narrowed her gaze. "She's not my momma."

"No, I know that," Daniel said. He met Amelia's gaze. "We both know that."

"No one can take the place of your mother," Amelia added gently. She didn't know why the child's statement bothered her, because Susie had just been speaking the truth. She felt bad that the relationship between her and Susie which had started out well had suddenly become fraught with tension.

"Don't be angry with Amelia because she's doing what I asked her to do."

Susie firmed her lips. "I don't need to be no lady," she replied stubbornly.

Daniel flashed Amelia a helpless glance. Amelia offered Susie a smile. "We'll forget the lessons then, shall we?"

The child looked at her with mistrust, before transferring her gaze to Daniel. He nodded.

"If the lessons bother you, then we'll forget about them for now."

With a jerk of her head in agreement, Susie informed them that she'd prefer that the lessons were forgotten indefinitely.

With that discussion between them over, Susie left for her room, leaving Amelia and Daniel alone.

"Did Reverend Whitely come with you?" Amelia asked, looking beyond Daniel's shoulder as if she expected the man to suddenly appear.

"No, Allen didn't want to come. Will isn't well enough to travel or be left alone." He studied her closely. "I'm sorry. I did question them, but neither one of them remembered seeing your father or Miriam that morning."

Amelia looked dejected by the news. "I thought—I'd hoped—that they'd remember something, anything, that might give us a clue to where we should start searching."

el," she said softly after a while.

?"

nk you."

nswer, Daniel kissed the top of Amelia's head.

"his man knows what happened to the mission. Your woman told me." He paused to accept a bark bowl of steaming rice from his sister, thanked her with a nod, and passed it to his friend. "Your woman said it was our enemy, the Sioux."

Daniel stared at his Indian friend and nodded. He watched Black Hawk's face darken. The warrior had been long seeking vengeance on the Sioux people, since he was a boy and a band of Sioux had ambushed an Ojibwa hunting party and murdered his father. It had been Black Hawk's first hunt, a memorable day—and a dark one. The young boy had witnessed his father and another adult member of the hunting party being tortured and killed slowly . . . and painfully. Black Hawk had managed to escape, taking with him a hatred of the Sioux and a need for revenge. The bitter hatred toward the Sioux that lay in the brave's heart continued to this day.

But Black Hawk picked his battles wisely. He was a ped Ojibwa war chief, and he was Daniel's good Daniel recognized what drove the warrior and that someday Hawk would know peace.

e has been no sign of them since, but I've asked feelings on this." He trusted Black Hawk. They'd ildren at the settlement at Michilimackinac when Indian had come to Robert Trahern's blacksmith is uncle.

nt men to scout the area. If there are Sioux people will find them." There was a glint

"There is no 'we' about the search. *I'll* look for your father and your friend. You will stay here where it's safe."

Her brown eyes flashed with anger. "He's my father."

"And you're my responsibility!" he replied with growing heat.

"Since when am I *your* responsibility?" she exclaimed.

He scowled. "Since the minute I saved you from that Sioux warrior!"

The reminder made Amelia pause. Daniel saw several emotions cross her face—anger, gratitude, frustration, and finally resignation.

"I must learn what happened to my father," she said, sounding choked up. Her gaze fell as if she didn't want him to read her thoughts.

His own anger with her dissipated. "I know." He moved closer, placed his hands on her shoulders, and drew her near. "I'm not insisting on this because I want you to feel frustrated or angry. The simple truth of the matter is that I won't be able to do what I have to do to find your father if I have to worry about you and Susie." He nudged her chin upward with his finger, forcing her to meet his gaze. "I was hoping you would take care of Susie for me. I know she seems resentful right now—"

Amelia brushed his concern aside with a shake of her head. "She and I got along quite well at first. She'll come around once she realizes that I don't really want to change her." She smiled, but he could see it was forced.

"I'm not sure that Susie needs to learn all those things that 'polite society' put so much stock in," she said. "Most of the folks back East have no idea what it's like to live out here, out anywhere beyond their city life. I can't see Susie ever wanting to live in the city. It's obvious to me that she loves it here in the wilderness." She hesitated, biting her lower lip as if she had something to say, but she wasn't sure she knew how to say it.

"Daniel, there is nothing wrong with Susie just as she is. She's a bright and inquisitive child. The thought of her in the midst of most people I used to know back in Baltimore frightens me. She's a sweet little girl, and you've done a wonderful job with her."

He felt an infusion of warmth as he held her gaze. "You mean that, don't you."

She nodded. "I do."

Daniel felt himself sway closer to her. He reminded himself that it wasn't wise to become involved with this woman, but argument and reason seemed to have escaped him in the face of his desire.

"Thank you," he said softly.

Her smile was tentative as she pulled back and put distance between them. "Are you hungry? I made you something to eat."

He was surprised. "You fixed me breakfast when you didn't know when I'd be back?"

She met his gaze with a grin. "I baked. Baked goods hold well for hours after they're done." She gestured toward the worktable. "Of course, I baked enough for three men, so I guess the three of us will be eating enough for five." She smiled crookedly. "Unless we share with Jack."

"If only Black Hawk would come," Daniel said. "He'd not say no to a baked pastry."

Something flickered across Amelia's expression. "Your friend—Black Hawk—he's back."

"Oh, did Rebb tell you?"

"Rebb?"

"Rebb Colfax? A grizzly bear of a man? Gray hair and whiskers? You met him when you first came."

She looked confused. "Oh, was he here? I haven't seen

him." She paused. "But I did s
looked embarrassed. "In fact, he
me when I opened the door this
standing there." She appeared reflec
who was more surprised by the encoun
or me."

Daniel frowned as he envisioned the sce
promised he'd stay and watch the house."

"If Susie hadn't woken up and recognized him
she did, I'm afraid I might have done something to cau
a war between you and your Indian friends. I thought he
was Sioux." She shuddered.

Daniel looked at her with regret. He understood about her fear after the attack. "I'm sorry you had to go through that. I didn't think he'd come himself. I figured he'd send Rain-from-Sky, and I'd be here when he came. You've met him, haven't you?"

Amelia nodded. "Black Hawk's brother. I must admit I'm confused about my feelings toward the Indians. I realize some of them are friendly. In fact, I've met those who are . . ." Her eyes fell, and her voice lowered. "P
the attack on the mission . . . I'll never be able to f
that. I'm afraid I'll feel terrified whenever I see
now. I wish it were different. Father and I
help." She trembled and hugged herself w
wonder how Father feels now." She cl
features contorted with grief.

"Please," she whispered, "do
Daniel pulled her into his
alive, Amelia. You must
harm."

·She leaned against him,
child. He enjoyed that she tru
ied in her hair, he hugged her

in Black Hawk's eyes. A look that said the man made a formidable enemy. Daniel was glad Hawk was his friend.

"So, Woman-with-Eyes-of-Deer resides in your lodge now," Black Hawk said.

Daniel raised his eyebrows.

"Woman-with-Eyes-of-Deer . . . the one Little Flower calls Am-e-lia."

"You gave Amelia an Indian name?" Daniel was surprised. He studied his friend and saw a man who attracted female attention. He began to wonder what Amelia thought of Black Hawk. Had she been drawn to the intelligence, the fire in his dark gaze? He narrowed his gaze, noting through the open doorway the way a passing Indian maiden stared at Hawk with unconcealed longing. There were several women in his community who would take Hawk as husband, but so far, Hawk had preferred a solitary life.

"You don't like my Ojibwa name for your woman?"

My woman. Daniel felt a burst of gladness at the thought. He quickly fought his feelings, knowing that it was the wrong time for him to have a woman. He recalled her glistening brown gaze, realized that Hawk's name was an appropriate one for Amelia. "It suits her." He turned his attention to the food before him. He ate a spoonful of steaming meat and wild rice. It tasted delicious.

He felt Black Hawk's continued gaze as he chewed and swallowed his food. He glanced at the brave questioningly. "What?"

Black Hawk eyed him thoughtfully. "You have another Indian name for Woman-with-Eyes-of-Deer?"

Daniel started to shake his head, but then he smiled as another name came to mind that accurately portrayed her. He was sure that of the two names Amelia would appreciate only Black Hawk's.

"Tree-That-Will-Not-Bend," he said finally. He grinned.

"Eya'," Black Hawk said with an answering grin. "She is beautiful like a tree but stubborn."

Daniel wasn't sure he liked the fact that his friend had noticed that Amelia was beautiful. Hell, he'd been blind to her true beauty at first. To realize that Black Hawk had seen something special in Amelia from the start bothered him.

Then he remembered that Black Hawk had also called Amelia "your woman," as if he recognized and understood that Amelia belonged to Daniel.

"You are wise for an Ojibwa," Daniel teased.

"And you are all right," Black Hawk began in a perfect imitation of the white man's English, "—for a *Wyaubishkizzidinin'e.*"

Fourteen

"What did Black Hawk say?" Amelia asked upon Daniel's return late that afternoon.

"He's sent out his men to scout the area."

They sat at the dining table in the main room of the cabin. Amelia was snapping some beans that Jack had brought over for them. Daniel had pulled up the chair across from her, and she was conscious of his continued study of her.

"How soon before we hear?"

"I honestly don't know. We're dealing with the Ojibwa, not the Americans. You can't rush them. As soon as Black Hawk learns something, he'll let us know."

"But that could be days, couldn't it?"

Daniel inclined his head. "Weeks actually."

"Weeks!" she exclaimed.

"More like days, but I can't promise you that."

Amelia's spirits plummeted. Her eyes filled, and she turned away.

"Amelia—" She felt his touch on her arm. She jerked away, unwilling at that moment to be comforted.

"My father is missing, Daniel," she said. "It's hard not to be upset, and it's even harder not to be able to do something to find him."

"Oh, but something is being done. Black Hawk's Ojibwa scouts are on the trail. They're excellent trackers, better than any white man I've ever known. If your father is nearby, then Black Hawk will find him. If not, then Black Hawk will help us search. In any event, Black Hawk will find your father in the end."

She felt mildly appeased. "You think so?"

"Yes, I do." Daniel looked about the cabin. "Susie all right?"

She nodded.

"What did the two of you do today?"

"I laundered clothes, and Susie ran around the house, playing Indians." Given what the child had suffered when she was three, Amelia was amazed that Susie could play such a game without evoking bad memories.

"Seeing Black Hawk made her think of her Indian friends," Daniel guessed.

Amelia smiled. "I suppose so. She seems quite fond of Black Hawk, too. If she hadn't come out of her room when she did, I might have brained your Ojibwa friend."

"Brained?" A twinkle of amusement lit up his blue eyes.

"I would have hit him over the head with my teacup."

Laughter erupted from his throat; the low musical sound made her tingle. Amelia knew that she was staring at him, but she'd never heard such a hearty laugh from him. It affected all of her senses. If she hadn't fallen in love with him before now, hearing his laughter would have clinched it. She couldn't stop her own grin or her laughter that followed.

"What do we do now?" she asked after their shared laughter had died down.

"Tomorrow I go back to work. I have several commissions I need to get done."

"So I'm just to wait?" She scowled with frustration.

Daniel eyed the woman before him, understanding how

she felt. "I know it'll be hard, but it's the best thing. I'm sure Black Hawk will get back to us in a couple of days. Until then, we wait and stay close to the house in case the Sioux take it into their heads to visit us."

"Do you think that's likely?" she asked, sounding worried.

"It's possible, but as for likely, I just don't know. The Sioux and I are not exactly friends."

"I see."

Did she? he wondered. She looked lovely today. Since she'd come to stay, she'd taken to wearing her hair unbound, a style that was much more fetching than the pinned-up knot she'd previously worn at her crown. For the first time in four days, Amelia wore something different than the gown she'd come to him in. When he'd left the mission yesterday morning, he'd brought back some of her personal belongings. When he'd given them to her, she'd been delighted. He didn't tell her that he'd found the infirmary in shambles with most of her father's medicines tossed or destroyed, nor would he tell her the destruction had continued into the Dempseys' living quarters in the back rooms. He'd accepted her thanks with a nod, glad to see her smile.

She'd made use of the change in clothes. Instead of the green-striped garment she had on the day before, she had donned a simple gown of blue calico with a scooped collar and lace along the neck edging and the hem of its short sleeves. With her hair down and her feet bare, she looked like a different woman from the city creature who'd come to the trading post with her physician father.

"Is something wrong?" she asked. She continued to snap beans, placing the ends in a pile off to her left side and the precious bean piece in a bowl to her right.

Daniel realized that he'd been caught staring at her.

Gawking would be more like it, he thought with self-reproach. "No, nothing's wrong." He made himself shift his gaze toward the doors to the back rooms. "Where's Susie?"

"Over at Jack's," Amelia replied. "She was anxious to get out of the house, so when Jack called with these beans and asked for her, I figured it was all right to let her go."

They were alone in the house, Daniel thought, pleased with the idea.

No, I must not act on this. She is vulnerable and hurt. She doesn't care for me. She's just grateful for the rescue and my help in the search for her father.

"Is there anything I can do to help?" she asked.

"No, I said I'd handle the search—"

"I meant in your shop," she said with a flicker of annoyance in her gaze. She hated to be reminded how helpless she was, he thought.

"You want to help me in the smithy?"

She set down a bean and steadily held his gaze. "Am I not capable of being of some assistance?"

Daniel blinked. This woman was forever surprising him. "Well, of course, you are," he said. "I just didn't think you'd want to is all."

"I'm always open to learning new things."

He arched an eyebrow. "And one of those things is to work at the forge?"

Looking haughty, much like she'd appeared that first day, she regally inclined her head. Her expression seemed to challenge him.

"Fine," he said with a smile. "If you're willing to help, then I'm eager for the assistance." He allowed himself the luxury of boldly running his gaze over her. "I hope you have something better to wear in the shop than that."

She frowned. "What's wrong with my gown?"

"Nothing," he assured her, "if you're visiting a neighbor or working in the house, but around the forge fire— no. You'll need something more practical for that."

"Practical?" She looked doubtful. "I'm not sure I have anything practical in my wardrobe." She paused. "You know what I have. Will any of those garments do?"

He shook his head. " 'Fraid not. I'll check with Jack to see if he has anything more appropriate."

"And what would be appropriate for the shop?" She must have read his mind, because suddenly her eyes widened. "Trousers? You want me to wear trousers?"

"Does the notion bother you?"

"No, no," she quickly reassured him. "If Jack has a pair of trousers that will fit me, I'll be happy to wear them in the shop."

"Good." Daniel pushed back his chair and stood. "There's a lot waiting for us to do." He didn't point out that a great deal of his commission work came from the mission and the missing and dead who would have no use for the items now. He planned to fill every one of his orders in case the owners were found alive. The items for the dead he'd use in trade if no else needed them.

She couldn't take it anymore. Not hearing or knowing anything upset her deeply. Lying in bed at night, Amelia stared at the rafters in her bedchamber. Two days had passed since Daniel had visited Black Hawk, two days and no sign of Daniel's Ojibwa friends.

She rolled onto her stomach and pounded her pillow in frustration. Living this close to Daniel, feeling the tension, the attraction, and fighting her feelings with her every breath was wearing on her nerves.

Not that he'd done or said anything to hurt her. She

scowled and flung herself onto her back again. On the contrary, Daniel had been solicitous and polite, allowing her time alone, while not pressing her when they were together.

Which is why this is all so difficult! she thought.

They'd sailed along fine, two crewmen on a ship cruising calm waters, sharing the same house, the same dinner table, as if they were friends and comrades and nothing more. But the physical ache was there; at least, it was for her. She attempted to hide it; yet, all the while she was afraid he'd see . . . not only that she was sexually drawn to him, but emotionally as well. The last thing she needed was for Daniel to realize the extent of her love for him. It would be too humiliating if he knew. He had lost a wife and at times appeared to be grieving for her still. Other times, it seemed that his wife had caused him nothing but anguish. She couldn't figure out just what he was feeling, and if she was confused, she could imagine how mixed-up he felt.

He hadn't touched her in the last two days, and she was glad. His gaze on her seemed like a physical caress, which was difficult to ignore. She was scared that if he touched her, she would instantly melt and beg him to love her.

Amelia hugged herself with her arms. She had to get away. The thought upset her, but then so did the battle going on inside her mind.

She sat up, swung her legs off the bed, and quickly, silently, pulled off her nightwear. She would go to the mission. She had to talk with the Reverend Whitely. He might have remembered something by now—or perhaps Will had.

Daniel wouldn't be happy with her, she knew, but she

had to go. She didn't think she'd be in danger—not if she was careful to stay hidden as she went.

Her gaze fell on the new pair of trousers she'd gotten from Jack. She was glad she had them; it would help her travel without skirts or petticoats to hamper her way.

She dressed in a shirt—another acquisition from Keller's—then donned the trousers and her black-leather boots.

Her fingers settled on the doorknob; she hesitated before carefully turning the knob. To her relief, the door opened quietly, and she was able to slip into the great room where there was little light. Her eyes were adjusted to the dark, so she was able to find her way to the outside door without mishap.

That door squeaked slightly as it opened, and she froze, listening to see if anyone had stirred at the sound. There was no noise but the *tick-tick* of the clock on the mantel. Putting aside her doubts, Amelia left the cabin with a pounding heart and hurried along the edge of the forest road toward the mission.

Daniel woke up with a start. He lay in his own perspiration, listening to his thundering heartbeat, and thought about the nightmare he'd just had. It had been a tangle of dreams, all of them frightening, with each segment featuring someone he'd loved or cared about.

There was Pamela, fleeing to escape him. His best friend James sat beside her in the carriage that careened over a cliff, sending the vehicle with two screaming occupants hurtling into the air and falling until the rocks below cradled their broken, bleeding bodies. *Which is strange, because their vehicle hit a tree.* In the dream, he'd heard a baby's wail as Pamela had been thrown, the cry of her unborn child—James's baby, the baby he'd called his own.

Just as quickly as that image faded, another one came, more terrifying than the last. This one featured Jane and Susie and the band of Indians who'd attacked them. He saw Jane being tied up and beaten, heard Susie screaming for the bad men to leave her mother alone. He saw an Indian reaching for the little girl, saw Susie scurry under her mother's bed. The Indian started after her, but a sharp word from another brave had him abandoning his chase, and Susie was left alone to weep and cry out for her mother.

After that, the images had become more confused. He saw Jack's face and Amelia's. He heard Rebb's voice, but the man who'd spoken didn't look anything like Rebb. Then, suddenly, he'd heard the wild cries of Indians on the attack. Oddly enough, it was the fur trapper Kertell who led them on their bloody massacre at the mission.

He woke up when Amelia appeared a tortured victim of Kertell and the Sioux Indians. Then, James Beck, his former best friend, was there, and he was laughing wickedly as he joined the others, where he stroked Amelia's face, fondled her breasts, and slapped her when she cried out and struggled.

This last part of the dream was more disturbing, more terrifying than the rest of the nightmare. *It's because of Amelia,* he thought. He was falling for her hard, and he was scared that she'd be hurt or killed, and he'd lose his heart and his soul.

"Amelia," he whispered. He had to see her, know for himself that she was all right. He rose naked from his bed and pulled on a pair of breeches. If she was awake, he didn't want to offend her sensibilities. She had kissed him like she'd known passion before, but her behavior afterward, her shy glances, the tide of red that swept her cheeks said she was an innocent.

He tread carefully as he moved to check on Susie first. He smiled and felt some of his concern ease. She looked so peaceful, like an angel with her hair of spun gold and her smooth babylike skin. He didn't approach the bed. He didn't want to wake her, for fear she'd be unable to go back to sleep. He closed the door and moved on to Amelia's room. Holding his breath for a heartbeat, he reached for the doorknob and found that the door hadn't been shut tight. He leaned his weight against the door and pushed, then stepped inside her room. He knew the bedchamber but wasn't as familiar with the layout of the furniture, for he'd built and furnished the room for Jane—in the event he ever found her . . . so she'd have a home to come to, a lovely room that would help banish the memories of four long years' nights of hell.

In here, he couldn't easily find his way, and there was not enough light to help him. He moved slowly, inch by inch, heading toward the bed—or so he hoped.

He released a sigh of relief as his knee touched the end of Amelia's bed. He paused to listen for the sound of her breathing. She must be a quiet sleeper, he decided, for she didn't make a noise.

Drawn by her image in his mind and the need to touch her, to reassure himself of her safety, Daniel followed the width of her bed, then moved down its length. He stopped and reached into the dark to find her, but came up with nothing but a tangle of bedcovers.

He froze, then slowly ran his hands along the bed in a search for Amelia's body, but again, all he came up with was empty air . . . and an empty bed. Where the hell was Amelia?

Daniel felt a burning in his stomach as he stumbled

across the room and out into the main living area. He stopped and searched the darkness, but there was no sign of Amelia. He went to the kitchen then in the hope that he'd find her raiding the pantry for a late-night snack.

But Amelia wasn't there. Anger battled with concern as Daniel returned to the great room and went to the exterior door. He threw open the door, expecting to see her on the porch, but her favorite place, the swing, was empty. He knew with a sudden certainty that she was gone.

Foolish woman, he thought, *didn't she listen to anything I said?* He should have seen this coming; Amelia had been feeling frustrated. He should have guessed she'd never take no for an answer when it came to her fear and worry over her missing father and friend.

He lit an oil lamp and placed it on the table. He pulled out a chair and sat, but rose again quickly, too agitated, too concerned to stay still. He couldn't go looking for her; he couldn't leave Susie alone, and Jack wouldn't appreciate another late-night wake-up call.

And so Daniel started to pace. The horrific images of his dream played on his imagination, increasing his fear for Amelia's safety.

How long had she been gone? he wondered. She must have gone to the mission; surely she'd not strike out into the wilderness and the unknown.

He experienced anger, terror, and an emotion he didn't want to put a name to. He wanted to grab hold of Amelia and hug her close. He wanted to throttle her for taking risks and traveling in the night—a lone woman.

He loved her, he realized. It was more than desire he felt for Amelia. He enjoyed her company, their conversations, even their heated arguments.

He reached his wit's end when an hour went by, and Amelia hadn't returned. He prayed to God for the second time in his life, asking for the woman's safe return, asking for the strength not to throttle her when she did finally appear.

What if she doesn't come back? What if she was ambushed by the Sioux . . . or kidnapped by that fur trader, Thomas Kertell? He couldn't stand it anymore; he had to do something, find her and bring her home.

He went to his room and put on a shirt, He grabbed his knife, slipping the sheath into the waistband of his pants.

He returned to the great room for his moccasins. Fear made him sick to his stomach as he bent over to put them on. He would have to wake Jack again. His friend wouldn't like it, but Daniel couldn't leave Susie alone, and he had to go. It was the only action that would save him from going insane with the worry.

He hurried toward the front door, was ready to open it, when he heard footsteps on the wooden porch planks. He threw open the door and heard a gasp, then the voice that belonged to the woman he loved. At least, he thought it was Amelia. It was hard to tell at first glance. She wore men's clothing: the breeches and the shirt she'd gotten to work in the smithy.

"Daniel!" she exclaimed. "You frightened me."

Now that he knew she was safe, anger overtook his concern. "Where have you been?" he demanded. "Foolish woman, don't you know it's dangerous to be running about at night unescorted?"

She stiffened her spine. "I'm well aware of that fact, sir. I'm not a complete idiot. I was well aware of the risk I was taking when I left!"

He gazed at her, saw her tears, her trembling mouth, and his anger melted away. "Come here," he said gently, opening up his arms.

"I'm tired. I'm going to bed."

He grabbed her, tugged her into his embrace. "Fine," he said huskily. "We'll go to bed then. Yours or mine?"

She stiffened, then gazed up into his face. There was tenderness in his expression . . . in his blue eyes. She saw something else, an emotion she couldn't identify. It thrilled her even while it frightened her.

"No," she moaned. She wasn't ready for these feelings. She had to think of her father; she couldn't allow herself a moment of happiness until he was safe.

"Please, Daniel, let me go. I shouldn't have gone, I know that. But please, please, allow me to go to my room."

"No," he said as he began to stroke her arm.

"No? Why not? Why won't you leave me be?"

"You're upset. You shouldn't be alone when you're upset."

"You're the one making me upset. If you let me go, I'll go to my room and be fine."

Daniel had no intention of releasing her. He'd just had a hellish time worrying about her, envisioning her injured and even dead. He was going to hold her until he felt absorbed by her presence. She was upset, but not because of him as she'd claimed. No, she had gone to the mission and seen what he hadn't told her. The row of crosses marking the dead. The senseless destruction of the interior of the mission buildings, including her own.

"I didn't want you to know yet. Not until I'd found your father."

Looking dazed, Amelia shook her head. "So many people . . . men, women, even young children."

Daniel knew how many crosses, how many dead, for he'd searched the area during his last visit. He'd helped the Reverend Whitely bury the dead. He hadn't spoken of it to her or to anyone for that matter. It had been a painful, horrifying few hours.

"Oh, Daniel," she wailed before she melted against him in acceptance of his comforting presence. "Anne Rose and her child. Pete . . . and Mr. Grutchly."

"Promise me you'll never leave that way again. Promise me," he growled.

She jerked back in surprise of his harsh tone. "I shouldn't have gone."

"No, you shouldn't," he said. "Promise me, Amelia. Swear it on my mother's Bible." He released her to fetch the book from a shelf beside the fireplace. He thrust it in her direction.

"Promise me, Amelia."

She stared at his face then lowered her gaze to the book in his hands. "I—"

"You scared me, Amelia, more than I've ever been scared in my life."

Amelia accepted the book as she looked into his anxious blue gaze. She placed her right hand on the book. "I promise I'll never leave the house as I've done tonight," she vowed softly. She handed back the book.

"I dreamt about you," he said. "A nightmare. Then I woke up and thought you were safe, only to find you gone."

She saw in his face the pain and fear he'd experienced because she'd been foolish enough to go out into the night. She touched his jaw. "I'm sorry, Daniel."

"Don't ever do that again," he said, trembling in the aftershock of what he'd been through that night.

Amelia, feeling terrible for what he'd suffered, rose to her toes and kissed him on the mouth.

Fifteen

The forest was rich with the scents and sounds of late summer. From high up in the treetops a bird sang to its mate. Below on the ground, a squirrel rustled the leaves as it ran, squawking, from its friend.

Amelia followed the trail behind Daniel and Susie, noting the landscape and wondering what lay ahead. They were on their way to the Ojibwa village, and she was excited but nervous. Black Hawk had issued the invitation for them to come; Amelia wondered whether or not the brave had received word of her father.

She'd never been to an Indian village before, and remembering the tales circulating back East about the savages, she was curious about how they lived, whether or not their living conditions were as crude and terrible as she'd been led to believe.

They had entered territory where Amelia had never been. Daniel and Susie seemed relaxed, so she wasn't overly concerned about safety. Daniel wouldn't have put his child at risk—or herself, for that matter. Besides, she had absolute faith in Daniel's ability to protect them should they encounter wild animals—or worse yet, unfriendly men.

Daniel paused, then moved off the path, and Susie followed him. Amelia stopped to wipe the perspiration from her brow with a handkerchief, then moved to join Daniel and Susie. Her gown bodice clung to her like a damp second skin. Amelia wondered what had possessed her to wear a gown when it would have been easier to wear the trousers she'd worn previously for her trip to the mission. Daniel and his daughter looked comfortable in their buckskins and beaded moccasins, more appropriate apparel for the journey.

About midmorning, Daniel called a halt for a meal and a brief rest. They had entered a small clearing, warmed by sunlight filtering through the trees, a cheery place, a beautiful haven for them to stop.

Amelia found a rock in the clearing and sat down to take the weight off her feet. Her toes felt cramped and her leather boots were chafing at her heels. She sighed with relief as she pulled off her footwear and wiggled her stocking feet.

She watched Daniel search through a satchel to pull out some bread and dried venison. He tore a hunk of bread for Susie and told her to sit and eat. He unearthed a tin cup from his pack and removed the waterskin that was strapped to his shoulder, then he filled the cup and gave it to the child. When Susie was seen to, he approached Amelia.

"How are you holding up?" he asked as he sat next to her on the large rock.

She managed a weary smile. "I'm doing fine." He handed her some bread and a portion of the dried meat. She accepted both with a murmur of thanks, then she proceeded to take a bite of bread.

He filled a cup for her and set it between them on the rock. "It shouldn't be too long now."

"I would have thought we'd already be there," she said. Daniel had made the trip there and back in a matter of a few hours. Today, they'd been walking all morning and part of the afternoon.

"Last time I borrowed Jack's horse," he said.

"I've heard that some tribes move from place to place. Do you know why?"

"For better hunting grounds and other food sources. They trap beaver. The pelts are prized, both by red men and whites. When beavers become scarce, they move in search for a place where the animals are more plentiful." He leaned back, stretching, his eyes closed. Amelia tried not to look, but her gaze was drawn to his muscles as they flexed, to the long line of him sprawled on the rock surface beside her.

"The Indians also move with the seasons. We're heading to their summer location. In the winter, they move deeper into the forest." He opened his eyes and smiled at her. She blushed that he'd caught her looking at him.

She pretended an interest in her surroundings. "Daniel, why did Black Hawk include Susie and me in his invitation?"

"Susie's been longing to visit the village again, and Black Hawk wanted you near in case he found your father."

She felt a bubble of excitement. "Is that possible? Do you think he'll find Father?"

"If anyone can find him, Black Hawk can."

"And you," she said with a smile.

His grin lacked humor as he picked up her cup from the rock and handed it to her. Amelia gratefully took a drink, then set the cup down.

Susie sat several yards away and made no effort to approach or join in their conversation. Amelia studied her with a frown. The young girl was still angry with her.

Daniel followed the direction of Amelia's gaze. "She still mad at you?"

Amelia nodded. "I don't understand. We were getting along fine, then suddenly she resented me. I thought it was the lessons, but now I'm not so sure."

She met Daniel's concerned gaze. "Has she had any more nightmares?"

"One."

"I'm sorry I didn't hear her. Maybe I could have helped." She studied Susie. "Perhaps not. Given her feelings for me right now, it's possible my presence would only make matters worse."

Amelia took her first bite of the venison jerky, tugging a piece free with her teeth. She'd never had dried meat before. It had a strange flavor, but not an unpleasant one. She paused to sip from her water cup, before continuing with her meal.

While she ate, she worried about her relationship with Susie. She thought back to the day it had seemed to go wrong. She realized that it was the day she'd asked Susie why she didn't have any dolls to play with.

"Daniel?" She turned to find him studying her with an odd expression. She blushed and looked down at her plate.

"Yes?"

She gathered her composure and met his gaze. "Why doesn't Susie have any dolls?"

He looked thoughtful. "She hasn't had any dolls since the day her mother was kidnapped." He frowned. "She'd had a doll then, but the Indians or whoever had attacked the cabin took Susie's doll and tore the head off."

Amelia felt a jolt. "The doll," she said. "She remembers that doll." She experienced a glimmer of excitement. "Daniel, Susie became angry with me after I asked why she didn't have a doll."

A look of understanding entered Daniel's expression. "Her nightmares," he said.

She nodded. "I'm so sorry. I had no idea."

He studied Susie with concern. "I'll talk with her about it later. For now, let's pretend we never had this conversation."

"But Daniel—"

He looked at her without expression. "Amelia, I appreciate your concern and your help, but please let me handle her, all right?"

Struggling not to feel hurt, she agreed. His smile was genuine and instantaneous. She was immediately appeased.

"How's your meal?" he asked her as he held up a piece of the dried meat.

"It's good, thank you."

Amelia glanced over and saw that Susie was studying her with a sour look on her face. Amelia caught her gaze; with a set look, Susie looked away.

"Are you ready to go?" Daniel asked.

She sighed. Everything was ready but her sore feet. She reached down for her boots. Her movements caught Daniel's attention, and he grabbed a boot from her hand and studied it. "Let me see your feet," he said.

Embarrassed, she tried to take back her boot. "I'm fine, Daniel. Let me have my shoe."

His mouth firmed. "Not until I've seen your feet."

With her cheeks flaming, Amelia lifted her foot for his inspection. Daniel grabbed her heel, and she gasped as he noted the abraded area. He shifted his grip and frowned as he saw the raw skin exposed by a hole in her stocking.

"Why didn't you tell me about this?"

She was taken aback by his gruffness. "I didn't know myself how bad it was until just a few minutes ago."

He held her foot cradled in the palm of his hand. She

could feel the warmth of his grip on her arch. Her skin tingled and burned, the sensation stronger than the pain of her heel.

Daniel turned to his daughter. "Susie! Bring me your bag."

"But Pa—"

"Now!" He carefully set Amelia's foot down.

The little girl rose to her feet with a frown, picked up the satchel she'd been carrying, and brought the bag to her father.

Daniel accepted the pack with a murmur of thanks. He rummaged through the bag until he came up with a pair of moccasins. "You're not going to wear those boots." He placed the moccasins on the rock between them and pulled out a shirt. To Amelia's astonishment, he tore two strips of cloth from the garment and set it on top of the moccasins. Then, he took hold of her right leg and foot and pulled down her stocking. Tugging the stocking free, he bound her foot with one of the fabric strips before he showed the same attention to her left foot. When he pronounced her heels sufficiently cushioned for the rest of their journey, he slipped the moccasins on her feet, then began to repack the satchel so they could leave.

Amelia was conscious of Susie's displeasure as Daniel worked on her feet, but she was powerless to say or do anything, for Daniel had insisted that he be the one to deal with his daughter. She wanted nothing more than to make peace with the child, for she had enjoyed Susie's company from the start. Susie's change of heart regarding their friendship was upsetting to her.

To her surprise, she found the moccasins easier on her feet. In fact, they were quite comfortable, and would be even more so, she decided, without the extra cloth bindings. She decided that she would find out if Jack could acquire a pair for trade as soon as they got back to the trading post.

They had traveled what seemed like an hour to Amelia. They had left the brush for a well-worn path. Suddenly, she smelled the scent of roasting meat.

Susie turned to her father with a grin. "We're here, Pa!" In her excitement, she included Amelia in her smile. Pleased, Amelia smiled back.

"Can I run ahead?" Susie asked.

"You'd better stay with us."

"Ah, Pa . . ."

Daniel reached out to ruffle Susie's unbound blond hair. "Honey, there's been some trouble with other Indians. Black Hawk and his men will be expecting trouble, not a little girl."

Susie nodded in understanding. "Will I be able to stay with Swaying Tree?" she asked.

"If she wants you." He grinned, then turned to Amelia. "Swaying Tree is Conner's grandmother. She took to Susie from their first meeting. She loves it when Susie comes to stay."

Amelia thought how wonderful for the motherless little girl to have a woman who cared for the child as much as the Ojibwa grandmother apparently did.

Her first sight of the village was through a small break in the forest where she glimpsed a wisp of smoke, which she decided came from the cook fire. As Daniel and Susie hurried ahead, Amelia lagged behind, unsure of herself and of what she'd find once she entered the village.

Noting her hesitation, Daniel paused on the path and waited for her to catch up. He took her hand as she came abreast of him, and she flashed him a grateful look as they entered the Ojibwa village together.

Amelia studied the encampment with interest as they

left the woods and entered the yard. Their houses were dome-shaped and covered with tree bark. Their doors were covered with flaps of animal furs. Each house had an open hole in the roof where small spirals of smoke curled up to dissipate into the air. There was no set pattern to the setup of the village. The houses were scattered about the clearing at the forest edge.

She didn't see anyone at first, but then movement to the right caught her attention, as a small group of children burst out of a wigwam, laughing and chasing one another in wide circles. Amelia gaped in shock as a bare-breasted Indian woman came out of the lodge to scold the boys before returning inside. A group of half-naked women and totally naked children appeared on the rise of a hill that sloped down from the village to water, a small glistening lake. Giggling and chatting among themselves, they walked together, carrying garments and waterskins. Amelia tried not to stare or feel horrified at their nakedness. She pretended, instead, that she was used to such sights.

As if hearing the noisy approaching group, a man stepped from a wigwam to greet them but spied the white newcomers instead. He gave a shout of welcome. Daniel called something back, and suddenly more Indians seemed to come out of nowhere. Amelia, Susie, and Daniel were surrounded by excited villagers. Amelia and Susie got separated from Daniel, who was encircled by the men. Fearful without his calming presence, Amelia grabbed Susie's hand, but the little girl pulled away in her gladness at seeing her old friends.

A woman ran her fingers through Amelia's hair. Amelia gasped and tried to pull away, but found herself in the same situation, being touched and pawed by the older Indian matron behind her. Amelia panicked as their half-naked bodies pressed close, stealing her air, blocking her in. "Susie!" she gasped.

"They will not hurt you," the child called back.

She flinched as someone touched her cheek. "What do they want?"

"They're curious is all."

A young Ojibwa maiden grabbed hold of Amelia's skirt. The woman began to speak rapidly. Another maiden answered her. They seemed to be having an argument. The first woman wouldn't release the fabric.

"Susie?"

"They like your gown. Little Turtle said it should belong to her. Morning Cloud says no, the white woman's garment should belong to her."

The Indian woman who had first taken hold of the gown stepped back from Amelia, giving her breathing room, as the two maidens continued their argument. She found Susie studying her thoughtfully.

"What are they saying?" Amelia asked anxiously.

"They are wondering which one you'll choose to give the gown to," she asked.

"No one." Amelia's throat tightened as she eyed the half-naked women. "I have no intention of giving my clothes to either one of them."

Eyes twinkling, Susie nodded. She said something in Ojibwa to the two women. The matrons stopped arguing to glare at Amelia. Then one woman said something to the other, and the argument started again.

Amelia looked to Susie for an explanation. To her astonishment and delight, Susie grinned at her. "They are arguing about something else now. They are sisters," she said.

A smile broke on Amelia's face. "I see."

Her answer brought another thoughtful look to the little girl's expression.

"Amelia! Susie!" Daniel's sudden appearance caught their attention. Amelia was never so glad to see him. "This way," he said, holding out both hands for them to take. Amelia captured his left hand, felt safe and secure as his warm fingers clasped her own.

"Are you all right?" he asked, sounding concerned.

The fear she'd endured must have shown some in her expression. "I'm all right now."

"They won't hurt you."

She met his gaze. "They don't know me."

Something flared in his blue eyes. "They know you are with me."

She glanced back over her shoulder to find several watching them, smiling and nodding as they spoke among themselves.

"Where are we going, Pa?" Susie asked.

"To say hello to Black Hawk. After that, you are free to go with Conner."

Susie grinned in obvious pleasure.

"Who exactly is Conner besides being Susie's playmate?" Amelia asked, having heard the name before.

"He is an Ojibwa boy. His real name is Barking Dog." Daniel grinned. "He and Susie took to one another from their first meeting. They even cut themselves to become blood brother and sister. Barking Dog gave Susie an Ojibwa name—Little Flower."

"That's beautiful," Amelia commented, turning her head to look at him.

Daniel met her gaze. "Yes, it is. Much better than Barking Dog. The boy wanted a white man's name as well, so Susie named him Conner."

"So Conner is an Indian."

"That's right."

Amelia looked beyond Daniel to his little girl. If she had heard their conversation, she gave no sign. She was too busy enjoying her surroundings—if her pleased expression was anything to go by.

Daniel stopped before one of the domed wigwams, perhaps a little bit bigger than the others, but Amelia wasn't sure. The animal-hide flap had been raised to reveal an open doorway. Daniel dipped his head under first, then waved Amelia and Susie inside.

At first glance, Amelia couldn't see much, but as her eyes became adjusted to the change in light, she saw the man who had come to the cabin while Daniel had been away—the brave who had nearly frightened her to death with his appearance.

Black Hawk remained seated as he and Daniel shook hands. "Dan-yel," he greeted his friend warmly.

Susie hurried to the brave's side, where she crouched down to sit and snuggle against the fierce-looking warrior. Without a word, Black Hawk hugged Susie against him and turned his attention to Amelia. She blushed under his piercing dark gaze.

"It is this man's pleasure to see you again, Miss Dempsey."

Amelia blinked, surprised that he knew her name. "Ah—thank you." She glanced about the wigwam, noting how he had made this crude structure into a comfortable home. "I am honored to be here."

The man's smile transformed his expression, and Amelia caught her breath at how attractive Black Hawk was. Conscious of Daniel's stare, she looked at him, only to be annoyed by his look of amusement.

She glanced away and struggled for something to say. She felt awkward as she stood while Black Hawk remained seated. As if reading her mind, the brave gestured for her and Daniel to sit. Checking to take her cue from Daniel, who nodded, Amelia took a seat on a woven-rush mat on the opposite side of the fire pit. Daniel settled himself beside her.

Daniel and Black Hawk began to talk in Ojibwa, and while Amelia thought it was rude of them, she didn't say anything. She took the moment to study the interior of the wigwam, noting the hole in the roof over the fire pit, the rush mats made from cattails on the floor and against the walls.

Suddenly, she felt as if she was being watched, and she glanced at each man to find them looking at her expectantly.

"I'm sorry," she said. "Did you say something to me?"

Daniel answered, "Black Hawk asked if you are hungry."

She was. "Yes, I am."

Black Hawk smiled and waved to someone at the entrance of the wigwam. It was then that Amelia saw the young, beautifully exotic Indian maiden who stood silently behind her.

Black Hawk's wife? Amelia wondered.

"This is Spring Blossom, my sister. She will feed you and show you to the place where you will sleep."

Amelia smiled at the woman, who smiled shyly back. Was this her signal to get up and leave?

Believing it might be, Amelia started to rise. When no one objected, she decided she had made the right move. "Does Spring Blossom speak English?" she asked.

"She speaks some," Black Hawk said. "I am sure the two of you will be able to understand each other."

Amelia flashed Daniel a glance. "Are you coming?" she asked.

He shook his head. "Not yet. I'll find you later."

Nervous at the thought of being separated from Daniel again, she nevertheless nodded politely and turned to leave. She paused suddenly to address Black Hawk. "I want to thank you for helping to find my father."

Black Hawk looked surprised by her statement, and she immediately wondered if she'd blundered . . . if Daniel had indeed spoken to the Indian about finding John Dempsey. Why else would he appear startled?

When the Indian spoke next, she knew. "It is not for the women to worry about such things. It is for their men to handle."

Amelia fought the urge to frown. She nodded instead and followed Spring Blossom from the wigwam. Outside, she scowled, wondering what Black Hawk meant by that cryptic remark. Then she felt Spring Blossom's concerned gaze and made an effort to smile. She would ask Daniel what his Indian friend meant later.

"This is sleep place," Spring Blossom said with a smile as she led Amelia into another wigwam.

Amelia took a brief moment to study it. It looked as comfortable as Black Hawk's living quarters.

There were three sleeping pallets. Amelia wondered who owned the wigwam, with whom she'd be sharing a home. Oddly enough, the thought of sharing the wigwam with Spring Blossom or another Indian woman didn't bother her as much as she'd thought it would.

"Whose home is this?" she asked.

Spring Blossom frowned as if trying, but failing to understand. Amelia tried to think of a way to rephrase her question.

She gestured about the wigwam. "Does this place belong to you?" She pointed to the woman and gestured about the Ojibwa house. "Will you and I be sharing?"

The Indian maiden still didn't understand, so Amelia tried again.

The two women engaged in a strange conversation of hand motions and chopped-up phrases until suddenly Spring Blossom understood what Amelia was asking her.

The maiden shook her head, and Amelia understood it to mean the wigwam did not belong to her. "Bear Woman," she said in heavily accented English.

"The wigwam belongs to Bear Woman?"

Spring Blossom nodded, smiling.

"All right," Amelia said. "Will Bear Woman come soon?"

The Indian woman frowned, then with a spark of understanding in her eyes shook her head. "Bear Woman no come. Gone."

Bear Woman was dead? Amelia frowned. She'd be staying in the house of a dead woman. She shivered even while she felt sad. "I'm sorry," she said with sincere sympathy.

Spring Blossom's brow furrowed as the woman continued to stare at her. Suddenly her expression cleared. "Bear Woman not dead. Gone to see clan sister."

Amelia laughed at her mistake. "That's good. I didn't want to think I'd taken over the woman's possessions."

Black Hawk's sister nodded, although it was clear to Amelia that she didn't comprehend a single word she was saying. She gestured toward a rush mat similar to the one Amelia had sat on in Black Hawk's lodge.

"Thank you, I would love to sit." The moccasins were much easier on her sore feet, but still the damage had already been done by her boots. She was grateful to be able to get off her own weight.

While she was seating herself, Amelia watched Spring Blossom rummaging through supplies stored beneath a

platform near one wall. She turned to Amelia with a vegetable that looked like squash. On closer inspection, Amelia
realized that was exactly what it was.

Spring Blossom started a fire in the pit in the center
of the wigwam, directly under the hole in the roof. Then
she began to prepare a dish of squash, corn, and beans
of some kind, cooking them together in a clay pot with a
small amount of water and some foul-smelling grease.
Amelia wrinkled her nose at the grease, wondering what
it was, but afraid to ask. As the mixture cooked, releasing
some of the vegetable smells, Spring Blossom sweetened
it with some maple sugar.

The smell emanating from the clay vessel was surprisingly pleasant; it made Amelia's mouth water and her
stomach growl.

Through all this, there was no sign of Daniel or Susie,
but she suspected that they'd been taken to a wigwam of
their own. Susie was perhaps with the boy Conner. Daniel
would probably be staying with his good friend Black
Hawk.

When the dish was fully cooked, Spring Blossom
spooned some of it into a wooden bowl, then handed the
bowl to Amelia along with a wooden spoon to eat it with.

The maiden didn't take any for herself, but watched
Amelia carefully, until Amelia realized that Spring Blossom was waiting for a judgment on her cooking. Amelia
brought a spoonful of the steaming mixture to her lips
and tasted it carefully so she wouldn't burn her mouth.

The mixture was surprisingly good. Amelia tasted the
different vegetable textures and enjoyed the sweetness of
the maple sugar. Whatever it was that Spring Blossom had
added that smelled so foul certainly didn't taste it. In fact,
she didn't taste it at all.

"This is delicious!" Amelia said.

Spring Blossom grinned in understanding. "Good?"

Amelia nodded. "Very good."

Someone called from outside, apparently for Spring Blossom, as the Indian maiden stood to leave. "Must go."

Amelia nodded. "Thank you," she said with a smile, holding up the bowl.

Spring Blossom murmured something in Ojibwa that Amelia took to mean "You're welcome." She started to duck out the door, when Amelia stopped her with a question that had been on her mind.

"Daniel," she said. "Where will he stay?" She asked again, rephrasing the question so that spring Blossom would understand.

"Daniel sleep place?" she asked.

Amelia nodded. "Yes, where is Daniel's sleep place?"

The Indian maiden started to giggle and said something that made Amelia start and nearly choke on the small bite of food she'd just eaten.

"Here?" Amelia said. "Daniel is sleeping here? With me?"

"Eya'." Spring Blossom nodded and smiled.

It didn't take a genius to figure out what the Indian word meant.

Yes.

Sixteen

Michigan
Late September, 1836

"Captain," a young soldier said breathlessly, "I've spotted the Sioux up ahead. They've got prisoners with them."

"Excellent!" The officer's eyes gleamed. "How many captives?"

"I saw five children and four adults—women, sir."

"Did the savages see you?"

The soldier nodded. "They did, sir. I spoke with the chief, Man-with-Crooked-Mouth—just as you told me to do. The savage asked about trading for guns."

The captain frowned. "I've got blankets, glass beads, and cloth to trade. I have no intention of arming the red bastards with dangerous weapons." He had saddles, too, issued by the US government for the Indians as promised by the latest treaty. He had no intention of giving away good saddles to a bunch of savages.

An unholy light entered the commander's eyes. He hated the Indians, but he was not above using them to further his own ends. He didn't see why the government gave the Indians goods and supplies when his men could use them more. He wanted the Indians killed or banished to a place where no white man would ever be forced to come in contact with one again. He was a captain in the

United States Army in charge of distributing supplies promised to the Indians in the most recent treaty with the Ojibwas and Ottawas, but he had his own agenda. He had no intention of giving the savages anything without getting something in return.

The government is too generous to the red dogs, he thought. If only his superiors would see reason, they'd soon get rid of all the savages.

"Sir," the young soldier said, drawing his commander's attention. "I told them we didn't have guns for trade, but that we had firewater."

A look of satisfaction entered the captain's expression. The smile that transformed his face was frightening. Whiskey didn't sit well with the redskins. A drunken Indian was an ornery one, bound to get into trouble, which was just what the captain wanted. "You've done well, Holton. Very well indeed."

The lad breathed a sigh of relief and beamed, for it was much better to please the captain than to anger him. Angered, the officer was a dangerous man.

"You said there are women among the Sioux?"

"Yes, sir. Four of them."

The captain smiled. "Ever been with a woman, Holton?"

The soldier, barely sixteen, blushed. "No, sir."

"We'll have to rectify that, won't we?" The officer held the private's gaze steadily. "I'll allow you first pick after I choose my own."

The younger man looked startled, then as understanding dawned, he appeared pleased. "Truly, sir?"

The officer was in the mood to be generous. He nodded.

"Thank you, Captain." The lad shuffled his feet and looked down. "Sir, what am I supposed to do?"

The man laughed. "You'll know when the time comes, Holton, but if it will make you feel any better, I'll allow you to watch me first." He chuckled at the lad's startled expression, before he dismissed him.

It should be an entertaining night, he thought. It had been a long time since he or any of his men had enjoyed the attention of females. With success so close at hand, the captain felt himself harden with lust. Tonight he'd celebrate a job well-done—whether or not the woman he'd chosen enjoyed it.

Daniel sat in the Ojibwa wigwam with his friend Black-Hawk-Who-Hunts-at-Dawn, the brave's two brothers—Rain-from-Sky and Thunder Oak—and the head chief of the Ojibwa village, Big-Cat-with-Broken Paw. The men were discussing the Sioux attack on the mission and how to find and rescue the missing white people.

The Indians were engaged in a discussion in Ojibwa. Daniel was quiet as he listened and tried to keep up with the rapid conversation. So far, he'd learned that one band of Ojibwa scouts had returned. Thunder Oak had been their leader. He'd reported that they had, indeed, found signs of their enemy, the Sioux. The only one of Black Hawk's brothers who did not speak English well, he spoke in Ojibwa. Daniel tried to make sense of what he was saying. He caught Black Hawk's gaze. His friend translated for him.

"Dan-yel, my father says he has found the tracks made by our enemy, the Sioux."

Daniel knew that the Ojibwa used the term *father* for all male family members. Thunder Oak continued his report, and Black Hawk kept Daniel informed.

Apparently, the Indians had followed the trail until

they'd reached a river, which they had crossed to check the other side. There were no tracks on the opposite shore, so they knew that the Sioux had left by canoe, canoes Thunder Oak claimed had been stolen from their Ottawa brothers.

After listening to the talk, Daniel realized that these Sioux would be difficult to find now, but he didn't give up hope. He had faith in his friends' ability to track, even under the worst circumstances.

As the Indians continued their discussion, Daniel felt someone's regard. He glanced toward the door opening and was startled to see Amelia.

"Daniel!" she exclaimed as she burst into the meeting of all men.

The group suddenly became quiet. Daniel rose to his feet and hurried to her side. "What is it?" He felt something between embarrassment and concern.

"I must speak with you!" she whispered.

"What's wrong?"

"Please, outside."

Daniel glanced at the men, who regarded Amelia with disapproval. "Amelia, you shouldn't have barged in on our meeting."

She tensed, and he saw her glance at the Indian men. "Tell them I am sorry for interrupting."

Daniel translated for Big-Cat-with-Broken-Paw. "My woman does not know your ways," he said in Ojibwa. "I will teach her. Please do not look too harshly upon her." He hesitated. "She is upset at the loss of her father."

"Go with her, Daniel," Black Hawk said in English. "I will explain to my chief and my brothers."

Daniel flashed Hawk a look of gratitude. *"Miigwech."*

"You are welcome, my friend."

Amelia had left the wigwam, sensing she'd committed

a terrible breach of Indian etiquette. She stood some distance from the door, waiting for Daniel to join her.

She had let emotion rule her head—and not her good sense. The last thing she needed was to alienate the Ojibwa. They were her hosts, and better yet, they were the only ones who could help Daniel find and rescue her father.

She waited, feeling nervous all of a sudden, wondering what Daniel would say about the way she'd burst in.

He came out of the wigwam, spied her immediately, and approached. "What is it?"

She flushed, feeling foolish. "Daniel, I'm sorry."

He sighed. "Amelia, this is a different culture than ours. Please let me handle this. I know it's difficult, but I—we—will find your father."

She nodded silently and looked away.

"Now what's wrong?" He had softened his tone. "What did you want to tell me?"

She drew a sharp breath before replying. "Daniel, they have us sharing a wigwam. They have us in the same room!" she exclaimed, sounding upset.

He stared at her without expression. She shifted uncomfortably under his intent study of her. "Amelia, they believe you are my woman."

"Well, then tell them I'm not!"

He raised an eyebrow. "I can't do that."

"Why?"

"For your own protection. As my woman, no one will bother you."

"I thought you said we'd be safe here—"

Daniel nodded. "I did, and we are." In a telling movement, he ran his hand over the back of his neck. "I'm sorry you're upset, but believe me—it's for the best that they've put us together." He smiled. "Besides, Susie will be with us."

A gleam entered his blue eyes, the first indication that he realized how difficult it was going to be for them to share such close quarters.

"Isn't Susie staying with Conner's grandmother?"

He looked alarmed. "I'd forgotten." He suddenly didn't look so sure of the situation. He shook his blond head, as if the problem was a minimal one. "It'll be fine, Amelia."

She hoped he was right. She looked behind him toward the wigwam. "Have they said anything about my father?"

"No," he said.

She frowned. "They haven't! Why not?"

"Amelia, you must be patient."

"I'm trying to be," she said, feeling dispirited.

He drew her face upward, stroked her cheek with his finger. "If it will make you feel better, I'll see about other sleeping arrangements."

She thought about it, then shook her head. "I don't want to be left alone."

"I'll be there if you need me," he said.

Amelia closed her eyes. *I need you. I don't want to, but I do . . .*

It was time in the Indian village for a naming ceremony. The son of a young Ojibwa couple had just turned one month old today, and it was time for the child to be given an identity. The event was cause for celebration. The festivities would include the ceremony, a feast, and a thanksgiving to *Gichi-manidoo,* the Great Spirit, and the spirits that govern all living things on the earth.

The Ojibwa had been preparing for this feast for several days. That evening, Amelia's first within the village, the festivities would begin with a gathering within the yard.

Amelia hadn't seen Daniel since she'd interrupted his meeting with Black-Hawk-Who-Hunts-at-Dawn. She'd returned to the wigwam and waited for him to come. Afternoon became dusk, and it was then that Spring Blossom came to help prepare her for the festivities. The maiden gave her a beautiful doeskin dress, held on by straps about the shoulders. The garment was adorned with bead- and quillwork in a variety of colors.

"It's pretty," she told the Indian maiden.

Spring Blossom looked at her blankly.

"Pretty," she said, stroking the skin. "Very nice. Very beautiful."

The maiden understood then and smiled. "Put . . . on," she instructed in hesitant English.

Amelia glanced down at her own green fabric gown and realized that she would feel less conspicuous if she changed clothes. She nodded and accepted the dress. She hesitated before undressing in the hope that Spring Blossom would take the hint and leave, but the Ojibwa woman was prepared to stay to help Amelia get ready.

Spring Blossom, herself, looked quite stunning in a similar tunic with separate attached sleeves. Her hair had been combed to a black glossy sleekness and made into a single braid. It looked as if she'd colored her cheeks pink with berry juice. She wore long beaded earrings, several strands of bead necklaces, a necklace of copper tubes, and a silver armband. There were several small yellow dots painted in a pattern across her nose and on her forehead.

Amelia's hands hovered on the buttons of her gown bodice. Although she'd seen most of the women without tops, Amelia was still uncomfortable at the thought of undressing before one. She realized that Spring Blossom had no intention of leaving, so she began to undress. Her fingers fumbled over the buttons.

Spring Blossom held out her hands. "Help."

Amelia shook her head, then concentrated on undoing her gown. She turned away as she stepped from the garment. Clad only in her chemise, she reached for the Indian dress and started to raise it over her head. She felt a tug on the back of her undergarment. She glanced at the woman over her shoulder.

"Take off," Spring Blossom said.

Amelia stared at her. "No, I—"

"Take off!" the maiden insisted.

She blushed as she pulled off the garment, then quickly slipped on the doeskin dress. Spring Blossom was waiting for her when she turned around.

The maiden smiled. "Pret-ty," she said.

"Thank you."

"Miigwech," Spring Blossom said, giving her the Ojibwa translation.

Amelia grinned. *"Miigwech."*

Wearing the dress wasn't all that was expected from Amelia. Spring Blossom combed and braided her sable brown hair into two plaits. Then to Amelia's amazement, Spring Blossom took some kind of red-and-yellow-colored substances and painted streaks in Amelia's hair.

A few more added touches to Amelia's appearance and Spring Blossom pronounced her ready. Without a looking glass, Amelia had no idea what she looked like, but she could guess. As she stepped from the wigwam behind Spring Blossom, she searched for Daniel and Susie, wondering if they'd recognize her in her Ojibwa dress.

The last half hour or so spent with Spring Blossom was enjoyable to Amelia. There was a language barrier to overcome, but she thought they'd managed to communicate quite well.

As the two women joined the gathering, Amelia felt slightly uncomfortable amidst the Ojibwa, many of whom looked fierce in their ceremonial finery. With faces painted and their hair adorned, they appeared as different from white men as any people she'd ever seen. On closer inspection, Amelia noticed a serenity about the Ojibwa, a gladness of being together in thanks for the child and for what the spirits had given them. She relaxed and followed Spring Blossom to where a group of women sat on rush mats. Someone placed a mat on the ground for her and Spring Blossom. She and her new Ojibwa friend sat down with the others. The Ojibwa had donned special dress for the occasion. Many of the women, usually bare-breasted, wore either dresses held on by straps worn over their shoulders or tunics with leggings. Sleeves to the dresses, like Spring Blossom's, were separate pieces tied on to each arm. Their jewelry was made from shells, dyed porcupine quills, copper, silver, and glass beads that they'd received in trade from the white settlement. Amelia noticed that some of the matrons wore the cross necklaces made by the missionaries and garments of linen fabric, obviously traded from the whites. She closed her eyes and said a silent prayer that those captured at the mission would be found and rescued.

Amelia heard the beat of Ojibwa drums, and the women, who'd been chatting among themselves, became quiet. All eyes became centered on the line of Indian men who danced in a line to take their places to form a circle with the women, the children, and the elderly.

Someone sat on the other side of Amelia. She glanced over and saw an elderly woman with gray hair fixed into two braids and a linen dress that had to have been acquired from a white trader. She watched the men as each took their place among the gathering, then she gestured toward one old man who stood in the center of the circle.

"He-Who-Came-from-Far-Away," the woman said.

Amelia studied her with surprise. "You speak English."

The matron nodded. "I was once one from among you. I have lived as an *Anishinaabe* since I was but eleven years."

Amelia regarded her with curiosity, noting what she hadn't before—the woman's light eyes. Other than the color of her eyes, she appeared as all the other Ojibwa—in dress, in stature, and in mannerism.

"My name is Woman-with-Hair-of-Fox." She smiled. "This old woman's hair is not so like Fox now." She fixed her gaze on the old man. "He-Who-Comes-from-Far-Away is *niwiidigegemaagan*. He is my husband. He has been asked by the boy's mother and father to give their child a name."

Amelia listened to the woman with interest. "Who is that?" she asked about an elaborately dressed man standing off to one side.

"He is our shaman. He will watch over the ceremony." She smiled as her gaze went to He-Who-Comes-from-Far-Away. "It is a great honor for my husband to name the child. In this way, he will honor the boy with his vision name. The child will use this name until he becomes a man and receives another. The boy will use the special gift given to He-Who-Comes-from-Far-Away by the spirits. When he becomes older, he will have his own vision name, a name that will honor and protect him with the spirits that he will see in his vision."

"Does your husband have a name for the child?"

The woman nodded. "It has long been in his mind . . .

since he was a young man and went into the forest alone to find his own identity."

The village chief joined Woman-with-Hair-of-Fox's husband. The Indian woman lowered her voice as she explained what was to occur.

The child's mother, a young Indian woman with her hair worn in a single braid, stepped into the circle with her baby. The boy-child was in his cradleboard, a wooden apparatus big enough for the baby, cushioned with furs and beaver pelts. A wooden bar protected the child's head. A footrest kept the child on the board whenever it stood upright—as when his mother carried him on her back or hung the cradleboard from a low tree branch where the boy could see his mother and rock gently back and forth as the cradle swung in the breeze.

The child's cradleboard was held up by his parents so all within the village could see. The drums went silent. Then, He-Who-Comes-from-Far-Away started to speak.

"This child's mother and father have asked me to give a name to their son. It is my honor that I should do this." He paused and looked around. "Many of you know me as He-Who-Comes-from-Far-Away. What you may not know is my Manitu, the name from my vision quest, a name I wish to share with this little baby. It is a good Manitu; it has protected me well when I hunted. It watched over me during my long journey from the village of my clan, the Loon."

He turned to the child and touched the boy's cheek with a gnarled finger. "You, boy, shall be given the name of Eagle-Who-Flies-through-the-Sun."

A murmuring throughout the gathering noted the village's pleasure with the child's name.

"The spirits shall be good to Eagle-Who-Flies-through-the-Sun," the old man said. "The spirits of the wind helps the Eagle soar to great heights in flight. It will watch over and protect this boy as he flies toward becoming a man. He will have this Manitu until he becomes a man with his own vision quest—his own name. Until that time, I give this Ojibwa son the use of mine."

He had appeared solemn as he'd given his speech, but now he looked at the child and smiled. "You, our son, will be an Eagle until the time you can soar on your own and become what *Gichi-manidoo* has decided."

Amelia listened to the old man speak and his wife's translation of what was being said. Woman-with-Hair-of-Fox was quiet as her husband became silent and the Ojibwa drummers began to play.

As the ceremony continued and the shaman began to speak, Amelia searched the gathering for Daniel. She became concerned when she couldn't find him, until she spied him among a group of Ojibwa men. She hadn't recognized him before, because, like her, he wore Ojibwa dress and had been painted with red, white, and yellow on his face, his hair, and across his bare, muscled chest.

Amelia's body warmed as she stared at him. She was still trying to take in that this painted warrior was Daniel, the blacksmith, Susie's father, and the man for whom she herself had strong feelings.

As if sensing her regard, he met her gaze. He looked as startled as she'd felt when she'd first caught sight of him. Apparently, he was as surprised by her appearance as she was by his.

He grinned, and she found herself grinning back; and for a moment, it seemed to Amelia that they were two people alone, aware of only each other.

Amelia felt a touch on her arm, and her attention turned from Daniel to Spring Blossom instead. The naming ceremony was over, and Amelia realized that she'd missed much of the last part. Her attention had been focused on Daniel and not the events taking place within the circle.

"We eat," the maiden said.

Amelia nodded then glanced at the older woman. "Thank you," she said. *"Miigwech."*

The woman's face brightened. "You are most welcome, Tree-That-Will-Not-Bend."

Surprised, Amelia stared. "That name—why did you call me that?"

Woman-with-Hair-of-Fox smiled. "It is the name your husband, Dan-yel, calls you."

Amelia's gaze returned to Daniel. "He called me that?"

"So says the child, Little Flower."

"Susie?"

The woman nodded.

"Should I be offended?"

The Indian matron frowned. "You do not like name? It is a good name, a strong one."

She hadn't thought of it that way. She smiled. "I like it, I think."

"You have not heard him call you by that name?"

Amelia shook her head.

"Then I would ask him about it." The woman's lips twitched. "You may have your own Ojibwa name for Dan-yel. Yes?"

She grinned. "Yes, I think I do," Amelia said as she narrowed her gaze on the white man across the way. "Man-with-Big-Head."

Seventeen

Night came quickly, and the festivities came to a close. Amelia had never seen such a celebration. There were all kinds of food prepared by the Ojibwa women and men, treats made with maple sugar, dishes made with meat and wild rice. After the naming ceremony, there was another occasion for celebration. A young Indian brave was being inducted into the Great Medicine Society of the Midewiwin, and the event was marked by the Great Medicine Dance, an interesting, wonderful sight to see.

After a morning of traveling and a day filled with new sights, scents, and meals, Amelia was tired. She longed for sleep, but she was nervous about the sleeping arrangements. She'd spoken with Daniel only twice during the course of the evening, and their conversations were short and not private as they were surrounded by his Indian friends.

As some of the Indian families retired to their wigwams, Amelia decided to return to hers and the Traherns'. She looked for Susie to see if the little girl was ready to go to bed, but there was no sign of the child anywhere. She wasn't worried. It had become apparent to Amelia from the start that Susie felt comfortable within the village, a fact that amazed her, because of what she'd learned from Daniel . . . Susie had witnessed the Indian attack when her mother had been taken. Astonished by the resiliency of children, Amelia was glad that Susie suffered no ill effects or felt any anger toward Indians.

As she headed toward the wigwam, Amelia recalled Susie's bad dreams. Perhaps the attack had left more scars on Susie than she'd first thought . . . if the mention of a doll had caused her to start having nightmares again.

One thing of which Amelia was certain: The Indians who took her mother couldn't have been Ojibwa, or Susie wouldn't feel so comfortable in their midst.

The fire in the pit had been banked to softly glowing embers. Amelia wondered if she should add wood, but decided she'd ask Daniel when he finally came in for the night. She eyed the rush mats covered by thick pelts and furs, and chose a sleeping pallet toward the back wall. She had brought some things with her, but it didn't seem right to change into a nightdress, not with the knowledge she would be sharing the wigwam with Daniel. Neither did she want to wear the doeskin tunic to bed. It was comfortable, but not for sleeping.

Amelia sat down on the sleeping pallet and worked to unbraid her hair. Tomorrow she'd have to find a place to wash it to get rid of the color. Glancing about the wigwam, she looked to see if there was anything she could use to comb her hair. When she didn't immediately find something, she settled for using her fingers. Outside, she could still hear the soft *tum-tum* of the Ojibwa ceremonial drums. Some of the people were still celebrating, mostly members of the child's clan—the Loon.

She stretched out on the sleeping mat and stared up at the domed ceiling of the wigwam. She was in the strangest surroundings, and she should have been afraid, but she wasn't. She'd been a little uncomfortable at some of the looks of the men, but they'd stopped staring after they'd seen her with Daniel. She understood now that it was best for the Ojibwa to believe she was Daniel's woman in order to have his protection from interested Ojibwa braves.

Amelia began to feel sleepy as she lay in the wigwam alone. She listened for Daniel's return, and when he didn't come, she got up and added fuel to the fire. She thought he might need the light when he came in.

She went back to her Indian bed and lay down. Her eyes drifted shut. She wondered if Daniel had found somewhere else to sleep as he'd suggested. She fell asleep, hoping that he hadn't, that she would wake up in the morning to find him sleeping within a few feet of her.

Daniel waited until it was late and most of the Ojibwa had sought their sleeping pallets, before he decided it was time to seek his own. The thought of sharing a wigwam with Amelia heated his blood and made his heart race. The sight of her earlier in Indian dress, adorned with Ojibwa jewelry and face paint, had surprised, yet pleased him. How different she'd looked from the prim and proper woman who had entered his smithy that first warm August day.

During the ceremony, he'd watched Amelia, saw the curiosity in her glistening brown eyes, and the ready smile on her lips when Spring Blossom or Woman-with-Hair-of-Fox had spoken to her. He couldn't stop thinking about her . . . or wanting her. He'd never felt such desire for a woman, not even his beautiful but treacherous late wife Pamela, who had so enthralled him from the first. Amelia Dempsey was a genuine woman, a warm and giving woman with underlying passion that, to his amazement, he was able to stir whenever they kissed.

He had even started to think about marriage, something he'd sworn he'd never do again . . . not after his disastrous relationship . . . not after seeing his sister Jane's un-happiness with her officer husband, Richard Milton.

He trusted Amelia. He'd seen her love and concern for her father, the caring she'd shown to Susie, his niece. The deterioration of Susie and Amelia's relationship upset him. He felt like it was his fault that Susie no longer liked or trusted Amelia, and he didn't know how to fix things.

Daniel rose from the remaining circle of men. His friend Black Hawk caught his gaze and he went over to speak with the Ojibwa briefly before seeking his bed.

"You look troubled, Dan-yel," Black Hawk said, as Daniel sat down beside him. "Did you not enjoy our feast?"

"I did," Daniel said. "The food and entertainment were excellent, as always. I have always said that the Ojibwa know how to enjoy themselves."

Black Hawk stared at him with his dark piercing gaze. "You are concerned about your woman," he said.

Daniel was amazed how his friend could easily read his thoughts. "I am worried about her father, and I am worried about her. Susie is angry with her, and it is my fault. I don't know how to make things better between them."

"You love this woman?"

He couldn't answer at first. He didn't want to say it aloud, although he knew it to be true. "Yes."

"My friend has not had a woman for a long time. He must not blame Tree-That-Will-Not-Bend for the wrongs made by Snake-Who-Strikes-When-One-Is-Not-Looking."

Daniel had to smile, as Black Hawk's name for his dead wife seemed an appropriate one. He'd never heard Hawk mention Pamela before, in any way.

"You are tired," the brave said. "You should seek your sleeping mat."

He nodded. "I'll see you in the morning."

"Come to the wigwam of Big-Cat-with-Broken-Paw. The chief wishes to speak with you."

"I'll come. *Miigwech.*"

Black Hawk inclined his head. "Go to your woman. Little Flower is with Swaying Tree. She and your woman will make peace, and all will be well."

Daniel rose. "I hope you are right."

"Do you doubt the wisdom of this man?"

A smile turned up the corner of Daniel's mouth. "How can I? You've never been proven wrong yet."

He left the small gathering and headed toward the wigwam and Amelia. He hoped that by the time he got there Amelia would have gone to sleep. *And temptation would be firmly out of the way.*

The door flap to the lodge was closed. Daniel raised the animal skin and stepped inside. The interior of the wigwam was bathed in the soft glow emanating from the fire pit. His gaze went to Amelia on the sleeping mat, and he felt relieved that she had fallen into slumber.

He approached to study her. She had released her hair from the braids she'd worn earlier, and her sable brown tresses were fanned out about her head and shoulders. She lay on her side, her face toward the fire, and he enjoyed her beauty . . . the thick crescent of dark lashes against her cheeks, her pink lips, her smooth white skin. Desire kicked him below his waistline hard, and he turned away to fight it.

He started to undress for bed, removing vest, armbands, and leggings, but leaving on the loincloth, before stretching out on the sleeping mat. He thought of his conversation with Black Hawk, realized his friend was right. He had to find his way with Amelia. Amelia and Susie would make friends again given time. He had to find Amelia's father, then search for peace within himself. If Amelia and he found that they could make each other happy, then he had to put the painful past behind him and follow his heart.

He rolled onto his side, where he could study Amelia in repose, and he saw to his surprise that she was awake and looking back at him. For a long moment, they just stared at each other. He felt his heart begin to beat faster. The fatigue he'd begun to feel as he undressed disappeared; he felt more energized and alive than he'd ever felt before.

Amelia sat up on the mat. She felt like a shameless hussy; she'd watched him undress. She'd been unable to take her eyes off him. "Daniel."

He didn't answer at first, but she knew he'd heard. He returned her stare. He looked wonderful. His muscled chest was bare. He had powerful shoulders and arms, a flat stomach. Her gaze traveled down to the loincloth. A wave of desire hit her so hard that she groaned softly and shut her eyes.

She wanted to touch him. She was conscious that she was alone with him. Where was Daniel's daughter?

"Susie—"

"She's staying with Conner," he said softly. He rose to a sitting position. "Are you all right? Are you comfortable?"

She gave an affirmative jerk of her head.

"The Ojibwa—they'd don't frighten you?"

Amelia shook her head. "I felt uncomfortable at first, but Spring Blossom and Woman-with-Hair-of-Fox made me feel welcome." Her mouth formed a little half smile. "Spring Blossom dressed me. Woman-With-Hair-of-Fox explained what was happening during the ceremonies." She shifted on the sleeping pallet and saw his attention shift to the outline of her breasts beneath the doeskin dress.

"I didn't realize that Woman-with-Hair-of-Fox is a white woman," she said. "She told me that she came to live with the Indians when she was only eleven."

"She told you she was a white woman?" Daniel frowned.

"Well, she probably wouldn't have, but I asked her where she learned to speak English."

Daniel's brow cleared. "She has been happy with He-Who-Comes-from-Far-Away for as long as I've known her."

Daniel couldn't keep his eyes off Amelia. She was appealing to look at with her tousled hair and sleep-softened face. As he gazed at her, he wanted her with a completeness that caused him pain. Several lustful thoughts passed through his mind, but there was more than lust in his feelings for Amelia . . . so much more.

Amelia gazed back at him steadily, and he fought the urge to pull her into his arms and make tender love to her.

"Tell me—who is Tree-That-Will-Not-Bend?" she asked, but it was clear in her expression that she knew.

He felt his face heat. "Where did you hear that?"

She smirked. "From Woman-with-Hair-of-Fox. She says it's your name for me. Is that true?"

Had he detected a note of hurt in her voice at the nickname? "Black Hawk called you Woman-with-Eyes-of-Deer. I thought Tree-That-Will-Not-Bend more appropriate." He paused, noting the way her face fell as he spoke. "Black Hawk agreed. Do you know what he said when I told him?"

She shook her head. Daniel felt like he was drowning in the watery depths of her lovely brown eyes.

"He said that it is a good name for you. A woman who is strong and as lovely and as a beautiful as a sturdy tree. Tree-That-Will-Not-Bend."

She looked surprised but pleased. "He said that?"

Daniel nodded. "He said it, and I meant it."

"Oh." She glanced away then, and he could tell she was embarrassed by this offhanded bit of praise. "I thought you were referring to my stubbornness."

"That, too." He grinned at her look of outrage.

"Am I that terrible?" she asked.

He was surprised to see tears in her eyes. She looked so pretty and vulnerable. He wanted to kiss her so desperately that it was a physical ache in his heart. "Amelia."

She didn't look at first.

"Amelia, please look at me."

She met his gaze then. "Yes?"

He rose to his knees and shifted toward her sleeping mat. A quick flicker of alarm passed over her features, and he hesitated until he saw the look of longing that quickly replaced her fear. "Nothing about you is terrible," he murmured huskily.

He slid next to her on the sleeping pallet, clad only in a loincloth, while she sat in the Ojibwa dress, secured by two single straps that ran over her shoulders. He eyed the curve of her shoulder and felt the strongest urge to press his lips to her skin. He gazed into her eyes and wanted to do more than kiss her. He gave in to the urge to put his mouth to her shoulders, and enjoyed the sound of the swift intake of her breath. He loved the way she trembled beneath the simplest contact with him.

He closed his eyes to savor the warm smoothness of her skin beneath his lips, the sweet scent of her that enveloped him as he buried his nose in her hair. When she turned to allow him access to the back of her neck and other shoulder, he groaned and continued to move his lips across her nape, back, other shoulder, and finally her ear.

She gasped as he nibbled on her earlobe, then moved on to turn her fully into his arms. He kissed her as he'd been wanting to do since their last kiss. He devoured her lips with his mouth, held her against him as if he was afraid if he released her he'd lose her forever. To his great joy, she wasn't frightened. She was enjoying the contact between them as much as he was. He lifted his head to study her and was elated to see the dreamy look in her eyes. Her pink lips were begging to be kissed again.

He felt himself harden beneath the breechclout. "Amelia," he said in a strained voice, "I'll leave if you want me to."

"No!" she exclaimed, while encircling his neck with her arms. She shifted to press herself closer to him.

Daniel thought that if he didn't have her soon, he would explode. "I'm sorry—"

"No." She pressed her lips against his mouth and kissed him. She began to kiss him all over his face, while straining to get closer to him. Her hands began to explore his naked chest, and he groaned at her delicate touch, then gasped with satisfaction as her caresses became bolder.

He thought hard to remember Pamela, and a lesson learned too late, but he couldn't picture his dead wife . . . or the best friend who had cuckolded him. All he could do was see and feel Amelia with his body and in his mind.

Amelia felt Daniel's strong hands lift her and lay her back on the sleeping mat. Clinging to his neck, she pulled him down to her, and they kissed, a frantic joining of open mouths.

Heat spiraled from her abdomen to all pulsing points of pleasure. Daniel raised his head, and Amelia's breath caught as he gazed into her eyes with desire. She wanted it, too. To be close to him, skin against skin. The feelings she had were frightening and new to her, but she didn't want them to stop. She'd been kissed before, but not like this. Never like this. She knew that the intensity of emotions she was feeling was all wrapped up in this one man.

She grabbed his head, cupped his jaw with her hands, so that she could capture his gaze with a look that revealed all that she was experiencing. A flame burned brightly in his blue eyes. As she ran her fingers tenderly over his features, he closed his eyes and sighed with pleasure.

When his dark lashes lifted, he gazed at her with blue eyes glazed over with passion. He caught her straying hand and held it to his cheek, then turned his head to press a kiss into the center of her palm. Amelia was moved by the romantic gesture.

"Daniel."

He wanted to take her, to bury himself deep into the softness between her thighs. He knew he shouldn't touch her, but for the life of him, he couldn't remember why. "Amelia, we—" *Shouldn't.* He couldn't say it.

"Touch me."

He shook his head. "I—"

"Touch me, Daniel. *Please.*"

"Yes," he said, unable to deny himself for even a moment longer.

She lay on her back, he on his side but half-draped over her. He moved to grant himself more access to her soft, feminine curves. Lifting himself away, he sat up and placed his hand on her leg where the tunic edge touched bare skin. Holding her glance, lest she want him to stop at any time, he caressed her knee, the area of lower thigh that was available to him. Then, he slowly, gently, began to raise the doeskin, revealing a form so beautiful that he had to remind himself to breathe.

She appeared unafraid as he lifted the tunic past her thighs and higher. He felt his mouth go dry as he saw the tiny nest of dark curls that sheltered her womanhood . . . the perfectly rounded curve of her hips . . . her flat white belly. He barely touched her, skimming her skin with the soft brush of his knuckles, but from the look on her face and the small sounds she was making deep in her throat, one would have thought he was touching and stroking her to his heart's content.

He released the garment hem when she was bared from the waist downward. He wanted to see all of her, but she would have to sit up to accommodate the removal of the Indian dress. He stared at her, his whole body pulsating with the desire to love her, waiting for a sign from her to continue.

Amelia felt a loss as Daniel moved away. One glance into his eyes and she understood what he was waiting for. Unashamed by her near nakedness, she sat up while holding his gaze, then reached for the garment hem and tugged upward. Daniel reached to help her, pulled the dress gently over her head. She heard his sharp intake of breath as he tossed the garment aside and stared at her body. She had a brief moment of embarrassment, until his eyes met hers and she saw the homage being paid to her by his hot look of longing and desire.

Her gaze locked with his, she lay back on the pallet as naked as the day she was born but for the small touch of hair and face paint. He took so long to look his fill that she began to feel a niggle of doubt and started to roll onto her side to escape his scrutiny.

"No," he said in a rasping voice. "Let me see you."

His hand cupped her hip and gently rolled her back. "Don't hide your beauty from me."

He hadn't removed his hand from her hip. His other hand joined the first one to span both of her hips and caress her along the curve up to stroke the outer sides of her breasts and downward again.

Daniel was tormenting her with his little touches. She wanted more of him. She wasn't a fragile china doll—she was a woman, and she wanted to feel his strength and the weight of his hot muscled length pressing her into the furs that lined her bed.

She started to rise up so she could touch and undress him as well, but he placed his mouth on her belly, and she gasped and fell back as hot coils of sensation filled her with pleasure and made her burn. He trailed kisses from her stomach up toward her breasts, but he had yet to capture a nipple. When he placed his mouth to suck, her nipple had already pebbled and peaked.

She grabbed his head, tilted his face up so she could see him. "Daniel, please," she gasped.

He nodded, then rose to untie the strings of his breechclout. As the garment fell away, Amelia felt a tightness in her chest for a brief moment before she felt her heart pound rapidly beneath her breast.

His manhood was thick and hard, rising from a nest of light brown curls. His arms, stomach, and legs, especially his thighs, were corded with powerful muscle. Dark blond hair covered his chest and formed a V that crossed his stomach until it joined the curly hair between his legs.

Amelia felt suddenly frightened. She'd never been with a man, and she experienced the impact of what she was about to do. Still, as he knelt on the mat by her side, she gave in to the urge to touch his leg. He bent and kissed her, and all her doubts disappeared in the glory and the rightness in her feelings for this man.

They came together, kissing gently at first, until desire spurred them on to greater heights. She didn't know when Daniel had stretched out beside her or how she'd ended up lying on top of him with their mouths joined, his hands fondling her from back to thigh.

She was aroused and unafraid, and it became more important to give him pleasure than to seek her own. But in giving she received, and soon it was she who lay beneath Daniel, feeling his weight as she'd dreamed.

They kissed, caressed, and fondled each other until both were gasping and wanting release. Amelia didn't hesitate in opening her legs when she felt a light nudge from Daniel's knee. She cupped his buttocks as he gently probed her with his staff. Wanting and needing him inside her, she arched up to force his entry, then gasped from the pain.

Daniel froze at her soft cry and started to pull away. He didn't want to hurt her.

"No!" she cried, and pulled him down as she raised herself to complete the joining. He felt big, stretching her to fullness, and while it had hurt, she didn't want him to leave her.

She met his gaze, saw his concern. "Are you all right?" She beamed at him, and he groaned and kissed her.

"I'll try not to hurt you."

Amelia nodded. "Just make love to me."

Daniel began to ease himself in and out of her, thrusting gently, then with more power when Amelia whimpered with pleasure and clung hard. He set a rhythm that she began to follow, and the two of them brought each other to the point of ecstasy and beyond using lips, teeth, tongues, hands, and their bodies.

Amelia felt the sweet ache of pleasure that pulsed through every part of her body. She gloried in the weight of him, in his hands and mouth on her breasts, in her hands and lips on his face, neck, and nipples.

She heard Daniel's rasping breath, then became aware of her own seconds later when the dizzying ride to the top reached the summit. She and Daniel shuddered and cried out, then clung to each other for the slow gliding trip back to earth.

He didn't say anything for several minutes, but she knew what he was feeling by the sounds he made, sounds that echoed her own . . . the rasp of labored breaths, the thundering of heartbeats.

He felt heavy, but she liked it. When he rolled to her side, she was disappointed by the feeling of loss, until he pulled her against his side, covered the both of them with a large fur, and nuzzled his face in her hair as they both drifted to the lazy plane that precedes sleep.

"Daniel?"

"Mmmmm?"

"Miigwech."

He moved her then and kissed her hard on the mouth, and then to her astonishment, she began to feel again. And so did he. This time their joining was slower, as though each wanted to savor every titillating moment, each caress designed to invoke pleasure in the other partner.

They came together smoothly, slowly, and the climax they reached was slow, satisfying, and stronger than the last one they'd shared.

Eighteen

"Pa? Pa!"

Amelia was jolted awake by the sound of Susie's voice. Startled, she lifted Daniel's arm from about her waist and scrambled out of bed to dress quickly.

"Pa?"

"Daniel! Wake up!" Amelia bent and shook his shoulder. "Daniel."

He stirred in his sleep, then opened one eye to gaze at her blearily.

She heard the little girl calling Daniel. She could tell from the sound that the child was approaching.

"Daniel, please. It's Susie!"

That seemed to bring him to full wakefulness. "What?"

She pulled on the first garment at hand—the Indian dress. "Your daughter will be here any minute."

"Pa?"

Daniel scrambled to his feet, then looked for his loincloth. Amelia pointed to where it lay in a heap close to the fire pit.

"Pa—"

Susie's plea was answered by softly murmured words in Ojibwa. Someone outside had captured the child's attention, turning it away from finding her father—at least for now.

"What did she say?" Amelia asked. She blushed as she

watched Daniel slip the leather breechclout between his legs, then fasten it into position with a string just above his hips. "It was Woman-with-Hair-of-Fox," he said. "She said that she has something to show Susie if the child will spare her but a moment of her time."

Amelia felt a wave of gratitude for the Indian matron. She closed her eyes in relief. "I thought Susie would find us—" Opening her eyes, she met his gaze, then hurriedly looked away. Memories of the night filled her thoughts, making her feel awkward in the light of day. She could feel Daniel's stare for several long seconds before he bent to strap on his leggings.

She didn't know what to say, how to ease the sudden strain between them. It was as if the time spent in each other's arms had added tension to their budding relationship. It was as if both had succumbed to an uncontrollable wave of intimacy and desire the night before, something which now gave them cause for regret.

Hurt, Amelia needed to escape. "I'll wait outside—"

"Amelia!"

She halted, then hesitated before she looked back. "Yes?"

He narrowed his gaze as he studied her. As he approached, she felt her heart trip, then thunder with joyful anticipation and a certain dread.

His voice was soft, husky as he spoke, "We cannot undo what we've done."

Her mouth quivered. She looked away as she nodded, unwilling to see his scorn.

He caught her chin with his finger, raised it up so that she had no choice but to meet his gaze directly. "You've done nothing to be ashamed of," he said. There was no scorn in his beautiful blue gaze, only concern . . . and some emotion she couldn't put her finger on.

Then he kissed her. Amelia felt fire in her belly. He held her head still, while he wreaked havoc on her mouth, her cheeks, her chin, her throat. Sensation rocked her back on her heels as she instantly came alive under his attention.

"We've got one more night together, at least, in this village. We'll have to make the best of it. I'll tell Susie she must spend the night here."

Amelia nodded. It was for the best, wasn't it?

Her throat, her lips, were still tingling from his touch, but she knew it was dangerous to want more of him. They'd become caught up in the moment of the night, and had made the grave mistake of succumbing to their passionate urges for one another.

Susie burst into the wigwam and pulled up short at the sight of Amelia and Daniel. "Pa? Can we go swimming in the lake?"

He turned to her with a smile. "Yes, of course, sweeting." He studied her attire, noticed the doeskin tunic and the way she looked like a little lady with her hair neatly done in blond braids that fell past her shoulders. "Did you have a nice time with Conner's grandmother?"

"I had a wonderful time!" she gushed, full of excitement. "Did you like the naming ceremony? Conner said it's a special occasion."

Amelia stepped forward. "It was a nice time, wasn't it?" Then she blushed as she felt Daniel's regard and the sure knowledge on his face that the wonder of the night came afterward, between the two of them in the privacy of this wigwam.

Susie avoided giving Amelia an answer, choosing instead to address her father. "Pa, do we have to leave here today?"

Daniel frowned. "We're not leaving today."

"We're not?"

He shot Amelia a glance. "For another day, at least."

The little girl was overjoyed.

"Have you eaten?" Amelia asked softly.

The child ignored her.

"Susie," Daniel said, "answer Amelia."

Susie pouted "I'm not hungry. I ate with Conner and his mother."

"Well, I'm hungry," he said, with a smile in Amelia's direction.

She managed to give him a weak smile. "I'll see what I can do about preparing us something to eat."

Daniel's lips twitched, even while he was angry at Susie for treating Amelia so badly. "Gaining confidence in your ability to cook?"

Amelia shook her head. "I'll ask Spring Blossom to help me."

He felt a tug on his legging strap. "Pa," Susie said. "Can't we go to the lake now? Please?" she added when she saw his dark frown.

He was going to have a long talk with Susie about respect and good manners whenever she spoke with adults.

"Later. I have to meet with Black Hawk and the chief. I'll find you as soon as the meeting is over."

Susie flashed Amelia an angry glance that accused the woman of stealing her father's attention, then she fled from the wigwam.

Daniel turned toward Amelia. "I'm sorry, Amelia. It's my fault that Susie has been hostile to you. I'm going to have a talk with her."

"No," Amelia said. "Don't be angry with her. Better that she be angry with me than hurting."

"I'll not have her treating you that way!"

Amelia's expression softened. "She needs you, Daniel. You—not me. It'll be all right."

He cupped the side of her face with his hand. He felt an overwhelming sense of affection as she rubbed her face against his palm.

"I have to go," he said.

She nodded. "I haven't forgotten my father," she said softly. "And I haven't forgotten all the help you've given me. I'm very grateful."

Tension marked his features. "I don't want your gratitude, Amelia," he said and left.

Stunned by his sudden sharp tone, Amelia stood gaping at the doorway. *What did I say that's wrong?*

She remembered with heat their night together . . . the glorious time they'd spent learning each other's bodies, pleasuring each other until they both lay gasping and soaring and wanting more.

The beginning of a headache centered between Amelia's eyes. "I have to find Father. How could I have been so foolish to become involved with Daniel, a man still tortured by the memory of his dead wife . . . a woman he doesn't want to admit is dead?"

Amelia was confused. If he wanted his wife so much, why did he make such sweet love to her? Unless his loneliness had prompted him to reach out for comfort . . . the comfort of a woman's arms . . . even if the woman wasn't his wife, the one he loved.

The headache was now a tight band across her temples. Amelia sat on the sleeping platform and rubbed her brow. She needed to find her father and her missionary friends. She couldn't think when she was so close to Daniel. When she was near him, she wanted nothing more than to spend time with him, to kiss him . . . and make love.

She lay down on the platform and closed her eyes. She could feel the soft fur beneath her head and back . . .

recall the brush of the fur against her naked skin as Daniel held her, kissed her, and made her cry out with ecstasy.

She didn't know what to do. She didn't want to have her heart broken, but she couldn't bear the thought of losing Daniel . . . he'd meant too much to her.

Daniel was at a meeting with the Ojibwa. Perhaps when he returned he'd tell her that they knew where to look for her father, and she could concentrate on getting him home. She could worry about her relationship with Daniel later.

". . . But, Daniel, it's been three days! There has to be something we can do . . . some news about my father!"

"They're working on it, Amelia. I'm sure it'll be soon. Finding him in this vast wilderness isn't easy."

Amelia's eyes filled with tears. "I know it's not easy. I never said it was." The tears overflowed to trail down her cheeks. It had been three tension-filled days of worrying about her father, of struggling with her feelings for Daniel. Since that night, Susie had slept in their lodging between them, but the little girl was no deterrent for the giant leap of sensation Amelia felt whenever she and Daniel innocently brushed hands.

He studied her with a soft expression. He opened his arms. "Amelia—"

"No, Daniel," she said, turning away. To be comforted by him now would only aggravate the situation. She wanted something more from him, something he wasn't ready to give. And he wouldn't be, she thought, unless he found out what had happened to his wife Jane.

"I'll check again with Black Hawk. If he thinks it'll be a while, then we'll go home."

Home, she thought, as if his wonderful cabin was her home as well as his. *Wishful thinking, Amelia.*

She turned to him then. "I'm sorry, Daniel. I don't mean to be difficult—"

"You're not being difficult," he said. Daniel was surprised by how well she'd adapted to their time in the Indian village. As for frustration, he knew it as well as anyone. Being this close to Amelia was slowly driving him mad. He wanted to touch her, hold her . . . love her all night long. He'd hoped Susie's presence would act as a buffer between them, but instead of feeling better, he found his longing for Amelia all the more.

"Dan-yel?" Black Hawk's voice drew their attention. The couple had been alone. Susie had gone to help Conner's grandmother, Swaying Tree.

Daniel lifted the deer flap. *"Aaniin.* Come in, Black Hawk. Amelia and I were just discussing her father."

The Ojibwa brave entered the wigwam, and his dark gaze fell on the white woman before he turned to his friend. "I would speak with you in this man's lodge."

"You may speak freely here," Amelia said.

Black Hawk shook his head. "My words are for the man—Dan-yel."

Daniel saw the anger in Amelia's face, saw how she opened her mouth to protest. He reached out to stroke Amelia's arm. "I'll be right back." His gaze pleaded with her to allow him to speak privately with Black Hawk. It promised that he would have news for her one way or another when he was done.

"I'll be down at the lake," Amelia said.

There was an awkward moment as the three looked at each other, as if each was waiting for the other to make a move.

Amelia gathered a few things, then excused herself and left.

Daniel gestured to Black Hawk to sit down. "She'll stay away until I look for her," he assured the brave.

"We must go to this man's wigwam," Black Hawk said. "There are others who wait for us."

Daniel nodded, then waited for Black Hawk to exit so he could follow him.

Black Hawk and Daniel crossed to Hawk's wigwam. Rain-from-Sky, Thunder Oak, Sleeping Bird, and three other Ojibwa warriors were waiting inside the domed structure for the two men. The Indians nodded in greeting, but did not speak until after Daniel and Black Hawk were seated. Big-Cat-with-Broken-Paw lit a pipe from the flame in Hawk's fire pit. The chief took a puff on the pipe, then passed it to the next man for a smoke. The pipe made its way to each man in the wigwam until it reached Daniel. Daniel drew from the pipe, then handed it back to the chief.

"We have found the Sioux village where many captives are being kept as slaves. We believe your John Demp-sey may be one of these white men."

Daniel felt a flash of excitement. "You've seen him?"

One brave, whom Daniel recognized as one called Thick Head among the Ojibwa, spoke up. "I have seen this village," he said in Ojibwa slowly so that Daniel would understand. "There are many white women, many children. This man thinks that there might be a white man as well."

His excitement dimmed a bit. "You didn't actually see the doctor." He forgot and spoke in English. Fortunately, through all of their years trading with the white man, all of the braves understood, at least, a small degree of English.

"He saw someone who could be a white man. It was

difficult to see. We could not go close, or we would have been killed or captured.

Daniel understood. "Do you know how to get back to the village?" he asked in Ojibwa.

Thick Head looked offended. "This brave knows how to find our enemy, the Sioux. He can find again and again, should his people ask him."

"Gaagiizom. This man did not mean to make you angry. This man forgets that the Ojibwa are much better at tracking than the white man."

The furrow across Thick Head's brow cleared. He nodded as he accepted Daniel's apology.

"We will leave this night," Black Hawk said, "when the sky is cloaked in darkness and the moon is high above us."

"Amelia, my woman—she will want to go with us."

"We must haste," Rain-from-Sky said. "Your woman cannot travel as fast as the great cat or as far as the great area where the land is flat and without trees."

Daniel hadn't expected them to want a woman along with them. Still he had hoped to avoid a battle with Amelia, but it was bound to happen either way. He wouldn't have taken Amelia with them even if the Ojibwa had said yes. He wouldn't put Amelia is such great danger.

"May Amelia stay here in the village while we are gone?" Daniel asked Black Hawk.

Black Hawk inclined his head as he accepted the smoking pipe on its second time around. "Tree-That-Will-Not-Bend will be safe here within our village. We will not take all of our finest warriors. Some will remain behind to guard our women and our children, to protect all that we own."

"Thank you," Daniel said, relieved.

There was no question about whether or not Daniel

would be going. The Ojibwa knew that he would; it was what they'd expected from a man who sought to regain his own.

After that, there was some discussion about how long they'd be gone and what they'd need to take. The journey to the village would take two full days. Much would depend on what happened when they got there, if their mission was successful in finding John Dempsey and the missionaries and bringing them home.

When the meeting was over, Daniel and the warriors stood. Daniel nodded to each warrior as they filed past him while they left. When everyone was gone, except for Daniel and Black Hawk, Daniel held out his hand to his friend. Black Hawk clasped it. "You have been a great friend to me, Black-Hawk-Who-Hunts-at-Dawn."

The brave smiled as he shook the man's hand, then released it. "You will have a chance to do much for this man," Black Hawk said. "You will make me a new knife?"

Daniel grinned. "Of course. And a new iron kettle for your cook fire."

"*Miigwech,*" the Indian said. "Dan-yel has been a good friend to this brave." He paused. "You will be ready to go when my people have taken to their sleeping mats?"

"I'll be ready." Daniel started for the door.

"Good." Black Hawk followed the white man outside. "You will have much to say to Tree-That-Will-Not-Bend."

The blacksmith eyed his friend solemnly. "I may have much to say. I can only hope that she will listen."

"You must make her listen to you, my friend. I say this for her protection as well as ours."

"I will make her listen," Daniel said.

* * *

Amelia stood at the edge of the lake and watched the pattern of ripples made by the stone she'd recently tossed into the water. It was a warm day for this area in September. The water looked inviting, but she knew it was cold to the touch. The autumn evenings had been chilly, giving little opportunity for the lake to stay heated from the day's sun.

It was not the first time that she'd come to the lake. On that initial occasion, Amelia had come with Spring Blossom and several other Indian women. That was two days past, when they'd come to bathe off their ceremonial face and greasepaint. The Ojibwa matrons had had no qualms about diving into the cold water. Amelia, thinking the water warm, had jumped in as well only to find the temperature too uncomfortable for her to stay long.

The lake was a good size, but it wasn't Lake Superior, the gargantuan body of water located near the end of the river they'd utilized near the mission.

Amelia marveled that this vast wilderness had so many lakes, rivers, and streams. There was an ample water supply for everyone . . . and a food supply as well. On the marshlands about the lakes, wild rice grew on long blades of swamp grass. Yesterday, Amelia had gone out with Spring Blossom to harvest the rice. She got her first ride in a birch-bark canoe, a light boat that was ingeniously made. She'd been scared initially, for the craft didn't seem strong enough to transport them safely across the water. Once seated with the Indian maiden and her brother, Thunder Oak, Amelia realized that the canoe was indeed safe, safe and easy to maneuver in the marshes where the rice grasses grew.

Usually there would be only one woman and one man in a rice-gathering boat, for the rice kernels were knocked off the grass into the hull of the craft, and a third person would take up room necessary for the harvest. Spring Blossom had suggested that Amelia come, to see how it was done, and to enjoy some time away from her worries.

It was a fascinating thing to watch—the harvest of the wild rice. While Amelia and Thunder Oak sat in the canoe, Spring Blossom stood with a *bawa'iganaak*—a stick that she used to knock the rice kernels from the grass into the hull of the boat. When the canoe was as full as having three people in it would allow, Thunder Oak brought the craft in, where Spring Blossom along with some of the other village women emptied the canoe and began the process of drying the kernels for use and storage. Once dried, the wild rice was packed in containers made of birch bark and either buried in the ground, kept in the individual's wigwam, or stored in a small hut built especially for that use.

Amelia had been fascinated with the whole process. As she learned more and more about the Ojibwa way of life, many of her fears concerning the Indians had died. She realized that the whites—be they American, British, or French—didn't fully understand the People, or they'd never have labeled them savages to be feared or killed.

As Amelia studied the water of the lake, she thought of how she'd felt when she first came here. The women she'd encountered had been bare-breasted. The children up to the age of seven or so ran about naked and without shame, unless it was chilly, in which case they wore moccasins on their feet and clothes made from the white man's fabric or fur wraps tanned by their mothers' own hands.

She glanced down at her pile of belongings and pulled out her green dress for laundering. With no soap as she knew it, she simply dragged the garment through the water, dunking and rinsing, until she thought it clean.

When she was done, she squeezed out the excess water and draped the gown over a tree branch to dry in the sun.

This day she wore the doeskin tunic. She found it more comfortable than she'd thought she would. She enjoyed the freedom of movement beneath the garment, where she wasn't hampered by chemise or petticoats.

She sat down on a rock baked warm by the bright sunshine, and thought about her father . . . and Daniel and Susie and even the missing Jane.

She closed her eyes, enjoying the heat of the day on her face, listening to the sounds made by the forest . . . a bird squawking from a distant tree . . . the leaves in the treetops rustling as a gentle breeze swept through them.

Amelia relished the quiet moment alone to think. Her mind filled with Daniel's image. Her skin tingled as she recalled how it felt to know his touch. Her blood warmed as she remembered how well they'd fit together as woman and man.

"I don't know what to do," she whispered. "In my heart, I know it was wrong to have done what I've done with him, but it didn't feel wrong." It felt wonderful and right . . . even though she was sure she had no future with him.

Remember your father, an inner voice taunted.

"How can I not? I came here to be with him, to take care of him. In this I've failed, because I don't even know where he is!"

"Amelia."

She gasped and spun around. Daniel had come up behind her so silently, she didn't know he was there until he'd spoken. She rose from the rock as she noted something in his expression. "What? What is it?" She bit her lip. "My father—he's not dead, is he?"

He came to her quickly and caught her by the shoulders. "No, love, no."

She frowned with concern as she studied him. "Then, what?"

He hesitated before answering. "We're leaving tonight. Black Hawk and the others believe they've found the village where the missionaries and your father were taken."

Her brown eyes brightened. "Do I sense a but?"

He nodded. "Amelia, I'm sorry, but you can't come with us. I know it's hard for you to understand, but we'll be traveling hard, and Black Hawk—and I—think it would be better, and safer for us all, if you stay here until we get back."

"All right."

"Please don't be angry—"

She shook her head.

"I know you have been going half crazy with worry about your father, but I'll be there for you. If he's there, I'll bring him home." He stopped and frowned, as if just realizing what she'd said. "Did you say—"

"All right," she said with a smile. "I'll be happy to wait here with Susie until you come back." She was happy and excited. Finally, someone would be looking for her father. She'd never expected to go with them; she just wanted someone, anyone, to go.

Daniel looked at her a moment as if he couldn't quite believe that she would agree so easily. "You're not planning on following us after we leave?"

Her shock must have shown on her face, for he instantly looked contrite. "I'm sorry. I just didn't expect you to be so reasonable about this."

"What? You were expecting an argument from Tree-That-Will-Not-Bend?" she teased him.

He chuckled, but it was a weak sound. He still looked unsure of her.

"How long will you be gone?" she asked. She wasn't angry that he doubted her. He knew how much she wanted to see her father again, but what he hadn't realized, perhaps until now, was that she trusted him completely. She wouldn't risk the life of the man she loved, or his child, just because she was impatient.

"It's a good two days' journey to the Sioux village. Add two days back and the time we'll have to spend rescuing your father—" He frowned as he thought. "A week, I'd say. Maybe sooner, maybe a few days more."

Amelia nearly groaned aloud. "A whole week?"

Daniel touched her face. "I'm afraid so." He studied her as if he was reading below the surface. "You'll stay here, won't you? You'll watch over Susie for me?"

She nodded. She would stay and care for Daniel's child.

"Miigwech," he said, before he kissed her.

She didn't answer him. She slipped her arms about his neck, and arched up against him, responding to the kiss. Desire flared; her love for him burned inside her, longing to break free in an admission of her feelings. She held it in check, allowing herself the luxury of touching him, kissing him. Until she had her father back and until she was sure of Daniel's true feelings for her . . . and for his dead or missing wife, she would hold on to the secret truth of her heart's desire.

Nineteen

Daniel left her that night with a kiss and a promise to return soon and, if possible, with her father. Amelia clung to him as they kissed. She watched as he hugged his daughter, then slipped away into the night with Black Hawk's band of Ojibwa warriors.

Susie forgot her animosity toward Amelia in her concern for her father. "He'll be all right, won't he, Miss Amelia?" she asked.

Amelia gave her a reassuring smile. "He's with Black Hawk," she said. "He'll be fine." She hoped she was right as she placed her arm around the little girl's shoulders and led her back to the wigwam. "I spoke earlier with your pa. Will you mind too terribly if we go back to the cabin in a couple of days?"

The child met her gaze. "I won't mind."

Her answer surprised Amelia, who had been certain that Susie would want to stay and play with her Ojibwa friends. "I thought it would be a good idea to keep an eye on the house and your pa's shop."

Susie nodded, and united by their concern for Daniel, they continued toward the lodge. Amelia felt hopeful that her relationship with Daniel's daughter would improve.

She hadn't lied when she told Susie she'd spoken to Daniel about returning to the house and shop. Because of her, Daniel had been absent from his home and his business for too long. She wanted to do something in return for him. Although Jack Keller and Rebb Colfax were nearby, Amelia felt it would be better if the house didn't remain vacant. Remembering that there were characters out in the wilderness like Thomas Kertell made her worry about the safety of Daniel's property. Who was to stop even the most innocent visitor from helping himself to some of Daniel's things?

When she'd approached Daniel with the idea of going home, he'd been hesitant at first. Then, to her amazement, he appeared relieved.

"Just stay for two days more until Thunder Oak returns from another village. I'll talk with Black Hawk. I'll feel better if I know that you and Susie will have Black Hawk's brother for an escort."

"All right," she said. "I'll wait." She didn't want to worry him.

"And you'll not leave the trading post until after my return? Not for anything? It's important that you promise me this, Amelia."

"I promise I won't leave. Not for anything."

She was glad she'd made the promise when she saw his relief.

As she'd stared into his blue eyes, she'd been overwhelmed with the magnitude of her love for him. "I'll take good care of Susie," she whispered.

"I know you will." He held her gaze captive. The sun made his blond hair glisten like a halo. His gaze was the most beautiful color of a clear autumn sky. His mouth tilted in a crooked smile.

"Come back safely, Daniel." She loved the way he looked. He was so handsome, he stole her breath. She couldn't think of him without remembering how perfectly their bodies had fit together, how wonderfully he'd made love to her.

His gaze glowed as if he'd shared her thoughts. "I'll be back soon—and with your father."

He didn't say it, but she heard the end of his thought. *If he is there, I'll return him to you.*

"We'll be waiting for you."

And then Daniel was gone. She wanted to go after him and beg him to stay. The realization that he was putting himself in grave danger to help save someone she loved upset her greatly. She felt torn between wanting her father's safe return and wanting Daniel Trahern to remain.

Thunder Oak returned to the village the next afternoon, and it was the day after that he, Two Teeth, and Little Squirrel led Amelia and Susie on the trail that would take them home.

When they arrived at the trading post, they stopped to see Jack Keller first. Jack was surprised, but pleased to see them. "Why good noon to you, little ladies," he greeted Amelia and Susie. He fixed his gaze on the Indians who'd accompanied them.

"Aaniin," Jack said with a nod for each of the braves. He asked after Daniel, and Amelia explained his absence.

"They've found a Sioux village where there were white captives," Amelia said. "He's gone with Black Hawk and a party of Black Hawk's men."

Thunder Oak stood silently behind Amelia as she spoke with Jack and waited for Daniel's key. He said something to Jack in Ojibwa. Jack answered, and the Indian seemed satisfied with his reply.

Amelia looked to Jack, then to Susie, for an explanation of what had been said, but neither offered a comment. Jack turned behind the counter to look for something.

"I don't know how long he'll be gone, Jack."

Jack smiled as he spun back with Daniel's key. "Here you go."

"Thank you." Amelia accepted the key, then with Thunder Oak and his men trailing behind her and Susie, she went to the cabin.

Thunder Oak stopped her from entering the house. He murmured some words in Ojibwa.

"He said he will check the house for unwelcome visitors," Susie said.

"Miigwech." Amelia gazed at the brave. He was a fierce-looking warrior with his head plucked of all hair but for a small tuft on his crown. He was Black Hawk's brother, but he didn't look like Black Hawk or even the other brother, Rain-from-Sky. As savage as he might appear, he'd treated her with nothing but respect. Nervous during the first leg of their journey, she'd quickly lost her fear as Thunder Oak and his friends proved themselves to be helpful and considerate escorts. They stopped whenever she needed a rest, ate whenever she decided she was hungry, and allowed her the privacy she desired when she needed to relieve herself.

Thunder Oak said something to his friends before he disappeared inside the house. One of the other braves apparently went to search out the smithy. The third warrior stayed on the front porch to guard the woman and the little girl. Soon, they all returned and through a series of hand signals and Ojibwa proclaimed both places safe for entry.

Amelia entered, holding Susie's hand, releasing the child's hand only when she herself felt safe. Amelia turned to the warriors with the intention of thanking them, only to note with surprise that they seemed to have settled in for a visit. She looked to Susie for help. Susie, understanding the silent message, spoke to the braves. Thunder

Oak replied, and Susie translated. "He said he will stay until Pa's return."

"Stay?" Amelia echoed. "Where?"

Susie knew the answer without asking. "They will make camp outside the cabin. It is his duty to protect us, and he is an honorable warrior."

Amelia was startled by the Ojibwa's intention to remain. "They're going to set up a wigwam outside?"

The little girl smiled. Thunder Oak said something to Susie, and Susie responded.

"Thunder Oak said that he and his friends would sleep under the stars."

"No," Amelia said. "Tell them they can stay in your pa's shop."

Susie nodded and translated. Thunder Oak stared at Amelia for a long moment, and Amelia gazed back, wondering what he was thinking. Finally, the brave gave an affirmative jerk of his head. He said something to Susie. Susie answered.

"He said that he will stay in Pa's smithy."

Amelia smiled. "Good." It would feel strange to have the warriors around for a time, but she understood and appreciated their concern for her and Susie's welfare. Amelia wondered if Daniel didn't have a hand in arranging this protection.

"Ask them if they are hungry. Tell them I will make them something to eat."

"Giwii-wiisin ina?"

One of the braves answered.

"He said that their bellies are still full from their last meal. If Tree-That-Will-Not-Bend will make food when the sun disappears from the evening sky, they would be grateful to eat then."

"All right," Amelia said, and everyone exchanged smiles.

They followed the river on which they'd learned the Sioux had escaped until they came to some abandoned canoes. There, Daniel, Black Hawk, and his men found tracks leading from the canoes into the wilderness—tracks made by men and horses. The Sioux were the people of open spaces; they used horses overland like the Ojibwa and other woodland tribes used their canoes over the waterways. Bringing their horses into this territory couldn't have been easy. Daniel wondered where they'd kept them during the attack, for he'd seen no sign of the animals. And they'd couldn't have taken them in a canoe.

The party followed the trail for a day and the morning of another until they came to wide-open land, the home of the Sioux Indians. Here the territory seemed drier, dustier, but Daniel decided it was perhaps an illusion produced by the lack of shade. Here keeping their presence hidden would be harder, as the woodland dwellers had mostly rocks and hills to hide behind.

They kept to the forest until dark, before venturing on Sioux land. The encampment was not far, located near a stream. They would check out the village at night, where their presence wouldn't be easy to detect. This wasn't the first Sioux village that Black Hawk had laid siege to, but their plan this day was not to attack, but to learn about the white captives. Later, they would execute a plan to rescue them. They would have to be careful, for the Sioux attacked their enemies at night; they would have guards to protect their own.

The time until darkness dragged slowly for Daniel. His desire to find and rescue Amelia's father and her friend was great. He had failed to find his sister; he would not fail this time. At dusk they moved into the rocky hills, where they drank from their waterskins, ate the pemmican they'd brought with them, and waited without speaking.

The night brought them a glimpse of the cook fire within the Sioux village, a beacon that would lure them directly to the encampment, and allow them a certain amount of light in which to observe the villagers and their captives.

Dressed in dark buckskin jackets, leggings, and loincloths, Daniel and his Indian friends smeared their faces with dark greasepaint, then headed out into the night to spy on the Sioux.

Daniel was gone an awfully long time, and Amelia was worried. She'd stayed close to the cabin and the trading post, tending a small garden she'd found that Daniel had planted, taking orders for Daniel's shop.

She missed him. She felt his presence in everything around her, but it wasn't the same thing. After a week had passed, and he still hadn't returned, she wished he'd come with or without her father. She had a missing father; the thought of Daniel never coming back frightened her as much as if they'd been husband and wife.

Husband and wife. Daniel had had a wife, a wife that he'd lost through tragic circumstances. A wife he couldn't forget until he'd learned the truth of her disappearance.

Amelia felt guilty. She wondered if Daniel's frustration in not finding Jane had made him anxious to rescue her father . . . so he wouldn't feel like he'd failed again.

Just come back to me. You may not want me in any way but the physical, but I don't care. I just want you

*back here and alive. Susie needs you, and I need to know
you're safe . . . even if you can never be mine.*

The situation with their Ojibwa guards had worked well
after the first day of her feeling awkward with them
around. They stayed mostly to themselves, entertaining
Susie when she went in to see them. They took their meals
in the shop, slept in the shop, but spent most of their time
outside, walking about the house, yard, and trading-post
area.

They had stayed for three days when a messenger came
from Thunder Oak's village requesting that the warriors
return. The brave was hesitant about leaving.

"Tell him it will be all right," Amelia said to Susie.
"Tell him we've Jack and guns to protect us, that his first
duty is to his people, who need him at this hour."

Susie translated what she could, and the brave finally
agreed.

"Miigwech, Thunder Oak," Amelia said, as the men
came to say their farewells. She handed him some cakes
she'd made. She'd seen how the Ojibwa had developed a
love of her sweet baked goods.

The fierce-looking warrior grinned, making him look a
bit like a little boy.

"Giminikwe na?" Susie said. She translated for Amelia.
"I asked if he is thirsty."

The brave gazed at Susie with an expression softened
by affection and shook his head.

Amelia thought how wrong the people back East were
when it came to the Indians. They were not savages; they
were people just like the whites. Their skin color was different, and so were their beliefs, but they rarely mistreated
their wives or children. Amelia scowled. Something that
couldn't be said about the "civilized" white men.

As she watched them leave, Amelia realized that she

would miss them. She understood Daniel's concern for the Ojibwa and all Indians who wished nothing more than to live their lives as they have for centuries. She'd learned a great deal from the People. It had been an experience she'd never forget.

Her thought went briefly to her sister Rachel back in Baltimore. Rachel would have been horrified to know that her sister had spent time in an Indian village. Her beautiful younger sibling enjoyed the finer things in life: the creature comforts of living in the city, the attention lavished on her by a series of handsome, sophisticated young men.

Amelia glanced down at herself and smiled. She wore the doeskin dress. Spring Blossom had insisted she take it when she left. Amelia had agreed, because despite her initial feelings about the dress, she'd found the garment more comfortable than her own wardrobe.

The two females were now alone, but for Jack Keller in his trading post across the way. Amelia glanced at Susie and smiled.

"I'm going to miss them," she said.

Susie looked surprised. "You will?"

Amelia nodded. "They've been wonderful to us."

The little girl agreed. "When will Pa be back, Miss Amelia?"

"Soon, Susie, soon."

Tears filled the child's blue eyes, eyes so like Daniel's that at times Amelia found herself looking at Susie because it made her feel closer to the man.

"I miss him," Susie said.

Amelia hugged the little girl to her side. "I miss him, too," she said softly. If he didn't return soon, she'd go out of her mind with worry. She wanted desperately for Daniel to return—with or without her father. She couldn't bear if anything happened to the man who'd become important to her.

"Captain, are you sure this is a good idea?" Private Holton watched as the Indians consumed more and more of the barrel of whiskey.

"Are you questioning my authority?" the officer said.

The younger man was suddenly frightened. His commander was good to the men, but occasionally a streak of meanness would arise out of nowhere in the captain. It was the meanness none of the men understood, but all of them feared. Warned by his fellow recruits, the soldier didn't want to anger his superior. "No, sir. Never, sir. I'm sorry, sir, if you thought that."

The officer's expression lost its fierceness. "Drunken savages are no threat to us, Private. We've got the guns. In their inebriated state, they can barely see their bows, much less shoot an arrow straight."

Holton smiled. "I see your point, Captain."

The captain raised an eyebrow. "I'm glad somebody sees the point, because the red bastards cannot see theirs."

The captain and Holton sat away from the others. The officer had promised that this night would be the night when the private would be initiated into the joys of manhood.

The officer spied his assistant as the man finished refilling the Indians' cups with spirits. Catching his attention, the captain nodded toward the group of slaves that sat, tied up, near the base of a tree. He crooked a finger, and his assistant, understanding the signal, went to the slaves and dragged two to their feet by the ropes binding their wrists at their back. The two slaves were women, one with jet-black hair and white creamy skin, the other was a pale, freckled-faced redhead.

Holton's heart started to thump hard as Lieutenant Rhoades jerked the two women toward where he and the captain sat.

"Private?"

Holton turned to find the captain watching his excitement with amusement.

"Are you ready?"

"Y-yes, sir."

The officer nodded and shifted his gaze to the two women. He was an attractive man, who didn't have to resort to force to gain the attention of women, but he enjoyed the game too much to allow nature to take its course.

"Good evening, ladies," the captain purred. "Nice night for a walk, don't you think?"

The women glanced at each other, unsure what to make of the captain's comments. "Yes, sir," one woman said. It was the raven-haired beauty.

"What's your name?"

"Mary," she said with a shy smile. "Mary Black."

"Untie Miss Black, Lieutenant."

The woman's face brightened as the lesser officer complied with his commander's wishes. "Ah, thank you, sir!"

The officer nodded, before he addressed the redhead. "And your name is?"

The other woman was not inclined to say much. "Cara, sir."

"Untie Cara as well, then take your leave of us."

"Aye, Captain," his assistant said. He didn't seem surprised by the officer's request. Apparently, he was used to doing strange things for his superiors.

"Ah, Cara. Do you enjoy a moonlight stroll?"

She gave a shy, hesitant nod.

"Excellent!" the captain said.

"Holton, choose your partner."

Holton's face reddened as he studied both girls. "Sir, please, I'd be happy if you'd choose first."

The captain stared at the private. Holton was suddenly afraid of creating the man's displeasure. "Cara?" he said, while studying the young girl. "You come with me." He looked at the private. "Holton, Miss Mary Black will go with you."

"Yes, sir."

The two women giggled girlishly.

The couples went in the same direction until they were far from the joint encampment of US soldiers and Sioux Indians.

When the first feminine scream rent the silent night, everyone within the camp, but for the bound captives, were too drunk to hear or to care.

Twenty

"Dr. Dempsey? John!" Miriam Lathom watched with horror as the two savages pulled the doctor from the group of captives and began to lead him away.

"It's all right, Miriam," he said. "Watch over the others. Be careful, and watch yourself."

They had all been taken during the Sioux attack on the mission. Five women, five children, and one man—John Dempsey. They'd traveled for days, by waterway to land, where they'd been forced to walk behind the Indians, who had acquired horses and rode, tugging their captives by ropes. They made few stops along the way. Occasionally, they would stop at an Indian village, where they were given food and water and forced to sit quietly as their captives visited their Sioux brothers, often trading for supplies, before they set off again to some unknown destination. If one of the captives became tired, they were pushed to continue. Thus far, none of the captives had suffered more than a broken bone, a serious complication had it been left untreated. John Dempsey had set the child's arm, and the Sioux had let him. Now the Indians were taking John away.

Miriam and the other women sat huddled together in the shade of a rock overhang. They'd left the forest days ago. They were in a land of barren hills and mountains, and some flatlands covered with short stubby grass. Sometimes, they saw buffalo, large beasts that roamed the plains in great numbers. The days were warm, but the nights were chilly. Miriam's only thought was how to escape and survive the ordeal. For now, her only option was to hang on and pray for a miracle from God to assist them.

They left the area after about an hour and were on their way again. Miriam had no idea where they had taken the doctor, and she prayed for his safe return. Their Sioux captors stopped in another village that apparently wasn't theirs. There was much conversation between the head of their group and the chief of the village. The discussion ended, and the women and children found themselves being inspected by the chief and several of his men. The leader of their captors said something to the chief, who shook his head and muttered something back. After several moments of what seemed to be an argument between the two men, the Indians reached some sort of agreement. Two of the women were taken from the group, along with one child, who cried out to be with his mother.

The chief shoved the child back into the group, then eyed the captives as if looking for another slave. Miriam shivered as she felt his dark eyes glide over her form, leave her, only to return to stare at her.

He barked something at her in Sioux. Miriam stared back without moving. Her heart raced, and her palms felt clammy. She didn't want to stay in the village. As long as she was traveling with the group, there'd be a chance of escape.

She had the choice taken from her when the brave who had captured her grabbed her roughly by the arm and shoved her in the chief's direction. Miriam stumbled and almost fell, but managed to gain her footing at the last moment.

Someone caught her by the arms, holding her so that

she couldn't get away. She saw the chief nod to a young brave, and the brave left, then returned with a single pony. Apparently, the chief had traded a horse for three female slaves and a child.

Miriam watched with a sense of dread as her captors left, taking with them two of her friends and their children. She wondered if she'd ever see them again, if they'd survive the trials yet ahead of them.

"Miriam?" a feminine voice whispered.

The young woman turned and saw it was Fiona York. "Fiona, are you all right?" Her gaze fell to the missionary's leg, which was bruised and swollen, and must be giving her great pain.

"I am healing," her friend said. She hesitated and glanced about, while they waited for direction as to what was expected from them. "What do you think they're going to do with us?"

Miriam frowned. "I don't know."

The two women looked at each other, their expressions mirroring their fear.

"Maybe we can escape when it's dark."

"And go where?" Miriam asked. "I know nothing about this territory, and until we learn something, I think we're just going to have to bide our time and plan our escape later."

Her friend shuddered and hugged herself with her arms. She gestured to the right with an abrupt nod of her head. "I believe we're being summoned."

"Oh, dear."

"Pray, sister," Fiona said.

She did, fervently, as she followed where the Sioux Indian led them.

* * *

"There's been another attack," Jack Keller said.

Amelia felt chilled. "On the mission?"

The trader shook his head. "A settlement about a half day's ride from here." He turned, grabbed a pouch, and shoved it across the counter in Amelia's direction. "You'd better keep this near your gun." He narrowed his gaze. "You do have a gun?"

She nodded. There was the flintlock rifle in the cabin, and she had her father's pistol, the one she'd taken from his bedchamber during the Sioux attack.

"How did you find out?" she asked.

"That young soldier, Cameron Walters," he said. "The fellow came to trade, then left this morning at first light."

"Cameron here?" she asked. Jack Keller nodded. "What did he say?"

"He said that his regiment were on the way to Fort La Pointe when they encountered a fur trapper by the name of Ralph Hewey. The man had come from the settlement just north of Green Bay. The raid had happened the day before. Two men were killed outright. Three women were taken captive before the villagers were able to run their attackers off."

"Where is Cameron's army?" she asked. Had they camped in the same area as they had last time?

"I believe they're at the mission."

Amelia felt a flicker of excitement. "Do you think they've been sent to help?" She picked up the heavy leather pouch.

"The army?" Jack asked. She nodded. "How would they have known?"

"Have there been more Indian attacks on white settlements?"

He seemed reluctant to tell her. "Four, that I've heard."

"Four!"

"Some within this territory, one between here and De-
troit."

"And do you think they're all Sioux?"

Jack frowned. "All Indian attacks. As for them being
all Sioux, I don't know."

"Why?" she asked. "Why are they doing this?"

He shrugged. "For slaves, perhaps. Or the white man's
supplies."

"Is the army at the mission there to protect what's
left?"

"Cameron didn't say. I got the impression that they
were just stopping on their way through."

Amelia became dispirited. "Oh." At the clank of the
Indian deer-hoof rattles that were tied to the trading-post
door to announce customers, she glanced back to see who
had entered.

Susie had been playing right outside on Jack's front
porch. She approached Jack and Amelia with a frown.

"Why, Susie, look how you've grown!"

The child's expression warmed. "You say that almost
every day, Jack."

"Because it's true. You have grown. When your pa gets
back, he'll not recognize you."

Susie looked alarmed. "He won't?"

Amelia reached to touch the little girl's arm. "Jack is
teasing you."

Daniel's daughter looked relieved. "Are you almost
done?" she asked Amelia.

"Yes, sweetheart." Amelia hesitated. "Why don't you
go outside, and I'll be there to join you in just a minute.
I have some unfinished business with this trader."

"All right." Susie left.

"Jack, do you think you could keep an eye on Susie
for me?"

Jack studied her with concern. "Of course. But why?" He narrowed his gaze.

"I'd like to go to the mission and speak with the officer in charge. Maybe he can help us."

"Help us do what?"

"Oh, I don't know." How could she make Jack understand that the feeling of being helpless was getting to her? At least, if she went to the mission, she'd feel like she'd done something. She could talk with the Reverend Whitely and Will, as well as ask for a little help from the US Army. After all, they were there to help, weren't they?

"Amelia, I'm not sure it's a good idea for you to leave the area."

"I'll only be going down the road. I should be safe with the army there, don't you think?"

"Wouldn't it better if you wait to hear something from Daniel?"

"Daniel was worried about Susie, but he can't be worried about her when she's with you. As for me, he was concerned about Indian attacks, but I hardly think the Sioux would attack with the troop of armed soldiers so near." She saw his doubtful expression.

"Please, Jack."

He stared at her hard for what seemed to Amelia like a long time, but must only have been seconds, because Susie hadn't returned to say she was tired of waiting. "All right, I'll watch Susie, but, Amelia—"

"Yes?"

"Take my horse. It'll be quicker and . . ."

"Easier to escape danger?"

He inclined his head.

"Fine, I'll take your horse."

"You do know how to ride?"

"Yes." *A little,* she thought, *but surely enough to get to the mission and back without mishap.*

"When do you want to leave?"

It was still early in the day. "Now?"

Jack didn't look happy about her going. "You'd better send Susie in to me, then."

Amelia agreed. "Jack, I'll be there and back before you know."

"I hope so, Amelia. I sincerely hope so."

The woman went out to the porch to call Susie in and inform the child of her plans.

"He's not there. None of the white people from the mission are there." Daniel battled his frustration as he spoke with his friend. If he returned without her father or any word, Amelia would be devastated . . . and the last person he wanted to hurt was the woman he loved.

"They cannot be far, Dan-yel," Black Hawk said. "We will not return to the village. I will send Thick Head ahead to find where they have gone."

Daniel calculated how long they'd been away. "Can you send word to Amelia?"

"Your woman will be concerned for you."

"Yes, but like you, I don't want to go home yet . . . not until we learn something."

A fire burned in the Ojibwa's gaze. "We will find them, and we will bring them home."

Black Hawk's expression might have frightened Daniel if he had been the object of Black Hawk's anger and revenge. He trusted his friend, but he knew that some dark emotion ate away at the Ojibwa war chief, and he wondered if he'd ever find the peace one needed to be happy.

Black Hawk sent the brave, Thick Head—who had

come with Thunder Oak the last time and had seen the white slaves—as scout to track the group who must have come, then left the Sioux village. The youngest, fastest runner left to get word to the village and the trading post about the delay in their return.

The rest of Black Hawk's band, including Daniel, waited where it was safe and where they could see travelers coming from the east.

The next day, Thick Head returned with the news that they had found another village where at least two white women were seen among the Sioux people.

An hour later, Daniel and the Ojibwa ventured farther into Sioux territory to find the missionaries and John Dempsey.

The soldiers were not at the mission as Jack had been told, but Amelia found Cameron Walters there talking with the minister.

Amelia entered the church after securing Jack's horse. The men were surprised, but pleased to see her.

"Miss Dempsey!" Cameron saw her first and hurried forward to clasp her hand.

"Mr. Walters." She smiled at the man behind him. "Reverend, it's good to see you." Tears filled her eyes as she approached him. "I'm glad you're all right." She caught a glimpse of Will Thornton. "Will, how is your injury?"

"Much better, Miss Dempsey," the young man said with a shy smile. "Thank you for asking."

"What are you doing here, Amelia?" Allen Whitely asked.

"I heard the army was staying at the mission." She frowned. "I guess the news was wrong." Her concern for

Daniel had become a clutching pain beneath her breast. She had to find him. Her father was gone; she couldn't lose Daniel, too. She had to know where he was.

Cameron smiled. "They're not far, Miss Dempsey. We're camped less than a mile from here."

Amelia's expression brightened. "Do you think the army can help find some people—some captives of the Sioux Indians?"

She, with the help of the Reverend Whitely and Will Thornton, explained to the young soldier exactly what had happened on the day of the attack, how women and children were taken . . . and Amelia's father, John Dempsey.

"Daniel and the Ojibwa left over a week ago to see if they could find the Sioux village where the Ojibwa believe the captives were taken. I expected them back days ago, and I'm worried. Do you think your captain will help?"

Cameron looked thoughtful. "The captain has had experience with savages, especially the Sioux," he said. "He'll most likely be interested in assisting you."

Amelia managed a smile. "When can I see him?" There was a chance that the captain could rescue Daniel and her father . . . and the missionaries who were still missing.

"Would you like to see him now?"

The young woman beamed. "That would be wonderful! Thank you." If anyone can help, then surely it would be the US Army.

It wasn't until she'd entered the soldiers' encampment and met the officer in charge that she remembered the horrifying story Cameron had told her about the man shooting an already dead soldier. But it was too late to change her mind. She was here, and there was nothing to do but plead her case, and hope for the best. To her relief, the captain was not the monster she'd thought, but an extremely handsome and charming man.

No doubt Cameron has a new commander, she thought, relieved. Then she pleaded her case.

Twenty-one

They watched the Sioux village from the cover of darkness. Daniel, Black Hawk, and the rest of the Ojibwa band crouched low and observed the noisy scene before them. To Daniel's surprise, there were white men in the village—fur trappers by the look of them. They had given the Sioux liquor; the Indians were drunk. Hooting and hollering, some danced about a central fire, while others passed around a jug. He watched as one brave swigged some spirits, which dribbled down his chin. The warrior next to him grabbed the jug from his friend's hands and drank deeply.

Daniel exchanged glances with Black Hawk, whose face could be seen in the dim light.

"Stupid Sioux who drink firewater," Black Hawk said. His grin shone white in the darkness.

He nodded. It would make it easier for them to enter the village and get out. Turning back to the scene, Daniel looked for a glimpse of white captives. *Where are you, John? Show yourself.*

A high-pitched scream gave the blacksmith goose flesh. He saw the flap of a teepee fly open and a woman run from inside the lodge, chased by a bearded white man. Daniel stared hard, then cursed. *Kertell!* What was he doing here? he wondered. It didn't sit well that the fur trapper was with the Sioux. The trapper staggered drunkenly as he chased the woman. A brave reached out and caught the captive by the arm and laughingly shoved her in Kertell's direction. Angry that the woman had tried to escape, the fur trapper grabbed the woman's arms and held them behind her. Securing her wrists with his hand, he reached around to the woman's left breast and squeezed, the woman shrieked, bucked, and kicked back with her right foot.

Kertell gasped as her heel made contact with his shin, and he released his hold as he reached to rub the pain. The dark-haired woman started to flee. Daniel saw the woman's face for the first time. He drew a sharp breath. *Miriam!* It was the missionary, Miriam Lathom, Amelia's friend. Joy spilled into his heart, and he felt the elation take hold, giving him renewed strength.

He glanced over at Black Hawk. The brave nodded; his dark eyes gleamed. He, too, had recognized the woman.

As several men scrambled to grab hold of the missionary, Daniel started to rise, wanting to help, but Black Hawk grasped his arm and shook his head. His eyes conveyed the message: *Not yet.*

His heart pounding with the need for action, Daniel watched the tussle between the woman and the men. A bellowing roar from a brave exiting a teepee had the men releasing Miriam, who ran off as soon as she was free.

Daniel searched the village for signs of the other missing people: Amelia's father, the other four women, and the children who had been taken.

Kertell laughed as the Indians shoved Miriam from one brave to the next. Miriam stumbled and tripped, but quickly righted herself, only to have someone grab and throw her again.

A regal-looking Sioux warrior called out something as he rose from the circle about the fire. The other braves got quiet, and Daniel suspected that the man held a position of authority, probably the chief. The silence lasted only a minute, as the liquor made the Indians crazy, and they disregarded whatever their leader had to say.

The Sioux got tired of their game with the white woman, and one warrior tossed her to the ground. The brave called loudly for the jug, and there was a tug of war and much laughter as he and another brave battled for the jug until one took a drink then handed it smilingly to his friend. Miriam scrambled to her feet and took refuge in the shadows, safe, at least, for now.

Two of the braves began to chant something loudly. From beyond Daniel's range of vision, two women entered the clearing carrying plates of food, which the warriors snatched away as the females approached. Daniel's pulse started to race as he noted one of the women had cropped blond hair and looked familiar, but he was afraid to hope, to believe. She was thinner than he'd remembered her. Her hair looked as if it had been chopped off with a knife. She wore ragged linen clothes and was barefoot. He stared hard, hoping to get a better glimpse of her face. She turned then, and he could see her blank expression. Something clenched in his gut, for he knew that face. He had almost given up hope; he'd been looking for her for so long.

He touched his Ojibwa friend's arm. Black Hawk started then relaxed when he saw it was Daniel. He frowned when he saw Daniel's expression.

Daniel pointed toward the blond white woman and said one word, which summed up what he'd seen and what he was feeling. *"Nishiime."* My younger sister. "Jane."

A flash of fire entered Black Hawk's jet-black eyes, for he knew Jane's story, and he had been searching, too, for four long years to help his friend.

Although he was disturbed by his sister's appearance, Daniel couldn't help the smile that curved his mouth or the joy of knowing that he had found Susie's mother and would soon be bringing her home.

They remained where they were until the other Ojibwa had slipped silently to a crouch behind their leader, Black Hawk, to wait for his command. Daniel knew that patience had become important if they were to succeed. They would wait until the Indians and the white men were asleep in their drunken stupor, then they would slip into the village, rescue the white captives, and slink out into the night, undetected.

Patience, Daniel thought, feeling everything but.

She shouldn't have come, and worse yet, she shouldn't have allowed the captain to talk her into bringing Susie. Amelia sat on a blanket on the ground, hugging Susie to her side, and watched as the soldiers sat around their campfire, laughing and swapping stories, passing around a flask of whiskey.

Susie shivered. Amelia glanced down at the child and was disturbed by her trembling.

"Susie, are you all right?" she whispered. She was glad they sat in the shadows, away from the attention of the men.

The little girl looked up, and Amelia was disturbed by her look of fear.

"It's all right, sweetheart," she said. "I won't let anything hurt you."

The child didn't speak, but Amelia saw a glimmer of hope in Susie's blue eyes, before she glanced away and burrowed deeper against Amelia's side.

Amelia knew Daniel was going to be furious that she'd

left the cabin, worse yet that she'd taken Susie with her. *I promised, and I broke my promise, putting Susie and myself at risk.*

She thought back to her meeting with the officer in charge of Cameron Walters' army regiment and marveled how the man had convinced her to come—and to bring Susie.

Her gaze went to the captain as he sat there among his men. Captain Richard Milton's good looks and charm had surprised her. He had been so sympathetic to her plight, promising to help her find her father . . . and Daniel who was overdue in his return home. She'd been captivated by his manners and his willingness to help. He had convinced her to come with him, telling her that he needed her to identify both Daniel and her father.

Amelia frowned as she tried to remember how Susie had entered their conversation, how Captain Milton had managed to persuade her that the child would be better off coming, too. As Amelia thought about it now, the idea of bringing a small girl on such a dangerous mission was ludicrous. How had he done it? Convinced her?

She closed her eyes with the realization that Daniel might never forgive her for being so foolish . . . and careless with his daughter's life.

She studied the captain and wondered what sort of man she'd entrusted with their well-being. He watched his men from his position, neither laughing nor partaking of the liquor that was being passed around. There was something vaguely familiar about him, but Amelia had no idea why she felt that way. In her mind, she compared him to a sleek cat, watching his prey, waiting, listening, for the right moment to pounce.

Her thoughts bothered her. When she'd left the army encampment outside the mission, she'd felt so sure, so convinced, that going with the regiment and bringing along Susie was the right thing to do. After all, how much safer could one be than in the midst of a regiment of thirty men?

Susie stirred within her arms, drawing her attention. It was late, and no doubt the child was exhausted. They had come a long way during their first day.

"Susie, sweetheart, why don't we get some sleep?"

Susie flashed her a look of alarm that startled her.

"It's all right. I'll sleep here, right by your side."

Some of the child's fear receded. Amelia saw her glance toward the group of men and look away. She nodded without meeting Amelia's gaze.

Amelia moved then to readjust their blanket and pull a second smaller wrap from the modest-sized satchel she'd brought with them. She didn't know what prompted her to put Susie on the other side of her, away from the men. She decided as she got comfortable that Susie needed to be shielded from the soldiers' bad behavior.

She pulled a blanket to cover herself and the little girl. Then she lay for a moment with her eyes closed, until raucous laughter from the men drew her gaze back to the group—and the captain. Almost as if pulled against her will, her attention focused on the commanding officer. He was almost too good-looking, Amelia thought, and then realized that it was a strange thing to ponder. Her gaze narrowed. It was true, though, she mused. Richard Milton had taken off his hat, but his dark hair looked unruffled, a black wave lying perfectly across his forehead as if it had been coaxed by expert hands.

While the rest of his men looked dirty, their uniforms rumpled, and their dispositions out of sorts, Captain Milton looked pristine and perfect—too perfect, and too polite. As she studied him, the man glanced her way. He stared at her, unsmiling, and she imagined she saw a hint of smugness in his expression. She held his gaze, refusing to be scared or intimidated. His face transformed as he smiled, radiating warmth. He gave her a nod, then turned his attention toward his men.

Amelia felt chilled as she raised the blanket higher around her and Susie, then moved closer to the sleeping child.

She lay curled on her side, facing the fire, wondering how she would sleep when she didn't feel safe, when the soldiers were getting drunker and drunker by the minute, their voices raised in laughter, coarse conversation, and song.

Someone touched her shoulder. "Amelia? Miss Dempsey?"

She gasped, opened her eyes, and flipped onto her back.

"I'm sorry. I didn't mean to frighten you."

"Oh, dear God, Cameron, you startled me!" She felt a rush of relief when she saw it was her friend.

Looking apologetic, he crouched down beside her. "I didn't mean to," he said sincerely. He shot an annoyed glance toward the group of men. "They're acting like drunken fools. I don't know why the captain is allowing this." He had a puzzled look on his face when he turned back to her. His brow cleared as he studied her. "Now, don't you be worrying about them, Miss Dempsey."

"Amelia," she said softly, recognizing Cameron as the only man here she could truly trust.

He nodded. "Well, Miss Amelia," he said, the *Miss* making her smile, "as I said, don't you be worrying. The captain . . . he sent me to look over you. He figured you were frightened and needed me to watch out for you."

Surprised by the officer's thoughtfulness, Amelia shot the man a glance. He spoke to the soldier beside him, then as if sensing her gaze, looked her way. His expression seemed to soften as their eyes locked for several long seconds until another subordinate caught his attention and he looked away. Strangely enough, Amelia felt comforted by the captain's look. She was left with the impression that he was concerned about her and wanted to assure her that she and Susie were safe and would remain so in his care.

"I'll just sit right over there," Cameron said.

She looked at him blankly. "I'm sorry."

He didn't seem offended by her lack of attention. "Don't let them scare you, Miss Amelia. The captain's allowed them their liquor, but he's taken away their guns."

Cameron patted his side where the barrel of a pistol had been tucked into the waistband of his trousers. "But not mine." He smiled. "The captain knows he can trust me."

Amelia nodded. "Thank you, Cameron," she said softly. She felt a little better that he was near. She didn't point out to him that a man's gun alone didn't make him dangerous, that there were worse things a man could do to a woman than shoot her. The truth was that having Cameron as guard was better than not having anyone at all . . . and for that she was grateful.

Miriam found temporary safety in a teepee with a Sioux woman and another white captive. The Sioux woman was an elderly matron, who was kind when none of the warriors was watching and mean when they were. The missionary woman understood Dancing Water's behavior, for she had seen the way some of the Indian men treated their women when they became displeased.

Dancing Water gestured for Miriam to move closer to

the other captive, a white woman with close-cropped blond hair and a blank expression that told Miriam that she must have suffered greatly at the hands of the Sioux. All Miriam knew about the woman was that her name was Jane.

She sat next to Jane, who met her gaze with blue eyes that were shadowed and lackluster. "Jane," she said, "are you all right? Did they hurt you?"

The woman blinked without showing emotion. Miriam got a sense that the pain inside Jane was so deep that she had ceased to feel lest she break down and never be able to recover.

Miriam had been in the village for only a little while. The other woman missionary who had been traded with her was gone, traded yet again to a band of Indians; she wasn't even sure they were Sioux. Miriam had stayed, because Dancing Water had wanted a slave and taken a liking to her.

"I'm all right."

The simple answer was the most Miriam had heard Jane say. She smiled in an offer of friendship. "Do they get like this often?" she asked, as if they were discussing the weather rather than the behavior of a bunch of men.

Dancing Water had left the teepee, leaving her alone with Jane. Miriam waited patiently for Jane, hoping to learn about the woman, the village, and how Jane had come to be in such a sorry state.

"They are bad when they drink whiskey. They drink when white men come and give it to them." Jane's words were stilted as if she hadn't spoken much English in a long while.

Miriam placed her hand on Jane's arm. "You've been with them a long time, haven't you?" she said softly.

Jane looked at her, and a spark of something came into

her blue eyes, the first sign of emotion she'd ever seen from this pale, pathetic woman with the beautiful-colored eyes.

"I've been here forever," she said.

Miriam patted her arm in sympathy. "I'm sorry."

Jane seemed surprised by her apology. "You did not bring me here."

The missionary held her gaze. "Who did?"

Something akin to pain crossed Jane's features, but then it was gone so quickly that Miriam wasn't sure she didn't imagine it. The woman's expression became shuttered, and Miriam had the impression that Jane was closing herself off from the past, the pain. She didn't want to remember, for to remember would be to suffer through her ordeal all over again.

Miriam wanted to be her friend. She shifted to sit where she and Jane faced each other, instead of sitting together side by side. "I'm Miriam Lathom. I was a missionary at Whitely Mission near Lake Superior in the Wisconsin Territory before the mission was attacked and I was captured." By speaking of her own experiences, she hoped that Jane would open up and speak of her own. She had the feeling that Jane desperately needed to talk about what had happened to her.

"I've seen Lake Superior," Jane said. "I spent some of my childhood there in the Michigan Territory. My father was a blacksmith." A soft look came to her expression as she looked inward to what Miriam decided must have been a recollection of happier times. She met Miriam's gaze with eyes suddenly sparked with life—just a tiny spark perhaps, but more life than Miriam had ever seen in Jane's expression. "My brother became a blacksmith, too." Sorrow dulled the blue eyes, but Miriam decided that the sadness was better than the dead look.

"Your brother is a blacksmith?" Miriam encouraged gently.

Jane's features took on a faraway look. "He was," she murmured. A small sob escaped from the woman's throat. "I don't know if he's dead or alive."

Sensing that the woman needed to be held, Miriam again shifted to Jane's side, placed an arm around her. "Won't you tell me about it?"

Jane shook her head.

"You've never told anyone, have you?"

"No."

"And it's eating you alive," Miriam said. "Has been for—"

"For what must be at least three or four years," Jane whispered.

"Four years!"

Miriam's distressed surprise had an unexpected effect on Jane. The woman began to talk for the first time about her experiences.

"I lived in a cabin in the woods. My husband—" Here, her breath hitched, and she seemed to sway with a fresh wave of pain. She inhaled sharply, pulled herself up, and continued. "Richard—he was—is—an officer in the United States Army. He was gone a lot. In fact, after only six months of marriage, I rarely saw him, except when he came home briefly, perhaps once a month for a day or two at a time." She got quiet, and Miriam could see that there was a battle of pain against emotion going on inside of her.

"Did you love him?" Miriam asked.

Jane pulled herself from the battlefield. "I did, at first. He was so handsome." Her expression took on a dreamy look at the memory. "He was so gallant and charming.

He made me feel special . . ." Her voice lowered. "And loved . . ."

Miriam waited for her to go on without saying anything. Jane gathered herself together and managed a weak smile. Miriam had a glimpse into a younger, more carefree Jane, one who would have dazzled a young soldier with the radiance of her smile. She was sure that the officer had been as charmed by Jane as she had been by him.

"It was lonely for me whenever Richard was away. It was hard until he came to visit. Then I felt . . . renewed. It hurt when he went away again, but I knew he'd come back. I lived for his visits. Then, two months went by, then three, and he didn't come. I learned shortly after he'd left that I was with child. I was so happy, and I was sure Richard would be happy, too. In my mind, I could see him asking to be assigned to a fort, where the baby and I could come to live with him." She closed her eyes and shivered. Miriam hugged her harder, began rubbing Jane's arms with her hands.

"He didn't come back, and I got scared. I wrote to my brother, told him that I was going to have a baby." She smiled softly with some other memory. "Danny packed up his things and came to live with me." She met Miriam's gaze with a look that told of her happiness with her brother's decision to come. "I didn't know it, but Danny's wife had died, and he was alone."

Jane frowned with concern for her sibling. "He came, and he seemed so different . . . as if he was afraid to show emotion. I thought he was in mourning, but then I learned later that there was more than that to his wife's death." She settled her hand over Miriam's on her arm. "She died during an act of betrayal," she said. "His wife was running away with her lover when she was killed.

She was with child when she died, and until that day Danny had thought the babe his."

"Oh, dear God," Miriam breathed, feeling the man's pain.

"Danny lived with me before my baby was born and after. I was happy to have him, and he changed after my daughter's birth. He was happy again. He loved Susie. She made him smile and laugh again." Jane smiled, but then her expression went dark. "Danny had been out hunting when they came, wrecked the house—" her breath hitched and her face crumpled "—killed my baby, and kidnapped me."

Miriam's eyes filled with tears as she listened.

"I didn't care anymore after I'd learned they killed my daughter. I wanted to die, wanted them to kill me. When I was raped . . . it didn't seem to matter."

Squeezing her eyes shut, Miriam held on to Jane as if she could help the woman forget the pain. "I'm sorry . . . so sorry," she mumbled.

Jane straightened and composed herself. "I'm all right."

"I don't know how you got through it. I always thought I was a woman of God, but after hearing about your suffering—" She shook her head. "I no longer know . . ." She released Jane's shoulders to clench her fists. "The savages! I always thought the Indians were worth saving, but now . . ."

"Did I say it was Indians who kidnapped me . . . who raped me?" Jane shook her head, and it was then that Miriam realized there was more . . . something so terrible that she wasn't sure she wanted to hear what it was.

"It was my husband's men."

Miriam blanched. *"What?"*

Jane wore a sickly smile. "My home was attacked, myself kidnapped, and my baby murdered by soldiers of the

US Army." She lifted a hand to run it raggedly through her closely cropped hair. "Then, when they were done, and the soldiers joined the Sioux Indians later that day, my husband, Captain Richard Milton—the only man I'd ever loved—raped me in full view of the Indians and a select group of his men."

Her features turned a ghostly shade of white, before Jane screwed up her face in an expression of anger and hatred.

"And he loved every agonizing minute of it."

Twenty-two

Patience paid off, and they crept into the village, slipping by the sleeping Indians and white men toward the teepees beyond the fire. Daniel moved quickly and quietly with the others. Although they had watched and waited for hours, there was no certainty that all danger had gone.

He glanced toward Black Hawk, nodded toward a certain lodge, and continued at an affirmative gesture from his Ojibwa friend. Together, they crept toward one teepee while the others checked another. Their quest was for white captives, all of them. Daniel's focus was to find Jane, John Dempsey, and Miriam, Amelia's friend.

The first lodge they came to was empty, they thought, until they saw the sleeping Sioux woman. They left as quietly as they'd come and went on to the next teepee. Daniel raised the flap, then entered first with Black Hawk following immediately behind him.

Daniel heard a gasp, saw the three women as his eyes became quickly adjusted to the light. One of them was an elderly Indian matron, who stared at them without fear. Daniel turned to the others.

"Daniel!" Miriam gasped.

He grinned in the darkness. His heart began to trip wildly as he recognized the woman beside her. He went to her, crouched low, and gazed into her eyes. His throat felt so tight; he wasn't sure he could speak.

"Jane?" he managed to rasp out. She looked so fragile, so full of pain. It hurt him to know that she'd suffered.

She shrank back toward Miriam and stared at him.

"Jane, it's me," he said hoarsely. "Danny." He used her nickname for him. She was the only one who called him Danny, the only one he'd allow to call him by that name.

"You're Danny?" Miriam asked.

He dragged his eyes from his sister to gaze at the missionary. He nodded.

"She thought you were dead," she said. A look of horror flashed across her face. "She believes Susie is dead."

Daniel's gaze shot back to his sister. Rage tightened his chest, swelled in his heart. He banked it down, for fear of frightening Jane. He reached out carefully, moving slowly so as not to scare her again. He cupped her face gently with his hands, holding her so that their gazes could focus only on each other. "Jane, it's me, Danny, and Susie—your baby—is alive."

She blinked. He could see the emotion warring on her face as she struggled to take in what he'd said, as if she was afraid to believe it, for fear it was some cruel joke that someone had been playing on her once again.

"Daniel," Miriam said. His gaze flew to hers. "There's more—"

"Dan-yel, my friend," Black Hawk interrupted. "We must not linger."

Daniel, meeting his glance, nodded. He released his sister. "Miriam, come on," he said, rising to his feet. He studied Jane, was barely able to focus on the task at hand. He wanted to take her away and hold her . . . to find out how terrible life had been for her and try it banish the horrible memories.

He heard Miriam scramble to her feet, was vaguely aware that Black Hawk was helping the woman up.

"Where's John Dempsey?" Daniel asked Miriam, dreading the answer.

Miriam's expression fell. "I'm sorry. I don't know. They took him away several days ago."

Daniel's gaze sharpened. "But he was alive then?" The woman nodded. "And the others? The women? Children?"

"One child—Johnny Black, Mary's oldest—he's here, but Mary and the others . . ." She looked concerned. "They were taken away . . . traded to another tribe."

"Was John traded, too?" he asked.

"I don't know. I'm sorry."

"Dan-yel."

Daniel nodded toward his friend. "What about her?" he asked, referring to the Sioux woman.

"Please, don't hurt her," Miriam said. "She's been kind to us."

Black Hawk and Daniel exchanged looks. "We'll gag and tie her up, so we have time to get away," Daniel said.

"They won't hurt her, will they?" Miriam looked worried. "I don't know," Daniel said. He needed, wanted, to get away; they'd been here too long already. He ran a hand across the back of his neck in a gesture that only those close to him would recognize as a habit of his when he was frustrated or worried.

A choked sob sounded in the teepee. "Danny?"

He looked down, saw the flicker of recognition in the blue eyes that matched his. He bent down, grabbed her gently by the arms, and pulled her to her feet. "Yes, sweet pea, it's me."

She started to cry softly. He looked at Black Hawk as he picked up his sister. Murmuring to Jane softly, he slipped out of the teepee and into the night.

They hurried from the village, Daniel with Jane, Black Hawk behind Miriam, who walked out on her own. They

met with the others where they'd waited earlier. With
Sleeping Bird, Thick Head, and the others sat a wide-eyed
beautiful little boy. "Hello, Johnny," Daniel said.

Johnny nodded without speaking, but when Miriam
opened her arms to him, the child ran to her for a hug
and some comfort.

Black Hawk surveyed the motley group. "We cannot
stay. The sun will be up in the morning sky, and the Sioux
will soon awaken."

Daniel studied his friend. He knew how much control
Black Hawk was exerting over his own feelings. He hated
the Sioux, wanted to kill them as they'd killed his father.
That he didn't take a single life was a testament to his
concern and consideration for the women and child they'd
rescued.

Jane had stopped weeping and fallen into a state of
exhaustion. She weighed next to nothing, so Daniel knew
he'd have no trouble carrying her as far as Black Hawk
wanted to go.

"Are you all right?" he said, addressing everyone in the
group. "All right, then, let's go."

They left the area, having rescued some, but not all.
Daniel was grateful for finding his sister, but he felt sorrow for the woman he loved, whose father was still missing and out there . . . a captive of the Sioux.

They traveled as quickly as they could, resting only
when they'd entered the forest and journeyed within its
shelter for an hour or more. They stopped and ate from
the food supplies that Black Hawk and the other braves
had brought with them.

Miriam accepted a piece of dried venison gratefully
from the brave Sleeping Bird, then followed a bite of meat
with a draw from the brave's waterskin. She smiled at the

Ojibwa warrior and sat back, took another bite, and closed her eyes as she chewed and swallowed.

She heard movement and sensed it was Daniel who settled down beside her. She opened her eyes and gazed at him. "Is Jane all right?" she asked softly, with sincere concern.

He nodded. "She's sleeping, poor thing." A look of pain crossed his features. "She's been through so much."

Miriam grimaced. "More than you know."

He looked at her. "You started to tell me something," he said. "Back there."

"Daniel, I already told you that she thought her daughter had been killed."

A furrow creased his forehead as he inclined his head. "The savages must have told her they'd murdered Susie."

Miriam shuddered, then hugged herself with her arms. What she had to tell Daniel was too terrible for anyone's imagination.

"Daniel," she said, "it wasn't the Sioux who attacked the cabin and kidnapped Jane."

Daniel frowned. "I don't understand. She was there, with the Indians."

"Yes," Miriam said softly. She placed her hand on his arm, a sympathetic gesture that was not lost on him.

A muscle ticked along his jawline. "Tell me."

"She was kidnapped . . . and raped," she began.

Daniel drew a sharp breath. His gaze flamed with anger.

"—by your brother-in-law."

He tensed, heard the heavy thundering of his own heart. *"What?"*

"Captain Milton ordered a band of his men to attack your home, kidnap your sister, and kill his daughter."

"No!" He stood, his fists clenched. "I'll kill the sonavabitch."

"And he's still alive." Miriam rose to her feet, captured his arm to hold his attention. "He hates the Indians, Daniel. Jane said that he's been playing Sioux against Ojibwa, encouraging an already existing animosity between the two nations. He convinces the Sioux to attack certain white settlements. Small farms he has some of his own men attack themselves. He stages those attacks to look like Indian attacks, so that the Indians—any of the tribes—will be blamed. He wants the government to lose patience with the Indians so they will drive them away, regardless of any agreements or treaties between then. He hates the Indians that much."

Daniel clamped his teeth together. "Bastard!" he hissed.

Miriam agreed. She released his arm, touched his shoulder. He flinched until his gaze came into focus again, his anger under control. "Amelia," she said, "is she—"

The lingering glaze over his eyes cleared. His hard expression softened at the mention of Amelia's name. He looked at Miriam, even managed a small smile. "She's safe . . . at my cabin, watching Susie for me."

Miriam closed her eyes. John Dempsey had been so worried about his daughter, wondering if she were dead or alive. "I'm glad."

Daniel nodded, relieved that through all of this he had that one constant that gave him no cause for worry. Amelia and Susie were at home, watched over by Thunder Oak and his friends, with Jack Keller close by to complete the circle of protection.

Thoughts of Amelia took him from the edge of horror. Images of their lovemaking warmed him, made him anxious to get back to her—the woman he loved.

When he got back, he would have to tell her that her

father was still missing. He would go out again to find John Dempsey, then he would return with Amelia's father so the man could stand by and give his daughter away . . .

After years of denying that he'd ever want to marry again, Daniel planned to take a wife . . . the only woman he fully trusted and truly loved in a way that wasn't brotherly . . .

He was going to spend the rest of his life with Amelia Dempsey. He smiled, felt his loins stir as he thought of her. Amelia Dempsey Trahern.

It was dark, and Captain Milton's regiment had settled in for the night. They had covered a lot of ground that day, and everyone was tired. Cameron Walters assured Amelia that they were getting near the Sioux village where her father—and perhaps Daniel—were captives. The captain had sent out scouts. The men's report had dictated the direction of the day's journey, and while Amelia felt edgy, she thought it had more to do with nervous anticipation in getting near rather than the uneasiness she'd begun to feel because of the officer in charge.

Amelia left Susie's side to seek the privacy of the bushes for relief, before returning to the encampment. It was late, and she didn't expect anyone to be up but her . . . and whichever soldier was on guard duty.

As she broke from the cluster of bushes into the open area of their camp, Amelia froze and felt her heart leap into her throat. Captain Milton had hunkered down beside Susie and was talking to the little girl, who looked terrified. The desire to protect rose up strong within Amelia, and she hurried to Susie's side.

"Captain Milton!" she gasped as she reached the sleeping pallet where the child must have been awakened from a sound slumber. "Susie's not feeling well. It would be in her best interest if you'd let her sleep."

The officer had tensed upon hearing Amelia's voice. "She had a nightmare. I was trying to comfort her." He looked up at her with an expression that seemed too slick, too unnerving to Amelia to convince her that he'd spoken the truth.

"Thank you, sir, but I'll talk with her now."

The captain stared at her hard. "I have a right to talk with her," he said, sounding petulant.

"She's a child, Captain Milton. A little girl. Little girls are often frightened by big men."

He opened his mouth as if he was about to say something, but then closed it again. "I'll leave her to you then," he said tightly. He rose, brushed off his pants, and moved away, back to his own bedroll.

Relieved, Amelia turned to Susie. "Susie, sweetheart," she said, holding out her arms. But Susie wouldn't move. She stared without seeing, her expression terror-stricken. When Amelia touched her, the child flinched, whimpered, and shrunk back away from her touch.

"Susie, did you have a bad dream?" she asked, keeping her voice soft.

Susie gazed at her, shook her head.

"Did that man—Captain Milton—" Amelia bit her lip. "Did he frighten you?"

The little girl nodded. Suddenly Susie reached out, grabbed Amelia's arm, her little fingers biting into flesh, her eyes filling with tears. "Bad man," she said, before she released her grip.

"Come here," Amelia said, offering her embrace.

Susie gasped out a sob as she flew into Amelia's arms and clung to the woman tightly. "Bad man. Bad men."

"I'll protect you, Susie." Amelia felt her own eyes sting

with the onset of tears. The poor child. How could that brute of a man frighten a little girl so? "I'll not let anyone hurt you."

Her sense of foreboding intensified. She had been feeling more uneasy with each passing hour. She'd dismissed the notion that the captain was at the root of her unease, convincing herself instead that it was the fact that each hour they'd traveled deeper and deeper into dangerous Sioux territory.

Funny, she thought as she hugged Susie tightly and nuzzled her face in the child's hair, *how the captain doesn't seem the least concerned or frightened of encountering Indians.*

It happened again. Amelia caught the captain with Susie during a brief rest midmorning the next day. She hurried to Susie's defense.

"Captain Milton!" she exclaimed. "I've already asked you to leave Susie to me." She frowned as she saw how frightened the child was of the man. "Why do you persist in bothering her?"

To Amelia's shock, the captain rose to his feet and roughly caught her arm. "Woman!" he growled. "I've got a right to speak with my daughter!"

Amelia gazed at him with disbelief. "Your daughter?" she replied. "Why that's ridiculous! She's not your daughter. She's—"

"Daniel Trahern's?" The man laughed harshly. "That child is no more Daniel Trahern's than she is yours." His light gaze glinted with an eerie light. "She's mine. Mine and Jane's."

Jane! "Are you saying that you . . . that you had a child by Daniel's wife!" She gaped, so startled by his tale that she wasn't sure how to react.

His laughter was almost maniacal. "Daniel's wife. Jane isn't Daniel's wife. She's his sister!"

Amelia glanced past Milton to study the little girl. "I don't believe you!" she hissed. She couldn't believe him. Susie was Daniel's daughter; she called him Pa. Amelia had referred to Susie as Daniel's daughter, and Daniel had never corrected her.

Captain Milton had to be lying . . . or else Daniel had lied to her.

She stared at Susie, then looked at Richard Milton. There had been something vaguely familiar about him . . . but Susie's father? *"No!"*

"I believe we're safe now," Daniel said to Miriam and his sister. "We're too far from the village for them to catch up with us—at least tonight."

Black Hawk and his men didn't have much to say. Miriam studied the Ojibwa leader, then focused her gaze on each of the braves. She felt safe among them. After her experience with the Sioux, she would have thought she'd feel afraid, but she wasn't. Her glance fell on Sleeping Bird, who had shared his food and water with her. She smiled at him, but his expression didn't change. She closed her eyes and leaned back against the tree, deciding that what she needed was rest, not to satisfy her curiosity about the Ojibwa.

"Sleep," she could hear Daniel urging his sister. "It'll be all right. I'll protect you. Nothing is going to hurt you again."

"How interesting that you should say that at this very moment," a stranger's dark voice said.

Miriam's eyes flew open. She heard a gasp, saw Daniel and the Indians spring to their feet. She turned her head, and felt a burning in the pit of her stomach. Indians and soldiers. And they didn't look friendly.

Daniel cursed as his hand reached for his pistol.

"I wouldn't try it, if I were you," the soldier said.

There were four soldiers and at least ten Indian braves. Daniel caught Black Hawk's glance and saw that what he'd feared was true. The Indians were Sioux. The soldiers, for reasons of their own, were the enemy.

"What do you want?" he asked.

The soldier who had spoken stepped out of the shadows and into the firelight. "You," he said with an evil smile. "Every one of you."

Twenty-three

Susie woke up, screaming. Amelia scrambled closer to her on the pallet and pulled the child into her arms. Tears filled the woman's eyes as she rocked the little girl.

"It's all right, sweetheart," she murmured. Susie's pain made her throat tighten. "It was just a bad dream."

Susie clung to Amelia and wept. Amelia's gaze fastened on Captain Milton and hardened. He was responsible for Susie's nightmares. That day, despite Susie's tears and Amelia's protests, the captain had made Susie ride on the saddle in front of him. He claimed it was his right as a father to have his daughter with him. Amelia wasn't convinced that Susie was his daughter, although he seemed to know a lot about Daniel and Susie's mother, Jane.

As she held the child tightly, Amelia debated what to do. She shouldn't have come with the army. She didn't even know if the captain was helping her as he'd said. She no longer trusted anything he said . . . no longer trusted him.

The captain sat by the fire, staring into the flames. Did the man never sleep? The rest of the men were sleeping, but perhaps for one soldier out there in the night somewhere keeping guard.

I don't care what he says tomorrow, Amelia thought, *I'll not let him have Susie. I'll not let him have this precious, frightened little girl.*

Once Susie had quieted within her arms, Amelia lay the child on the sleeping pallet. Susie cried out, unwilling to be released, and with soft words of comfort, Amelia wrapped her arms about Susie and stretched out so that the two lay together side by side, Amelia holding Susie against her breast.

I'm sorry, Daniel. I should have listened to you. I should have stayed at the cabin. She had lost her father; she hadn't been able to bear the thought that Daniel might have been captured, too. She'd had to know. She'd had to help him.

But all I did was put Susie and me in danger. I shouldn't have listened to the captain. I should have gone with my instincts and left Susie with Jack. Her tears filled her eyes to overflowing.

I'll never forgive myself if something happens to Susie. She would protect her with her life. She'd even kill if she had to. Nothing was going to happen to this child, she vowed silently.

A commotion woke her at first light. Amelia released the still sleeping child and sat up to see what was happening.

A young soldier walked by on his way to the bushes.

"What is it?" she asked him.

He gave her a smirk. "We've got company. Jed, Rob, and Mack and some Injuns with their captives." Acting as if such visits were commonplace, the soldier continued on his way.

Captives? Amelia thought. She rose to her feet and strained to see. The regiment had gathered a group. The captain was gone from his usual place by the fire. She assumed he was at the head of the regiment greeting the newcomers. *Who are Jed, Rob, and Mack?* she wondered.

Susie made a sound as she started to wake. Amelia

hunkered down to draw the child into her arms. She stood, holding Susie.

There was laughter among the men. The thought of the Indians bothered her, but she waited without moving, clutching Susie as if the child would give her comfort.

The sea of men parted and revealed the captain before the group swarmed together again. Amelia saw the captain heading in her direction. He met her gaze, and she didn't care for the look on his face.

"Well, Miss Dempsey, it seems we have one problem solved, at least."

"Problem?" she echoed, feeling uneasy.

"Daniel Trahern."

She felt a rush of relief so great she became light-headed with it. "Daniel? You know where he is?"

Without a change in expression, Captain Milton nodded.

"Why, that's wonderful!" she gushed. "How did you learn of this? By some of your men?"

The officer nodded slowly, and Amelia didn't like the sudden slow smile that curved the man's lips as he glanced back to his regiment.

"Where is he?" she asked, wondering if she had reason to be grateful to this man after all. "When can we rescue him?"

"I'm afraid that's impossible."

Her heart tripped. "Excuse me?"

"He can't be rescued."

Horror balled in throat, waiting to be released. "Why?" she cried.

Richard Milton removed his hat and studied the brim as he ran a finger around the felt edge. "Because, Miss Dempsey, like you and Susie, Daniel Trahern and a few others are now my prisoners."

"Your prisoner!" she gasped.

He turned, and as if he'd commanded it, the sea of men parted once again, and there stood Daniel, tied up and looking disheveled, but no less handsome . . . no less than the man she loved.

Her gaze flew to the captain. "I don't understand." She felt weak and stumbled, but she held on to Susie as she righted herself.

"It's quite simple, my dear. You and your"—he glanced toward Daniel with a grimace—"blacksmith have bothered to stick your nose in where it's not wanted. But now the cards are in my favor."

Amelia felt herself pale as she looked at Daniel. He still hadn't seen her at the edge of the clearing. When he did, she realized, he wouldn't be happy.

Just then, he turned and found her. He stared a long moment at her and disbelief entered his expression as he slowly recognized her. His disbelief turned to shock, then to anger as he looked at the captain, before his hardened gaze fastened on Amelia once again.

"Daniel!" she whispered, and she started to rush forward.

Milton grabbed her arm, squeezed it until she cried out in pain. "I'm afraid not, my dear. I'll not have you two together, not until I have what I want from each of you."

Amelia shivered. And what was that? she wondered. As she turned back to gaze at Daniel, she found that the man she loved was studying her with a look that could only be described as hatred.

Her stomach burned. Her head spun, and she reeled with the dizziness. "No," she gasped.

Milton grabbed Susie just as Amelia stumbled and fell to the ground. As darkness enveloped the world around her, she was conscious only of the sound of the man's wicked laughter and the weeping of a little girl.

No, Susie, don't cry, she thought as her mind began to fade. *I'll protect . . . you.*

"Amelia?" a soft voice urged. "Wake up, Amelia."

Amelia groaned softly. She had a splitting headache. She wanted to open her eyes, but couldn't.

"Amelia."

She recognized that voice. It was Miriam's. Father must have a patient, she thought, and he needs my help.

She cracked open one eye. "Miriam?"

The woman's face swam in and out of focus. As she struggled to see, Amelia was able to make out her nod. "Tell Father I'll be right there," she said groggily. She attempted to get up, but her head swam and she fell backward.

A warm feminine hand held her down. "Don't move. Give yourself a few moments," Miriam said.

Without opening her eyes, Amelia nodded.

"Is she all right?" The voice sounded as if it belonged to an Indian. *Black Hawk,* Amelia thought.

"She'll be all right in a minute," Miriam replied. "She's had a terrible shock. I'm not sure, but I wouldn't be surprised if her ordeal was as bad as ours."

As ours. Amelia frowned. What were they talking about? Ordeal? What ordeal? Why was Black Hawk here? Where was Father?

She allowed herself another second to regain her balance, then she opened her eyes . . . and understood instantly where she was and how she'd gotten here.

She closed her eyes again. "Daniel."

"He is here, little one," Black Hawk said, "but he is . . . busy."

She lifted her eyelids and encountered compassion in

the Indian's dark gaze. She shivered. Her gaze swung from Black Hawk to Miriam on the other side of her. Miriam's expression was filled with pity. "He hates me."

"He is angry," Black Hawk said. Amelia looked at him. "He thought you were safe. It almost killed him to know that you are here . . . with the soldiers."

With Susie, she thought. He would never forgive her for involving Susie.

Tears filled her brown eyes and spilled over. "I'm sorry." Miriam touched her hair. Amelia grabbed her arm. "Please! Tell him that I'm sorry. I shouldn't have come. I shouldn't have brought Susie."

How could she make them—him—understand that the captain could be utterly convincing when he wanted to be? The perfect picture of charm, he had swept away her fears and persuaded her that it was in her and Susie's best interests to entrust their lives to his army regiment. How wrong she'd been to trust him, she thought as the sobs started to come from deep in her throat. How, oh, so, wrong . . .

Black Hawk stared down at the weeping woman, then slipped away to talk with his friend. He found Daniel under a tree, gazing off into the distance. Captain Milton had untied him and all the other prisoners. It had amused the officer to see the main players interact with each other, to see the anger and the theatrics played out before him.

Daniel didn't turn when Black Hawk approached. The Indian took a place by his friend's side. "She is awake, but crying."

There was no comment from his friend, not that Black Hawk expected one. He knew how much anger simmered beneath the surface of Daniel, but he also realized that some of that anger, whether the man liked it or not, was rooted in his concern for Amelia Dempsey.

"Susie is with her mother," the brave said.

Daniel turned then. "How is she?"

"Both are doing well. Little Flower recognized her mother right away." Black Hawk smiled. "They have not let go of each other."

The blond blacksmith's eyes became misty. "I never thought I'd find her, Hawk. She's been gone such a long time."

Black Hawk understood that his friend referred to his sister. It had been a shock for Daniel to see her, a reason for great joy. A knot of anger began to burn in the pit of his stomach. How could it have happened? He had not heard them coming . . . four smelly white men and a band of nasty Sioux. He had failed Daniel, failed his own men. Sleeping Bird had escaped, but how could he leave their rescue entirely to one brave?

"No," Daniel said, touching Black Hawk's arms. "I can read your thoughts, and you are wrong. I should have heard them, but I was tired." He held Hawk's gaze. "We were both tired."

"It is no excuse. I have failed you, failed my people."

"You found Jane," Daniel said. "And Miriam."

"But now we are all captives." Hawk frowned. "Except Sleeping Bird."

Daniel allowed a spark to enter his blue eyes. "This day is early yet, my friend. We will get away before the night is late."

Black Hawk felt a flicker of shock. Since when did he—Black-Hawk-Who-Hunts-at-Dawn—give up so easily? Daniel was right. He was tired.

In the near distance, they could hear Amelia sobbing. From another direction, they could hear the satisfied laughter of the men.

"You will have to talk with her," Black Hawk said,

drawing Daniel's attention. It was then that Daniel realized that he had turned and was staring in Amelia's direction.

He scowled. "I have nothing to say to her."

"But she has much to say to you."

"I'm not interested."

Black Hawk raised his eyebrows. "Ah, but I think you are. A man's heart does not stop beating for his mate, just because she has done something to displease him."

"Displease me!" Daniel boomed. "For God's sake, Hawk, she broke her promise. She put not only her life but Susie's in the hands of these"—he grimaced—"men."

"She did it with a good heart, Dan-yel."

"She does not have a heart—just like Pamela. You think you can trust one, then you realize that you're a fool to trust any of them."

"You are a hard man, my friend," Black Hawk said.

Daniel's blue eyes glinted. "She has hardened my heart again, Hawk, and I'll not allow it to soften for anyone but Jane . . . and Susie . . . and my Ojibwa friends."

Amelia peered into the darkness to find Daniel. The day had turned into night. The soldiers had taken them west, toward the village from where the others had escaped. They'd been forced to walk, almost dragged behind the soldiers' horses and the Indians' ponies. Jane was allowed to ride. The captain put her before an Indian, while he took the woman's weeping daughter. Susie had cried until she'd received a slap from her father. The child had whimpered for a moment, then become quiet.

Susie's and Jane's unhappiness along with Daniel's intense anger and contempt for her ate away at Amelia's heart. She loved Daniel and regretted what she'd done. She loved Susie. She didn't know the child's mother, but felt that she and Jane could have been friends if circumstances had been different.

It was true. Amelia had learned from Miriam that Susie was, in fact, Richard Milton's daughter, that Jane was Daniel's sister and not his wife.

As she struggled to fight her self-pity, Amelia knew somewhere in the back of her mind was her own anger with Daniel. He had lied to her, made her believe that Susie was his daughter, that Jane was his loving wife. She had been led to think that the man she loved was so grief-stricken over the loss of his wife that he'd never find it possible to love—or desire—another.

Oh, but he had desired her, Amelia thought, recalling the passion of his lovemaking. He had desired her, and he'd taken her . . . even if he hadn't been happy about it.

Had Daniel been married? Or had that been a lie, too?

Did it matter if he had been? He didn't want her; he hated her, because she'd broken his trust, put those that mattered most to him in danger.

Amelia rose to her feet to get a better view in the darkness. *My father is missing and may be dead, but all I can think of is you,* she thought. *You!*

It had always been Daniel, she realized. She could have stayed in the cabin if she'd known that he was all right, but she hadn't known. His continued absence had made her believe the worst . . . and she hadn't been able to bear it. She would have gone again with the soldiers if she thought her going would give her a chance to find Daniel, to see that he was all right. Her biggest mistake was not in leaving, but in taking Susie with her.

She understood now what had motivated the captain to persuade her to bring Susie. She realized, too, why the man had been so convincing. He was a consummate actor, and he had much at stake . . . his relationship with his daughter.

Only Milton was going about it the wrong way. He'd never get Susie to come to him willingly, to want him as her father, if he continued to frighten and force his wishes upon her.

She saw Daniel there, in the night, leaning against a tree, not far from the others, yet all alone.

Amelia started to approach him, wondering if the captain or any of the soldiers would see and stop her. If the captain's Sioux Indians saw her, would they, too, try to stop her?

It didn't matter if they did. She had to try. It had been a hellishly long day. She needed to talk with Daniel. He didn't want to see or speak with her, but it didn't make a bit of difference to her. She deserved a chance to give her side of things.

She slipped from the area where her sleeping pallet lay near Miriam's bed toward the spot where most of the male captives lay within a fair distance to the army guard. There was a large tree near the men. Daniel leaned against the back of the tree, while most of the others lay crowded several yards from its other side. It was as if all of them had sensed Daniel's fierce anger and had chosen to distance themselves from him.

Amelia was ready now to face his fury. She'd had over sixteen hours to think about it, to prepare herself to encounter the full force of his ire. She wanted to do it now, before she changed her mind and took the coward's way out.

It wasn't until she got closer to him that she saw that Daniel's arms were tied behind his back, but she couldn't tell if his ankles were bound. *Well,* she thought, *if they*

*are, he'll not be able to run away. He'll have to stay and
listen.*

She hunkered down beside him. He didn't move, and
she wondered if he slept, wondered if she should wake
him. Amelia stared at him, drinking her fill of his handsome features . . . his tousled blond hair . . . the furrow
across his brow, as if he slept with painful thoughts.

She swallowed as her gaze drifted to his eyelashes then
to his masculine nose . . . his sensual lips. She shivered,
remembering how that wonderful mouth of his played
havoc with her senses . . . her flesh.

She reached out to touch him, hesitating before her fingers made contact with his jaw. Her eyes misted, and a
lump formed in her throat. She loved him. With all of her
heart, she loved him, but he hated her . . . everything
about her.

She closed her eyes, felt the wave of pain that made
her gasp and shudder. She hugged herself with her arms
and rose to leave, to return back into the night.

A hand clamped on her arm. She shrieked and spun to
see who it was that held her. Her eyes widened and she
trembled.

It was Daniel who had the painful hold of her arm,
Daniel who gazed at her as if she was the lowest form
on earth . . . his enemy. Somehow, he had managed to
unfasten the ropes that had bound his wrists. His grip on
her flesh was like a manacle of hot steel.

Twenty-four

"Daniel!" she breathed.

"You were leaving so soon?" His blue eyes glared at her without affection, without the least bit of the admiration she'd come to appreciate in his gaze.

"I thought you were asleep." She struggled to pull away, but he refused to release her.

"Here?" he said mockingly.

"Please," she gasped, "you're hurting me."

"You'll stay if I let go of you?"

She stared at him, nodded.

He released her, and she rubbed her sore arm.

For a long time, neither spoke. Their silence was painful to Amelia. She wanted to crawl onto his lap and beg his forgiveness. She wanted to grab him and kiss him, then pull him down to lie on her. She wanted, needed, to feel him deep inside her.

Never again. The thought made her clench her eyes tight and nearly cry out with the pain. *Never again will he love me.* If he'd ever felt anything remotely like love for her while they'd been passionately involved, she thought.

She could feel him staring at her in the darkness. She studied him, shivered at his dark look. This was her chance to explain, and she had yet to start telling him.

She held her breath; she released it in a shuddering sigh. "I'm sorry," she whispered brokenly. "I'm so sorry."

Their eyes locked and held in the darkness. There was enough moonlight to see that Daniel's glittering gaze held no warmth. Amelia reached out to touch him, saw him flinch when her fingers brushed his arm. She drew back as if burnt.

"I shouldn't have brought Susie," she said.

His gaze narrowed. "You made a promise," he replied after a long moment of silence. "You broke that promise. You destroyed my trust."

"Daniel—"

"Why?" he said brusquely. "What possible reason could you've had for leaving the cabin?" She saw his hands fist on his lap. "In leaving with the man—"

"Captain Milton."

"I know who he is!" he rasped.

A surge of anger rose behind her pain. "That's right, you do, don't you?" She looked at him accusingly. "He's Susie's father." She grabbed his arm. "Not you. Richard Milton!"

His arm muscles balled beneath her fingers. He glanced down at her grip as if she were poison and he wanted to be rid of her, but she didn't release him. She couldn't let go of the warmth of his flesh. At the moment, it was the only thing that was warm about him.

"You talk about trust," she said, "yet you couldn't trust me with the truth." Her anger dissipated, and the pain rose to choke her. "You couldn't trust me with the truth," she repeated in a rasping whisper. "You never trusted me." Tears filled her eyes, but she made no effort to dash them away.

Her voice broke as she continued. "You led me to believe that Susie was your daughter . . . that Jane was your wife . . . the woman you'd never get over loving." The tears slipped down her cheeks. "All along Jane was your sister and Susie your niece." She allowed a flash of anger to shimmer through her tears. "You were never married, were you?"

Emotion worked on his face as he stared at her. "I was married."

She felt a flicker of surprise.

"But I'm not about to discuss Pamela with you."

Amelia closed her eyes. *Pamela*. He was married and his wife had a name.

"I don't know what I can say to make you understand," she said. *Because you were gone, and I was so scared, so frightened that something had happened to you. That you'd never return.*

"What possible reason could there be for putting a little child in danger?"

"I didn't know she'd be in danger!" she cried.

He shook off her hand, grabbed her by the shoulders. He dragged her closer so he could glare into her eyes. The heat between them sizzled and burned.

"You didn't trust me to find your father. You wanted to come; and when I wouldn't let you, you decided to get that scum over there to help you. Admit it." He shook her until her teeth rattled. "Admit it!"

"All right!" she gasped. "I admit it. I did go to the captain for help—"

He thrust her away from him in disgust.

"But it's not what you think!" she cried.

"I don't want to hear any more."

She realized then that she'd do anything to make Daniel listen. It had become suddenly more vital than her own life that Daniel understood and believed her. If he heard her out, then sent her away, at least, she would have had the satisfaction of knowing she'd had her say.

"Daniel, please, you must listen to me." She no longer cared if the captain or any of his men heard her. She scrambled back to him on her knees, latched on to his arms.

He didn't move. He was unyielding. Despite her hold on him, he wouldn't look at her or acknowledge her, not even by shoving her away. His rejection, his adamant refusal to listen, was more than she could bear. She began to sob his name, begging him to listen to her.

"Please, Daniel," she cried. "Please, listen to me."

Daniel held himself firmly in check as Amelia begged and pleaded to be heard. He'd heard enough, he thought. He was furious with her; he'd never known such fury. It curled in the pit of his stomach; it shook him to the depths of his soul.

He wanted her. Damn, but he wanted her despite her lying, deceiving heart. She'd done the unthinkable, put herself and Susie in the heat of danger. She was selfish, just like Pamela. He shook his head; he didn't particularly want to think of his dead wife.

As Amelia's soft cries hammered at his ears, he realized that it was Amelia's safety that caused him the most worry. Despite the fact that Milton was a monster, he didn't think that Richard would actually stoop to hurting his own daughter. Maybe his wife, but not an innocent child.

But Amelia . . . with her glistening brown hair, sparkling eyes, and pink lips. She was a woman whom Milton would enjoy. Daniel's jaw clenched. The thought of his brother-in-law's hands touching Amelia's skin, kissing her mouth . . . *raping her* . . . made him want to strike something.

The night was quiet but for her. No one had heard them; everyone was sleeping. He looked down at her. She lay against him, crying softly, pitifully. Something stirred in his gut. He was angry, but his anger was rooted in his concern for her. Seeing her within Milton's clutches nearly destroyed him.

He loved her.

He didn't want to love her; he didn't want to be that vulnerable again.

Daniel grabbed her arms to angrily thrust her away, but he found himself lifting her instead, slowly, carefully, so that their bodies brushed against each other and their faces were even. He shifted her so that she straddled him.

She whimpered. He didn't want to feel sorry for her; he didn't want to care that she was hurting . . . and that the reason for her pain was him.

She seemed to realize that he'd moved her. She stopped crying, gazed at him with watery eyes, and he heard her gasp at the fury she must have seen in his expression . . . the fury and the desire . . . for his body had hardened with a mind of its own.

From somewhere in his thoughts came the notion that it wasn't just lust driving him at the moment, but he refused to recognize it.

"No, Daniel," she gasped with fear in her eyes.

She must have seen some of the violence in his gaze. He felt violent, was ready to explode at the least bit of provocation. She blinked, struggled to get away, but he tightened his grip. Her bid for escape only empowered him. It inflamed him all the more.

"No."

He pulled her closer, so that her breasts were crushed against his chest. "Yes," he said. He could hear her little gasps in his ear.

"Daniel, ple—"

Her cry was muffled by his lips as he crushed her mouth, tasted her sweetness. He filled himself with her fragrance, her flavor. No matter how hard he tried to get closer to her, it wasn't enough.

He dragged his mouth from her lips to her throat, nipped the throbbing pulse there. She moaned and ceased to fight, and he knew he'd have her . . . not slow and easy, but fast and hard. Just like his anger.

He dipped his head, encountered the neckline of her gown, and released her long enough to rip the bodice off one shoulder. He would have torn the dress free, but he knew the damage would be too noticeable. She'd have nothing to wear when it was over, and she'd be exposed and vulnerable to Milton's men.

As his fingers fumbled to undo the buttons of her bodice, he wondered if Milton had seen Amelia leave her bed to come to him. As he jerked open the gown to expose her chemise, he hoped that if anyone was awake, they were truly blocked from view by the tree . . . and that no one would decide to check on him.

The thought spurred Daniel on to urgency. He grabbed hold of the chemise collar and jerked it downward to expose her white breasts. He fastened his mouth on a dark pink nipple.

She cried out, and fearing discovery, he reared back and clamped a hand over her mouth. She stared at him with glazed eyes; fear and passion warred with each other to shimmer in the brown depths.

"Don't make a sound," he growled. "Do you hear me?"

Her eyes widened as she stared at him. The haze in her expression started to lift. He released her mouth, and his gaze narrowed as it followed the path his hand made as it trailed down to her breast. He took her nipple between his fingertips, pinched it, then when she gasped, he softened his touch, rubbing the sensitive nub until it perked up and the passionate glaze returned to her eyes.

"You were made for this," he whispered. He transferred his attention to her other breast. "See how you respond to me?" His eyes gleamed. "You hate me with your mind right now, but your body . . . your body is telling me something else."

Amelia stifled a moan as Daniel played her body with the expertise of one who knew exactly how to please her. She gasped when he latched on to her nipple with his mouth, bit lightly, then laved the sensitive nub with his tongue.

There was leashed violence in his movements. It was as if any moment it would erupt and send him hurtling over the edge. Her anticipation became laced with excitement at the danger. She jerked when his hand slipped into her gown to her belly, where he splayed his fingers as if stating his possession of her. He rubbed her skin, then groaned, as if frustrated with the constriction of fabric, and pulled his hand out.

She was aware of the dampness on her breasts and nipples. She gazed at him, but could barely see for the passionate haze clouding her own vision.

He dipped his head again to suckle her breast, drawing upon the nipple hard. Her hands floundered in the air, then her fingers settled in his hair as she clutched him to her. Her head fell backward as sensation after sensation poured through her. Hot pleasure spiraled in her core and fanned outward. As the pulsing waves continued to spread, she found it difficult to think, to breathe. She tried not to cry out, felt the scream building in her throat, looking for release.

No! she thought. She couldn't control it. The pleasure

was too dark, too strong. As if sensing that she'd had enough, Daniel let go of her nipple. She shuddered and gasped in air, but then he was attacking her damp breast's twin. Using lips, teeth, and tongue, he continued the pleasure. She felt the cry rising again with the ecstasy . . . the pleasure-pain.

Her gasping moan was captured by his mouth. The heat of his breath filled her nostrils. The wild masculine scent of him drugged her, bullied her into a world of mindless bliss.

He raised his head and touched her already sensitive breasts. He shifted her on his lap and she could feel the male bulging heat of his desire.

He jerked his hips a bit, and her eyes widened as the shimmering sensation was compounded by the ache in her groin area. "Daniel," she breathed, shivering in his arms.

Daniel studied Amelia, and smiled darkly. She had her head thrown back, exposing the long lovely line of her throat. He could hear her panting breaths. His gaze dropped to the rise and fall of her wet, swollen breasts.

A sound from the camp behind him reminded him where they were, who they were with . . . how precarious their position was.

They were making love in the midst of villains.

If he didn't have her soon, he feared the moment would be lost for him to ever have her again.

He pulled her forward, cradled her face with his hands, and kissed her, a hot mating of tongues that spoke of his desire to possess her, to punish her.

She whimpered softly beneath his mouth. While he continued to kiss her, he slid his hand down her side, over her skirts, along hip and thigh, past knee and calf to the hem of her garment. Bunching the fabric in his fist, he began to raise the fabric, baring leg, then thigh. He didn't stop kissing her; he didn't pull away and look down, for he knew that the sight of her nakedness would unravel him.

He delved his fingers into her secret warmth. She bucked and tightened her leg muscles. He found her nub, and rubbed it gently but with friction, until she shuddered, and his mouth caught her wild little cry as she soared into a climax.

He could feel her shock. He caught her jaw, made her look at him. He sent her a look that told her he wasn't done with her yet . . . not by a long shot.

Another sound pierced his consciousness. He saw by Amelia's horrified expression that she'd heard it, too. Someone had moaned in his or her sleep.

Amelia started to get up, but he held her down, caught her gaze, then kissed her deeply.

The noise beyond their intimate world had filled Daniel with the urgency to have Amelia now, to take her.

He jerked up her skirts just as he raised his head. He sensed Amelia's surprise at his roughness, but it didn't matter. The throbbing heat of wanting her propelled him to continue.

He kissed her, delving deeply with his tongue, while he worked with one hand to undo his loincloth. His fingers fumbled at the string on this side, but couldn't find the knot. He lifted his head, cursed, and shifted Amelia so that he had access to his other side. Then, his lips fastened on her left breast as his fingers made quick work of the string.

He lifted Amelia, brushed the breechclout out of the way, then lowered her quickly until he had fully impaled her on his staff and felt himself throb painfully in the moist softness between her thighs.

Daniel bit back a groan as he felt her muscles contract

around him. He heard her breath come quickly as he started to move. He held her hips to keep her steady, arched his spine to thrust hard and deep between her legs.

He felt the hot pleasure that began in his staff suffuse his whole body with heat. He smelled her fragrance, tasted her on his lips, and, as he thrust up hard, he grabbed on to her breast with his mouth and began to draw on the nipple deeply.

He let go of the breast to catch his breath. He had heard the thundering sound of Amelia's heart as he'd suckled her, realized with a burst of surprise that his heart was tripping as wildly as hers.

Daniel felt himself spinning out of control. He caressed her wildly, touching everywhere he could gain access, relishing her soft cries, her urgent whimpers. As his own pleasure rocketed, he realized he couldn't hold on much longer.

No! he thought. *Not yet. Not without her.*

But he was caught in a whirlwind of ecstasy and couldn't stop himself. With one last thrust of his hips, he surged upward. She gasped as he buried himself to the hilt.

As he was raised over the precipice and lifted high on a passionate plane that surpassed all earthy pleasures, he realized that he'd not traveled alone. He had taken Amelia with him.

Daniel pulled her to lie on his chest. She lay there with thundering heart as she fought to draw precious air into her lungs. He couldn't move then; he felt nearly dead. Her loving had almost killed him.

After a time, Amelia sat and pulled up her bodice without looking at him. He felt a growing sense of dread as he attempted to assist her. When she stood and straightened her skirts without meeting his gaze still, Daniel felt a burning ache of shame that he had taken her in anger.

He stared at her, realized that she would leave without a word, without a look, if he didn't stop her.

"Amelia."

She glanced at him then.

He felt contrite. For him, their rough joining had been wonderful. For her . . . what else could it have been but an act of hurtful shame? "I'm sorry."

She didn't flinch, nor did she acknowledge that she accepted his apology.

Earlier, she had begged, pleaded, with him to listen and accept her apology, but he'd ignored her. Then he'd taken her without thought for her loss of pride, without murmurs of understanding or declarations of love.

How could she forgive him?

He watched her turn away. He cursed as he closed his eyes, for he'd realized something that he didn't want to admit before.

He loved her . . . more than he'd ever loved another . . . and he'd taken her in anger, not love. He'd sought to punish her for a wrong *he'd* decided she'd committed.

And in punishing her, he'd enjoyed the most memorable passionate joining in his life . . . but in so doing, he'd driven his woman away.

Twenty-five

"Are you all right?" Miriam asked.

Amelia glanced at her and smiled. "I'm fine," she lied, glad when the woman seemed convinced.

She wasn't all right, but she didn't want her friend to worry. It was difficult enough coming to terms with her emotions, in what she'd done, without having to discuss it.

They had stopped for a brief rest. For some reason, Captain Milton was in a sudden hurry to get to their destination—wherever that was—and so now they all rode.

The regiment had met up with another group of Sioux where they'd acquired two more horses in exchange for goods, including whiskey. Fortunately, they hadn't stayed with that particular band of Indians long enough to witness the effects of the firewater, but had continued on the journey westward.

As she sat down to rest on the damp ground, Amelia was aware that Daniel watched her from a distance. Since they'd left early that morning, she had avoided his gaze. She was ashamed of her behavior the night before, was well aware what he thought of her . . . what he must think of her after last night's wild, wanton mating of their bodies. He'd been angry when he'd taken her. That alone should have kept her from making a fool of herself over him, but it hadn't. She had not only enjoyed what he'd

done to her, she'd gloried in it. And because of that she'd
lost all remnants of her pride . . . Now she had nothing
left.

After she'd left him the previous night, she had realized
what they had done . . . what they had said to each other,
and she had lain on her pallet and shed silent tears. Daniel
hated her. He hated her, yet he desired her, and for that,
he loathed not only her but himself as well.

You can't hate me more than I hate myself, Daniel.

She'd done a terrible thing, and while she'd thought she
had a good reason at the time, she'd realized since that it
had been a foolish thing to do—breaking her promise to
stay with Susie in the safety of Daniel's cabin.

Now, because of her, they were all in the clutches of
a madman. If she'd been back at Daniel's cabin, she and
Susie would have been safe, and Milton wouldn't have
had the leverage to keep his other prisoners in line.

A surge of contempt for the army officer filled her,
had her looking in his direction. He was so suave, so
charming when it suited him . . . until he got what he
wanted. He stood, speaking with one of his men, a young
private by the name of Holton, who hung on his superior's
every word.

He's even convincing enough to fool his own men, she
thought. It was amazing, for some of them must have
wondered about his actions, his commands.

Amelia scowled. That morning, Milton had displayed
more of his true character when he'd forced Jane to ride
before him on his horse, forced his daughter Susie to ride
in front of a Sioux. Poor Susie had been terrified. She'd
cried and put up a fight. Watching the captain, Amelia
was afraid that Milton was going to beat his daughter.
Fortunately, Black Hawk had intervened. He said something to Susie in Ojibwa. Whatever the brave had said

calmed Susie, and she didn't complain when one of the soldiers lifted her onto the Indian's horse.

Rather than be grateful for the Indian's help, Milton wasn't happy with Black Hawk's interference. He'd demanded to know what Hawk had said to the little girl. When the Ojibwa refused to tell him, Milton had struck the brave with the butt of his rifle, and Black Hawk had fallen to the ground with a wounded shoulder. Milton then muttered something about black-hearted savages and left the Ojibwa to be helped up and seen to by one of his men. Black Hawk hadn't said a word, but Amelia had seen the hatred in Hawk's dark gaze.

Daniel rode with Miriam. Amelia had been ordered to ride with Cameron Walters. She thought herself fortunate in this, as it would have killed her to share a horse with Daniel.

During the morning's ride, Amelia wondered if they'd ever find the chance to escape. If Daniel or Black Hawk were planning anything, they hadn't seen fit to inform her. Richard Milton was a crafty man; he knew that as long as he kept control of Jane and Susie, he had control of the whole group. Daniel wouldn't do anything rash and risk the lives of his sister and niece. Neither would Daniel's friends.

"All right, all of you have had enough rest," Milton barked. "We need to get moving. Now get up off your lazy arses, and let's go!"

As Amelia rose to her feet, she saw from the corner of her eye Daniel helping his sister. Amelia wouldn't glance at him directly. She was afraid of what she'd see if she did. She'd already experienced his condemnation; she didn't have the desire or the strength to experience it again.

She felt vulnerable and raw . . . and guilty.

A dark-haired, bearded soldier appeared at her side. "You can ride with me," he said.

Amelia cringed. He was filthy and smelled; his uniform was rumpled and torn. She was surprised that the captain tolerated him, but she supposed the man was the kind that served Milton's purpose well.

She didn't like the way the soldier was studying her. His gleaming gaze was lustful; it made her suspect with growing horror that he might have heard her and Daniel in their last act of intimacy together.

"Thank you, but I already have a ride," she said with a gracious smile.

"What's the matter—" He hawked up wad of spit and spat on the ground near her feet. "Ain't I good enough fer you?"

She swallowed and stepped back. "I don't have any idea what you mean." Dear God, she hoped he hadn't heard her cry out with passion. She had tried so hard not to scream, but the pleasure Daniel had elicited had been so great . . . so overwhelming.

"Amelia." Cameron Walters approached. "Are you ready to leave? I adjusted our saddle." He smiled. "It seemed a little loose when I helped you down earlier." He frowned. "Are you bothering Miss Dempsey, Barker?"

The man glared. "I was trying to be friendly, is all. Thought since she had to ride with someone, maybe she'd like to ride with me."

"She's riding with me," Cameron said, his voice cold. "The captain asked me to look out for her, and I intend to do just that."

Barker shrugged. "No need to get in a snit about it," he said gruffly. "I know when to back off."

"Good," Cameron said. "Then back off." He turned to Amelia once the man had left. Amelia stood, shivering, hugging herself with her arms. "Are you all right?" he asked gently. "He didn't hurt you—"

Amelia shook her head. "Other than spit on my shoe."

In a gallant gesture, Cameron knelt and wiped the bit of spittle that had splattered on her leather boot with a cloth handkerchief. He rose with a grin and offered his elbow.

Amelia took his arm and thought that the whole situation was like a bad dream. She was a captive of a hate-crazed captain; yet, she was being treated with consideration by one of his men. Of course, the man was Cameron Walters, someone she'd met previously, someone who'd already offered his friendship.

"Did the captain really ask you to look after me?" she asked, curious.

"No," he said. "Not since the others joined us anyway." Cameron lifted her up onto the saddle, then he climbed up behind her. "My looking after you right now is my own idea."

"Thank you," she murmured, grateful.

The young soldier didn't answer. He surrounded her with his arms to take the reins and with a light kick of his heels urged the horse forward. The warmth of Cameron's arms around her had little effect on her other than to feel pleasant. Nothing about Cameron evoked even the most remote feeling akin to the tingling she felt whenever Daniel touched her.

She stole a glance in Daniel's direction, saw him staring straight ahead. His arms were around Miriam much like Cameron's arms surrounded her. She wondered with a niggle of jealousy if Miriam felt the way she did when she was within close proximity to Daniel Trahern.

Amelia's gaze went to her friend. Miriam didn't seem overly enthralled with being close to Daniel. Amelia watched as Miriam turned to speak to Daniel, saw the man's smiling response. Just as her spurt of jealousy became a wild surge, she saw Daniel's gaze wander, then finally focus in her direction.

The smile fell from his lips, a tautness appeared around his eyes. Amelia's jealousy vanished, and despair took its place.

I love you, she thought. *God help me, but I love you.*

Cameron shifted in the saddle behind her. "At least, the weather's holding," he murmured in her ear.

She nodded. She didn't really feel like polite conversation, but right now she needed Cameron's friendship. It was the only thing that made her feel like a decent woman.

"We should be stopping before dark," Cameron said.

She decided to ask something that she'd been thinking about for some time. "Cameron—" She hesitated.

"Yes?" She could sense his smile.

"The captain . . . what is he doing? Why has he taken us prisoners?"

She turned then, so that she could see him. The soldier looked worried. "I don't know," he said, "but I'm sure the captain has a good reason for all this."

She could see his doubt; she decided to build on it. "I think what he's doing is wrong. Jane—she's his wife. Do you know where she's been for the past four years? With the Sioux . . . as a captive." Miriam had told her yesterday, before Amelia had sought out Daniel.

The path became a rough incline, and Amelia had to look forward to keep from losing her balance. Cameron tightened his arms about her to hold her in place. Once the horse was on even ground again, Amelia glanced back at Cameron. "I don't understand your captain," she said. "I trusted him, and look what he's done."

Cameron's face became set. "I'm sure the captain knows what he's doing," he said.

With an inward sigh, Amelia faced front. "I hope you're right," she said, but she didn't believe it for a second. Richard Milton was a madman, an army officer gone bad. She could only hope that someone else within the army recognized it as well and that something was done before anything bad happened to Daniel, Susie, and the others.

"She is friendly with that soldier Wal-ters," Black Hawk said. "She may be our only hope."

It was dusk. They had stopped for the evening. Black Hawk had sought out his friend where Daniel sat on the edge of the clearing, alone.

Daniel scowled at the Ojibwa. He was all too aware of Amelia's friendship with Cameron Walters. In fact, it angered him every time he saw them together, which was most of the time given the fact that Amelia had chosen to ride with the man.

As the day had worn on, and the journey had become monotonous, Daniel had found himself taking frequent glances at Amelia Dempsey. The sight of her sitting within the circle of Cameron's arms had made him jealous. He'd felt his jaw tighten when he'd caught them deep in conversation with smiles on their lips.

Daniel couldn't forget what it had been like to make love to Amelia, to hear her gasp and feel her quiver within his arms. The thought of her being touched and kissed that way by another man made his teeth snap and his eyes see a red haze.

Thank goodness for Miriam. As if sensing his upset, the kind, unassuming missionary woman had drawn him into conversation. He'd smiled for her sake, but his heart hadn't been in it. If she'd noticed, she didn't mention it.

"Amelia may not agree to help us," he said.

Black Hawk gave him a strange look. "She is still your woman, is she not?"

Daniel shrugged. "Miss Dempsey is her own woman. I have no control over her actions." *Or whom she wants,* he thought.

"But you will talk with her," Black Hawk said. "Each day we get farther from our people." He frowned. "Sleeping Bird escaped, but we do not know if he returned safely to our village. We must use every opportunity presented to us, my friend, or we will die at the hands of that officer."

"We will not die by that man's hands," Daniel vowed. "I'll kill him first."

"And none of us left will get out alive, for his men will still be here to shoot us."

"I'll talk with Amelia," Daniel said, dreading the moment.

Black Hawk nodded. "Tree-That-Will-Not-Bend cares for you. She will not turn you away."

Daniel's mouth firmed. She wouldn't even look at him, he thought. Hawk had no idea what had happened between him and Amelia the night before. The brave didn't know that Amelia no longer wanted anything to do with him . . . and Daniel understood why. He didn't blame her for it.

He sought her out later, when the sky had darkened and many of the others had gone to sleep. This time the captives were kept closer to the soldiers. Captain Milton was starting to get nervous, Daniel suspected. He wondered why. Still, he thought as he rose from the hard ground, Milton's anxiety might ultimately work in their favor. A nervous man was often a careless one. They might lose their only opportunity for escape if they didn't take it soon. With that in mind, Daniel approached where Amelia lay on her sleeping pallet. A soldier glanced his way, but he must have decided that Daniel posed no threat, nor would he try to escape. *And the man is right to think that,* Daniel thought, *at least for the present.*

Amelia faced away from the circle. She had no cover; she'd given one of her blankets to Jane and Susie. He thought she might be sleeping, and he debated what to do if she was. He decided he'd wake her. Time was running out; there was little opportunity during the day for them to talk. It might be easier for her, anyway, to face him in the darkness . . . since she wouldn't look at him in the daylight.

He moved slowly, carefully, so as not to disturb anyone he passed. He must have made a sound with his footfall, for when he drew near to her, she spun over and sat up.

Daniel saw the fear glistening in her fire-lit brown eyes, realized that it wasn't him she feared when her gaze cleared as she recognized him. The fact that she didn't appear afraid amazed him . . . considering the circumstances of their last meeting.

"Daniel," she breathed. It was more a silent opening of her mouth forming his name than sound.

He sat beside her, reluctant to meet her gaze. "I'm sorry to disturb you, but I have to talk with you."

Amelia studied the man before her and felt her heart kick into high gear. What did he want to talk about? What was so important that he'd waited until late to confront her?

"You and Cameron seem friendly," he said carefully.

She frowned. He didn't appear to be jealous. "He's been kind to me," she said.

Daniel turned to her then, took her hand. She caught

her breath as she gazed at him, remembering the passion . . . the anger. Only the anger appeared to be gone. "Amelia, we need your help—Cameron's help. We need Cameron to stage some kind of disturbance, so we can get away."

She felt disappointment. "You want me to speak with Cameron."

He nodded, seemed glad that she understood. She saw him try to gauge her reaction, but she must have hidden it well, as he waited politely for her answer. *So it's come to this, Daniel. Now we are strangers . . . polite strangers.* She suffered a pang of pain that things had gone so wrong between them. She blamed herself. She was sure that Daniel blamed her, too. And that was what was difficult to live with.

"I tried talking with him once," she said, her voice quiet. "He seemed . . . disinclined to believe anything ill of the captain."

Daniel's brow furrowed as if he hadn't anticipated that. "He did, however, appear worried."

Daniel raised his eyebrows. "Do you think he can be convinced?"

"Perhaps," she said. "I can try."

He looked at her gratefully. "Thank you."

She shrugged. "Considering our position, I agree . . . he may be our only chance of escape." *And since it's my fault that we're all here . . .*

He rose to his feet. Something close to a smile touched on his lips, close to but not quite. "I'll tell Black Hawk." He glanced back to see if anyone was watching them.

"Will you tell me what he says?" he asked. "So we can plan what to do?"

She nodded. "Of course."

"Amelia, I just wanted you to know that I . . . regret what happened last night."

"I do, too," she said. She regretted his anger, the fact that she'd lost all chance of having a relationship with him. But then again perhaps she'd never had a chance, she thought.

He hesitated, as if he wanted to say more. She held her breath in hope. "Good night," he said.

She forced a smile. "Good night, Daniel," she replied. When he left, she lay back on her side, as he'd first found her, and cried. Again. For what would never be.

Twenty-six

Everything was set. At least, Daniel hoped it was. Amelia had somehow managed to convince her soldier friend Cameron that the captain wasn't stable, that Cameron needed to help them escape.

It was dusk, the day after he'd first spoken about this to Amelia. Daniel was amazed at how quickly she'd worked, how rapidly she'd been able to persuade the young man.

Gazing at her from his horse, Daniel realized with a pang that he knew why she'd been able to convince Cameron Walters. She was a beautiful woman. What man could resist giving in to the lady's wishes?

Amelia rode, once again, with Cameron. It still bothered Daniel to see her within the young man's arms, but he couldn't very well complain . . . not given the soldier's intended assistance.

He had learned of Cameron's agreement only hours before, when she'd come to him during their midday meal stop. They'd not been able to talk long. His brother-in-law had been watching them, and Daniel had been afraid that once Milton recognized his interest in Amelia that the good captain would use Amelia next to make him squirm. So Amelia and he had barely spoken two sentences when Daniel had dismissed her with the harsh whisper that they'd talk more later. Daniel had been aware of two things—Amelia's hurt expression at his quick dismissal of her, then the sudden look of understanding in her eyes when she'd realized that Captain Milton had been watching them intently.

She'd been given the chance to say little earlier except to tell Daniel that Cameron had consented to help and that he had a plan. Daniel was waiting now for them to stop for the night, so that they could continue their conversation under the cover of darkness.

Miriam shifted in the saddle before him, and Daniel readjusted his arms to give her room.

"Tired?" he asked her.

He saw her dark head bob. "Exhausted."

"It's getting dark. It won't be long now."

He heard her sigh. "I hope you're right." After a moment's pause, she said, "The captain has been acting oddly lately." She turned to look at him. "Odder than usual, I mean."

He gave her a nod. "He's unstable."

Miriam shivered and faced the front. "He's like a powder keg, waiting to be lit."

"Well, then," he said, "we'll just have to make sure that nothing enflames him."

This time it was her turn to nod.

Normally, they stopped when it was still dusk, but in keeping with the commanding officer's strange behavior, Milton forced them to continue, until it was well after dark. When one of his soldiers began preparing a fire like they usually did, Milton flew into a rage, telling them that there would no fire that night. They would camp and sleep with complete darkness. Milton also ordered his men to camp in a circle around the prisoners.

Daniel and Black Hawk had locked gazes at Milton's announcement. The darkness would give them the cover they needed to finalize their escape plan. Daniel wasn't worried about the soldiers. He'd have been more concerned if Milton had decided to tie the captives. Grouped together in the center of the army, they could still whisper secrets, make plans.

After they'd set up camp, Daniel looked for an opportunity to talk with Amelia, but Milton's continued sharp gaze kept him from approaching her. He went to Black Hawk.

"Walters will cooperate," he told him softly. "Talk with Amelia. Milton's been watching me."

His Indian friend had nodded and waited for the right time.

Black Hawk came back to him later. "Walters is going to create a disturbance. We won't know if it'll be tonight or tomorrow."

The two men quietly discussed what they'd do, which man would be responsible for which woman and child. They had to break off their conversation abruptly when Milton came into the circle to stare at his prisoners, especially Daniel.

"I've got my eye on you, Trahern," the captain said. "Your sister will pay if you try anything funny."

Enraged, Daniel sprang to his feet. "Don't you be threatening me, you bastard!"

Even in darkness, Milton's eyes gleamed. "Private Holton! It seems my brother-in-law is having a problem with his behavior."

The young man appeared instantly at his side. "May I have your rifle please," the officer said politely.

Watching from a short distance away, Amelia's heart leapt in fear. *No, Daniel,* she thought.

The man took the rifle from the soldier and raised the gun to Daniel's temple. Amelia gasped, then felt a hand clamp firmly onto her arm. She glanced over, saw the brave Thick Head's warning glance, and nodded in understanding. With a silent shuddering sigh, she closed her eyes and prayed.

"I could kill you, Daniel," Milton said. "I could kill you as easily as I kill the enemy." He smiled grimly. "But then you are the enemy, aren't you?"

"Richard," a soft quivering voice said, "please let him alone. He's done nothing. It's me you're angry with, not him."

Milton smirked as he looked at his wife. "You overestimate yourself . . . and your charms, my dear. Still, you do have your uses." A quick move of his arm and the gun was now trained on Jane, his wife. He glared at his brother-in-law. "One wrong move, and I'll kill her, Trahern—and I won't bat an eyelash." His gaze narrowed. "You know I'll do it."

Daniel held up his hands and lowered himself carefully to the ground. "Just don't hurt her."

Amelia could hear the aching in his voice; she wanted so desperately to take him into her arms and comfort him. A flutter of pain in her breast reminded her that he wouldn't want her comfort. He didn't want her.

Milton was grinning. She could see the flash of teeth in the darkness, for even without the fire, it wasn't all that dark.

"I could hurt you," Milton said. Daniel nodded. "I'm smarter than you. She preferred me over you, and it was so easy . . . so damnably easy."

Daniel's gaze went to Jane. He frowned. "It wasn't a question of preference, Richard. You married her. She loved you."

Richard Milton's grin widened briefly. "Oh, she loved me all right, but I didn't marry her." He paused as if to allow the effect of what he had to say next sink in. *"You did."*

The captain's eyes glistened as he smiled again. "You didn't know, did you?" He shook his head. "Idiot! She said you'd never guess. That you were a fool, and she was right."

Amelia saw that Daniel had become very still.

"What are you saying, Richard?" he said in a quiet voice. *Too quiet,* Amelia thought.

"You don't know? You still haven't guessed?" In his feeling of power, he lowered the gun away from Jane. "You are stupid, aren't you? Pamela said you were, but I thought she'd underestimated you."

Pamela. Amelia froze with shock. Something was happening here, a revelation of some kind.

"Pamela?" Daniel kept his voice light and even. He didn't let on that he understood, that there was rage building inside of him. At all costs, he must control his anger.

"Pamela." A flicker of something changed Milton's expression.

Love? Regret? Pain? Daniel wasn't sure what he'd seen, but he realized that it was connected with Pamela, his late wife.

"Yes, Pamela," Milton repeated. "Your wife. My lover. The mother of my child."

"You bastard," Daniel growled angrily. Some display of anger was expected of him. And he was angry, but not because of Pamela. He'd long gotten over her lying, cheating heart. But because of James. He had misjudged his best friend, had believed the man had cuckolded him.

The captain laughed. "You thought it was that good-for-nothing friend of yours, James Beck!" His amusement faded abruptly. "He killed her." His mouth tightened; his gaze glowed. "He killed her. They said it was an accident, that the carriage went wild before it crashed into the tree, but I don't believe it." His gaze glistened with madness. "James Beck loved her; he must have. How could he have not? He loved her, so that when she went to him for help, he gave it to her, hoping she'd turn to him . . . stay with him when she was coming to me. But she didn't want him. She loved me!"

"But you were married to Jane!" Daniel said.

His vision clearing, the captain shrugged. "And you were married to Pamela, but that didn't stop her from lying in my bed . . ." An evil grin. "Beneath me."

"You'll burn in hell, Richard," Jane hissed, surprising Daniel with her strong outburst. He saw no fear, no horror, just anger . . . and something else he recognized in her gaze, but he had trouble believing it of his sister. *Murder.*

Richard laughed as he handed Holton back his gun. "Watch them," he said. He grabbed Jane by the hair, dragged her to her feet, and toward the place where he'd set his bedroll. "Susie!" he'd barked. "Your momma and I want you to come over here. *Now!*"

"Pa?" From the circle of Thick Head's arms, Susie shot a fearful gaze at Daniel.

"Go on, sweeting. Just listen to what he says." Daniel gave her an encouraging smile. "I love you," he mouthed silently. "Hold on a little longer."

"Susie!" Milton shouted impatiently.

The child scurried to her feet and ran in the direction of her parents.

"That's better, little girl," her father said, his voice turning pleasant. "Now come lie down here next to your mother."

The fury rose within Daniel, making it difficult to breathe.

Amelia saw that Daniel was seething; she wanted to go to him, help him, even though there was every likelihood that she would become the focus of his anger. He needed to release his feelings. She would gladly bear the brunt of his fury one more time, something she'd sworn she'd never be able to do again. This would be different. This would be to help her beloved . . .

She glanced over at Cameron, caught the soldier's gaze, and saw that he was upset by the scene that had just occurred. Frowning with concern, he nodded at her. She gave a slight nod in return. Cameron moved his lips. *Tonight,* he said silently.

Amelia felt a little thrill. She had to alert Daniel.

Tonight, she thought. Tonight they would escape.

"Mr. Holton! Mr. Walters," Captain Milton said. "May I have a moment of your time."

"Yes, Captain," Cameron Walters said, quickly approaching his commanding officer's side.

"Yes, sir," Holton said, hurrying to the captain with a gaze that was eager.

Milton glanced down at his man. "Cover these two prisoners, Barker. If they move, shoot them."

"Aye, Captain." The man grinned evilly at Jane and the little girl.

"Soldiers," Milton said to his two waiting men, "come with me."

Cameron followed the captain from the group, into the dark stillness of the night. When the captain halted, he waited for the man to speak, hoping that the officer couldn't read his thoughts or his concern about his commander's sanity.

"Holton, Walters," Milton said. "You're the only men

I can trust now. The others may do what I say, but as you might have guessed, they're not regular army. They're men my superiors have allowed me to recruit in order to serve a special purpose, to control and distribute supplies to the Indians." Richard Milton smiled. "Sometimes, our measures may seem . . . questionable, but I assure you that I do have my orders . . . a master plan."

Cameron nodded, and he saw Holton bob his head, his brown eyes gleaming with admiration for their commanding officer. He himself wasn't convinced that Richard Milton was following orders issued by the US government, but he wasn't going to put himself in a position to be beaten, killed, or court-martialed by a crazy captain.

"Sir, is there something specific you'd like us to do?" Cameron asked.

"I want you to keep a special eye on the prisoners, Mr. Walters, especially that one, Black Hawk. I can handle Daniel Trahern and his sister." A gleam came and went in the man's eyes. "Can you do that?"

"Of course, sir," Cameron said. "It will be a pleasure to do so."

"But at the same time, I want you to watch our men. If you note any trouble, hear anything out of the ordinary, I want you to come and tell me directly. All right?"

Cameron nodded.

"And me, Captain?" Holton gushed. "What shall I do?"

Captain Milton looked at the private with half annoyance and half tolerance. "You, Holton, I want to make sure that a special shipment of supplies I've been waiting for, and which should arrive shortly, is kept under guard until we can dispose of it."

"Dispose of it?" Holton asked, and Cameron was glad it was the private who'd asked and not him.

Richard Milton's expression darkened. "When I want

you to know all the details, Mr. Holton, I'll tell them to you."

A look of fear shadowed the man's eyes. "Yes, Captain. Yes, sir."

The captain's features cleared and a smile curved his lips. "Good," he said. "Now let's get back to those ruffians before they do something we can't hold them accountable for."

Cameron managed a grin. His humor restored, Holton did also.

As they headed back to camp, Cameron thought of the conversation and realized that there was a lot about Milton that he didn't know about or understand. He had a feeling that the captain was selling the goods meant for the Indians, and that he was on his own private quest for revenge.

He was glad now that he'd agreed to help Amelia and the others. Any doubts he'd had were banished earlier when Captain Milton had lost his temper, nearly killed an innocent man in cold blood, then had turned a gun on the man's sister, the captain's own wife. If that wasn't the behavior of a man gone mad, then he didn't know what was. Now it was up to him to do something about it . . . without alerting Milton to his own role in the game.

The soldiers back at camp had pulled out their food rations and were washing them down with whiskey.

Cameron had promised Amelia a diversion. He'd had no idea what it would be or how he'd arrange it . . . until now . . . as he caught sight of two soldiers who could barely tolerate the sight of each other, drinking rotgut whiskey. He knew the two's drunken behavior well, knew it wouldn't take much to induce a fistfight between the two men. And to involve the rest of the regiment in a drunken brawl, which would justify taking Cameron's attention away from his prisoner charges to the captain's men, whom he was supposed to keep in line.

Everything was falling into place perfectly. Cameron smiled as he, Captain Milton, and Private Holton rejoined the regiment.

"Captain Milton!" A young soldier raced up to him, gestured back to a stranger that Cameron had never seen before. "The goods are here."

Cameron turned in time to see Milton's eyes gleam.

"Excellent!" A grin curved the officer's lips. "Mr. Holton," he said, "you come with me. And, Cameron, tell the men that they may have their fire now."

Cameron nodded, amazed by the transformation within his commanding officer. "I'll tell them, sir."

As he watched the captain and Holton disappear with the stranger, he realized that these goods were what Captain Milton had been waiting for.

He turned to the men with a smile. "Fellows, the captain said it's okay for us to have a fire." And while the captain was gone, he had another fire to light, one that would ignite a brawl among the inebriated members of Captain Milton's regiment.

Twenty-seven

"Smith, apologize to Rogers," Cameron said. "That's no way to talk about a man's mother!"

"What?" Rogers exclaimed angrily as he turned to the soldier named Smith. "You've been insulting my mother again? I told you what I'd do if I ever heard you say anything bad about her again!"

Cameron backed away as the two men rose to face each other with fists raised. The first punch came from Rogers, clipping Smith on the shoulder. Smith swung back, hitting Rogers in the nose, sending the man sprawling into a group of soldiers who had a taste for liquor but no tolerance for having a body hurled at them. Soon, others came into the brawl, and it became a drunken free-for-all, with some of the men circling to watch, cheering for their favorite fighters.

Daniel turned to Black Hawk. "That's it. Let's go."

The men scrambled to help the women and children. There were four Ojibwa and Daniel; there were three women captives and two children to escape with the men. The numbers would have been even, but one of the braves had slipped out of camp to get to the horses.

In the excitement, their plan of who was to rescue whom went awry, and each man was forced to rescue the nearest captive. Daniel grabbed for the boy Johnny, and ran toward Thick Head who stood on the fringe of the camp with the four horses he'd managed to secure. Black Hawk had already swung into a saddle with Miriam up in front. Daniel handed Johnny up to his friend, who placed the boy into Miriam's arms.

"Go!" Daniel said as he prepared to return. "Go and don't look back."

Black Hawk's dark gaze glistened as he nodded. Daniel could see in his eyes that Hawk didn't want to go, not without exacting vengeance. But the brave knew he'd have to wait for his revenge. "May the Great Spirit protect you, Dan-yel. I will meet you where the stream forks in the forest." He didn't kick the horse into a wild gallop but eased him on slowly, so as not to draw attention to the others.

Behind them, the fight continued with the noise of solid thuds, the occasional outburst of vicious curses, and the wild cheering from the onlookers. Daniel searched for Jane, Susie, and Amelia. With a feeling of relief, he saw Amelia and Jane being urged toward the horses by Rain-from-Sky. Broken Bow was going in for Susie. Thick Head had moved the horses closer to the camp.

One of the soldiers turned, saw the horses and the fleeing prisoners, and shouted. Thick Head swung up onto a horse. The beast shifted restlessly beneath the brave, who fought to control his mount as well as keep hold of the other two.

Daniel caught Walters' glance, knew he had little time as the soldier slowly raised his gun to fire it into the air. He understood that Cameron had given them their chance, but that the soldier had no other option but to fire his gun soon, to alert his commander or else risk having his role in the escape discovered.

Cameron shot off the gun. Running to help save the

two women, Daniel prayed that Broken Bow had reached
Susie and made their escape in time.

A soldier fired his gun, hitting Broken Bow in the
heart. Jane screamed as the brave fell dead, leaving Susie
behind and helpless.

"Go on!" Amelia shouted at the woman. "Run! I'll get
her."

Rain-from-Sky, Black Hawk's brother, turned back to
help.

"No, go!" Amelia cried. "See to Jane!" The woman
sobbed hysterically, as she fought to get back to her baby.
"Please, Rain."

The brave took Jane to the horse.

Daniel raced forward, his heart in his throat, as he saw
Amelia turn around and rush back toward the danger.
"No, Amelia! No!"

There was another gunshot. The bullet whizzed by
Daniel's head, just missing him by inches. He watched
Amelia pick up little Susie, saw her spin and run to escape. A soldier jumped her from behind, catching hold of
her skirts and dragging her down with him as he fell.
Amelia released Susie as she tumbled to the ground,
shoved her in Daniel's direction. "Run, Susie. Run to Pa!"

"Pa!" the child screamed, running, obeying without
question.

Daniel scooped his niece up into his arms and ran to
thrust the child at Thick Head. Rain-from-Sky was already
in the saddle with Jane. Daniel spun to return for Amelia,
saw with horror that the man who'd tripped her had risen
to his feet and held a gun to Amelia's head.

The soldier grinned as he saw Daniel coming. Amelia
turned then, saw Daniel, and her eyes widened in horror.
"No, Daniel! Leave! Go! Damn it! Save yourself and the
others!"

"Dan-yel!" Thick Head said. "Come."

"Amelia!" Daniel cried.

Amelia saw his indecision, prayed that he'd make the right choice and leave. She saw the other soldiers scrambling for their weapons. "Go!" she screamed. She'd never be able to live with herself if he'd gotten himself killed while saving her. It was too late for her rescue.

"Dan-yel," the brave urged.

"Pa, please!"

Susie's plea reminded him about the others who depended on him. He wanted to stay for Amelia. He had to leave for the others, but he'd return. He'd be back for Amelia, and no one would be able to stop him then.

I'll come back for you, my love! he cried silently. *I'll be back.*

She had risked her life to save Susie and Jane . . . and now himself.

His heart squeezed painfully. *I love you, Amelia. I love you . . .*

Amelia saw him turn toward the horse and felt an overwhelming wave of relief as he escaped with the others. She closed her eyes and cried happy tears. If she'd nothing else good in her life, at least, she had this. Daniel and the others were safe. That was all that mattered.

"Well, well, well," a soldier said, and she turned and saw with shock that it was Cameron Walters, who had taken over for the soldier holding the gun. He jabbed her in the side with the barrel. "Move, woman," he growled cruelly, loudly.

She stiffened, glared at him in fury, then slowly obeyed him to wherever he ordered. The fight had stopped at the first sound of gunfire. Several soldiers, she saw, lay on the ground, groaning from their injuries. Another was puking up his stomach contents, while a second soldier laughed at the other man's sickness.

Nice friend, Amelia thought. Then, she jumped and cried out as Cameron hit her in the back with his gun.

"Keep going," Cameron commanded harshly.

She kept going, but her anger at him nearly blinded her, making her stumble and almost fall to the ground. Cameron grabbed her arm and hauled her to her feet. "I'm sorry," he whispered, before he let her go, and Amelia understood. She'd been caught, so now her friend had to play his part, so no one, especially Richard Milton, would realize that the young soldier had been instrumental in the prisoners' escape.

She released her anger toward Cameron, gathered it up for Richard Milton instead. She should have been afraid of the man, but right now the only thing she could think about was how vile the captain was, how he'd hurt people she cared about . . . how she'd love to see him pay and the authorities get their hands on him.

She heard the sharp bellow of rage before she saw the officer. He must have only returned to see the destruction and hear about the missing prisoners.

"Walters! Barker!" he screamed angrily. *"What is the meaning of this?"*

"Rogers and Smith got into a fight, sir," Barker volunteered, and Amelia recognized him as the man who'd nearly accosted her, who demanded that she ride with him instead of with Cameron. "It sparked off the others."

The captain looked livid. He didn't realize that they still had one prisoner, Amelia thought. She saw him in the firelight—a devil with bulging demonic eyes, fury on his face, and his hands clenching and unclenching at his sides.

The man stared at Barker in such a way that the soldier cringed and backed away. The captain reached into his holster, grabbed his pistol, then raised it toward the soldier's head.

"I caught one of the prisoners, Captain," Barker said in a fearful, quivering voice.

Milton froze. "One of them didn't escape?" Barker nodded, then sighed with relief as the officer lowered the gun. "Who?" the captain asked calmly, more rationally.

Cameron Walters stepped forward. "I've got her here, sir," he announced loudly as he prodded Amelia in Milton's direction with his gun.

Richard Milton's expression cleared of his anger, and he was suddenly the charming, handsome officer again. The quick change in him made Amelia shiver and hug herself with her arms.

"Why, Miss Dempsey, is it?"

She nodded, controlling her emotions as she gazed into the laughing eyes of the dark devil himself.

He turned his attention from Amelia to smile approvingly at his two men. "Excellent," he said. "Trahern will be back. They're lovers."

Amelia opened her mouth to object, closed it again when she saw Milton turn a mocking light glance in her direction.

The officer then barked orders to his men to organize a party consisting of half of his men to recapture the escaped prisoners. When the band of fear-sobered men had left the camp, Milton turned to Rogers and Smith. While Amelia and his army watched with horror, he fired his pistol into Smith's neck. He then ordered the shaken Rogers to care for the wounded soldier and bury the man if he died.

Captain Milton returned to Amelia, who stood with Cameron behind her, his gun now held to her nape. The

horrible memory of Smith's neck injury had turned Amelia
pale and queasy.

"Now, Miss Dempsey," Milton said with extreme po-
liteness. He waved Cameron away, before he smiled at
Amelia. "I think we should get to know each other better."
He held out his arm for her to take, as if they were a
gentleman and lady at a ball instead of two adversaries
in the wilderness.

Amelia stared at the navy coat sleeve, then took the
man's elbow, because she knew she had no other choice.
She wouldn't cross the army officer, for Captain Richard
Milton was a madman and a cold-blooded killer.

"I'm going back for her," Daniel declared to the others.

"No, Daniel!" Jane cried.

"No, Pa!"

He caught his sister by the shoulders. "I am going back
for Amelia," he said. "I love her."

A flash of awareness entered Jane's eyes. "Oh, Daniel."
He released her, and she turned away to hide the onslaught
of tears. "It's not that I don't want her saved."

"But you'd rather see one of the others do it?" he said
quietly. "Miriam perhaps?"

She spun with a hurt expression. "You know that I
didn't mean her."

Daniel studied his sister with sympathy in his blue gaze.
"Who then? Black Hawk? Thick Head? It's all right if
one of the savages go, but not me?"

Her face reddened with shame. "I'm sorry," she said
miserably.

Oddly enough, it was Black Hawk who comforted her.
"He will not go alone, my sister. I will go with him."

She blinked as she looked at him. "I didn't mean for

you to put yourself in danger. I . . ." She glanced away, feeling helpless.

The brave touched her arm. "This man wishes to go. I have a score to settle with the white man." He smiled when she again turned to him. "A score to settle for all of us."

"He's an evil man, Black Hawk," she said softly.

"I am not afraid of the white man's devil. I am not afraid of the white army officer. Dan-yel and I will rescue Tree-That-Will-Not-Bend, and we will return safely to our villages and to the people who love us."

Despite the fire in his gaze, Black Hawk's expression was gentle.

Jane nodded. "Go with God then."

The Ojibwa brave inclined his head. "And may *Gichimanidoo* protect you as well."

The group had never made it to their original agreed-upon meeting place in the forest. The others caught up with Black Hawk and the child Johnny within miles of the regiment, in the first hiding place where the brave could keep watch for the others without being seen by the enemy.

Just moments ago Sleeping Bird had found them. He'd brought Ojibwas and their friends, the Ottawas, to help rescue the remaining captives. It had been a surprise to see them.

Sleeping Bird's party decided to split into two groups, one that would go with Daniel and Black Hawk, one that would stay and protect those who remained.

Daniel hugged his sister and niece, then embraced Miriam briefly. "Take care of yourselves. Listen to Thick Head and Rain-from-Sky in the event of danger. They'll know what to do."

He went to climb on top of his horse. Black Hawk

would ride with him, so they could leave behind the remaining three animals for the others. Black Hawk climbed into the saddle behind Daniel, but allowing Daniel full control of the animal. The two men would act as scouts while the others followed on foot.

"Good-bye," Daniel said softly. "Keep safe."

"Danny!" Jane ran to the horse just as Daniel had nudged the animal forward with a gentle kick to the gelding's side.

Daniel drew up on the reins and turned to his sister.

She placed a hand on his knee. "I love you," she whispered achingly. "Please, please, come home safe. I've only just found you again."

Her brother grinned. "Just try to keep me away," he said. He bent and touched her cheek. "Give Susie another hug for me."

She nodded, unable to control her tears. "I never thanked you for taking such good care of her."

"I love her," he said simply. "And I love you."

Daniel straightened in the saddle, then with a jaunty wave, he spurred the horse into a gallop, and he and Black Hawk disappeared as the first hint of dawn brightened the new day's sky.

"I don't know what your game is, but you're never going to get away with this," Amelia said to the army officer.

"Game?" Milton's smile was cruel. "Who said this is a game, Miss Dempsey? This is serious business here. Government business."

They were breaking camp and heading out. The captain stood with Amelia close to his side, watching his men put out their campfire and gather their things.

Amelia heard a low rumbling of wheels and from the woods a soldier manned a horse-drawn cart that she'd never seen before.

Shortly after the others' escape, she'd overheard a conversation between Milton and Holton, the young private. She'd learned that the goods were being sold and traded for money to pay Milton's soldiers, not dispensed to the Indians for free as stipulated and promised by the March treaty. Amelia realized then that this army's current actions weren't sanctioned by the United States government. Only its soldiers didn't know that. As long as they received solid pay for obeying orders, Milton's army believed that the captain's commands were direct orders from the army superiors.

She recognized, too, that the only other person who might know enough to see Captain Richard Milton hang for his deeds was Private Holton. Milton had chosen his assistant well, Amelia thought, for there was no denying Holton's loyalty and extreme devotion to the captain.

Holton was the only one who knew exactly what Captain Milton was up to. Except her. Amelia shivered. Which made her situation extremely dangerous should the officer ever realize how much she knew and understood about his operations.

"Shall we go, Miss Dempsey?"

She saw the captain's extended elbow, looked up into the light-colored eyes that studied her strangely and chilled her to the bone.

She accepted his arm. "Thank you, Captain." She forced a smile. He knows, she thought. He allowed her to overhear last night's conversation for a reason, and that was to make her see how extremely vulnerable she was.

What does he want from me?

He led her to his horse and placed his hands possessively at her waist, allowing them to remain there for several seconds, before he lifted her up onto the animal. He held her attention as he released her slowly, easing his hands free, but not his gaze. Then, he smiled, and Amelia's breath fisted into a ball of fear that became lodged in her throat.

Dear God, he wants me. She closed her eyes and fought the panic, as she felt the shift of the horse as the captain climbed onto the saddle behind her.

He leaned forward until his breath whispered in her ear, his chest was pressed firmly at her back, and his hands brushed the sides of her breasts as he controlled the reins and horse.

God help me, she thought. Daniel and the others were safe, she told herself, that was all that mattered. Then, to banish the thought of Richard Milton touching her, violating her, Amelia closed her eyes and remembered those times when she and Daniel had come together with sweet longing and passionate kisses.

Twenty-eight

Daniel and Black Hawk found the army, then together with the band of Ojibwa and Ottawa warriors, followed it for a time until dark.

It nearly killed him thinking of Amelia with Richard Milton, but Daniel knew it would be foolish to attack the army in the daylight. Milton and his men had the advantage of horses and guns, while Daniel and his Indian friends had only two trade rifles with limited ammunition, bows and arrows, war clubs, and knives. They would be at a disadvantage if spotted from a distance, but at close range, their weapons and skill would prove deadly.

Daniel sat, watching from high on a rock outcropping, studying Milton's army as it passed below. They had sent their only horse back to the others with an Ottawa warrior, preferring to continue on foot, once they realized that Milton's army no longer traveled in a hurry.

He noted with a frown a horse-drawn cart driven by a soldier and guarded by two others on horseback. The back of the cart appeared to be packed with wooden crates, and Daniel wondered what was in them. Then, he hazarded to take a guess. Could it be guns?

He saw Amelia seated on Milton's horse. His first feeling was one of joy that the woman he loved was alive and apparently unharmed. His emotions turned quickly as he saw his brother-in-law lift a hand and run it slowly down the back of Amelia's unbound hair. Even from this distance, Daniel could sense Amelia's resistance.

Rage stirred within Daniel that Milton would dare to lay a finger on her. His hand fisted on the rock face until he scraped his skin on the rough surface.

His gaze shot to his friend. Black Hawk nodded as they shared a silent message, before Daniel looked away, back toward Amelia.

He loved her, Daniel thought, and somehow, some way, he'd convince her to forgive him. He wanted her for always, to live with her, eat with her, and sleep with her by his side.

I want to take you to wife, my love. Just hold on until I can come for you.

Night seemed forever in the coming, but then finally it came, and Daniel and the Indians mentally prepared themselves for attack as they watched the soldiers set up camp for the night. Daniel had told Black Hawk his suspicions about the guns earlier, and they used the knowledge to caution the other Indians.

Apparently, there were other items in some of those boxes as well, Daniel thought, as he and Black Hawk watched, in the firelight, as Milton ordered one of his men to pry open one crate. The soldiers cheered as their captain reached into the box and pulled out a glass bottle.

Wine? Whiskey? Daniel wondered. All he knew for certain was that it was some kind of spirits that they drank and passed around to share.

"A toast!" he heard Richard Milton exclaim. "To the finest men in the United States Army. I'm proud of each and every one of you."

Several more bottles were uprooted from the straw-cushioned crate. There was much laughter and swigging from the bottles. Richard Milton wore a grin as he chuckled with the others in a celebration of the day's successful acquisition.

"But, Captain," one man was bold enough to ask. "What of the others?"

Milton's grin wavered for only a moment. "I'm sure they've recaptured the prisoners and are on their way right now to our next meeting stop."

They weren't, Daniel stopped. The small army had been apprehended by a large band of Ottawa and Ojibwa warriors only a few hours after they'd left camp.

"And where's the meeting place, sir?" the same soldier queried.

The captain apparently didn't like the men asking so many questions. He scowled, then his expression brightened. "Where the women are, Mr. Barker!"

The men all laughed and the matter was dropped as they continued to drink and eat from supplies they had garnered from somewhere. No doubt from in another one of those wooden boxes, Daniel thought, unamused.

The Indian band and Daniel bided their time, as they'd had once before, until the soldiers became drunker and drunker, even the captain. Daniel, noting Milton's behavior, thought the taking of this army would be easier, giving their drunken state and their reduced number, but he feared that his inebriated brother-in-law was now more of a danger to Amelia than ever before.

Daniel glanced at Black Hawk, smiled grimly when he saw what he wanted to see. Then, shrieking wildly at the top of his lungs, he rushed forward with the Indians, his hand raised with a deadly Ojibwa war club, the sharp point aimed to kill.

Amelia heard the wild cries and froze as fierce-looking painted figures came out of the darkness with weapons raised. Her first thought as she saw the first soldier fall was that she was going to die at the hands of real savages. They were all going to die. Then she saw Daniel, and her heart gladdened as she screamed his name.

She cried out as someone grabbed her around the throat from behind.

"I told you he'd come back," Milton said, sounding almost gleeful. "Don't move," he hissed. He tightened his arm, strangling her airway. Amelia's world blackened as she struggled for breath. "He's coming," he said *"Ah, he's already here."* He smiled.

"Hello, Trahern. I knew you'd not be able to resist coming back." Milton released Amelia's throat so she could breathe and gaze blearily at the man she loved standing before her.

Daniel's face was painted black, but his blond hair fell in its familiar short waves about his head . . . and his eyes were still the brightest shade of blue she'd ever seen.

The blue orbs were cold, deadly, without an ounce of emotion, but a great deal of intent. "Let her go, Richard, or you'll never make it out of this alive."

Richard laughed and squeezed his arm. Amelia gasped and futilely, without strength, put her hands to the arm that was slowly choking the life out of her.

Around them came the sound of fighting as Indians battled soldiers. In an eerie scene out of somebody's nightmare, the two men stood eyeing each other with venom in the midst of the fighting, while the woman in the mad one's arms fought to stay alive.

"Don't!" Daniel cried as he watched Amelia's eyes widen and glaze over. "Don't hurt her."

The army officer laughed, a sick sound that echoed in Daniel's ears and chilled his blood.

"What do you want?" His heart tripping, Daniel stared at Amelia. "You're killing her, you bastard!" he roared.

"Haven't you killed enough innocent people?" *He's drunk . . . and he's killing her!*

"Richard, please," Daniel pleaded. He thought quickly and grabbed for the only subject that he'd ever seen have any great effect on his brother-in-law. "For Pamela."

Looking shocked, Richard released his arm. Amelia slumped back against the officer, until he shook her hard, and she came to, sobbing and gasping for breath.

"You're not Pamela!" Milton said. His eyes sparkled with tears. "Pamela is dead." He shoved Amelia until she stumbled and fell. "Our baby is dead."

Daniel cursed and made a move to go to her, then lunged for Milton instead, grabbing his hand just as the man reached for his gun.

The two men struggled, but Daniel, the stronger and the only sober one of the two, easily subdued his brother-in-law.

Daniel had dropped his club, when he'd had no choice earlier because of the risk of endangering Amelia further. But he still had his knife, which he drew from his legging string with one hand. He had Richard with the other arm in a choke hold similar to the one the man had had Amelia in.

I can choke the living breath out of him and feel the life ease out of him, or I can stick him quickly and cleanly, Daniel thought. *Which way do you want to die, bastard!*

"No, Daniel!" Amelia rasped as she lurched to her feet. "Don't kill him!"

Daniel blinked and came out of the haze of blind rage. "Amelia—" Her beautiful face swam before his gaze. She looked upset. Distressed, he thought. No, horrified.

"He deserves to die."

"Yes. Perhaps," she said hoarsely. "But not by your

hand." He could see that she struggled for every word. *"Not by your hand!"*

He stared at her, wavering. The desire to kill remained strong within him. Milton's men had attacked his home, kidnapped his sister. The captain himself had raped Jane. He'd taken Pamela, and because of Milton and Pamela, Daniel had doubted and hated his best friend.

He raised the knife as if to plunge.

"No, Daniel!" Amelia screamed.

"No, my friend." Black Hawk stepped into the line of Daniel's vision, approached, and reached for the knife. "Tree-That-Will-Not-Bend is right, my friend. You are not like this Ojibwa man. Richard Milton is a cruel man. He is an evil man, but he is still your sister's husband, and while he deserves to die, you should not be the one to kill him."

The Indian took the knife and raised it high. He stared into Milton's fear-stricken eyes. "Let me kill him for you." Milton's eyes bulged as he gazed at the sharp blade.

"No, Black Hawk!" Amelia cried. "Let his own people deal with him. I know what he's been doing. With my testimony to the government, he'll hang."

The Ojibwa met her gaze, before he turned back to his friend. "You will consider this?" he asked Daniel.

Daniel nodded, then released Milton's throat to grab hold of the man's arms and force them behind his back. He realized that the fighting was done. Whoever hadn't been killed by the Indians was now a prisoner. Cameron Walters was among the prisoners, held by an Ojibwa who didn't know about the young soldier's earlier vital assistance.

"Thunder Oak, Mr. Walters is a friend." Daniel's gaze met the soldier's frightened one. "Isn't that right, Cameron?"

A flicker of hope entered the young man's face as he nodded.

Daniel allowed the barest of smiles to surface. "Then, I trust I can place Captain Milton in your capable hands. You will see that he is presented to the proper authorities?"

"Yes, sir," Cameron said.

Amelia, seeing Milton's look of hatred toward Cameron, went up to the soldier and took hold of his arm. "And I'll tell them what I know about the captain's criminal acts . . . and about how Cameron"—she gazed smilingly into his eyes—"protected us as best he could and did everything he could to help all of us escape."

The young man's expression cleared of doubt. "I'd be much obliged, Miss Amelia," he said. He grinned.

"No," she returned quietly with a squeeze of his arm. "We are much obliged."

Milton was bound by the wrists and loosely by the ankles, then handed over into Cameron's care. Furious, the officer struggled against his ropes.

"You're a fool, Trahern," the captain cried. "A fool, you hear me! She was never yours. She was mine—long before you even met her. Her father was one of my commanding officers. We were to have been married, but I had orders and was sent away. I was coming back to her. We would have married . . ." To everyone's surprise, the man released a sob.

He glared at Daniel. "Then, you came along, and you had to have her. She thought I was gone—dead!" Richard Milton's voice rose and his eyes filled with tears. "So she listened to you . . . married you, but she never loved you."

Milton's gaze went to other members of the group. "She loved me. When I found that she had moved with her father to another fort, I followed her there. But she was married." He grinned then, the grin of an emotionally wounded and insane man. "So I married Jane—your sister. It seemed a fitting thing to do. You got my woman, so I took your sister . . ."

Daniel moved as if to hit him, but Amelia grabbed his arm. He looked down at the small, feminine hand and settled back into place, his anger bumping around inside of him crazily.

Richard seemed oblivious to everything but his loss. "But then I learned that Pamela still loved me . . . so we started to meet secretly. I even moved Jane away from the settlement. Away from you. It would be easier for Pamela and me to meet then. With Jane gone and me on active duty, it was a simple thing for me to leave Jane home and spend time with Pamela."

Amelia watched and listened with horror as Daniel's past and the source of his pain was revealed.

"Things were wonderful between Pamela and me," Milton said, "but I couldn't stop being angry that she was your wife. Then, she told me she was with child—my child. She seemed so happy. I was exhilarated when I learned that she had plans to leave you, Daniel. Leave you and come to me."

Everyone within the camp was quiet as Milton continued to talk. "James Beck, your friend." He paused to chuckle as if he found what he had to say next amusing. "It was so easy for Pamela to convince Beck to help her get away."

His face darkened as he relived some inner pain. "But damn it, he killed her instead . . . her and our baby. They must have fought for the carriage reins when he learned she was coming to me . . . and not leaving with him."

Richard Milton broke down then, and Amelia studied

the crying, pitiful excuse of a man and felt no sympathy for him. He had hurt Daniel, the man she loved, and he had hurt others as well. The only feeling she'd have concerning him would be satisfaction once she'd learned that justice was finally served.

Amelia glanced at the man she loved and ached for him. There was anger and heartache between them, she thought, but she would always love him.

He looked at her as if he barely noted her existence, and her pain was swift and went deep. *Good-bye, Daniel. I will always love you.*

Twenty-nine

"What happened between you two?" Jack Keller stood in the smithy, watching Daniel hammer a tool into shape with skill but with a vengeance he'd never seen before in his friend.

"Nothing happened between us," Daniel grated out between hammerblows.

"Sure, nothing much," Jack mocked. As Daniel continued to hammer metal that had cooled—a fruitless and noisy step in properly manipulating steel, Jack sighed, then he went over to pump up the bellows to heat up the forge fire.

Without comment, Daniel transferred the metal to the fire for warming, then returned it to the anvil and went back to work.

"Nothing, my arse, "Jack muttered darkly, with concern for his friend.

The blacksmith stopped. "What?" he said. "Did you say something?"

"I said, 'Nothing, my arse.' " He didn't allow Daniel's scowl to upset him. "You watch the woman as if you want to either shake her or kiss her senseless. The latter, I think . . . while Amelia gazes at you with longing and fear."

Daniel tensed. "She doesn't gaze at me with longing."

It was Jack's turn to scowl. "All right, then she looks

at you with fear. Is that what you want to hear? Me, I don't believe that," he said. "Oh, it's not that I don't think she isn't afraid of something . . . but it's not you. Perhaps of losing you . . ."

Jack's gaze narrowed as his friend looked away. "Did you do something to make you think she fears you?" He felt a flicker of surprise when he saw Daniel blush. "What did you do?"

Daniel glared at him then. "None of your damn business!"

"Fine!" Jack threw his hands up in the air and started to walk away.

"Wait," Daniel said, his voice suddenly gone quiet. "I'm sorry. I'm angry with myself, and I've taken it out on you."

Jack nodded. "You're so much in love with her, it's eating you up inside."

"I don't deserve her," Daniel said. Then, he managed to smile when he caught his friend gaping at him. "I don't," he said.

"Hell, Dan. Who's to say who deserves whom?"

"I didn't bring back Amelia's father." Daniel whacked the metal with his hammer, then cursed when it raised a mark in it that would need to be worked out.

"You tried, Daniel," Jack said quietly. "You tried." He paused, felt something kick in his gut as he got a mental vision of a woman with cropped blond hair and a blue gaze filled with pain. "And you brought back Jane," he said so softly his friend couldn't hear him.

"But trying isn't enough, is it?" Daniel returned shortly. "At least not for me, it isn't. And I'm sure it's not for Amelia either."

"Is that all that's keeping you two apart? John Dempsey's disappearance?"

Daniel couldn't admit to his friend about the other thing that had happened between him and Amelia Dempsey . . . when he'd loved her until he'd burned and shivered . . . and had known that he was hopelessly in love.

"Isn't that enough?" he said.

"If the man came back, then you'd talk with her? Ask her to marry you? It is what you want, isn't it?"

With all his heart, Daniel thought. "I'd talk with her," he said.

"You'd have to promise that you'd talk with her if you expect me to believe you mean it. Or are you too cowardly to do such a thing?"

Daniel became angry. "I said I'd talk with her, and that's all I can promise."

"If her father came back," Jack said. When Daniel nodded, his friend grinned, a stupid grin that had Daniel raising his eyebrows.

"What?" Daniel growled.

"He's back."

Daniel blinked. "Excuse me?"

"I said John Dempsey has returned safe and sound." Jack looked smug. "If you don't believe me, go to the mission and see for yourself."

"When? How?"

"The Sioux had him, but apparently they were friendly Sioux. John Dempsey had once helped save one of their young sons. It was by chance that the band of Indians met up with the others and recognized our good doctor."

Chance? Daniel wondered, reeling from the impact of the news. *Or fate?*

"He's all right then?" he asked, his thoughts, his concerns with Amelia.

"He's fine," Jack said. He jerked a thumb to the smithy

doorway. "You'd best get moving, Trahern, so you can just 'talk with her' before it gets too late."

Daniel stared at his friend, then down at the misshapen tool on the anvil. He laid his hammer beside the cooling black metal and grinned over his shoulder as he headed toward the door. "I reckon you're right. I'd best be on my way."

Daniel approached the missionary infirmary building with his heart thundering in his chest and his hands clammy at his sides. He knocked, then held his breath as he waited for someone to open the door . . . for Amelia.

To his disappointment and pleasure, it was John Dempsey himself who answered his knock.

"Mr. Trahern!" the doctor exclaimed. "How nice to see you! Come in. Come in!"

"How are you, sir?" Daniel said as he entered the front waiting area.

"Fine, fine," the man enthused. "I must say I had my moments of fear, but all in all I was all right." He grinned. "Am all right. See? I'm as healthy as a horse."

The doctor's comments made the younger man smile.

"My daughter says I have a great deal to thank you for." John's brown gaze, so like Amelia's, met Daniel's. "You rescued her, took her into your home. In fact, you rescued her twice."

Daniel broke away from that gaze. "I did nothing." He couldn't take credit for what came naturally . . . just as he couldn't take credit for loving Amelia . . . for loving her came naturally to him as living and breathing.

"I didn't rescue you."

John snorted and waved that notion aside. "Can't be rescuing what you can't find to rescue," he said. "Besides, son, you tried." His voice lowered. "You tried," he murmured, sounding grateful.

The man's gratitude made Daniel feel ashamed. He knew the last thing the doctor would feel was gratitude if he knew what Daniel had done to his lovely daughter.

"Sir, may I ask where Amelia is?"

John's gaze grew sad. "I suspect she's walking about the compound, probably toward that little stream she loves so much. The one in the forest behind the church. She's got something on her mind. A decision to make."

Daniel's stomach clenched. Was it safe for her to be out walking?

"She's not far. I'm sure you'll be able to catch her."

Daniel suddenly recalled hearing something about a decision. "A decision, sir?"

The man nodded. "As much as it will pain me to lose her, I've suggested to Amelia that she return East to live with her sister and aunt. I'm an old man, and I've learned from this experience that I'm not very good at taking care of her. And since she has nothing to hold her here, but me . . ."

Back East. Daniel panicked. Amelia going back to Baltimore?

"No!" Daniel caught himself protesting the idea out loud. He saw that John was watching him strangely, almost with expectation. He drew a deep breath as he made the decision to tell the man how he felt. "I'm in love with your daughter."

John smiled, a warm smile that gave Daniel encouragement, hope. "Then, son, I suggest you get to her before she makes her decision final."

Daniel nodded and felt himself grin. "Yes, sir." He turned to leave.

"Daniel?"

The blacksmith froze and glanced back.

"Don't take no for an answer, do you hear?"

Daniel's teeth flashed. "No, sir. I mean yes, sir."

Then, he hurried toward the stream with fear in his heart that the woman he loved would never forgive him.

It was a lovely autumn day with a soft breeze rustling the treetops, carrying with it the scent of dried leaves and damp earth. Amelia walked along the stream, listening to the trees and the soft burbling of the water that rushed by her.

Back to Baltimore. She had a decision to make. Should she go or stay? Go, return to her aunt's house and a life that held no meaning for her? Or stay, where she could see Daniel and experience a surge of pain each time she saw him and realize what she'd lost?

It wasn't really much of a decision, actually. Amelia had known soon after her father had suggested the move that she wouldn't go. Couldn't go. If all she could have of Daniel was a brief glimpse on occasion, it was better than nothing. Better than not ever having the chance to see him again, hear his voice . . . watch him work. As a customer even, she'd be able to indulge herself in watching him work.

She should be happy. Her father was back, healthy and alive, and so were the other women captives and children, having been returned at John Dempsey's request.

Amelia thought of her father's tale with amazement. Apparently, Runs-with-the-Wind, the father of John Dempsey's late-night patient—the little injured Sioux boy, Little Cloud—had been among the band of Indians who'd traded for John Dempsey. The grateful father, a firm believer in the doctor's healing ability, had taken John to another patient, a young Sioux woman who had contracted some strange white man's disease.

The first thing her father had done was quarantine the woman to keep the others from contracting the illness. Then with patience, prayer, and the right medicines, he'd helped see the woman through the medical crisis, thus earning the Sioux's gratitude once again.

With the woman cured, John has asked to be returned to the mission and for help in finding Amelia and the other missionary captives, who, once found, would be returned as well. Runs-with-the-Wind had agreed, and it had taken until just recently to find those who had survived the ordeal. All but Amelia. It wasn't Runs-with-the-Wind's men who'd attacked the mission, a fact that Amelia had already learned after the business of Richard Milton.

Amelia sat down on a rock near the stream's edge and trailed her fingers in the water. She should have been happy, she thought. And she would have been, should have been, since her decision to stay had come so easily to her. But the decision didn't alter the fact that Daniel hated her, that he desired her but would never love her as she wanted to be loved.

Not that I can blame him. He'd been hurt so much. First by Pamela. Amelia felt intense anger as she thought of Daniel's dead wife. Next when he'd lost his sister. And because of her, he'd nearly lost not only his sister for the second time, but Susie, Jane's child. The little girl Daniel loved like a daughter.

"I love you, Daniel." She closed her eyes and sought comfort for her tears in the wind and the sounds and the scents of her surroundings. "I love you."

"Amelia."

She gasped and shot to her feet. "Daniel." Her pulse

began to hammer wildly. Her skin burned, and her spine tingled as she shyly met his gaze.

He stared at her intently, his blue eyes burning with some emotion that Amelia didn't recognize but feared. "I saw your father," he said. His expression softened. "He told me you were here."

She nodded. Had he heard her declaration of love? No, she decided. She didn't know, couldn't tell what was on his mind, but she was certain it wasn't worry that the woman he distrusted loved him.

"You're going back to Baltimore," he said.

Amelia was intrigued. It had sounded more like an accusation than a statement.

"I've been thinking about it." It wasn't a lie, for she had been thinking about it. Thinking about it and dismissing the idea. She decided to be truthful. "But I'm not going."

His blue gaze flickered. "You're not?"

Gazing at him, wondering what she saw, she slowly shook her head. "No."

"Why not?"

"I, ah, have things here that matter to me." *And people,* she thought. *You.*

He approached until he was only inches away. "Amelia," he murmured. He reached out and, studying his own actions, touched her face. "I'm glad."

She felt surprised. "You are?"

He nodded, then leaned in closer until she could barely breathe. He turned her head so she could feel the soft whisper of his breath against her neck and ear. "Do you know you have a little mole here behind your left earlobe?" he asked.

She frowned. "I do?"

He drew back so she could see him nod. "A little tiny

one. And you have a larger one at the base of your spine."
He reached around her, placed his hand at the small of
her back, and rubbed her through the fabric. "A brown
mark. Like an angel's kiss."

He smiled. "Do you believe in angels?"

Staring at him, caught up in his mesmerizing blue
glance, she could only nod.

"Me, too," he murmured as his gaze fastened on her
mouth. His head loomed closer. "Angels are fragile," he
said huskily. "You must be careful with them. Treat them
with care."

His breath hitched before his head lowered and he
kissed her gently on the mouth. Startled, then fascinated,
Amelia wanted harder kisses and more.

"Angels are wise," he said. "You must always trust that
angels will never hurt you. Trust them. They act in good
faith, and one must never forget that."

Amelia began to tremble as he cupped her behind the
ears, used his thumbs to caress the sensitive areas. She
tingled. She burned. She closed her eyes and wondered if
this was a dream, a cruel dream that would be punishment
for her sins when she awakened.

But it didn't feel like a dream when his mouth captured
hers in a hot, searing kiss that rocked her to her toes and
made the hair at her nape stand on tingling end. Nor did
his blazing blue gaze look angry . . . the flame in his
eyes was desire.

Daniel released her mouth to bury his face in her neck,
where his lips worked their magic on her shoulder and
throat.

He raised his head. "Angels are special. You have to
care for them." He paused as his hand cupped her throat
and felt the throbbing pulse there at the base. *"Love them."*

His expression changed. He looked suddenly concerned,

wary. "Angels are rare. If a man is lucky, he'll find one only once in a lifetime."

His face cleared as he studied her, apparently pleased with what he saw in her features. "Angel. Amelia," he murmured. "Coincidence that both words begin with *a?* I think not."

He kissed her then with unconcealed longing. She felt the mindless pleasure, lifted her hands and sank her fingers into his hair to hold him still. While he ravaged her mouth, she gave back to him, and their guttural groans filled the tiny hidden forest glade.

Daniel lifted his head and frowned. "I'm sorry. I didn't mean to be so rough with you." There was a heartbeat of silence in which Amelia sensed that he was apologizing for more than just this one solitary kiss, that his apology was also for the last time they'd come together.

"I'm not," she said. Amelia raised her hand, touched his cheek. "Sorry for the roughness."

He seemed startled by the admission. "Amelia?"

She nodded. "That night, you didn't hurt me—not physically. I—" She blushed. "I loved it."

He stared at her hard, groaned when he saw she meant it, and clutched her to him tightly.

"Amelia . . . Angel, will you marry me?" he asked. His voice had turned raspy as he was overcome with emotion.

Amelia's eyes filled with tears as she nodded. "Oh, Daniel, I thought you'd never ask."

And they kissed and felt their passion returning, building. Then, they clamped it down and reluctantly pulled apart. They wanted to tell the others their news. They wanted, quite simply, to share their joy with the other people they loved.

Epilogue

The rippling sound of childish laughter filled the quiet afternoon outside the Trahern residence. Amelia sat on her front porch swing, observing Daniel playing with their blond, blue-eyed daughter. She watched as Daniel swung the little girl high into the air, where she hovered for a moment in laughing glee. The child cried out with happiness as she fell downward, confident in her father's efforts to catch her.

She and Daniel had been married for two years. Amelia had given birth to baby Cecily nine months after the day she'd become Daniel's wife. She'd been wary, at first, wondering how quickly Daniel wanted to be a father, grateful when he'd been overjoyed at the news. She'd thought that perhaps Daniel had wanted a son. He loved Susie like a daughter, and Amelia wanted to take nothing away from Jane's little girl.

Daniel's face when Cecily was born banished any of Amelia's lingering doubts that this child wouldn't be wanted or loved by her father.

Jane remained still quiet and withdrawn—except with Susie. Her four-year ordeal had scarred her emotionally. Amelia hoped that Daniel's sister would someday find the peace and happiness Jane needed so desperately in her life.

It didn't help that no one had ever heard what happened

to Richard Milton. The last news had been that the
authorities had shipped him back East for trial. It would
have been nice to know for certain what method of justice
had finally taken the man in the end. *Jane needed to know,*
Amelia thought, and made a silent vow to write to her
aunt back East to ask if the woman could use her social
contacts to make polite inquiries.

Daniel's deep musical laugh drew Amelia's attention
back to her beloved family. He had put Cecily on the
ground and was tickling her.

Amelia's gaze went to Susie, now ten years old. The
child stood off to one side, watching father and daughter
not with envy but with a loving smile on her beautiful
little face. *You're a treasure, Susie.* And Amelia knew that
Jane thought so, too, for she had the feeling that Jane
would have long given up the will to live if not for her
overwhelming love for the daughter she'd been separated
from for four years.

Daniel rose to his feet, eyed his niece with a wicked
gleam. "Your turn," he growled, before he went after Susie
with tickling fingers.

Both man and child went down in the yard, rolling,
tickling each other, their laughter rising high on the warm
spring afternoon air. Amelia watched fondly as Cecily tod-
dled over on unsteady legs to jump on the tangled heap
of bodies and limbs. Her own childlike giggles joined the
other two. The sweet, musical sound of all three was so
merry, so full of happiness and love, that Amelia's eyes
filled with tears.

"Ho! Are those my little ladies?"

Amelia glanced over to see her smiling father coming
up the path. Two heads lifted from Daniel's chest as Cecily
squealed with delight as she spied her grandfather.

Daniel rose to his feet with a grin, then meandered over

to Amelia as John Dempsey assumed with great pleasure the duties of a doting grandpapa.

"Hello, little momma," Daniel said, then he bent to kiss her on her protruding belly. He straightened, then took a seat next to her on the swing.

Amelia smiled and patted her stomach, knowing in her heart, that if she could have wished for it, life couldn't have been any better. She had her father back, and she had a wonderful husband, a beautiful daughter and niece, and another baby on the way.

She sighed and reached out to pat and squeeze Daniel's knee. "I love you, Daniel."

He covered her hand, then trailed his fingers seductively up her arm until she had to look at him. The desire in his blue gaze made her catch her breath and caused her pulse to beat rapidly.

He still makes my heart go crazy, she thought, looking forward to the time when she and Daniel could be alone.

She gave him a flirtatious smile. Life was good.

ABOUT THE AUTHOR

Candace McCarthy lives in Delaware with her husband of 24 years, and she has a son in college. She enjoys hearing from her readers. You may write to her at:

P.O. Box 58
Magnolia, DE 19962.

She also has a Web site on the Internet.

ROMANCE FROM FERN MICHAELS

DEAR EMILY   (0-8217-4952-8, $5.99)

WISH LIST   (0-8217-5228-6, $6.99)

AND IN HARDCOVER:

VEGAS RICH   (1-57566-057-1, $25.00)